Table of Contents

Principle Woods, Inc.
One San Jose Place, Suite 11
Jacksonville, Florida 32257
www.pwimpact.com

Contributors:
Jon Kern, Tori Friedrich, Heather Martin,
Laura Jacqmein, David Whitlock,
Susan Anderson

ISBN 0-9719228-6-1

Suggested Teacher Guide for Using *Impact!*

Step One
Teacher leads students through the Before Reading activities in the Reading Instructional Guide.

Step Two
Students individually read the article. Teacher leads students through During Reading activities in the Reading Instructional Guide.

Step Three
Teacher leads students in class discussion using the Discussion Starter Questions in the After Reading Section of the Reading Instructional Guide.

Step Four
Teacher discusses the Reading Strategy sheet. Students work together in groups to complete the strategy sheet and then participate in class discussion about the answers.

Step Five
Students work in groups to discuss the Reading Comprehension multiple-choice questions and come to a group consensus on the answers. Students participate in class discussion about the answers.

Step Six
Teacher discusses the Interpreting the Data section and gives mini-lessons on each section. Students work individually or in pairs/groups to complete each section.

Step Seven
Students participate in class discussion about the short and extended Interpreting the Data responses using the rubrics. Teacher uses rubrics to grade responses and monitor student progress.

Step Eight
Students complete Look Inside and Grow section. Teacher uses rubric to grade responses. Students participate in class discussion using the Look Inside and Grow section as the prompt.

Step Nine
Students individually read Technical Extension and complete multiple choice questions to test their comprehension and critical thinking. Students participate in class discussion about the answers.

Step Ten
Students individually read Vocational Extension and answer Looking Forward and Ethical Dilemma questions.

Step Eleven
Students participate in class discussion about the Looking Forward and Ethical Dilemma questions. Teacher uses rubrics to grade writing responses.

Syllable Guide

The Syllable Guide is an instructional tool designed to help students learn to break unfamiliar words into manageable parts. With this tool, uncertain readers can learn to sound words out to identify them.

Lesson One	Lesson Two	Lesson Three
Beginner's Guide to Breaking Words Into Syllables	Beginner's Guide to the Detailed Rules of Breaking Words Into Syllables	Quick Reference Guide
1. Count the vowel sounds in the word. 2. Subtract any silent vowels (like *e*). 3. The final number should be the number of syllables. 4. Break the word into that many chunks. 5. The chunks should be small parts you can say.	1. Count the vowel sounds in the word. 2. Subtract any silent vowels (like *e*). 3. The final number should be the number of syllables. 4. Slash between parts of compound words. 5. Slash after beginning parts. 6. Slash before end parts. 7. Slash between two middle consonants (except for two different consonants that make one sound, like *ph, th, ch, wh*). 8. Sometimes slash before a single middle consonant (except for short vowel sounds, like *cabin: cab-in*). 9. Slash before a consonant-*le* (like - *ble, -cle, -tle*). 10. Try to say the words using these small "chunks."	1. Circle vowel sounds (don't count silent vowels). 2. / compound parts (*cup/cake*) 3. prefixes/ & /suffixes (*con/fine/ment*) 4. C/C (*inves/tigative*) (not *ph, th, ch*, etc.) 5. Sometimes /C (*trau/ma*) 6. /Cle (like *-ble, -cle, -tle*, etc.) 7. Say the word using these "chunks."

Basic Vowel Sounds

ai (raid) *au* (taught) *ay* (may) *ea* (bread, seat) *ee* (sleep) *oa* (road) *oi* (coin) *oo* (soon, look) *ou* (proud)	*ow* (cow, flow) *oy* (toy) *ar* (harm) *er* (perm) *ir* (sir) *or* (horn) *ur* (burn) *a*(c)*e* (date) *e*(c)*e* (eve)	*i*(c)*e* (slide) *o*(c)*e* (note) *u*(c)*e* (accuse) *a* (hat, carry, father) *e* (let, merry) *i* (tin) *o* (go, to, mop) *u* (up) *y* (sky)

Basic Beginning Parts (Prefixes) and Their Meanings

ab-: from *ad-*: to, at, toward *an-*: not *be-*: to make, about, by *co-, col-, con-, com-*: together/with *de-*: from, down, away, off *dis-*: apart, not, opposite	*en-*: in, into, make *ex-*: out *fore-*: in front, before *in-, im-, il-, ir-*: in, into, without, not *mis-*: wrongly, incorrect *post-*: after *pre-*: before	*pro-*: moving forward, in front of, defending *re-*: back, again *sub-*: under *trans-*: across, through, beyond *un-*: not *uni-*: one

Basic End Parts (Suffixes) and Their Meanings

-al: relating to, process (adj.) *-ance*: action, state of (n.) *-ar, -er, -or*: one who/that/which (n.) *-ate*: make, cause (v.) *-cide*: kill (n.) *-dom*: quality (n.) *-en*: make (v.), made of (adj.) *-ful*: full of (adj.)	*-fy*: make (v.) *-ice*: condition (n.) *-ion, -sion, -tion*: state of (n.) *-ish*: a characteristic of (adj.) *-ism*: system, condition (n.) *-ive*: related to, tending (adj.) *-ize*: to cause or make (v.) *-less*: without (adj.) *-like*: resembling (adj.) *-ly*: manner of (adv.)	*-ment*: process, result of, act of (n.) *-ness*: state of (n.) *-ous*: having (adj.) *-ology, -alogy*: study of (n.) *-tude*: condition of (n.) *-ward*: in a particular direction (adj.) (adv.) *-y*: having (adj.)

Queen Latifah & Mariah Carey

Reading Instructional Guide

BEFORE READING

Front-Loading Background Knowledge Through Read-Aloud-Think-Aloud

Search the internet for recent articles on Queen Latifah and Mariah Carey.

Check out articles at the following websites to determine if they would be appropriate for your RATA:

- http://www.queenlatifah.com

- http:// en.wikipedia.org.wiki/Mariah_carey#2001.E2.80.932004:_Personal_and_professional_struggles

(Please keep in mind that it is the responsibility of the teacher to determine if articles from suggested sites are appropriate. The sites may have changed content since this publication. The publisher takes no responsibility for the current content of the site.)

Looking at the Words

Determining How the Word Sounds (Phonics)

With your students, use one of the sets of steps from the Syllable Guide at the beginning of the book to determine how to break a word into manageable parts. The goal is to break the words into syllables that the students can say. Then they can put those parts together to "sound the word out." However, remember that the rules for syllabification do not always work because our language is so diverse. The rules can also become rather complex for low readers, so keep in mind that their overall objective is just to figure out how the word sounds. They may not be able to break the word into its syllables perfectly, but they should at least be able to figure out how to say the word based on their attempt at following one of these sets of steps. Lesson One is a more basic set, while Lesson Two attempts to give the students the more specific rules without becoming too complicated. Take your time when teaching either set, and understand that many of the lower readers are not going to understand right away. It will take time, practice, and repeated application before many of them are able to make use of these strategies on their own.

Determining What the Words Mean (Vocabulary)

After students have spent time breaking the words apart to figure out how they sound, use the lists of prefixes and suffixes and their meanings found in the Syllable Guide to have students try to add whatever meaning they can to the words before actually looking at their definitions. After giving the students the definitions, have them see if they can figure out which words truly apply the meaning of any of the prefixes or suffixes.

Words to Study	Breaking into Syllables	Short Definition
Diva	di-va	(n.) a leading female singer
Altercation	al-ter-ca-tion	(n.) an angry or heated discussion
Feminist	fem-i-nist	(adj.) relating to the belief in political, economic, and social equality for women
Pillar	pil-lar	(n.) a main support of something
Debuted	de-buted	(v.) to publicly appear or formally introduce

Activating Background Knowledge

Anticipation Guide
Mark each of the following statements True or False:

1. ____ Mariah Carey's and Queen Latifah's careers have been stagnant for several years.

2. ____ Queen Latifah employs minorities in her production companies.

3. ____ Mariah Carey's brother was killed in a car accident.

4. ____ Queen Latifah has been in trouble with the law on more than one occasion.

5. ____ Mariah Carey has sold over 100 million records.

Starter Questions
After completing the anticipation guide, have a group or class discussion with the students using the following questions:

1. What is a diva?

2. Whom would you consider to be a diva?

3. Can you name any of Mariah Carey's songs?

4. Who is Queen Latifah?

5. Can you name any movies Queen Latifah has been featured in?

Make a prediction about what you think the article will be about.

DURING READING

- Have the students skim the article. Give them about 45-60 seconds to do this.

- As they skim the article, tell them to circle any words they don't know how to say.

- When they are finished, talk about how to chunk the words they don't know how to say by sounds they now know and then sound them out.

- Have the students skim the questions. Give them only about 30-45 seconds to do this.

- Ask the students to predict what the article is about.

- Have the students read the article. They should question, summarize, clarify, and predict as they read. Instruct them to jot their questions, summarizations, clarifications, and predictions in the margins as they read.

- Remind students to constantly ask themselves if they know what the article is about right now. If they don't, they must reread to clarify. This is called monitoring for understanding.

- After they have finished reading the article, they are ready to answer the questions.

The Strategy Sheet

You may choose to have students complete the strategy sheet for each section before they answer the multiple-choice questions. Or you could have them complete the questions, work on the strategy sheet with a partner, and then go back over the questions to see if the use of the strategy sheet helped them more easily find the answers to any of the questions.

Queen Latifah & Mariah Corey

AFTER READING

Discussion Starter Questions

1. Do you have a passion in life?

2. Have you ever experienced any personal struggles in your life? How did you learn to cope with them?

3. What would you do if the one thing you wanted to achieve in life was taken away? Would you give in to defeat?

4. Think about a time in your life when you just gave up on something. Do you regret making that decision? Would you go back and change your decision if you could?

5. On whom do you rely to find personal strength? Do you have a support network, such as family?

Teacher Reflection

When you are finished with the article, strategies, and questions, ask yourself the following:

1. Did I get the students to THINK about what they have read?

2. Did I teach them (even a little bit) about how to read more effectively?

If you answered "Yes" to both questions, you can feel good about the day.

Failure and the Sweet Smell of Success:
Queen Latifah & Mariah Carey

Failure hurts. But any celebrity could probably sit with you for hours and go over the list of failures they've suffered to get where they are today. Falling down is just a necessary step in the process of getting back up. And the higher you want to get, the more painful the falls may become. Your character determines how quickly you bounce back into place and soar above others.

Two entertainers who have seen good times, bad times, and then good times again are Queen Latifah and Mariah Carey. Both performers have proven that nobody is perfect, but the key is to be strong enough to deal with our lives when we become something we aren't proud of.

Mariah Carey

Too successful? Too fast? Too early? Too young?

No matter how one would describe it, it was all too much to handle for the 20-year-old Mariah Carey. Her single "Vision of Love" became an immediate hit when it debuted in 1990. From there, her career took off. She eventually married the president of Sony Music in a glamorous wedding in 1993. That was also the year she sold 10 million copies of her third album, *Music Box*.

In 1995 she became the first female to have a single become number one on the charts the first week it was released. Then another single from the same album spent 16 weeks at number one. The album the songs appeared on, *Daydream*, also debuted at number one. Her great start in the 1990s helped her eventually sell 110 million records.

Unfortunately, life has a way of knocking people down when they least expect it. And Carey was no exception. In 1997 she split with her husband. Her music

career remained on track for a couple of years with her albums *Butterfly* and *Rainbow*. But things were starting to unravel.

Carey let the money get the best of her, and she signed a record contract with Virgin Records for $80 million. The contract was the largest in history at the time. She later expressed her belief that the deal kept her from releasing the types of songs she thought would be successful.

Her first attempt at the movies, the film *Glitter,* was a disaster. Unfortunately, it won her a Golden Raspberry award for the Year's Worst Actress of 2001. The soundtrack she released for the movie fared no better. It was heavily criticized and sold only 1 million copies in the United States.

Carey's downfall was painful after living as one of the world's top divas. The media released reports of her

suffering emotional and physical breakdowns, the worst of which came in 2001. Of course, rumors then started to fly about other problems she may have been dealing with. As is often the case, some people seem to take joy in the suffering of others, and the late-night talk show hosts made her a favorite target.

But, demonstrating the truth in the saying "Whatever doesn't kill you will make you stronger," Carey regained her strength. She kept her spiritual faith and relied on the well wishes of the fans that still believed in her. In 2002 she signed a new deal with Island/Def Jam. They gave Carey her own label. This gave her the ability to have more control over what she sang.

She soon released *Charmbracelet*, which performed moderately. The album served only as a warm-up to what was to come. In 2005 she released *The Emancipation of Mimi*. This new CD put her right back on top. "We Belong Together," the album's first single, spent 14 weeks at number one. And just when no one thought 50 Cent's *The Massacre* would ever be knocked from the top of *Billboard's* Top 100 List, Carey's album did just that. It sold 404,000 copies in its first week alone, swiftly taking the spot from 50 Cent.

Carey's return has been labeled the "Comeback of the Year." She talks humbly about her turn-around. She suffered publicly through painful failures. But she did what only strong people do: she learned from them.

Queen Latifah

She would tell you she was born a queen. It all has to do with her self-esteem. Possibly, no entertainer is prouder of herself than Queen Latifah.

Born Dana Owens in New York in 1970, her cousin later gave her the nickname Latifah, which in Arabic means "delicate" or "sensitive." She was raised by her father, a policeman, and her mother, a teacher. Both of them served as role models from whom she learned the value of strong heart and desire.

She recently starred in the films *Last Holiday* and *Beauty Shop*. Each movie earned over $38 million and spent three weeks on top-ten lists. Her other top accomplishment in 2006 was being the first rap artist to be awarded a star on the Hollywood Walk of Fame.

Unfortunately, her life hasn't been full of bright spots. Like Mariah Carey, she has found herself in dark holes from which she had to drag herself out.

Her music career began in 1989 with her debut album, *All Hail the Queen*. She was nominated for a Grammy Award for the album. In 1991 she released *Nature of a Sista*, which also gained respect in the music world. The following year, she was nominated for Best Rap Solo with "Fly Girl." She was enjoying life and included her family in her success. Her brother was a motorcycle fan, so she purchased a motorcycle for him. But this part of the story didn't end happily for Latifah. Her life was changed forever when her brother had an accident on the motorcycle and was killed. This event would haunt her for years and force her to remain strong in order to hold on to her career and her soul.

As if things couldn't get worse, she was carjacked in 1993. She was left unharmed, but her friend was shot and killed during the altercation.

To the public, things seemed okay for Latifah following these tragic events. She won a Grammy Award for her album *Black Reign*, which she dedicated to her brother. She also played parts in several movies and was seen as a symbol of feminist strength. But inside she was battling to overcome the uncertainty about life that the death of her brother and friend had left her.

In 1996 she was pulled over for a traffic violation. The officer found a loaded gun and marijuana in the car. After being punished for the incident, she continued to act and sing. In 2002 she was arrested again. This time it was for drinking and driving. She later admitted that her abuse of drugs and alcohol was due to her inability to accept her brother's death. But she relied on her family and her talents to help bring her back.

In the past few years, not only has Latifah enjoyed success in movies, but she also won the Harvard Foundation Artist of the Year Award for being an excellent role model and inspiring others to succeed. She has been noted as a pillar of female strength. She gives back to society by contributing her time and efforts to the Lancelot H. Owens Scholarship Foundation, which aims to help minority students. She also tends to carefully pick the employees of her production companies, opting for African Americans she thinks may not elsewhere be given the opportunities they deserve.

Queen Latifah and Mariah Carey have been to dark places through different routes. But they have both emerged as models of strength and the ability to learn from mistakes. They have proven that pain isn't something to just sit and cry about, but something that can make us stronger.

Reading Comprehension

After reading "The Sweet Smell of Success: Queen Latifah and Mariah Carey," choose the options that best answer questions 1-14.

1. Read this sentence from the article.
   But they have both emerged as models of strength and the ability to learn from mistakes.

   What is the meaning of the word *emerged* as it is used in this sentence?
   A. faded
   B. vanished
   C. come forth
   D. earned fame

2. Read this sentence from the article.
   She has been noted as a pillar of female strength.

   What does the author mean by this sentence?
   F. Queen Latifah is stronger than most men.
   G. Queen Latifah works out regularly to maintain her strength.
   H. Queen Latifah is looked at as a mentally and emotionally strong role model.
   I. Queen Latifah lost her strength after her brother's death and never really regained it.

3. From the article, the reader can tell that Queen Latifah has used the pain caused by her brother's death
   A. to make herself a stronger person.
   B. to destroy herself emotionally and physically.
   C. as an excuse for her drug and alcohol abuse.
   D. to prove that anyone can live through painful periods of time.

4. How did Mariah Carey overcome her obstacles?
   F. She looked for the easy way out.
   G. She worked hard and relied on the strength of those who love her.
   H. She allowed other people to take care of her and plan her life out for her.
   I. She was rude to those people who wouldn't do what she wanted and demanded that everyone do things her way.

5. With which statement would the author of the passage most likely agree?
   A. Carey and Latifah proved that not giving up made them stars again.
   B. Carey and Latifah will never be able to have the fame they once possessed.
   C. Carey and Latifah are role models for other celebrities, but not for normal people.
   D. Carey and Latifah were unique in facing struggles that most people will never have to face.

6. The author organizes the article by
   F. describing the barriers faced by many different people.
   G. discussing events in reverse chronological order to point out similarities.
   H. listing the awards received by two celebrities and the hardships they overcame to earn them.
   I. describing two individual celebrities' struggles and the ways they persevered through their rough times.

Queen Latifah & Mariah Carey

7. Why does the author use facts and statistics about Mariah Carey?
   A. to show how the data can be used to trace the ups and downs of her career
   B. to illustrate how data can be used to define the pop star's amount of character
   C. to demonstrate how much better Mariah Carey has performed than Queen Latifah
   D. to prove that Mariah Carey's success can be traced back to her single "Vision of Love"

8. Which statement BEST expresses the main idea of the article?
   F. Some celebrities are able to make incredible comebacks.
   G. Mariah Carey and Queen Latifah are examples of people overcoming life's challenges because they emerged from difficult times as stronger people.
   H. Mariah Carey's recent album, *The Emancipation of Mimi*, is an example of the ability of a pop star to renew her career when she has struggled with life's challenges.
   I. *The Emancipation of Mimi* and *Last Holiday* were successful for Mariah Carey and Queen Latifah because they are celebrities with the strength to overcome life's obstacles.

9. What is significant about the death of Queen Latifah's brother?
   A. It destroyed her career.
   B. It caused her to focus on her career and become a better actress.
   C. It caused her to become weak, but when she accepted it she regained her strength.
   D. It caused her to focus on helping others by starting the Lancelot H. Owens Scholarship Foundation.

10. According to the article, what was the reason Mariah Carey's career fell apart around 2000?
    F. She attempted to become an actress.
    G. She made a big deal with a company she later felt she couldn't be successful with.
    H. She received a Golden Raspberry Award for being the Year's Worst Actress of 2001.
    I. She suffered emotional breakdowns in 2001 and was a target of late-night talk show hosts.

11. What is true of both Queen Latifah and Mariah Carey?
    A. Both have been successful actresses.
    B. They have both had albums that have debuted at number one.
    C. They both felt guilty about something that happened to a loved one.
    D. They both relied on support from others to regain their strong character.

12. Which sentence from the article offers the best evidence that Mariah Carey is one of the world's most successful singers?
    F. Her great start in the 1990s helped her eventually sell 110 million records.
    G. That was also the year she sold 10 million copies of her third album, *Music Box*.
    H. In 1995 she became the first female to have a single become number one on the charts the first week it was released.
    I. And just when no one though 50 Cent's *The Massacre* would ever be knocked from the top of *Billboard's* Top 100 List, Carey's album did just that.

13. According to the evidence in the article, which of Mariah Carey's career moves was possibly the most damaging?
    A. winning a Golden Raspberry Award
    B. the release of the album *Charmbracelet*
    C. the release of the movie *Glitter*, in which she performed
    D. splitting up with her husband who was the president of Sony Music

14. What fact does the author use to support the idea that Queen Latifah is a strong role model?
    F. She received a Grammy Award for her album *Black Reign*.
    G. She was awarded the Harvard Foundation Artist of the Year Award.
    H. She has learned from her mistakes and become a great singer and actress.
    I. She relied on her family and her talents to help her restore her successful career.

Reading Strategy

The Highs and Lows

Cities such as Los Angeles and New York are built for celebrities like Mariah Carey and Queen Latifah. Most people who have used those cities to help them become famous can tell you that their careers are full of highs and lows similar to the skylines of the cities themselves. You have just read about the ups and downs of the lives of two famous celebrities. Use the diagram below to compare the highs and lows of their lives. Write the highs and lows that are unique to each celebrity in the boxes as marked. Fill in any highs or lows that both of them share in the boxes marked "Both." This strategy activity is similar to a Venn diagram, but it takes it one step further by having you compare and contrast not only two individuals, but two different aspects of those individuals' lives.

Teacher's Notes: Student answers should include facts from the article such as those indicated.

HIGHS ~ HIGHS ~ HIGHS ~ HIGHS ~ HIGHS

Mariah Carey	Both	Queen Latifah
- Sold 10 million copies of *Music Box*. - In 1995 became the first female to have a single reach #1 in its first week. - Sold 110 million records in the 1990s. - "We Belong Together" spent 14 weeks at #1. - *The Emancipation of Mimi* sold 404,000 copies in its first week.	Overcame emotional distress and hard times in their lives with the help of their faith in family, friends, and fans.	- Nominated for a Grammy Award for *All Hail the Queen*. - Nominated for Best Rap Solo with "Fly Girl." - Won a Grammy Award for *Black Reign*. - Played in *Last Holiday* and *Beauty Shop*, movies that each earned over $38 million. - First rap artist to be awarded a star on the Hollywood Walk of Fame. - Won the Harvard Foundation Artist of the Year Award.

LOWS ~ LOWS ~ LOWS ~ LOWS ~ LOWS

Mariah Carey	Both	Queen Latifah
- Split with her husband in 1997. - Her deal with Virgin Records kept her from releasing the types of songs she felt would be successful. - Her movie, *Glitter*, was a disaster. - When she failed, she was a favorite target of the media.	Suffered emotional distress when bad things happened in their lives.	- Brother was killed driving the motorcycle she had bought for him. - She was carjacked in 1993. Her friend was killed during the carjacking. - Arrested in 1996 for having a loaded gun and drugs in her car, and in 2002 for drinking and driving. - Her inability to deal with her brother's death led to her abuse of drugs and alcohol.

Queen Latifah & Mariah Carey

Interpreting the Data

PART I

15. When did Mariah Carey have the most difficulty with her career? Include details from the article to support your answer.

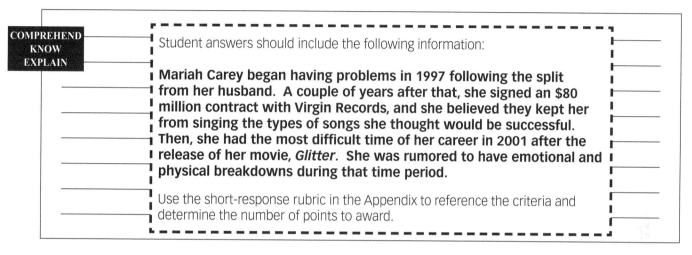

COMPREHEND KNOW EXPLAIN

Student answers should include the following information:

Mariah Carey began having problems in 1997 following the split from her husband. A couple of years after that, she signed an $80 million contract with Virgin Records, and she believed they kept her from singing the types of songs she thought would be successful. Then, she had the most difficult time of her career in 2001 after the release of her movie, *Glitter*. She was rumored to have emotional and physical breakdowns during that time period.

Use the short-response rubric in the Appendix to reference the criteria and determine the number of points to award.

16. When did Queen Latifah have the most difficulty with her career? Include details from the article to support your answer.

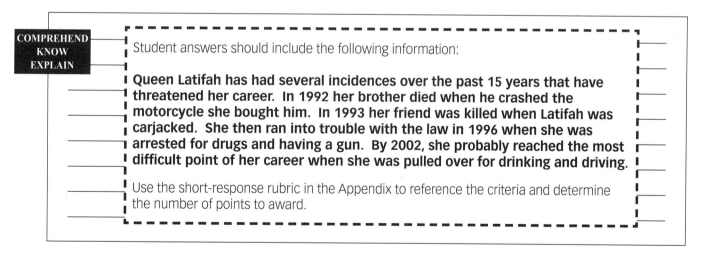

COMPREHEND KNOW EXPLAIN

Student answers should include the following information:

Queen Latifah has had several incidences over the past 15 years that have threatened her career. In 1992 her brother died when he crashed the motorcycle she bought him. In 1993 her friend was killed when Latifah was carjacked. She then ran into trouble with the law in 1996 when she was arrested for drugs and having a gun. By 2002, she probably reached the most difficult point of her career when she was pulled over for drinking and driving.

Use the short-response rubric in the Appendix to reference the criteria and determine the number of points to award.

Now look at the following table which shows the number of hit singles Mariah Carey had over the past 16 years.

Year	Title	Billboard Hot 100	Hot R&B/ Hip-Hop Songs	Hot Dance Club Play	Adult Contemporary	Hot Latin Tracks
2005	Don't Forget About Us	1	1			
2005	It's Like That	16	17			
2005	It's Like That (D. Morales Mixes)			1		
2005	Mine Again		73			
2005	Shake it Off	2	2	23		
2005	We Belong Together	1	1		3	
2005	We Belong Together (P. Rauhofer Remix)			42		
2005	We Belong Together (P. Rauhofer / Atlantic Soul Mixes)			1		
2003	Boy (I Need You)		68			
2003	Bringin' On the Heartbreak			5		
2003	Through the Rain	81	69			
2003	Through the Rain (Mixes)			1		
2002	Irresistible (West Side Connection)		81			
2002	Through the Rain				17	
2001	Don't Stop (Funkin' 4 Jamaica)		42			
2001	Loverboy	2	44	45		
2001	Never Too Far				17	
2001	Never Too Far/ Hero (medley)	81	66			
2000	All I Want for Christmas Is You	83				
2000	Can't Take That Away			6		
2000	Crybaby	28	23			
1999	Heartbreaker	1	1	2		
1999	I Still Believe	4		1	8	39
1999	I Still Believe (Pure Imagination)		3			
1998	Fly Away (Butterfly Reprise)			13		
1998	My All	1	4	5	18	
1997	Butterfly				11	
1997	Honey	1	2	1		30
1996	Always Be My Baby	1	1	6	2	
1996	Forever				2	
1995	All I Want for Christmas Is You				6	
1995	Fantasy	1	1	1	8	
1995	Heroe (Hero)					40
1995	Joy to the World			17		
1995	One Sweet Day	1	2		1	
1994	Anytime You Need a Friend	12	22	1	5	
1994	Hero		5		2	
1994	Never Forget You / Without You	3	7			
1994	Without You				4	
1993	Dreamlover	1	2	1	2	
1993	Hero	1				
1992	Can't Let Go	2	2		1	
1992	I'll Be There	1	11		1	
1992	Make It Happen	5	7	16	13	
1991	Emotions	1	1	1	3	
1991	I Don't Wanna Cry	1	2		1	
1991	Someday	1	3		5	
1990	Love Takes Time	1	1		1	
1990	Vision of Love	1	1		1	

Mariah Carey's Top Singles — Best Position of Songs by Categories/ Charts

17. Examine the table and determine which year was Mariah Carey's most productive. Explain what criteria you used to determine her most productive year.

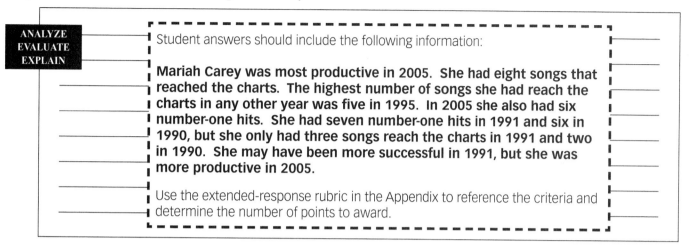

ANALYZE EVALUATE EXPLAIN

Student answers should include the following information:

Mariah Carey was most productive in 2005. She had eight songs that reached the charts. The highest number of songs she had reach the charts in any other year was five in 1995. In 2005 she also had six number-one hits. She had seven number-one hits in 1991 and six in 1990, but she only had three songs reach the charts in 1991 and two in 1990. She may have been more successful in 1991, but she was more productive in 2005.

Use the extended-response rubric in the Appendix to reference the criteria and determine the number of points to award.

18. Create a line graph that shows how many hits she had in the top 20 of all listed charts for each year.

Mariah Carey's Top Singles by Year

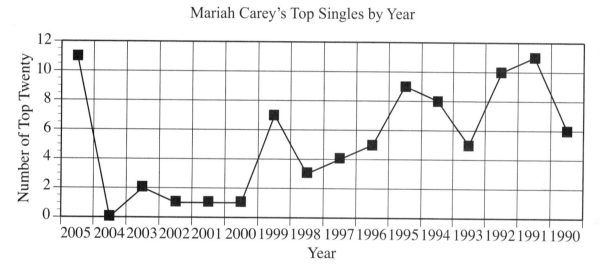

19. Analyze the information shown by the graph you have just created. Would you consider 2005 a "comeback" year for Mariah Carey? Explain your answer using data from the graph and table as support.

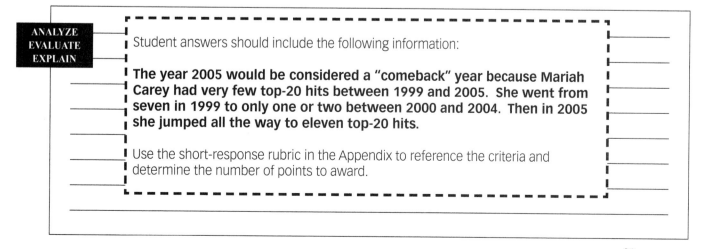

ANALYZE EVALUATE EXPLAIN

Student answers should include the following information:

The year 2005 would be considered a "comeback" year because Mariah Carey had very few top-20 hits between 1999 and 2005. She went from seven in 1999 to only one or two between 2000 and 2004. Then in 2005 she jumped all the way to eleven top-20 hits.

Use the short-response rubric in the Appendix to reference the criteria and determine the number of points to award.

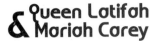

PART II

Use the following data table to answer Part II questions.

Look at the following table depicting the appearances of Queen Latifah's songs on various charts over the last several years.

Queen Latifah's Top Singles						
		Best Position of Songs by Categories/ Charts				
Year	Title	Billboard Hot 100	Hot R&B/ Hip-Hop Songs	Hot Dance Club Play	World Jazz Top 20 Singles	Hot Rap Singles
2004	California Dreamin'				3	
1998	Bananas (Who You Gonna Call?)					2
1998	Paper	50	23			
1997	It's Alright	76				
1994	Black Hand Side					20
1994	Just Another Day	54	37			11
1994	U.N.I.T.Y.	23	7			2
1994	Weekend Love	70				
1994	Weekend Love / Black Hand Side		29			
1993	What Cha Gonna Do?					14
1992	How Do I Love Thee		32	19		
1992	Latifah's Had It Up 2 Here		13			8
1991	Fly Girl		16			19
1990	Come Into My House		81	7		21
1990	Ladies First		64	38		5
1989	Dance For Me					14

20. Create a line graph that shows how many hits she had in the top 20 of all listed charts for each year. Also fill in the x-axis and y-axis headings.

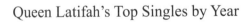

Queen Latifah's Top Singles by Year

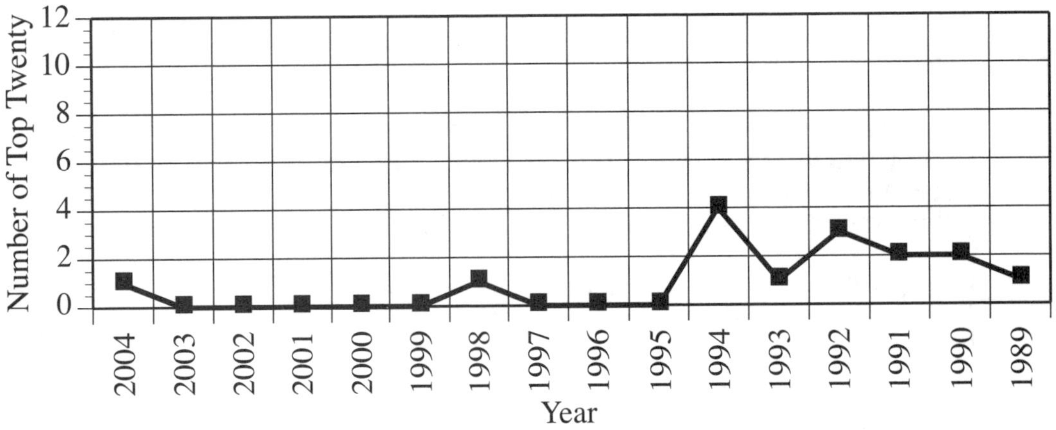

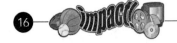

Queen Latifah Movies				
Movie	Peak Position on Charts	Date	Total Gross	# of days on the charts
Last Holiday	2	1/13/2006	$38,360,195	52
Beauty Shop	2	4/1/2005	$36,310,118	47
Taxi	4	10/8/2004	$36,609,013	138
Bringing Down the House	1	3/7/2003, 3/14/2003, 3/21/2003	$132,675,402	157
Living Out Loud	6	11/6/98	$12,902,790	122

21. Analyze the information from the table above and the graph you created on the previous page. Was Queen Latifah's entertainment career in decline during the years she appeared absent from the music scene? Include details from the tables and the graph to support your answer.

ANALYZE EVALUATE EXPLAIN

Student answers should include the following information:

According to the graphs and the table, it appears that Queen Latifah was spending more time working on movies than singing in 1998 and again between 2003 and 2006. The movie she was in during 2003 was very successful, which would indicate that her overall entertainment career was not in a huge decline, although her musical career was.

Use the short-response rubric in the Appendix to reference the criteria and determine the number of points to award.

22. Using the numbers in the table entitled "Queen Latifah Movies," create a list that ranks the movies in order from most productive to least productive. Determine productivity based on the amount each movie made on average for each day it was on the charts. Explain how you determined the order.

ANALYZE SYNTHESIZE EXPLAIN

Student answers should include the following information:

I would rank the movies in the following order from most productive to least productive: *Bringing Down the House, Beauty Shop, Last Holiday, Taxi,* and *Living Out Loud*. Based on the total gross amount divided by the number of days on the charts, *Bringing Down the House* grossed on average $845,066.24 per day. *Beauty Shop* grossed $772,555.70 per day. *Last Holiday* grossed $737,696.05 per day. *Taxi* grossed $265,282.70 per day. And *Living Out Loud* grossed only $105,966.39 on average per day.

Use the extended-response rubric in the Appendix to reference the criteria and determine the number of points to award.

23. Based on your list and the preceding tables and graphs, which year of Queen Latifah's life seems to have been the most successful? Explain your answer with support and details from the unit.

ANALYZE EVALUATE EXPLAIN

Student answers should include the following information:

Students could argue 1994 or 2003, but they should make sure to include data to prove their point. The year 2003 could have been Queen Latifah's most successful year because she starred in a movie that grossed over $132,000,000. This was over three times as much money grossed by any other movie she appeared in. The year 1994 was very successful for her due to the number of appearances she had on the top charts (9) and the number of top-twenty hits (4).

Use the extended-response rubric in the Appendix to reference the criteria and determine the number of points to award.

Use the following tables as additional data to help you answer question 24.

Queen Latifah's Top Albums

Year	Title	Best Position of Songs by Categories/ Charts	
		Billboard 200	Top R&B/ Hip-Hop Songs
2004	The Dana Owens Album	16	11
1998	Order in the Court	95	16
1994	Black Reign	60	15
1990	All Hail the Queen	124	6

Mariah Carey Movie

Movie	Peak Position on Charts	Date	Total Gross	# of days on the charts
Glitter	11	9/21/2001	$4,273,372	38

24. After looking at the previous tables and graphs, decide whether the data supports the claims made in the article about the struggles Mariah Carey and Queen Latifah suffered in their careers and their subsequent "comebacks" following those difficult times. Use data and statistics to support your answer.

ANALYZE EVALUATE EXPLAIN

Student answers should include the following information:

The article tells us that Mariah Carey had her most difficult times in 2001 and Queen Latifah had the lowest point of her career in 2002. Mariah Carey hit a low point in 2001 following the reception of her movie *Glitter*. It never made it above number 11 on the charts and grossed just over $4 million. In 2001 she also had the least amount of top-20 hits of her career. However, by 2005 she jumped up to eleven top-20 hits, which shows that 2005 could be considered her "comeback" year. Likewise, Queen Latifah had a visible break in the productivity of her career as shown by the charts and graphs. Her break was roughly between 1998 and 2003. Those years saw her have few, if any, top-20 hits and no real activity in movies. However, before 1998, she had several top-20 hits, and she began making good money in the movies around 2003 and after.

Use the extended-response rubric in the Appendix to reference the criteria and determine the number of points to award.

---

*Quick*thought

No amount of failure can erase the dreams of someone who holds on to his or her HOPE that things will get better as long as hard work and effort are continually put forth.

Look Inside and Grow

25. What lessons can be learned from the life of Queen Latifah? What mistakes did she make? What allowed her to overcome those mistakes and make her life successful? What qualities do you think you and Queen Latifah might share? How might Queen Latifah be an inspiration to you?

> **Look Inside and Grow**
>
> Student answers may vary.
>
> The student should address each section of the question to the best of his/her ability. The question is meant to elicit strong classroom conversation about character. Students should be able to demonstrate that they have learned a lesson through the inspirational model Queen Latifah has provided through her comeback.
>
> Use the character-education rubric in the Appendix to reference the criteria and determine the number of points to award.

Notes

"Mariah Carey Top Singles" (chart)…: Billboard.com.
http://www.billboard.com/bbcom/retrieve_chart_history.do?model.chartFormatGroupName=Singles&model.vnuArtistId=48340&model.vnuAlbumId=668708.

"Queen Latifah Top Singles" (chart)…: Billboard.com.
http://www.billboard.com/bbcom/retrieve_chart_history.do?model.vnuArtistId=79058&model.vnuAlbumId=286097.

"Queen Latifah Movies" (chart)…: The Numbers.
http://www.the-numbers.com/movies/2006/LHDAY.php,
http://www.the-numbers.com/movies/2005/BESHP.php,
http://www.the-numbers.com/movies/2004/TAXI.php,
http://www.the-numbers.com/movies/1998/LIVLO.html,
http://www.the-numbers.com/movies/2003/HOUZE.php.

"Queen Latifah Top Albums" (chart)…: Billboard.com.
http://www.billboard.com/bbcom/retrieve_chart_history.do?model.chartFormatGroupName=Albums&model.vnuArtistId=79058&model.vnuAlbumId=286097.

"Mariah Carey Movie" (chart)…: The Numbers.
http://www.the-numbers.com/movies/2001/GLITR.html.

Technical Extension

Tracking Billboard

Since 1936, *Billboard* magazine has been publishing a list of the most popular songs. In the summer of 1940, they published the first chart that visibly showed which music was popular. Since then, charting music has become a way of life for the American music industry. The Hot 100, a list of the most popular singles, was first published in 1958 and has been published weekly ever since. Since then, many different charts have been added.

Billboard publishes many different charts to cover the different genres of music. There are charts for singles, albums, and even for individual artists and performers. As new music comes about, new charts are created to keep track of it. While some music can be found on several different *Billboard* charts, the diversity ensures that all music will have a place. Each chart uses the same basic formula to determine the order of popularity. What makes the charts different is which CDs and stations the chart uses, decided by a *Billboard* chart manager. For now, we'll just focus on how the Hot 100 chart is created.

For many years, keeping track of the sales and radio airplay of songs was very difficult. *Billboard* got its information for ranking music from manual reports recorded and sent by stores and radio stations. This was a tedious and time-consuming process.

New technology has made the charts less work and more reliable. *Billboard* now uses Nielsen SoundScan, a system that registers sales every time a CD, video, DVD, or single is bought. To track radio airplay, *Billboard* owns a system called Broadcast Data Systems (BDS). BDS assigns each song its own musical "fingerprint" and records each time that fingerprint is played on the radio. At the end of each week, the numbers from both SoundScan and BDS are added up and statistically analyzed to rank the music. In 1990 the Country Singles chart was the first to use SoundScan and BDS. Today, all *Billboard* charts use this technology.

Billboard charts are based on airplay and sales. The days included in each week's chart are complex. The tracking week for sales begins on Monday and ends the following Sunday. The tracking week for radio airplay begins on Wednesday and ends the following Tuesday. New charts are compiled through the week and released in *Billboard* magazine on Thursday of each week.

At the end of the year, the results of each chart are added up and tallied. At the annual *Billboard* Music Awards in December, the top single, artist, and albums are given awards according to the highest tally in that category.

The music industry spends a great deal of time trying to get to the top of the *Billboard* chart. The chart can make or break an artist's career. *Billboard* shows the connection and artist has with his or her listeners. But a good understanding of that chart takes some concentration.

Reading Comprehension

After reading "Tracking Billboard," choose the options that best answer questions 1-14.

1. Read this sentence.
   This was a tedious and time-consuming process.

   What is the meaning of the word *tedious* as it is used in this sentence?
   A. rare
   B. tiresome
   C. motivating
   D. interesting

2. Read this sentence.
   Billboard **shows the connection an artist has with his or her listeners.**

   What does the author mean by this sentence?
   F. The *Billboard* chart is the single most important factor in an artist's success.
   G. Artists rely on radio airplay alone to increase their ratings on the *Billboard* chart.
   H. The *Billboard* chart tells artists how popular they are by showing whether people are listening to their music.
   I. If an artist is not listed on the top part of a *Billboard* chart, he or she must not be successful or have any fans.

3. According to the article, the *Billboard* charts are most influenced by
   A. weekly records of radio airplay and sales.
   B. the commercial popularity of a singer or album.
   C. the executives who compile the data for the chart.
   D. other magazines that publish similar music rating systems.

4. What has made *Billboard* a part of music industry history?
   F. *Billboard* is the only magazine to ever publish a list of the top 100 songs of the week.
   G. Artists have allowed *Billboard* to determine which songs they should put on their albums.
   H. *Billboard* has published a list of the most popular music every week since the mid-1900s.
   I. *Billboard* magazine professes that they are the most important part of the music industry today.

5. With which statement would the author of this passage most likely agree?
   A. The *Billboard* charts are an important part of popular music in all genres today.
   B. SoundScan and BDS are difficult technologies to use when creating the *Billboard* charts.
   C. The *Billboard* Music Awards give an unfair advantage to favorite artists of *Billboard* chart managers.
   D. The weekly *Billboard* charts are probably less accurate than when the statistics were recorded manually.

6. The author organizes this article by
   F. posing a question about the *Billboard* chart and then answering that question.
   G. explaining the process of compiling a *Billboard* chart as well as its significance.
   H. comparing and contrasting the elements of the different types of *Billboard* charts.
   I. using one artist as an example of how the *Billboard* charts affect the music industry.

7. Why does the author explain the process *Billboard* uses to collect its data?
   A. to compare *Billboard* to other music rating systems
   B. to reveal how expensive it is for *Billboard* magazine to operate
   C. to show how much easier technology has made the data collection process
   D. to show that the Country Singles chart is the most technologically advanced

8. Which statement BEST expresses the main idea of the last paragraph?
   F. *Billboard* is a profitable business that makes a lot of money.
   G. *Billboard* magazine was popular many years ago but isn't today.
   H. People who are in the music industry don't pay much attention to *Billboard*.
   I. The *Billboard* charts can be a determining factor of the success or failure of an artist or album.

9. What is the significance of *Billboard* using BDS and SoundScan technology?
   A. Collecting music data will be slower, but more accurate.
   B. They make *Billboard's* charts more accurate and less complicated to compile.
   C. Every time a song is bought or played, it will be on a *Billboard* chart released the next week.
   D. They both assign "fingerprints" to music, which allows *Billboard* to know the age of the person buying the music.

10. Why might a new *Billboard* chart be created?
    F. Chart managers get tired of the old charts, so they create new ones.
    G. New music that comes out doesn't fit in on any of the existing charts.
    H. There are too many songs and albums to fit onto the current number of charts.
    I. Not all of the radio stations and stores report in time to get on the current charts.

11. All *Billboard* charts are ALIKE in that they
    A. began in 1958.
    B. rank the same music.
    C. began using BDS and SoundScan in 1990.
    D. use the same technology and formula for data collection.

12. Which statement provides the best evidence that *Billboard* charts are an important part of today's music industry?
    F. *Billboard* charts are statistically analyzed.
    G. *Billboard* charts are based on airplay and sales.
    H. *Billboard* charts can make or break and artist's career.
    I. *Billboard* charts are published weekly in *Billboard* magazine.

13. According to the article "Failure and the Sweet Smell of Success," Carey had a single at number one on the charts the first week it was released. Using information from the article you just read, what can you deduce about that single?
    A. The single was on only one *Billboard* chart.
    B. The single was popular because Carey had just gotten married.
    C. The single sold many copies in stores, but had not been played on the radio yet.
    D. The single was played often on the radio and sold many copies in stores that week.

14. Which of these statements supports the idea that *Billboard* magazine has helped shape 20th and 21st century music?
    F. Keeping track of a single's radio airplay is very difficult.
    G. The Hot 100 is the most important chart because it has been published the longest.
    H. *Billboard* charts identify which songs and artists are popular with listeners at any particular time.
    I. Most artists get into the music business only so that one day they will be named on a *Billboard* chart.

Vocational Extension

You read in the article "Failure and the Sweet Smell of Success: Queen Latifah and Mariah Carey" that Queen Latifah's father was a policeman. You also read that he served as a role model to her and passed along his values, heart, and strength to persevere. People have many different views on who and what police officers are. Police officers are dedicated and hardworking. They believe in the safety of their communities. They take seriously their positions as role models. Most of all, police officers put the needs of others before their own.

Being a police officer is a challenging and exciting job. When an officer goes to work, he or she never really knows what to expect for the day ahead. Being a police officer is also rewarding. Those who become officers genuinely feel a need to help people. They are called to work daily for the good of others. Another reward of the job is that police officers are highly respected people in society. That respect is earned as officers uphold the law and help protect citizens.

There are several mandatory requirements for becoming an officer. Applicants must have education equivalent to a high school diploma. They must be at least 18 years old and citizens of the United States. Most states require applicants to have a valid driver's license and a safe driving record. Those who are accepted to the police force will have to apply and test for a Class E driver's license. Police candidates cannot have ever had a felony conviction. They must be examined by both a physician and a psychologist and be in good physical and mental health.

One who is interested in becoming a police officer may use the following checklist:
- Finish high school.
- Take college or continuing education courses in business, math, computer applications, and/or behavioral sciences.
- Consider military service prior to police work.
- Have a background check.
- Take a physical exam testing vision, hearing, strength, agility, and general physical fitness.
- Take the written civil exam for police officers.
- Take a lie detector test.
- Take a drug test.
- Have an entrance interview.

With all of the emotional rewards of being a police officer, there are other benefits as well. Police are usually offered medical insurance for themselves and sometimes even their family. They are provided with life insurance to care for their family in the event that something happens to them. Police are also allowed to retire after 20 years on the force and are provided with retirement income for up to 30 years. Many police forces also provide restricted college tuition reimbursement.

There are opportunities every day to make a difference. Police officers get to exhibit this every day. Is this an opportunity you'd like to take?

Looking Forward

15. Imagine that all you've ever wanted to do is become a police officer. You've taken the courses in high school that will allow you to be successful. You've stayed out of trouble and maintained your physical health. Think about your plan after you graduate from high school. What will you do to ensure that you become a successful police officer? Will you go to college? Will you join the military? What will you study? Craft a plan that includes not only educational experiences, but other experiences as well. Use details from the article and your own experience.

Looking Forward

Student answers may vary.

The student should address the question to the best of his/her ability using the article and personal experience. The question is meant to encourage students to explore areas of interest for their future and begin to determine how they will prepare for a future career.

Use the extended-response rubric in the Appendix to reference the criteria and determine the number of points to award.

Ethical Dilemma

16. You are a police officer with two years of experience. A gas station attendant calls the police to report that a young man has been disturbing his customers. The young man has been washing car windows without asking in hopes that they will give him some money. He lives with his grandmother and is trying to help her pay the bills. The attendant wants the young man arrested for harassing his customers and scaring away business. Knowing the man is desperate to earn money, you are caught in a struggle between reacting with compassion and enforcing the law. What do you do?

Ethical Dilemma

Student answers may vary.

The student should address the question to the best of his/her ability using background knowledge from the article as well as personal opinion and experience. The question is meant to encourage students to contemplate scenarios and make ethical decisions.

Use the character-education rubric in the Appendix to reference the criteria and determine the number of points to award.

Reading Instructional Guide

BEFORE READING

Front-Loading Background Knowledge Through Read-Aloud-Think-Aloud

Search the internet for recent articles on piracy and use them to model the effective habits of readers through a Read-Aloud-Think-Aloud.

Check out articles at the following websites to determine if they would be appropriate for your RATA:

- http://www.riaa.com/issues/piracy/penalties.asp
- http://www.pro-music.org/copyright/faq.htm

(Please keep in mind that it is the responsibility of the teacher to determine if articles from suggested sites are appropriate. The sites may have changed content since this publication. The publisher takes no responsibility for the current content of the site.)

Looking at the Words

Determining How the Word Sounds (Phonics)
With your students, use one of the sets of steps from the Syllable Guide in the beginning of the book to determine how to break a word into manageable parts. The goal is to break the words into syllables that the students can say. Then they can put those parts together to "sound the word out." However, remember that the rules for syllabification do not always work because our language is so diverse. The rules can also become rather complex for low readers, so keep in mind that their overall objective is just to figure out how the word sounds. They may not be able to break the word into its syllables perfectly, but they should at least be able to figure out how to say the word based on their attempt at following one of these sets of steps. Lesson One is a more basic set, while Lesson Two attempts to give the students the more specific rules without becoming too complicated. Take your time when teaching either set, and understand that many of the lower readers are not going to understand right away. It will take time, practice, and repeated application before many of them are able to make use of these strategies on their own.

Determining What the Words Mean (Vocabulary)
After students have spent time breaking the words apart to figure out how they sound, use the lists of prefixes and suffixes and their meanings found in the Syllable Guide to have students try to add whatever meaning they can to the words before actually looking at their definitions. After giving the students the definitions, have them see if they can figure out which words truly apply the meaning of any of the prefixes or suffixes.

Words to Study	Breaking into Syllables	Short Definition
Permission	per-mis-sion	(n.) authorization
Piracy	pi-ra-cy	(n.) the unauthorized use of copyrighted material
Incredibly	in-cred-ib-ly	(adv.) unbelievably
Legitimate	le-gi-tim-ate	(adj.) lawful
Device	de-vice	(n.) a piece of equipment
Convenient	con-ven-ient	(adj.) easy to use
Content	con-tent	(adj.) satisfied
Entertainment	en-ter-tain-ment	(n.) something that entertains, especially a performance

Activating Background Knowledge

Anticipation Guide
Mark each of the following statements True or False:

1. _____ Copying and selling a CD is illegal.

2. _____ Copyright laws are only for books.

3. _____ China makes a lot of money from CD sales.

4. _____ You can download movies from the internet for a fee.

5. _____ The entertainment industry is responsible for making CD and DVD prices go up.

Starter Questions
After completing the Anticipation Guide, have a group or class discussion with the students using the following questions:

1. What are your favorite music groups?

2. What is a pirate?

3. How might CDs become less expensive in the future?

4. Can you think of a time when you were given a "free" copy of a CD or video? Explain.

5. Why might entertainers sign endorsement deals with different companies?

Make a prediction about what you think the article will be about.

DURING READING

- Have the students skim the article. Give them about 45-60 seconds to do this.

- As they skim the article, tell them to circle any words they don't know how to say.

- When they are finished, talk about how to chunk the words they don't know how to say by sounds they now know and then sound them out.

- Have the students skim the questions. Give them only about 30-45 seconds to do this.

- Ask the students to predict what the article is about.

- Have the students read the article. They should question, summarize, clarify, and predict as they read. Instruct them to jot their questions, summarizations, clarifications, and predictions in the margins as they read.

- Remind students to constantly ask themselves if they know what the article is about right now. If they don't, they must reread to clarify. This is called monitoring for understanding.

- After they have finished reading the article, they are ready to answer the questions.

The Strategy Sheet

You may choose to have students complete the strategy sheet for each section before they answer the multiple-choice questions. Or you could have them complete the questions, work on the strategy sheet with a partner, and then go back over the questions to see if the use of the strategy sheet helped them more easily find the answers to any of the questions.

AFTER READING

Discussion Starter Questions

1. What can you do to help keep the cost of CDs and DVDs from increasing?

2. What should happen to people who make illegal copies of CDs and DVDs? Does imprisonment fit the crime?

3. What can you do to help stop illegal copying of CDs and DVDs?

4. Should someone who has copied or received a copy of a work by a particular music group be allowed to purchase that group's future CDs? Why? Why not?

5. Should we be allowed to copy a CD, with no intention of reselling it, just to be able to listen to the music for our own private use? Why? Why not?

Teacher Reflection

When you are finished with the article, strategies, and questions, ask yourself the following:

1. Did I get the students to THINK about what they have read?

2. Did I teach them (even a little bit) about how to read more effectively?

If you answered "Yes" to both questions, you can feel good about the day.

Pirates on the Sea of Technology

Mason loves listening to Nickelback and 50 Cent. Mackenzie listens to Pink and Shakira. They both enjoy going to the movies. If a movie has Vin Diesel or Angelina Jolie in it, it is instantly one of Mason's favorites. Mackenzie will watch anything with Orlando Bloom or Johnny Depp.

Mason likes to share some of the music he listens to with his friends. As soon as Mason buys a new album (today he bought Yellowcard's latest), he rushes home, throws it in his computer, and burns several copies of it to give to his friends. Maybe he'll even be able to make a few dollars from some of them by selling the CDs for a few bucks to those kids on the soccer team. They'll buy anything. He was even able to get them to buy that copy of *King Kong* his uncle had copied for him last summer. Mason's uncle, by the way, gets to vote for various awards for the Motion Picture Academy. So all the major studios like Universal, Warner Brothers, and Disney send him copies of the films before they are released on DVD so he can watch them and decide which ones he likes best. But he's not just voting. He's making early copies of the movies and selling them or sharing them. After all, he believes he should have the right to make some money for the work he's doing for them.

On the other hand, Mackenzie buys and downloads her songs from iTunes. If she wants to share her favorite music with her friends, she can publish a list of songs on the iTunes Music Store. Then her friends can look at the list and legally buy the songs they like. Mackenzie also downloads her movies from iFilm, a company she found on the internet that allows her to pay for and download movies. Who would Peter Jackson, the producer of King Kong, like having as his fan?

Mason is a fan, for sure. But Mason is a pirate. Oh, he doesn't make people walk the plank or carry a sword singing funny songs, but he is what people in the music and movie industry call a thief. According to them, what he is doing is no different than walking in a music store and stuffing CDs and DVDs in his pockets and walking out without paying for them. He steals money from the industry every time he illegally downloads a movie or copies a CD and sells it to his friends. It is even wrong when he copies music and just gives it away.

But Mason can't afford the high prices of CDs and DVDs. It's cheaper for him to go to an internet site that provides the music for free. Or he can trade CDs or video game software with his friends. They all do it. None of them think it is wrong. After all, they paid for the first copy. They believe they should be able to do whatever they want with it. They can hardly afford to buy CDs at $20 a pop. They see the music videos. They know music artists ride around in fancy cars, sporting all kinds of bling. People like Mason think that guys like 50 Cent or Kanye West won't miss the few extra bucks they'd make from him.

The problem is that what Mason is doing is against the law. The government has laws that say you can't take someone else's work and make copies of it. You can't pass out copies of it. You can listen to it. You can watch it. You can talk about it. But you can't do much else with it without the permission of the artist or the owner of the piece of work. These laws are called copyright laws. They protect the rights of the person who has done all of the hard work to make all of the money. When someone makes a copy of the music or movie without permission, it is called piracy. For every illegal copy that is made of a CD, DVD, or software, money is taken from the people who created it. It is not just the music artists who lose out when Mason burns a CD and sells it or shares it with his friends. It is also the producer, the editor, the record company, the person that develops the art work for the CD cover, the store that sells the CD, the employee at the store, and the list could go on. The music industry guesses that they lose a total of about $4.2 billion to piracy every year.

The sad thing is that Mason's parents think he is incredibly smart. He makes great grades in school. He knows more about computers than any adults they know. He even ordered a tool online that will let him make copies of videotapes directly onto DVDs. The company is legitimate and even provides telephone support. His parents figure if it is legal to buy the device, it must be legal for him to use it. Almost anyone you ask would believe the same thing. There are no laws that say someone can't sell tools like this. The technology

China's Music Industry

Piracy has become so bad in China that performers no longer expect to make much money from the sales of CDs. Almost as soon as they release a CD, someone has made mass copies of it and has begun selling it illegally for half the cost of the real CD. This means that those real CDs are vanishing. The musical performers are finding new ways to make money. They perform more concerts. They sign endorsement deals with different companies, having their faces printed on the sides of water bottles and other products. They create their own limited CDs with their inexpensive recording equipment and sell them at their concerts. Some American artists are resorting to this tactic and even claim that they are now actually making money on their CDs for the first time in their careers.

Some entertainers are just accepting the fact that they will never become fabulously rich by selling CDs and performing. They are content with the fact they are doing what they like to do, even though they aren't living in mansions.

What Drives Piracy?

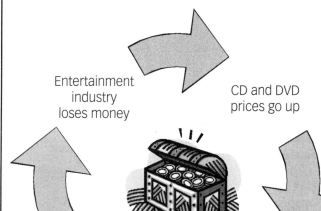

Entertainment industry loses money

CD and DVD prices go up

People copy CDs and DVDs to share or sell "free" copies of music or movies

New equipment/ software is invented to make cheaper copies of CDs and DVDs

are used to make illegal copies?

This issue means the entertainment industry may eventually have to duke it out with the technology industry in court. Both groups have tons of money to hire lawyers. The problem is that it may never be possible to decide who should win. The entertainment industry should be able to protect their work. But the technology industry should also have the right to sell equipment that could be used in a positive manner. So, right now, the music and movie people are going after people like Mason and his uncle. They are clearly breaking the law. And Mason and his uncle don't have a fighting chance in court.

We live in a convenient society. Things come pretty easily to us. As technology gets better and better, it is easier for people like Mason to be tempted to take advantage. Hopefully each of us has enough of Mackenzie in us, however, to know the difference between right and wrong. The problem is, with all of this convenience, the lines between right and wrong get much more difficult to see.

giants such as Sony, Microsoft, and Apple all have the right to make and sell equipment like this for today's world. The question is who is responsible when the tools

Reading Comprehension

After reading "Pirates on the Sea of Technology," choose the options that best answer questions 1-14.

1. Read this sentence from the article.
   They are content with the fact they are doing what they like to do, even though they aren't living in mansions.

   What is the meaning of the word *content* as it is used in this sentence?
   A. happy
   B. unhappy
   C. displeased
   D. knowledgeable

2. Read this sentence from the article.
   We live in a convenient society.

   What does the author mean by this sentence?
   F. We get most things for free.
   G. We don't have to work as hard for things now.
   H. It is very difficult to determine right from wrong.
   I. Technology makes the sound of copied CDs almost perfect.

3. According to the article, why do many young people make copies of CDs?
   A. They don't believe they are truly breaking the law.
   B. They can easily download them from sites like iTunes.
   C. It is cheaper for them to copy them and share with a friend.
   D. Musical artists like 50 Cent or Kanye West won't miss a few dollars here or there.

4. What is the purpose of copyright laws?
   F. to ensure people like Mason will go to jail
   G. so someone can get permission to make copies of a CD
   H. to protect the rights of people like Mackenzie who copy CDs legally
   I. to protect the rights of the people who have done all of the work on something

5. With which statement would the author of the passage most likely agree?
   A. Mackenzie and Mason understand how to use technology efficiently and fairly.
   B. Mason uses legitimate companies to purchase his copying tools. So, what he does is legal.
   C. Mackenzie understands the difference between right and wrong when it comes to the use of technology.
   D. Mason's uncle works for the Motion Picture Academy, so he deserves to make money on the DVDs he burns for his friends.

6. The author organizes the article by
   F. listing the reasons pirating is wrong.
   G. describing the copyright laws to prove a point.
   H. comparing two young people's use of technology.
   I. placing events in the order in which they occur to show why pirating is wrong.

7. Why does the author include the passage entitled "China's Music Industry" with the article?"
   A. to prove why piracy should be declared illegal all over the world
   B. to encourage people to purchase CDs directly from the musical performers
   C. to emphasize how much worse piracy is in China than in the United States
   D. to demonstrate the effect piracy is having on musical performers in different parts of the world

8. Which statement BEST expresses the main idea of this article?
   F. We must remember the difference between right and wrong when we use technology.
   G. Things come pretty easily to us because of technology, and it is easy for people like Mason to be tempted.
   H. Copyright laws make it illegal to make copies of CDs or DVDs without the permission of those who produced them.
   I. Make sure you use legitimate companies when purchasing software and equipment to make copies of CDs or DVDs for your friends.

9. Why does technology make it difficult for people like Mason and Mackenzie to live with high moral standards?
   A. Technology makes it easy to do things that are against the law.
   B. The legitimate companies are allowed to sell illegal equipment.
   C. Companies like Sony, Microsoft, and Apple have the right to sell copying equipment.
   D. The entertainment industry and the technology industry are going to court to decide who is right and who is wrong.

10. Why is it easy for Mason to copy CDs and DVDs?
    F. The companies he buys from provide telephone support.
    G. His parents think he knows more about computers than most adults.
    H. Copyright laws were created to protect the rights of people who create original pieces of work.
    I. There are no laws that say companies can't create software or equipment that allows people to copy CDs and DVDs.

11. Mason and Mackenzie are DIFFERENT
    A. because both teenagers enjoy popular music and movies.
    B. because Mason's parents have made it easier for Mason to be tempted to steal.
    C. because Mason has a much better understanding of technology than Mackenzie.
    D. because one knows the difference between right and wrong and acts appropriately.

12. What statement proves that piracy may cause a problem for the future of the entertainment industry?
    F. Mason and his friends can't afford CDs and DVDs.
    G. The music industry guesses it loses $4.2 billion per year to piracy.
    H. Major studios like Universal send copies of movies to people to vote for their movies.
    I. Some entertainers are even accepting the fact that they will never become fabulously rich by selling CDs and performing.

13. According to the article and the graphic entitled "What Drives Piracy?" what is responsible for young teens copying CDs illegally and sharing them?
    A. teenagers who copy CDs and DVDs illegally
    B. the invention of new software by companies that makes it easy for teens to copy music and DVDs
    C. a combination of factors, including higher CD and DVD prices and new software that allows people to easily copy CDs and DVDs
    D. musical performers like Kanye West and 50 Cent who don't see a need for stopping young teens from copying their music illegally

14. Based on the information from the article and additional passages, which conclusion is most accurate?
    F. Kanye West may eventually have to stop selling CDs.
    G. We will soon be able to get music so cheaply that we won't have to make illegal copies.
    H. Eventually, the entertainment industry may not be able to compete with the pirates, which will affect the type of entertainment we receive.
    I. The technology industry and the entertainment industry must settle their differences in court so we can have laws that will protect the entertainers.

Reading Strategy

Making Comparisons: Authors make comparisons between two people or things to make a point. We can use different tools to help track the comparisons we should be making as we read. Use the following diagram to compare Mackenzie and Mason from the article.

- Write the characteristics that are unique to Mason on the sword to the left-hand side and the characteristics that are unique to Mackenzie on the sword to the right-hand side.
- Write the characteristics they share on the flag in the middle of the two swords.
- Then answer the question below on the treasure chest using the information you've written on the rest of the diagram.

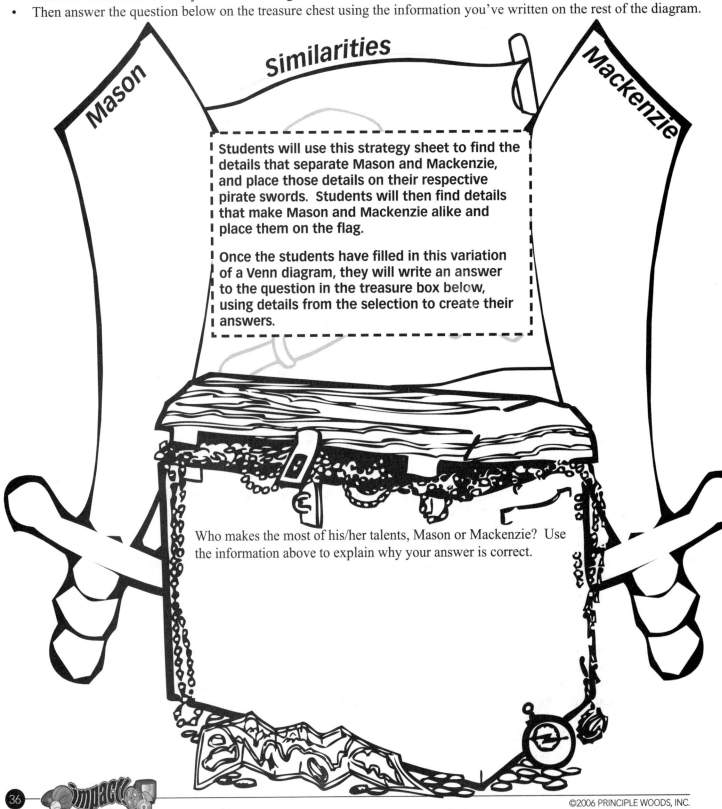

Mason

Similarities

Mackenzie

Students will use this strategy sheet to find the details that separate Mason and Mackenzie, and place those details on their respective pirate swords. Students will then find details that make Mason and Mackenzie alike and place them on the flag.

Once the students have filled in this variation of a Venn diagram, they will write an answer to the question in the treasure box below, using details from the selection to create their answers.

Who makes the most of his/her talents, Mason or Mackenzie? Use the information above to explain why your answer is correct.

Interpreting the Data

PART I

The following graphs compare the number of legal CDs sold in 2000 and 2003 to the number of illegal CDs sold in those same years.

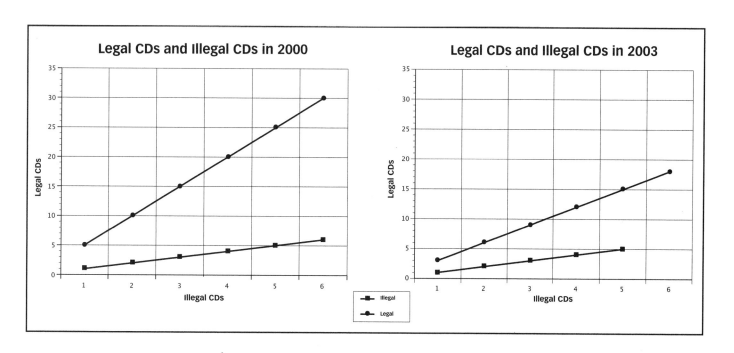

15. Using the information from the graphs, determine what has happened to the ratio of legal CDs to illegal CDs between 2000 and 2003.

COMPREHEND ANALYZE EXPLAIN

Students should answer something to the effect that in 2000, for every five legal CDs sold, there was one illegal CD sold. By 2003 the ratio had increased to three legal CDs for every one illegal CD.

Use the short-response rubric in the Appendix to reference the criteria and determine the number of points to award.

16 – 19. Make a prediction. Based on the article and your background knowledge, create a line graph that indicates what you think the price of the average CD has been between 1995 and 2005.

16. Value of the Average CD from 1995 - 2005

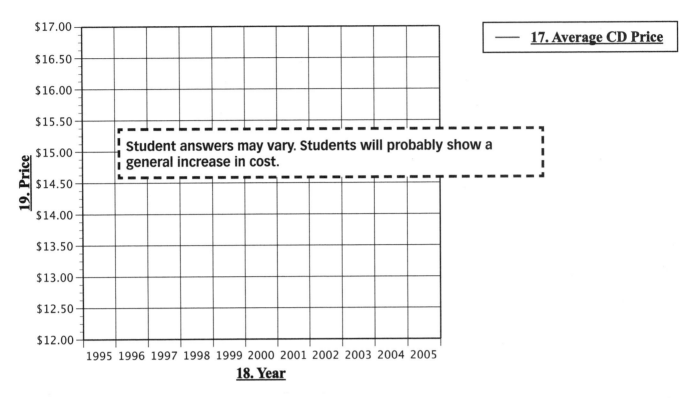

┌─────────────────────────────┐
│ ――― **17. Average CD Price** │
└─────────────────────────────┘

19. Price

Student answers may vary. Students will probably show a general increase in cost.

18. Year

20 - 30. Now look at the data below, provided to the public by the Recording Industry Association of America, and determine the value of the average CD each year from 1995 to 2005. Write the value in the column on the right.

	TABLE A		
Year-End Statistics of the Recording Industry Association of America			
Year	CDs Shipped (in millions)	Dollar Value (in millions)	Value of Average CD (Dollar Value/ CDs Shipped)
1995	722.9	$9377.4	20. **$12.97**
1996	778.9	$9934.7	21. **$12.75**
1997	753.1	$9915.1	22. **$13.17**
1998	847	$11416	23. **$13.48**
1999	938.9	$12816.3	24. **$13.65**
2000	942.5	$13214.5	25. **$14.02**
2001	881.9	$12909.4	26. **$14.64**
2002	803.3	$12044.1	27. **$14.99**
2003	746	$11232.9	28. **$15.06**
2004	767	$11446.5	29. **$14.92**
2005	705.4	$10520.2	30. **$14.91**

31 – 34. Create a line graph below that depicts the actual value of the average CD between 1995 and 2005.

31. Value of the Average CD from 1995 - 2005

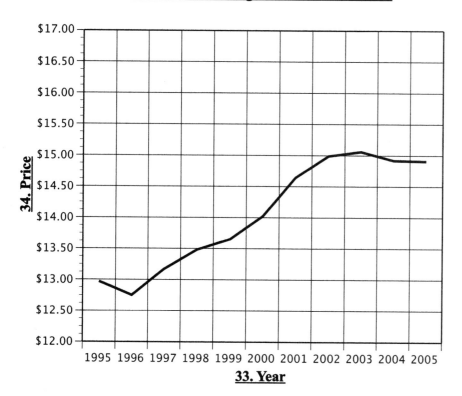

— **32. Average CD Price**

35. Was your prediction from the preceding page correct? **Answers will vary.**

36. How might the actual value of CDs over the last 10 years be related to piracy? Analyze the data to determine what the music industry has had to do to fight piracy.

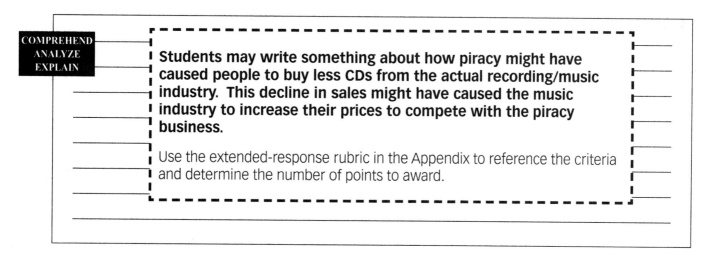

COMPREHEND ANALYZE EXPLAIN

Students may write something about how piracy might have caused people to buy less CDs from the actual recording/music industry. This decline in sales might have caused the music industry to increase their prices to compete with the piracy business.

Use the extended-response rubric in the Appendix to reference the criteria and determine the number of points to award.

PART II

Use the data below from the Recording Industry Association of America to determine the amount of counterfeit, pirate, or bootleg CDs they have seized from 2001 through 2004.

TABLE B The Recording Industry Association of America's Year-End Anti-Piracy Statistics				
Illegal CDs and CD-Rs Seized	2001	2002	2003	2004
Counterfeit[1]/Pirate[2] CDs	121,939	246,452	781,724	1,232,487
Counterfeit/Pirate CD-Rs[3]	2,795,693	5,298,368	5,069,637	3,713,522
Bootleg[4] CDs	16,795	1,863	2,659	59,053
Bootleg CD-Rs	93,520	200,239	14,182	63,236
Total # of Illegal CDs and CD-Rs Seized	37. **3,027,947**	38. **5,746,922**	39. **5,868,202**	40. **5,068,298**

[1]Counterfeit Recordings: When someone illegally makes a copy of the music on the CD and copies the packaging to try to make all of it look like the real deal.
[2]Pirate Recordings: When someone illegally makes a copy of just the music on the CD. They don't copy the packaging, etc.
[3]CD-R (Compact Disc-Recordable): A blank disc that can be used on a personal computer to easily make a copy of a CD or CDs.
[4]Bootleg Recordings: When someone illegally records a concert or live performance and puts it on a CD to sell to people.

41. Use the space provided below to add the categories together for each year. Write the total number of illegal CDs and CD-Rs for each year in the bottom row on the table. Then determine the average number of illegal CDs and CD-Rs seized each year between 2001 and 2004.

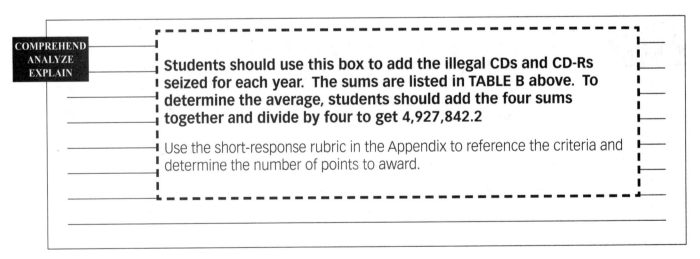

COMPREHEND ANALYZE EXPLAIN

Students should use this box to add the illegal CDs and CD-Rs seized for each year. The sums are listed in TABLE B above. To determine the average, students should add the four sums together and divide by four to get 4,927,842.2

Use the short-response rubric in the Appendix to reference the criteria and determine the number of points to award.

42. What was the average number of CDs and CD-Rs seized each year between 2001 and 2004? **4,927,842.2**

43. Look at the preceding table entitled "TABLE B: The Recording Industry Association of America's Year-End Anti-Piracy Statistics," the footnotes, and the article, and tell which category creates the most problems for the music industry. Explain why that category might be the most damaging to the music industry and why it is the most difficult for the music industry to overcome.

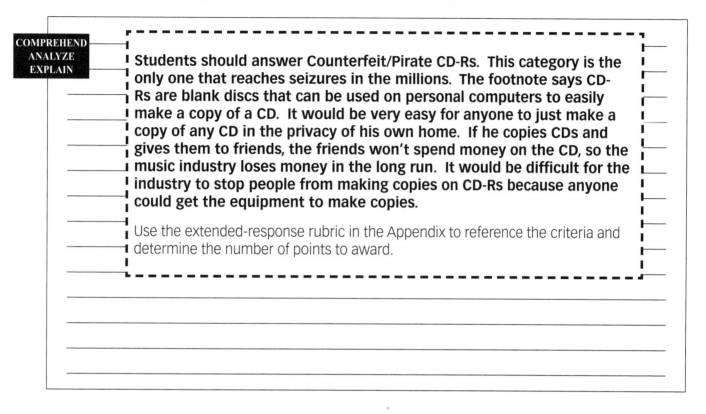

COMPREHEND ANALYZE EXPLAIN

Students should answer Counterfeit/Pirate CD-Rs. This category is the only one that reaches seizures in the millions. The footnote says CD-Rs are blank discs that can be used on personal computers to easily make a copy of a CD. It would be very easy for anyone to just make a copy of any CD in the privacy of his own home. If he copies CDs and gives them to friends, the friends won't spend money on the CD, so the music industry loses money in the long run. It would be difficult for the industry to stop people from making copies on CD-Rs because anyone could get the equipment to make copies.

Use the extended-response rubric in the Appendix to reference the criteria and determine the number of points to award.

Use the preceding table entitled "TABLE B: The Recording Industry Association of America's Year-End Anti-Piracy Statistics" to determine which graph (A through F) illustrates each of the following questions. (Circle the letter of the graph that is represented by each category. One graph will not be used.)

44. Counterfeit/Pirate CDs   A   B   C   **(D)**   E   F

45. Counterfeit/Pirate CD-Rs   **(A)**   B   C   D   E   F

46. Bootleg CDs   A   B   C   D   **(E)**   F

47. Bootleg CD-Rs   A   **(B)**   C   D   E   F

48. Total   A   B   **(C)**   D   E   F

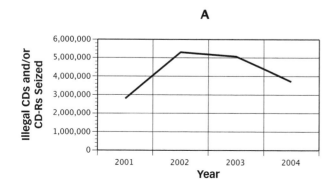

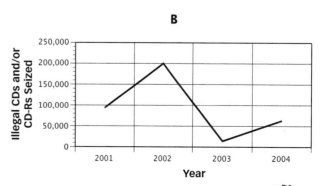

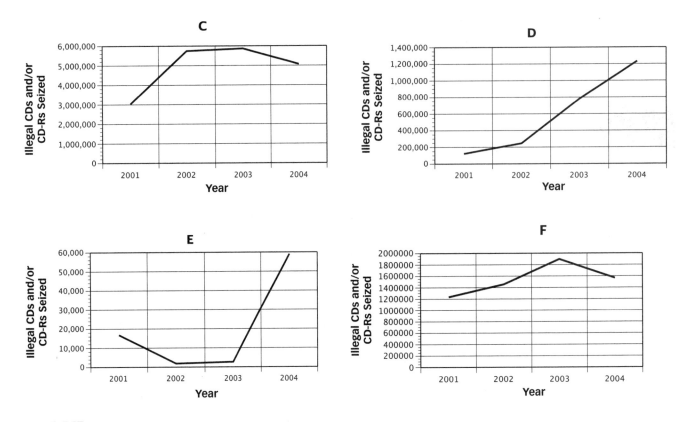

PART III

49. Look at the table entitled "TABLE A: Year-End Statistics of the Recording Industry Association of America." What was the value of the average CD during 2004? **$14.92**

50. Look at the table entitled "TABLE B: The Recording Industry Association of America's Year-End Anti-Piracy Statistics." What was the total number of illegal CDs seized by the Recording Industry Association of America in 2004? **5,068,298**

51. If the illegal CDs that were seized in 2004 had been sold by pirates, how much money could the RIAA claim to have lost that year to piracy? (Assume that all of the illegal CDs would have been sold and that consumers would have originally bought the real CDs instead of the illegal ones.) Show and explain your work.

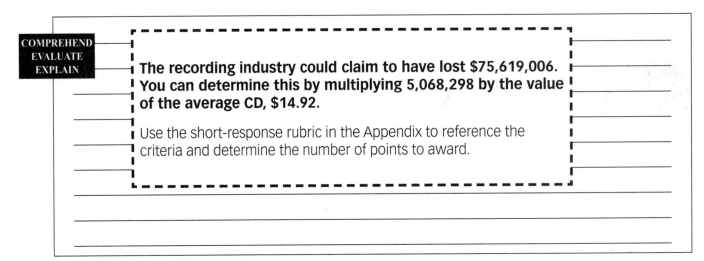

COMPREHEND EVALUATE EXPLAIN

The recording industry could claim to have lost $75,619,006. You can determine this by multiplying 5,068,298 by the value of the average CD, $14.92.

Use the short-response rubric in the Appendix to reference the criteria and determine the number of points to award.

52. Analyze the dollar value of CDs shipped during 2004 (from TABLE A) and the answer you came to in Question 51. Based on those two amounts, make a conclusion about whether illegal CDs damage the music industry. Explain whether or not they damage the music industry and how you decided on your answer.

ANALYZE EVALUATE EXPLAIN

> **Students should find that the dollar value of CDs shipped in 2004 was $11,446,500,000. The amount the recording industry would have lost in 2004 if they had not seized the illegal CDs would have been $75,619,006. This is roughly $150 made on legal CDs for every dollar of illegal CDs seized. That doesn't look too bad, but $75,619,006 is still a lot of money.**
>
> Use the extended-response rubric in the Appendix to reference the criteria and determine the number of points to award.

PART IV

Look at the following table of information, provided to the public by the Recording Industry Association of America, that depicts the number of CDs shipped (in millions) from the United States between 1995 and 2005.

Determine how many gains or losses the music industry had in the number of CDs shipped from year to year by subtracting the number of CDs shipped from the number of CDs shipped during the previous year. Write the number of gains or losses in the row labeled (+/-). Write a (+) before the number if the industry had a gain that year. Write a (-) if the industry had a loss that year.

The Recording Industry Association of America's Year-End Statistics											
	1995	1996	1997	1998	1999	2000	2001	2002	2003	2004	2005
CDs	722.9	778.9	753.1	847.0	938.9	942.5	881.9	803.3	746.0	767.0	705.4
(+ / -)		53. +56	54. -25.8	55. +93.9	56. +91.9	57. +3.6	58. -60.6	59. -78.6	60. -57.3	61. +21	62. -61.6

63. From the table, when does it appear that pirating of CDs may have begun having an effect on the recording industry? **2001**

64. What trends or patterns do you notice in the shipment of CDs by the Recording Industry over the last 10 years?

COMPREHEND
EVALUATE
EXPLAIN

Students should recognize that the Recording Industry went through a rough year in 1997, regained its footing from 1998-2000, and then dropped off for three years. It went up in 2004, then dropped sharply again in 2005.

Use the short-response rubric in the Appendix to reference the criteria and determine the number of points to award.

65. According to the Recording Industry Association of America, the music industry loses an estimated $300,000,000 a year in the United States due to piracy. What facts can you compile that show whether this could be an **accurate** claim? Explain whether or not you think it could be an accurate statement based on the data provided to you. (Hint: You must multiply the number of CDs shipped by the average price and look at the losses. Are there close to $300,000,000 in losses?)

SYNTHESIZE
EVALUATE
EXPLAIN

Students should show work that reflects the following:

Year (+/-)	Avg. Value	Dollar Value (+/-)
1996 +56 X	$12.75	+714,000,000
1997 -25.8 X	$13.17	-339,786,000
1998 +93.9 X	$13.48	+1,265,772,000
1999 +91.9 X	$13.65	+1,254,435,000
2000 +3.6 X	$14.02	+$50,472,000
2001 -60.6 X	$14.64	-$887,184,000
2002 -78.6 X	$14.99	-$1,178,214,000
2003 -57.3 X	$15.06	-$862,938,000
2004 +21.00X	$14.92	+$313,320,000
2005 -61.6 X	$14.91	-$918,456,000

Based on the drops in shipping, it would be difficult to say that piracy costs them only $300,000,000 a year. In the years they had losses, they were in the $800 million to $1 billion range. So, it doesn't look like an accurate statement.

Use the extended-response rubric in the Appendix to reference the criteria and

66. Based on everything you've looked at in "Pirates on the Sea of Technology," how would you suggest that the entertainment industry deal with piracy? Use details from the article and data to support your ideas.

COMPREHEND SYNTHESIZE EXPLAIN

Answers will vary, but should reflect the students' comprehension of the article and an understanding of the data.

Use the extended-response rubric in the Appendix to reference the criteria and determine the number of points to award.

*Quick*thought

Taking something from someone without permission and without paying for it is stealing.

Look Inside and Grow

67. What are your thoughts? When is it okay to copy CDs or DVDs, and when is it not okay? Do you agree that it should be illegal to make a copy of a CD you purchased (as the music industry claims)? Should it be considered theft to make a single copy of a CD you spent your own money on? Why or why not?

Look Inside and Grow

Student answers may vary.

The student should address each section of the question to the best of his/her ability. The question is meant to elicit strong classroom conversation about character. Students should be able to demonstrate that they have learned a lesson about what is and is not morally right when it comes to what you can do with today's technology.

Use the character-education rubric in the Appendix to reference the criteria and determine the number of points to award.

Notes

The music industry…: Recording Industry Association of America. www.riaa.com.

Year-End Statistics (charts, definitions)…: Recording Industry Association of America. www.riaa.com.

CD Cross-section (diagram)…: Brian, Marshall. "How CDs Work." howstuffworks.com. http://electronics.how-stuffworks.com/cd.htm.

Technical Extension

What's In a CD?

You probably can't remember a time when CDs didn't exist. But that wasn't always the case. There was a time when CDs and CD players could be afforded only by the very wealthy.

Engineers working for Philips and Sony started experimenting with the idea of audio discs as early as the 1970s, naming them compact discs, or CDs for short. At that time, music was being recorded and sold on records, before cassettes even hit the market. As CDs evolved and became more sophisticated, they came into play as a source for pop media. One of the first all-digital recordings by a major act was released in 1985 by the rock band Dire Straits. It appealed to the consumer because the format of the CD allowed more and longer tracks than the same album's cassette release. Today, nearly all music sold in stores is on CD. The CD industry has expanded from only audio to discs that carry information (CD-ROM), user-recordable discs (CD-R), and beyond. In 2004 the annual worldwide sales of all types of CDs reached about 30 million discs.

A CD is mostly just a simple piece of plastic. Standard audio CDs are made from a 1.2-mm-thick disc of polycarbonate plastic. This plastic makes up the majority of the CD's thickness and weight. During manufacturing, the plastic is impressed with tiny bumps. The bumps are arranged into a spiral to hold information on the CD.

The next layer is called the data layer, where music and information are stored. This is the layer that a CD player reads to produce the appropriate sounds, graphics, etc. The data is arranged by track in a spiral that moves from the inside out. A thin metallic layer (123 nanometers) is on top of the data layer. This aluminum makes the disc reflective and allows the disc to reflect the CD player's laser. The metallic layer makes the play side of the CD shiny and reflective.

Next is a layer of hard, ultra-thin protective coating made of acrylic. This layer protects the CD from potential damage and makes the CD top smooth so label information can be printed. Finally, a label is printed on top of the protective plastic. This label is what you see when you look at the top of a CD, and it may contain the title, graphics, and other information that identifies the disc. There is a 15-mm hole in the center of the disc, usually clamped into place and rotated by a motor.

CDs are usually packaged with a combination of a jewel box, a tray card, the disc, and an informational booklet. A finished product is shrink-wrapped and fixed with security stickers. This is how you'll find it in the store. Next time you pick up a CD, you'll understand the complex procedure it took to create it.

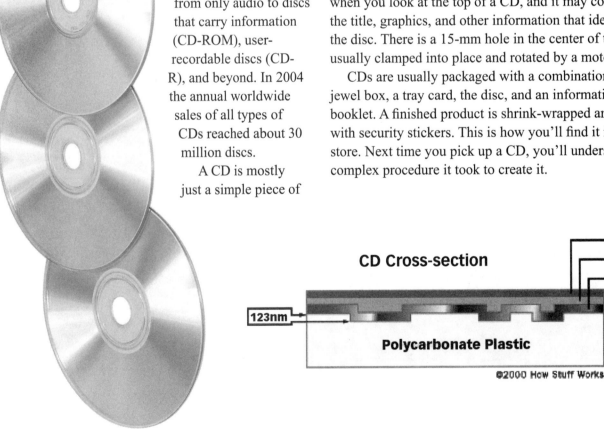

CD Cross-section

Label
Acrylic
Aluminum
123nm
1.2mm
Polycarbonate Plastic
©2000 How Stuff Works

Pirates on the Sea

Reading Comprehension

After reading "What's In a CD?" choose the options that best answer questions 1-14.

1. Read this sentence.
    As CDs evolved and became more sophisticated, they came into play as a source for pop media.

    What is the meaning of the word *sophisticated* as it is used in this sentence?
    A. refined
    B. colorful
    C. expensive
    D. exaggerated

2. Read this sentence.
    You probably can't remember a time when CDs didn't exist.

    What does the author mean by this sentence?
    F. CDs are difficult to understand and use.
    G. CDs were a secret when they first hit the market.
    H. You don't have as good of a memory as the author.
    I. CDs were probably already around when you were young.

3. According to the article, what makes up the majority of the weight and thickness of the CD?
    A. the plastic
    B. the acrylic
    C. the labeling
    D. the graphics

4. What is the role of the thin layer on top of the data layer?
    F. It reflects the CD's laser.
    G. It protects the CD from damage.
    H. It lays the foundation for graphics.
    I. It adds the needed weight for the CD.

5. With which statement would the author of the passage most likely agree?
    A. Most people listen to CDs in their cars.
    B. Most people spend too much money on new CDs.
    C. Most people download their music from the internet.
    D. Most people do not understand how complicated it is to create a CD.

6. The author organizes the article by
    F. describing the manufacturing layers of the CD.
    G. listing the reasons people like compact discs.
    H. comparing and contrasting CD sales to technology.
    I. presenting a chronological list of music devices and pop media.

7. What is the purpose of the illustration on the page?
    A. to explain the labeling procedure
    B. to show the different layers of the CD
    C. to tell the reader there are new guidelines
    D. to emphasize the size and dimensions of the CD

8. What statement best expresses the main idea of the article?
    F. CDs are easier to manufacture than cassettes.
    G. CDs have a clearer sound than vinyl records.
    H. CDs will eventually be replaced by the new iPod.
    I. CDs have evolved into a complex industry standard.

9. What is the significance of the evolution of the CD?
    A. to show why they are so expensive
    B. to show why nearly all music in stores is on CDs
    C. to emphasize the importance of manufacturing costs
    D. to emphasize the portability of CDs as opposed to records and tapes

10. Why is the CD impressed with tiny bumps during manufacturing?
    F. to hold information
    G. to reflect the CD player's laser
    H. to protect against potential damage
    I. to lay a foundation for the label to be printed

11. According to the article, what is the main advantage of CDs over cassettes?
    A. CDs sound better
    B. CDs have less working parts
    C. CDs are smaller and stackable
    D. CDs hold longer and more tracks

12. Which statement about CDs is LEAST accurate?
    F. They are packaged in a jewel box.
    G. The finished product is shrink-wrapped.
    H. CDs are not bought as often as cassettes.
    I. CDs usually contain an informational booklet.

13. According to the illustration, which of the following is NOT one of the layers of a CD?
    A. the acrylic layer
    B. the ceramic layer
    C. the aluminum layer
    D. the polycarbonate plastic layer

14. Based on the article, which statement is most accurate?
    F. CDs are more expensive than cassettes.
    G. CDs last longer than records or cassettes.
    H. CDs can be used in cars and portable players.
    I. CDs are manufactured with multiple complex layers.

Vocational Extension

Job Description

Star Recording is seeking a full-time sound engineer to join our production team. The employee will be required to do the following:

- mix and edit voices and music using sound mixing boards
- setup, test, and adjust recording equipment for recording sessions
- reproduce sound recordings from original media

Applicants must have a high school diploma or GED with three to five years experience directly related to the duties and responsibilities of the position.

Have you ever wondered how all the sounds on a CD are combined to make your favorite song? Do you have a good ear for music and enjoy technical tasks and attention to detail? Perhaps a career in sound engineering is for you.

A sound engineer has many responsibilities. He or she must be an expert in operating the mixing board, track recorder, and other recording equipment. Engineers participate in every detail of the recording process. Below are just a few of the engineer's responsibilities:
- translate the artistic vision of the artist/producer into sound
- set up and adjust recording equipment
- record musicians (one track at a time) and mix the tracks into one final product
- repair sound equipment

The training needed to become a sound engineer can occur in several ways. Some may elect not to continue their education after high school, but to begin gaining hands-on experience. Other future engineers may elect to pursue a two-year degree at a technical school. Another option is to attend a university program and major in recording arts, a division of the communications department. Those serious about learning more may even go on to get a master's degree as an engineer. Jobs vary in difficulty, and a person's level of education and experience will determine which jobs he or she will look for.

Because of the technical nature of the job, there is little experience other than actual engineering work to prepare a person for the position. This experience can be conducted as on-the-job training or learned while in a technical school or college. A job as a technician in a sound-recording studio or at a radio station provides helpful hands-on experience.

There are also classes and activities a student interested in sound engineering can participate in during high school. These opportunities will help the student learn about different components involved in sound technology. They will also help the student determine if he or she wants to pursue sound engineering as a career.

Sound engineers and technicians have very detail-oriented jobs that seem almost magical. They take many different components and combine them into a complete song. It's a fulfilling and challenging career.

Looking Forward

15. You are a high school student who would like to become a sound engineer one day. You haven't decided yet whether you will go to college or technical school, but you want to get as much experience as possible while you are in high school. Design a schedule of six classes and one after-school activity, and explain how each class or activity will give you experience toward becoming a sound engineer. Don't forget to include classes required for graduation!

Looking Forward

Student answers may vary.

The student should address the question to the best of his/her ability using the article and personal experience. The question is meant to encourage students to explore areas of interest for their future and begin to determine how they will prepare for a future career.

Use the extended-response rubric in the Appendix to reference the criteria and determine the number of points to award.

Ethical Dilemma

16. You're a sound engineer working for a premier record producer. Your assignment is to record the tracks of a popular rap artist's new song. The lyrics of the song contain hate words about women, and the sound effects include sounds that imitate violence against women. These issues go against your ethical position on violence. What do you do?

Ethical Dilemma

Student answers may vary.

The student should address the question to the best of his/her ability using background knowledge from the article as well as personal opinion and experience. The question is meant to encourage students to contemplate scenarios and make ethical decisions.

Use the character-education rubric in the Appendix to reference the criteria and determine the number of points to award.

Reading Instructional Guide

BEFORE READING

Front-Loading Background Knowledge Through Read-Aloud-Think-Aloud

Search the internet for recent articles on paparazzi and use them to model the effective habits of readers through a Read-Aloud-Think-Aloud.

Check out articles at the following websites to determine if they would be appropriate for your RATA:

- http://people.howstuffworks.com/paparazzi.htm

- http://peoplehowstuffworks.compaparazzi3.htm

(Please keep in mind that it is the responsibility of the teacher to determine if articles from suggested sites are appropriate. The sites may have changed content since this publication. The publisher takes no responsibility for the current content of the site.)

Looking at the Words

Determining How the Word Sounds (Phonics)

With your students, use one of the sets of steps from the Syllable Guide at the beginning of the book to determine how to break a word into manageable parts. The goal is to break the words into syllables that the students can say. Then they can put those parts together to "sound the word out." However, remember that the rules for syllabification do not always work because our language is so diverse. The rules can also become rather complex for low readers, so keep in mind that their overall objective is just to figure out how the word sounds. They may not be able to break the word into its syllables perfectly, but they should at least be able to figure out how to say the word based on their attempt at following one of these sets of steps. Lesson One is a more basic set, while Lesson Two attempts to give the students the more specific rules without becoming too complicated. Take your time when teaching either set, and understand that many of the lower readers are not going to understand right away. It will take time, practice, and repeated application before many of them are able to make use of these strategies on their own.

Determining What the Words Mean (Vocabulary)

After students have spent time breaking the words apart to figure out how they sound, use the lists of prefixes and suffixes and their meanings found in the Syllable Guide to have students try to add whatever meaning they can to the words before actually looking at their definitions. After giving the students the definitions, have them see if they can figure out which words truly apply the meaning of any of the prefixes or suffixes.

Words to Study	Breaking into Syllables	Short Definition
Clashing	clash-ing	(v.) to conflict; disagree
Paparazzi	pa-pa-raz-zi	(n.) photographers who take candid shots of celebrities
Tabloid	ta-bloid	(n.) a newspaper, often with sensational news stories
Restraining	re-strain-ing	(adj.) holding back from action
Allegedly	al-leg-ed-ly	(adv.) according to what has been declared, but without proof
Stalking	stalk-ing	(v.) to pursue a person in a persistent, harassing, obsessive manner

Activating Background Knowledge

Anticipation Guide

Mark each of the following statements True or False:

1. _____ Loopholes in the law allow paparazzi to stalk celebrities.

2. _____ Arnold Schwarzenegger signed a law that severely punishes paparazzi for causing harm to celebrities.

3. _____ Paparazzi take and sell photos of celebrities.

4. _____ Courteney Cox was caught driving away with her baby on her lap trying to avoid the paparazzi.

5. _____ Lindsay Lohan crashed her Mercedes into another vehicle while trying to avoid the paparazzi.

Starter Questions

After completing the Anticipation Guide, have a group or class discussion with the students using the following questions:

1. Who are the paparazzi?

2. What celebrities can you think of that have had run-ins with the paparazzi?

3. What rights does freedom of speech entitle a person to?

4. What rights should celebrities have in protecting their privacy?

5. What rights should paparazzi have in obtaining photographs of celebrities?

Make a prediction about what you think the article will be about.

DURING READING

- Have the students skim the article. Give them about 45-60 seconds to do this.

- As they skim the article, tell them to circle any words they don't know how to say.

- When they are finished, talk about how to chunk the words they don't know how to say by sounds they now know and then sound them out.

- Have the students skim the questions. Give them only about 30-45 seconds to do this.

- Ask the students to predict what the article is about.

- Have the students read the article. They should question, summarize, clarify, and predict as they read. Instruct them to jot their questions, summarizations, clarifications, and predictions in the margins as they read.

- Remind students to constantly ask themselves if they know what the article is about right now. If they don't, they must reread to clarify. This is called monitoring for understanding.

- After they have finished reading the article, they are ready to answer the questions.

The Strategy Sheet

You may choose to have students complete the strategy sheet for each section before they answer the multiple-choice questions. Or you could have them complete the questions, work on the strategy sheet with a partner, and then go back over the questions to see if the use of the strategy sheet helped them more easily find the answers to any of the questions.

AFTER READING

Discussion Starter Questions

1. Celebrities are viewed as public figures. This means they have fewer rights to privacy. Does seem fair? Should they have more right to privacy because they are celebrities?

2. Do you feel paparazzi have the right to take pictures without permission? Does this invade privacy?

3. Should paparazzi be allowed to sell and make money from celebrities' photos?

4. Paparazzi often have to stalk celebrities to get their photograph. Stalking is a crime. Should paparazzi be punished for targeting celebrities?

5. Should celebrities be forced to use anti-paparazzi tactics, such as disguises and decoys, to avoid recognition in public places? Should they pay a higher price because of their fame?

Teacher Reflection

When you are finished with the article, strategies, and questions, ask yourself the following:

1. Did I get the students to THINK about what they have read?

2. Did I teach them (even a little bit) about how to read more effectively?

If you answered "Yes" to both questions, you can feel good about the day.

The Founding Fathers Never Met
THE PAPARAZZI

Congress shall make no law… abridging the freedom of speech, or of the press…

The quotation above is part of the First Amendment to the U.S. Constitution, guaranteeing the rights to freedom of speech and of the press. This freedom means that the media has the right to report any newsworthy event without having to worry about being punished by the government or anyone else. It sounded good to our founding fathers, but it is now being tested because of the same people it was meant to protect. Now this right given to the American people over 200 years ago is clashing with the right to privacy for some top celebrities. Those celebrities want the right to be treated like normal people. They also want others to remember the unwritten rule to treat everyone the way you would like to be treated.

The problem lies in the fact that the press doesn't see our celebrities as normal people. Our celebrities make millions of dollars, live in extravagant homes, and are known by billions of people around the world. That is hardly what you would call normal. This lifestyle makes everything they do seem newsworthy to the press. So they chase them and take their pictures. They stalk them and take their pictures. Some even run their cars into them and take their pictures. These people are known as the paparazzi, a word that literally means "buzzing insects."

The paparazzi have caused serious problems for celebrities over the past few years. In 1997 the darling of the English people, Princess Diana, was killed in a car crash when her driver was attempting to get away from members of the paparazzi who were taking Diana's picture. It was later revealed that her driver was under the influence of alcohol, which was blamed for her death. However, the aggressive photographers were at the root of the accident.

Since then, celebrities such as Cameron Diaz, Lindsay Lohan, and Arnold Schwarzenegger have fought the paparazzi in and out of court. Schwarzenegger is governor of California, a state that recently put into effect a law that more severely punishes photographers if they cause someone to be hurt while they are taking pictures.

Some members of the media think this law is unfair. They think it goes against the freedom the press needs to be able to report all stories. However, the celebrities don't think the intimate details of their lives are stories the media should be reporting on to begin with. When a star is at a restaurant with family and friends and someone shoves a camera in his face, he feels like his rights are also being taken away. In essence, celebrities are being forced to give up their privacy just because they are famous.

The paparazzi see the situation as "I'll scratch your back if you'll scratch mine." They claim that up-and-coming stars will practically throw themselves in front of a camera in order to be seen by the public. The more they are seen, the more famous they become. Once they become ultra-famous, however, many of them no longer want their pictures to be taken. That is when magazines start offering between $10,000 and $500,000 for pictures of them, the amount varying according to their level of fame.

So photographers become more and more aggressive in their approach. They run over people. They block them with their cars. They sneak into their weddings. They pretend to be family members to get in hospitals and see celebrities when they are having babies. All so they can get that exclusive picture. Then they can sell the picture to a publisher for big money. The publisher will then print the photo in their magazines that sell to the public who will happily buy anything that gives them an inside look at the lives of their favorite idols.

Unfortunately, the fans don't realize the hassle they are creating for their favorite singers, actors, and actresses just to read the latest gossip about them. It seems unfair, but when people become famous, they have to accept the fact that their lives are anything but normal. To be famous means to be widely known and talked about. That is what the media does. They tell the public about people. They take pictures of people. They try to prove to everyone that they can get the best story. And they often do all of this without any sympathy for the people who get in their way.

When people become famous, they must remember that they live in a world of people who think they have the right to know everything about them. They can only hope that their loved ones will not get physically or psychologically hurt. It is the price celebrities pay when they open themselves up to a world that doesn't live by that unwritten rule that begs us to treat others the same way we would want to be treated.

THE OFFENDED

GEORGE CLOONEY

He tried to get people to boycott *Entertainment Tonight* and *Hard Copy* because of the paparazzi's footage of him and his girlfriend in 1996. In 2005, however, he claimed to just ignore the paparazzi because he doesn't want to cause issues with freedom of speech.

MICHAEL DOUGLAS AND CATHERINE ZETA-JONES

A tabloid magazine crashed their wedding and took unauthorized pictures and published them. The couple had originally made an agreement with a different magazine to publish the photos of their wedding for a set amount of money.

JENNIFER LOPEZ

After much exposure about her break-up with Ben Affleck, she ducked the media's attempts to determine whether she was married to Marc Anthony.

SCARLETT JOHANSSON

She hit a vehicle at Disneyland when she swerved to get away from photographers. The cars were damaged, but no one was injured.

COURTENEY COX

She took pictures of her newborn baby and sold them to the media so they wouldn't chase her trying to get photographs and possibly cause harm to her baby daughter. She gave the money she made with the pictures to a charity.

BRITNEY SPEARS

Photographers circled her, her mother, and her sister while they were in her car outside a pet store. One of the photographers was supposedly hit by her car. A spokeswoman for Spears placed the blame on the paparazzi.

During another run-in with the paparazzi, she was criticized for placing her baby, Sean Preston, on her lap and driving away. She said she was trying to get away from photographers and was afraid for her son's safety.

CAMERON DIAZ

She snatched a photographer's camera from him when he surprised her and her boyfriend, Justin Timberlake, outside a hotel. She turned the camera in to police.

LINDSAY LOHAN

In October 2005 her Mercedes crashed into another vehicle in West Hollywood when she was trying to get away from a photographer. Lohan and the driver of the van she hit were taken to the hospital, but neither was severely injured.

In May 2005 she was involved in a crash in when she attempted to get away from a photographer. He hit her car with his own car as he followed her. The photographer was arrested for assault with a deadly weapon. This incident helped the California government pass a law making the punishment for such crimes much more severe. However, the photographer in Lohan's case was eventually cleared of any crime.

REESE WITHERSPOON

She was surrounded by about half a dozen vehicles full of photographers who were trying to photograph her leaving a gym. She was able to pull away, but they drove aggressively around her. When she got home, one of the cars blocked her front gate. Her security finally chased them off. One of her representatives called the police and filed a report for false imprisonment.

When she was at Disneyland, two park employees were allegedly assaulted by a photographer who was trying to get a picture of her and her family. The photographer became aggressive and pushed the employee when she tried to move Witherspoon's group away from him. He was charged with misdemeanor assault and battery.

JUSTIN TIMBERLAKE

In 2004 he obtained a restraining order against a photographer who was supposedly stalking him.

ARNOLD SCHWARZENEGGER

The Governor of California and former actor claims he and his two children were once forced off the road by people trying to take photos of them.

GWYNETH PALTROW AND CHRIS MARTIN
(lead singer of Coldplay)

Martin supposedly hit one photographer in the face and damaged another's car on Paltrow and his wedding day. He was charged with damaging a photographer's car in a later incident, but the charges were dropped.

Reading Comprehension

After reading "The Founding Fathers Never Met the Paparazzi," choose the options that best answer questions 1-14.

1. Read this sentence.
   Celebrities don't think the intimate details of their lives are stories the media should be reporting to begin with.

   What is the meaning of the word *intimate* as used in this sentence?
   A. small
   B. secret
   C. personal
   D. unauthorized

2. Read this sentence.
   However, the aggressive photographers were at the root of the accident.

   What is the meaning of the phrase *at the root of the accident* as it is used in the article?
   F. caused the accident
   G. were possibly to blame
   H. were hurt most by the accident
   I. susceptible to injury from the accident

3. What do people find MOST acceptable about the paparazzi?
   A. their skill in taking hard-to-get pictures
   B. their right to freedom of speech and of the press
   C. their desire to bring the public all the news they need
   D. their ability to take any photos they want regardless of the price

4. What happened to Princess Diana that didn't happen to the other celebrities mentioned in the article?
   F. She was killed.
   G. She was involved in a car accident.
   H. Her incident caused new laws to be written.
   I. She was being aggressively chased by the paparazzi.

5. What is the author's point of view in this article?
   A. He opposes the paparazzi.
   B. He believes in the freedom of the press as long as they are considerate of others.
   C. He believes celebrities need to be more understanding of the rights of the media.
   D. He favors the rights of the media to get a story regardless of the effect it has on others.

6. What method of organization does the author use for the short stories about the celebrities?
   F. The author arranges the events by type of offense.
   G. The author arranges the events in order of importance.
   H. The author uses chronological order to relate the events as they occurred.
   I. The author lists the events in no specific order to emphasize the variety of offenses.

7. Why does the author repeat "and take their pictures" three times in the second paragraph?
   A. to make the reader remember the point
   B. to create a poetic rhythm for the reader
   C. to illustrate the persistence of the paparazzi
   D. to cause the reader to feel sympathy for celebrities

8. What is the main idea of the first paragraph?
   - F. Celebrities believe the rights given to the press should be changed.
   - G. The media must be more considerate of our modern-day celebrities.
   - **H. Celebrities are troubled by the way the media uses the rights given to them in the Constitution.**
   - I. The Constitution gave the American people the freedom of speech and of the press over 200 years ago.

9. What is the central conflict of this article?
   - **A. the freedom of speech and of the press vs. the right to privacy**
   - B. rights of modern-day celebrities vs. the public's right to a free press
   - C. the Constitutional rights of celebrities to sue aggressive photographers
   - D. the beliefs of the founding fathers vs. the rights of modern-day celebrities

10. Some celebrities provide pictures of their babies to the media at a fee because
    - F. they want to make their children famous.
    - G. they believe in the rights of the public to be informed.
    - **H. they believe it will make photographers stop chasing them.**
    - I. they want to make as much money as they can from their fame.

11. According to the paparazzi, how are up-and-coming stars different from very famous stars?
    - A. Up-and-coming stars believe in the rights of the media.
    - **B. Up-and-coming stars feel the paparazzi can help their careers.**
    - C. Up-and-coming stars are less noticeable and more difficult to photograph.
    - D. Up-and-coming stars want to be photographed because of the freedom of the press.

12. Which of these facts supports the idea that the paparazzi can be dangerous?
    - F. Courteney Cox sold pictures of her baby to the media.
    - **G. A photographer was arrested for assault with a deadly weapon after causing an accident.**
    - H. The media used the paparazzi to overly publicize the break-up of Jennifer Lopez and Ben Affleck.
    - I. A tabloid magazine upset a celebrity couple by crashing their wedding and taking unauthorized pictures.

13. People who read this article will learn
    - **A. about laws protecting the media.**
    - B. about the private lives of all celebrities.
    - C. about laws protecting the public from the media.
    - D. the difference between the American press and the European press.

14. Based on the information in the article, which of the following conclusions is most accurate?
    - F. Pregnant celebrities are more susceptible to the paparazzi.
    - G. Male celebrities more aggressively handle the paparazzi than female celebrities do.
    - H. George Clooney now believes freedom of speech is more important than the right to privacy.
    - **I. Accidents involving high profile celebrities led to tougher laws in California involving the media.**

Reading Strategy

THE SHOOT AND THE SCOOP
(Visualizing and Summarizing)

When a reader can't follow everything in a reading selection, it may help him to break it down into little parts and visualize what is happening. After "seeing" the selection in his head, he is then ready to summarize. Pick four paragraphs or separate parts from the article. Then, in the newspaper below, draw what you visualize for each part. After you have visualized, review your drawing and write a sentence or two that summarizes that part.

Edition IV Volumn III

The Daily Gossip

For Minds That Need to Know

Serving 2 Million Daily

The Shoot: *Paragraph #:*

The Shoot: *Paragraph #:* _____

The Scoop: _____

_____

_____

_____

_____

The Scoop: _____

_____

_____

_____

_____

The Shoot: *Paragraph #:* _____

The Shoot: *Paragraph #:* _____

Teacher's Notes:
Students should be able to pick four parts and adequately illustrate each paragraph/part to show that they have thought about what the author is trying to tell them in that part.

Drawings need not be perfect, but should demonstrate an ability to pull the most important parts out of a paragraph/part. It may help to have students add lines connecting parts of the drawings with verbal descriptions of what those parts of the drawings are meant to represent.

The Scoop: _____

_____

_____

_____

Interpreting the Data

PART I

An entertainment magazine recently purchased photographs of Brad Pitt and Angelina Jolie's new baby, Shiloh, for nearly $4 million. The two celebrities sold the photos to the highest bidder in hopes of reducing the number of photographers who would buzz around them trying to take pictures of the baby. Now that the photos are out there, there is less of a chance that photographers will hunt them down. They also donated the money to a charity to help other young children.

Was it worth it for the magazine?

Take a look at the data to determine for yourself.

Following are the newsstand prices (the price you pay for a magazine if you buy it in a store) and the 12-month subscription prices (the price you pay if you order the magazine and have it delivered to your home) of four magazines. Determine the newsstand price per individual issue and then determine the subscription price per issue for each magazine. Complete the chart with the prices you find.

Average Cost of Most Popular Entertainment Magazines During Summer 2006 According to Amazon.com					
Magazine	12-Month Newsstand Price	12-Month Subscription Price	Number of Issues	Newsstand Price Per Issue	Subscription Price Per Issue
People	171.08*	113.88	52	15. $3.29	19. $2.19
Us Weekly	181.48	69.97	52	16. $3.49	20. $1.35
In Touch	103.48	77.48	52	17. $1.99	21. $1.49
In Style	47.88	23.88	12	18. $3.99	22. $1.99

*This total does not account for all of the special editions published by *People*.

23. Which magazine offers the best rate through its subscription price? Explain how you determined your answer.

READ COMPREHEND APPLY

Student answers should include the following information:

Us Weekly offers the best rate through its subscription price. I know this because when I divided the subscription price by the number of magazines sold, their subscription price per issue ($1.35) was the cheapest when compared with the newsstand price per issue.

Use the short-response rubric in the Appendix to reference the criteria and determine the number of points to award.

24. Based on the preceding prices, which magazine do you think could most afford the $4 million price tag attached to the photos of the Pitt-Jolie baby? Explain why you chose the magazine you did.

> **ANALYZE EVALUATE EXPLAIN**
>
> Student answers will vary. They should support their predictions with some facts or details from the chart.
>
> Use the short-response rubric in the Appendix to reference the criteria and determine the number of points to award.

25. Assume that the magazine that purchased the photos used all of the money it collected on its magazine subscriptions to pay for the photos. Determine which magazine would have to sell the least amount of subscriptions to pay for the photos. How many subscriptions would they have to sell? How many subscriptions would the next closest magazine have to sell?

> **READ COMPREHEND EVALUATE**
>
> Student answers should include the following information:
>
> **People would have to sell the least amount of subscriptions. I know this because their subscription price is the highest. If you divided $4 million by their price ($2.19), you get 1,826,484 issues. So they would have to sell only that number of issues. The next closest magazine, *In Style*, would have to sell 2,010,050 subscription-priced issues.**
>
> Use the short-response rubric in the Appendix to reference the criteria and determine the number of points to award.

PART II

Use the following data table to answer Part II questions.

Cost to Run an Advertisement One Time in Entertainment Magazines			
	Half-page ad in color	Full-page ad in color	Full-page ad in color on the outside back cover
People	$154,100	$228,275	$294,400
Us Weekly	$140,510	$84,310	$182,665
In Touch	$64,910	$99,860	$129,810
In Style	$7,165	$11,020	$14,875

26. Based on the preceding numbers, which magazine appears to be best suited to pay the $4 million price? Explain how you came to your conclusion. Write about other factors that might affect your answer.

> **ANALYZE EVALUATE EXPLAIN**
>
> Student answers should include the following information:
>
> *People* appears to be the best suited to pay the $4 million because it charges the highest prices for its magazine advertisements. I am assuming that *People* sells more ads in its magazines than the other magazines. But if other magazines sold more ads, they might be better suited. For instance, if *Us Weekly* sold twice as many ads as *People*, it could be better suited to buy the photos.
>
> Use the extended-response rubric in the Appendix to reference the criteria and determine the number of points to award.

The magazine that purchased the photos could have used their advertising money to pay for them. The table below shows the different types of advertisements it ran in the magazine that included the photos of the Pitt-Jolie baby. (Assume that all advertisers had to pay the typical one-time fee and there were no discounts or additional costs because the baby photos were in the magazine.)

Advertisements (by type) Run by the Magazine That Purchased the Pitt-Jolie Baby Photos			
	Number of ads	Price per ad	Total
Full color, full page	66	$228,275	27. $15,066,150
Full color, 2/3 page	1	$194,350	28. $194,350
Full color, 1/2 page	7	$154,100	29. $1,078,700
Full color, 1/3 page	4	$104,650	30. $418,600
Full color, inside front cover	1	$271,975	31. $271,975
Full color, inside back cover	1	$248,975	32. $248,975
Full color, back cover	1	$294,400	33. $294,400
Black and white, full page	4	$156,000	34. $624,000
		Total:	35. $18,197,150

36. Analyze the data given so far. Was the $4 million cost of the photos expensive when you look at the amount of money the magazine made? Use data to explain your answer.

ANALYZE EVALUATE EXPLAIN

Student answers should contain the following information:

The cost of the photos doesn't seem that expensive after you add up all of the advertising money. When you add up the prices of the ads, you see that *People* magazine potentially collected $18,197,150 in advertisements alone.

Use the short-response rubric in the Appendix to reference the criteria and determine the number of points to award.

Look at the following table depicting the total audience of each magazine:

Total Audiences (readers) of Four Entertainment Magazines	
Magazine	Total Audience
People	40,259,000
Us Weekly	10,713,000
In Touch	4,271,000
In Style	65,390

37. *People* magazine actually bought the photos and paid a reported $4 million for them. Assume that after they subtracted the costs of running the magazine, they earned about 40 cents per magazine. Explain whether they could have paid for the photos with just the money they earned through selling the magazine. (Assume they used all of the money they made on the subscriptions to pay for them.)

APPLY EVALUATE EXPLAIN

Student answers should include the following information:

If they earned 40 cents (.40) per magazine, and you multiply that by the total audience (40,259,000), you see that *People* earned $16,103,600 on the issue, which is four times the price of the photos. So they definitely could have paid for the photos with the money they made selling the magazine.

Use the extended-response rubric in the Appendix to reference the criteria and determine the number of points to award.

38. Consider what you read in the article and examine the data to determine who ultimately pays for the photos. Then explain who ultimately pays the paparazzi. Use facts and data to support your answer.

**ANALYZE
EVALUATE
EXPLAIN**

Students should come to the conclusion that, even though the magazines pay the paparazzi, the consumers buy the magazines. We also buy the products that are advertised in the magazines, so we ultimately pay for the photos. Our money eventually finds its way to the paparazzi. So we are indirectly responsible for the loss of privacy that many of our idols suffer.

Use the extended-response rubric in the Appendix to reference the criteria and determine the number of points to award.

*Quick*thought

When you die, you can't take your money with you. While it is nice to have money, it is more important to build positive relationships in this life. Don't let money get in the way of that.

Look Inside and Grow

39. How much money would someone have to give you to be a total nuisance to someone else? Would you be willing to tell your best friend's secrets if someone paid you for them so they could announce those secrets to the school? What would your price be? Decide whether the paparazzi have a right to bother people the way they do. Explain why you think they do or don't.

Student answers may vary.

The student should address each section of the question to the best of his/her ability. The question is meant to elicit strong classroom conversation about character. Students should be able to demonstrate that they have learned a lesson about what is and is not morally right when it comes to making money at the expense of someone else's privacy or comfort.

Use the character-education rubric in the Appendix to reference the criteria and determine the number of points to award.

Notes

These people are …: "How to Spot the Celebs." BBC.CO.UK. http://www.bbc.co.uk/london/entertainment/celebrity/paparazzi.shtml.

The paparazzi see …: "Snap, Crackle, Pop." *The Sun-Herald*, October 4, 2004. http://www.smh.com.au/articles/2004/10/03/1096741893853.html?from=storyrhs.

That is when …: "Paparazzi: Going Too Far?" CBSNews.com, June 10, 2005. http://www.cbsnews.com/stories/2005/06/10/earlyshow/leisure/celebspot/main700831.shtml.

In 2005 he …: "Clooney Fears Fighting Paparazzi Will Create Freedom Issues." World Entertainment News Network, October 11, 2005. http://www.hollywood.com/news/detail/id/2446207.

The Governor of …: "DiCaprio Fears Death by Paparazzi." BBC.CO.UK, November 22, 2004. http://news.bbc.co.uk/1/hi/entertainment/film/4032567.stm.

Average Cost (chart)…: The subscription and newsstand prices for each magazine were found on Amazon.com in June 2006.

Cost to Run (chart)…: The advertising costs were found in the 2006 media kits for *InStyle*, *People*, *Us Weekly*, and *In Touch* magazines.

Total Audiences (chart)…: The total audience numbers were found in the 2006 media kits for *InStyle*, *People*, *Us Weekly*, and *In Touch* magazines.

Technical Extension

Rights and Responsibility

Freedom of speech was once a privilege reserved only for the rich and powerful. In the early days of the American colonies only a powerful few were allowed to express their views. Today, thanks to the Bill of Rights, freedom of speech is viewed as a right instead of a privilege and is protected for everyone. Having free speech means having the right to freely express your thoughts, views, and opinions. This doesn't include just fancy speeches and newspaper articles. Today this can include anything from movies and artwork to music or even the way you dress.

One part of the Bill of Rights is the First Amendment, which you may read below. The original text of the Constitution faced some conflict because it didn't specifically talk about the rights of the people. The founders of the country believed in a tradition of rights. The Bill of Rights was crafted under the leadership of James Madison and proposed by Congress in 1789. Two years later, it was officially adopted as an amendment to the Constitution. It's amazing that something written over 200 years ago still has such a huge impact on our lives today.

The First Amendment addresses five basic rights:

- Freedom of religion—There isn't an official national religion.
- Freedom of speech—You have the right to share your opinion.
- Freedom of the press—You have the right to get information from many sources with different views.
- Freedom of assembly—You have the right to gather in public or private places.
- Right to petition—You have the right to ask for changes in the government.

Often, people see the Bill of Rights as their permission to do or say anything they would like. But the Bill of Rights doesn't entitle Americans to unlimited rights. Think about a familiar situation. You probably know that you can't yell "Fire!" in a crowded place like a theater. The government defends its right to prohibit this because it would likely cause harm to others. The government is allowed to restrict your freedom when what you are saying or doing could hurt one or more people.

There's another side to free speech, however. There are hundreds of court cases every year examining the boundaries of controversial free speech. Some speech the government allows, and some it doesn't. Many of these cases revolve around the responsibility of a particular view being communicated. For example, is it responsible for a celebrity who serves as a role model to promote controversial political or social views? The celebrity's right to do that is protected and legal. But is it fair? Is it any more or less fair than a celebrity supporting a well-accepted, non-controversial view?

The fact that we can even have a discussion about this subject shows that we live in a society shaped by inherent freedoms and rights. The boundaries of free speech continue to be stretched every day. What are your views?

First Amendment

Congress shall make no law respecting an establishment of religion, or prohibiting the free exercise thereof; or abridging the freedom of speech, or of the press, or the right of the people peaceably to assemble, and to petition the Government for a redress of grievances.

Reading Comprehension

After reading "Rights and Responsibilities," choose the options that best answer questions 1-14.

1. Read this sentence.
   The fact that we can even have a discussion about this subject shows that we live in a society shaped by inherent freedoms and rights.

   What is the meaning of the word *inherent* as it is used in this sentence?
   A. inborn
   B. allowed
   C. artificial
   D. incapable

2. Read this sentence.
   It's amazing that something written over 200 years ago has such a huge impact on our lives today.

   What does the author mean by this sentence?
   F. It is too old to mean anything.
   G. It has had such a lasting impression.
   H. It hit with such force that it damaged our lives.
   I. It hasn't been used enough to make an impression.

3. According to the article, when is the government allowed to restrict your freedom?
   A. when you are in a place you shouldn't be
   B. when what you are saying or doing could hurt people
   C. when you do not have the same opinion as everyone else
   D. when you do not have the same religion as everyone else

4. What is the purpose of the right to petition?
   F. to share your opinion
   G. to ask for changes in the government
   H. to gather information from many sources
   I. to gather in public places or private places

5. With which statement would the author of the passage most likely agree?
   A. Citizens should responsibly use the right of free speech.
   B. Freedom of speech is a privilege that only some citizens deserve.
   C. Citizens have no right to express themselves through offensive clothing styles.
   D. Citizens should be able to freely yell anything in public places without concern for the welfare of others.

6. The author organizes the article by
   F. listing the ways the First Amendment protects your rights.
   G. comparing and contrasting the First Amendment and the five basic rights.
   H. describing Freedom of Speech and how it is part a of the First Amendment.
   I. presenting the chronological list of events linking the Bill of Rights to the First Amendment.

7. What is the purpose of the illustration on the page of the Technical Extension?
   A. to encourage the reader to read it first
   B. to tell the reader there are five basic rights
   C. to explain to the reader why the First Amendment is the best
   D. to emphasize to the reader the importance of the First Amendment

8. What is the main idea of the first paragraph?
   F. The First Amendment addresses five basic rights.
   G. Freedom of speech is only for the rich and powerful.
   H. Freedom of speech gives you the right to express your thoughts, views, and opinions.
   I. Today, thanks to the Bill of Rights, freedom of speech is viewed as a right instead of a privilege.

9. What is the role of the Bill of Rights?
   A. to protect your rights
   B. to restrict your freedom
   C. to promote social views
   D. to place boundaries on your rights

10. Why are people prohibited from yelling "Fire!" in a movie theater?
    F. People cannot see the fire in the dark.
    G. It involves the safety of a particular action.
    H. It is not polite to talk until the movie is finished.
    I. People will think you are rude for talking during the movie.

11. What do artwork and music have in common?
    A. In both, you can exhibit your talent only in performances.
    B. In both, you can share your artistic work only with close friends.
    C. In both, you have the right to freely express your artistic views.
    D. In both, professional people are allowed to showcase their artistic work.

12. Which statement about James Madison is LEAST accurate?
    F. He created the Bill of Rights.
    G. He believed in the tradition of rights.
    H. He was a founding father of our country.
    I. The Bill of Rights was developed under his leadership.

13. Which of the following is not an example of free speech?
    A. giving fancy speeches
    B. saying "Bomb!" on an airplane
    C. expressing controversial political views
    D. writing a sports column in the newspaper

14. Based on the article, which statement is MOST accurate?
    F. The Bill of Rights was designed only for the rich.
    G. The First Amendment entitles you to limited rights.
    H. The Bill of Rights was created to give you unlimited rights.
    I. The First Amendment allows you to do whatever you want.

Vocational Extension

Job Description

The *Springfield Daily Tribune* is seeking a full-time photojournalist to complete our news team. Applicant must have a degree or equal experience in the field of photography or visual arts. Responsibilities will include the following:

- obtaining photography assignments from news editors and journalists
- researching and covering complex news events
- exploring new opportunities and accepting ownership for tasks

Applicants must display photographic and layout skills, creativity, deadline-oriented behavior, attention to detail, digital technology proficiency, and quality focus. If you are interested, please e-mail your resume and electronic portfolio to hr@sfdaily.com.

Paparazzi have a bad reputation for stalking celebrities. They intrude upon private lives and use devious schemes to get photos. These so-called "professional photographers" then sell their photos to tabloids for tons of money. In short, paparazzi give many news photographers a bad name.

However, there are truly professional photographers in the news business. They are called photojournalists. A photographer takes pictures of things. A journalist tells stories. Therefore, a photojournalist uses a photo or photos to tell a story. Photojournalists are visual reporters. News journalists are expected to give accurate, truthful accounts of events. Photojournalists give the same unbiased account, only visually.

Photojournalists document history through their camera lenses. They get to travel the world and see many momentous events. Their primary job is to photograph people, places, and events in modern history. Usually their work is published in newspapers, journals, or magazines. It's not an easy job. It's more than taking a picture of an inanimate object, or even a person. They must capture the essence of a subject. Their work has an impact on the understanding of all who see it.

Many paths of training and study can lead to work in this field. Positions for photojournalists usually require a college degree in journalism, photography, or both. However, degrees in other areas are common because they give the photojournalist a special knowledge in a specific field. For example, a photojournalist might study earth science and specialize in photos of hurricanes or volcanoes.

Photojournalists must learn a unique set of skills to be competitive in their field. They obviously need excellent photography skills. In addition, good photojournalists are creative, intuitive, and knowledgeable about current events. Today, photojournalists will often need training in digital photography. They must be proficient in digital and print layout software. A photojournalist looking for a job should keep an up-to-date portfolio (print and electronic) showing a broad array of subjects, as well as a resume detailing any experience.

Competition is high in the photojournalism field. Young people wanting to enter it should try to get the best education and experience they can. The reward will be a career that impacts the lives of many.

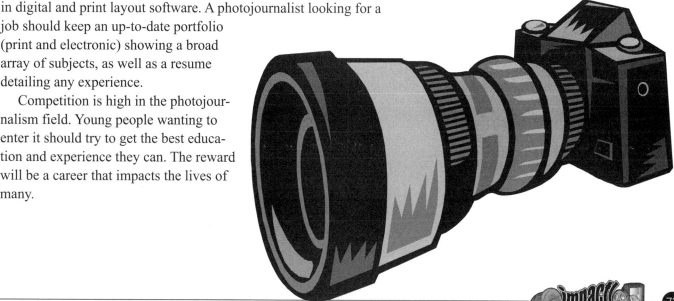

Looking Forward

15. Imagine you're a college student who wants to be a photojournalist. You're building your portfolio and need to cover a major current event. Choose a current event and describe what you will do to portray a story through pictures. Use information from the article and personal experience to explain you answer.

Looking Forward

Student answers may vary.

The student should address the question to the best of his/her ability using the article and personal experience. The question is meant to encourage students to explore areas of interest for their future and begin to determine how they will prepare for a future career.

Use the extended-response rubric in the Appendix to reference the criteria and determine the number of points to award.

Ethical Dilemma

16. You're a photojournalist working for a major national newspaper. You're on assignment in a developing country where you've witnessed human hunger and suffering. You've taken a heart-wrenching picture of a mother sobbing as she holds her young child who has died from malnutrition. The picture would be important internationally to help show the tragedy of hunger. It would also be a potential prize-winning photograph. On the other hand, it has captured a very personal moment of a mother's private grief. Do you publish it? Defend your answer.

Ethical Dilemma

Student answers may vary.

The student should address the question to the best of his/her ability using background knowledge from the article as well as personal opinion and experience. The question is meant to encourage students to contemplate scenarios and make ethical decisions.

Use the character-education rubric in the Appendix to reference the criteria and determine the number of points to award.

Reading Instructional Guide

BEFORE READING

Front-Loading Background Knowledge Through Read-Aloud-Think-Aloud

Search the internet for recent articles on skateboarding and use them to model the effective habits of readers through a Read-Aloud-Think-Aloud.

Check out articles at the following websites to determine if they would be appropriate for your RATA:

- http://www.etniesgirl.com/team/elissa-steamer/interview/
- http://www.etniesgirl.com/team/lauren-perkins/

(Please keep in mind that it is the responsibility of the teacher to determine if articles from suggested sites are appropriate. The sites may have changed content since this publication. The publisher takes no responsibility for the current content of the site.)

Looking at the Words

Determining How the Word Sounds (Phonics)

With your students, use one of the sets of steps from the Syllable Guide in the beginning of the book to determine how to break a word into manageable parts. The goal is to break the words into syllables that the students can say. Then they can put those parts together to "sound the word out." However, remember that the rules for syllabification do not always work because our language is so diverse. The rules can also become rather complex for low readers, so keep in mind that their overall objective is just to figure out how the word sounds. They may not be able to break the word into its syllables perfectly, but they should at least be able to figure out how to say the word based on their attempt at following one of these sets of steps. Lesson One is a more basic set, while Lesson Two attempts to give the students the more specific rules without becoming too complicated. Take your time when teaching either set, and understand that many of the lower readers are not going to understand right away. It will take time, practice, and repeated application before many of them are able to make use of these strategies on their own.

Determining What the Words Mean (Vocabulary)

After students have spent time breaking the words apart to figure out how they sound, use the lists of prefixes and suffixes and their meanings found in the Syllable Guide to have students try to add whatever meaning they can to the words before looking at their definitions. After giving the students the definitions, have them try to figure out which words truly apply the meaning of any of the prefixes or suffixes.

Words to Study	Breaking into Syllables	Short Definition
Propel	pro-pel	(v.) to push or drive forward
Endorsement	en-dorse-ment	(n.) money or support given to someone by a company
Deface	de-face	(v.) to hurt something's appearance
Apathetic	ap-a-thet-ic	(adj.) not interested in anything
Exhibition	ex-hi-bi-tion	(n.) public display of something
Franchise	fran-chise	(n.) a business with the right to sell
Consistency	con-sis-ten-cy	(n.) acting the same way over and over
Beloved	be-lov-ed	(adj.) much loved
Nuisance	nui-sance	(n.) something that causes trouble

Activating Background Knowledge

Anticipation Guide
Mark each of the following statements True or False:

1. _____ Skateboarding on the street is illegal in many cities.

2. _____ Snowboarding is not yet an event in the Winter Olympics.

3. _____ Tony Hawk is a fictional character made popular through video games.

4. _____ Skateboarders can make a living through endorsements.

5. _____ Skateboarders cause damage to public property.

Starter Questions
After completing the Anticipation Guide, have a group or class discussion with the students using the following questions:

1. Who is Tony Hawk?

2. What are the dangers of skateboarding?

3. Why might skateboarding be good for some people?

4. What video games do you know that are related to skateboarding and snowboarding?

5. Can you name any famous skateboarders and/or snowboarders?

Make a prediction about what you think the article will be about.

DURING READING

- Have the students skim the article. Give them about 45-60 seconds to do this.

- As they skim the article, tell them to circle any words they don't know how to say.

- When they are finished, talk about how to chunk the words they don't know how to say by sounds they now know and then sound them out.

- Have the students skim the questions. Give them only about 30-45 seconds to do this.

- Ask the students to predict what the article is about.

- Have the students read the article. They should question, summarize, clarify, and predict as they read. Instruct them to jot their questions, summarizations, clarifications, and predictions in the margins as they read.

- Remind students to constantly ask themselves if they know what the article is about right now. If they don't, they must reread to clarify. This is called monitoring for understanding.

- After they have finished reading the article, they are ready to answer the questions.

The Strategy Sheet

You may choose to have students complete the strategy sheet for each section before they answer the multiple-choice questions. Or you could have them complete the questions, work on the strategy sheet with a partner, and then go back over the questions to see if the use of the strategy sheet helped them more easily find the answers to any of the questions.

AFTER READING

Discussion Starter Questions

1. What are other sports or types of entertainment where people have negative perceptions of the participants?

2. Why do people "judge a book by its cover"?

3. What can you do to help change people's perceptions of others?

4. Name an athlete or movie star who gives his/her profession a bad name because of his/her actions. Name one who gives his/her profession a good name because of his/her actions. Is it easier to think of the bad ones than it is the good ones? Why?

5. Should a professional athlete who has been arrested be suspended for a season? Why? Why not? Can that same athlete make people look at other athletes and think poorly of them? Is that fair?

Teacher Reflection

When you are finished with the article, strategies, and questions, ask yourself the following:

1. Did I get the students to THINK about what they have read?

2. Did I teach them (even a little bit) about how to read more effectively?

If you answered "Yes" to both questions, you can feel good about the day.

impact!

Image – Don't Judge a Skater

Image is everything, isn't it? Without it, we would all be just alike. That is the positive side of the freedom to express ourselves. The problem that arises when we choose to grow our hair long and shabby or roll it into tight braids is that people are quick to judge. Can you really tell everything about someone just by the way he or she dresses?

One sport that may always suffer from an image problem is skateboarding. People say skateboarders cause a nuisance, reduce public safety, and deface public property. This causes cities to make laws against skateboarding in public places.

Many cities are erecting community skateparks. However, street skating still remains a popular form of the sport. Street skating is when skateboarders perform tricks using anything available such as curbs, benches, planters, and rails. The concern from outraged citizens is that they are destroying those things as they skate.

The way many skaters dress and act causes these same citizens to think they are lazy and apathetic. Unfortunately, these people see skaters and immediately think "criminal" or "drug user." This is obviously not a fair assessment of all skaters. But it only takes a few to ruin the image of many. And, unfortunately, it takes an entire army to restore the image of that same group.

Lately, skateboarding has become more popular because of the X-Games. Skaters like Tony Hawk and top young skater Ryan Sheckler are working hard to be positive role models for the sport.

Shaun White is also doing his part to help win the image battle. The Olympics has adopted snowboarding as one of its events. This has propelled White, one of skateboarding's phenoms, into the spotlight. He has successfully combined his talent for skating the ramps with snowboarding to become one of the world's best in both sports.

White's road was paved by the hard work and determination of Tony Hawk. He is the best known skateboarder the sport has ever seen. In 2005 Hawk was ranked number 22 in CNN's list of top sports figures. That same year, he received his fourth Kid's Choice Award by Nickelodeon for Favorite Male Athlete. These were big accomplishments, considering that the sport itself was nearly dead just 15 years earlier. But Hawk had helped bring it back from the ashes of its lost popularity.

Ryan Sheckler

Ryan Sheckler was born in December 1989. He started skating in 1993 and began competing in 1997. By 2003 he'd turned pro, and in 2004 he became the youngest pro-skater to win gold at the X-Games. By the age of 15, he'd won over 150 events in skateboarding, surfing, and snowboarding. He has toured with one of his main sponsors, Etnies. He has also toured with Tony Hawk and appears to be following in the skateboarding star's footsteps.

Sheckler has accomplished all of this while still in high school. He states that one of the keys to his success is consistency in his skating. He also advises young skaters, "Don't ever give up. You gotta keep trying, and never give up."

Hawk was born in 1968 and turned pro a mere 14 years later. By the age of 17, he had earned enough money through his sponsors to buy his own house. In 1991 the skating world fell apart. It seemed to lose its appeal. Sponsors backed off their endorsements. Tony began to lose all he had worked so hard to gain. But in the end, though, this just made the determined Californian even stronger. He started his own company, Birdhouse. He waited out the storm and had faith that his sport would regain its popularity.

His patience paid off. Eventually Birdhouse became one of the largest skateboarding companies in the world. By 1998 he started Hawk Clothing, which has since been bought by Quicksilver. In 1999 he signed a deal with Activision to create Tony Hawk's Pro Skater video game for PlayStation. The game was an instant hit. Since then, several newer editions have been released. The line has become one of the best-selling game franchises of all time. In 2005 his game Tony Hawk's American Wasteland was named the Best Individual Sports Game at the 2005 Spike TV's Video Game Awards.

In 2002 he started the Boom Boom Huck Jam. This is a tour featuring skateboarders, BMX, and motocross in an exhibition of X-treme sports. He also created the Tony Hawk Foundation. This charitable organization has spent more than a million dollars building public skateparks in low-income areas across the country. All in all, he's made it through the sport's rough times. With his creativity and determination, he has helped make his beloved sport popular again.

Shaun White, Tony Hawk, and Ryan Sheckler represent what the image of skateboarding could be. They work very hard to be three of the top skaters in the world. They are educated. They are well-mannered and proud, yet humble. They have a sense for business and how to market themselves, making large amounts of money on endorsements alone.

Too often one sees a teenager failing school, hanging out with friends, doing everything but what he should be doing. In his mind, he is living that skater lifestyle, like "hanging out" is all that matters. It is a lifestyle that appears to be glorified by the top-name skateboarders and X-game athletes. However, it is the exact opposite of their real lives. Tony Hawk, Shaun White, and Ryan Sheckler may make a living off of skateboarding and snowboarding, but they don't make a living by slacking off.

One thing young people need to remember is that even though these modern-day heroes of the X-sports portray a laid-back lifestyle, they are anything but lazy. Somehow their images become distorted by the way they seem to perform so effortlessly. They are just that good. But effortlessness doesn't translate to laziness.

They are setting the example for X-treme achievement. It is up to young skaters to follow.

Shaun White

He's been called the Flying Tomato, the Egg, Future Boy, and Señor Blanco. But it doesn't really matter what you call him now. Regardless of the nickname, he will forever be known first as Olympic Gold Medal Winner. Whether he's performing the McTwist or a backside 540, Shaun White lives for the moment. His boyish smile, wavy red hair, and laid-back attitude are only a cover for the amount of hours he has put into honing his craft.

At the age of 7, he won his first amateur snowboarding contest in the 12-and-under age group. He finished 11th that same year in the national championships. But that was only the beginning for Shaun. The next year, he returned to the nationals and won his first of five titles.

He has been successful in the world of skateboarding also. He won the gold in skateboarding at the Dew Tour in Louisville, Kentucky in 2005. He also took the silver medal in the vertical competition at the 2005 Summer X-Games.

White topped all of his accomplishments in February 2006 when he traveled to Torino, Italy and competed in the Olympic Winter Games. He nearly fell out of the competition in one of his semi-final runs. But he turned it around and performed a gold medal winning run in the finals, claiming his first Olympic gold medal in snowboarding.

And he has accomplished all of this before the age of 20. White reportedly earns more than a million dollars per year in endorsements and owns as many as three homes. His sponsors include Volcom, Oakley, Target, and Playstation. He has released his own DVD, The White Album, about his skateboarding and snowboarding adventures.

Though he works harder than he'd ever admit, he performs effortlessly both on and off the slopes and ramps. But don't mistake his smooth manner for a lack of effort. No one could be as successful as Shaun White without pushing himself to the limit nearly every day.

Reading Comprehension

After reading "Image: Don't Judge a Skater," choose the options that best answer questions 1-14.

1. Read this sentence.
   This has propelled White, one of skateboarding's phenoms, into the spotlight.

   A *phenom* must be
   A. someone who beats everyone.
   B. someone who is very successful at something.
   C. someone who tries very hard but is not very good.
   D. someone who makes himself look better, while making everyone else look bad.

2. Read this sentence.
   They have a sense for business and how to market themselves, making large amounts of money on endorsements alone.

   What is the meaning of the phrase "market themselves" in this sentence?
   F. create new endorsements
   G. make money by being successful
   H. become strong business people by advertising themselves
   I. use their image to make money by advertising for different companies

3. According to the article, Shaun White
   A. should be most thankful to Tony Hawk.
   B. should be most thankful to Ryan Sheckler.
   C. has been one of Tony Hawk's toughest competitors.
   D. should be thankful that Tony Hawk has done so much for the sport of snowboarding.

4. Which statement about Shaun White is LEAST accurate?
   F. Shaun White probably looks up to Tony Hawk.
   G. Shaun White has not been as successful as Ryan Sheckler.
   H. Shaun White doesn't have to spend much time working to be successful.
   I. Shaun White must truly believe in his abilities as an athlete and entertainer.

5. With which statement would the author of the passage most likely agree?
   A. Tony Hawk and Shaun White are responsible for skateboarding's rebirth.
   B. Tony Hawk and Ryan Sheckler have made young people lazy and apathetic.
   C. Tony Hawk, Ryan Sheckler, and Shaun White are ready to make skateboarding the most popular sport in the world.
   D. Shaun White, Tony Hawk, and Ryan Sheckler are positive role models in a sport that many see as having a bad image.

6. The author organizes the article by
   F. listing the reasons skateboarding has gotten such a bad reputation.
   G. comparing the lives of three of skateboarding's greatest athletes and showing how they have used their own style to recreate the sport of skateboarding.
   H. describing the problems faced by the sport of skateboarding and then showing what different people have done to help save it and try to restore its image.
   I. listing the accomplishments of Shaun White, Tony Hawk, and Ryan Sheckler so that the reader can easily see how each athlete was responsible for the rebirth of skateboarding.

7. What is the purpose of the information provided on Ryan Sheckler?
   A. to compare him to Shaun White
   B. to show how he has become a young star
   C. to prove why he is the best pro skateboarder
   D. to show the success he has enjoyed and the attitude he takes to help him become successful

8. Which statement BEST expresses the main idea of this article?
   F. Young people should follow the positive examples set by hard-working role models.
   G. Skateboarders always get a bad reputation because of the way they damage public property.
   H. Shaun White and Ryan Sheckler have much to be thankful for. Tony Hawk has provided them with the ability to make money on the sports they love the most.
   I. Role models can be picked by the amount of success they have had over a number of years. Only choose role models who have been successful for a long period of time.

9. Which statement best describes the determination Tony Hawk showed in order to help the world of skateboarding?
   A. By the age of 17, Tony Hawk had earned enough money to buy his own house.
   B. Tony Hawk started his own skateboarding company when the sport had lost nearly all of its appeal.
   C. Tony Hawk's charitable organization has spent more than a million dollars building public skateparks.
   D. Tony Hawk's American Wasteland was named the Best Individual Sports Game at the 2005 Spike TV's Video Game Awards.

10. Why might street skating be bad for the sport of skateboarding?
    F. Street skaters are destroying benches, planters, and rails.
    G. It is a dangerous form of the sport and only adds to its poor reputation.
    H. Street skating still remains a popular form of the sport even though many communities are erecting skateparks.
    I. Citizens are concerned that street skaters are destroying public property, which is hurting the image of the sport.

11. The major difference between Shaun White and Tony Hawk is that
    A. they both turned pro at a young age.
    B. they've both won medals at the X-Games.
    C. White has been more successful at snowboarding.
    D. White has a more positive attitude about his sport.

12. Which statement about street skating is LEAST accurate?
    F. It can cause damage to public property.
    G. It can lead to people's poor opinion of the sport of skateboarding.
    H. It has helped to make the sport more popular among average citizens.
    I. It is performed on things such as street curbs, benches, planters, and rails.

13. According to the article and the passage on Ryan Sheckler,
    A. Ryan Sheckler has won more events than Tony Hawk.
    B. Ryan Sheckler and Tony Hawk turned pro at about the same age.
    C. Tony Hawk is probably a better skater and snowboarder than Ryan Sheckler.
    D. Ryan Sheckler and Tony Hawk have both seen the sport of skateboarding through its rough times.

14. Based on the sections about Shaun White and Ryan Sheckler, which of these conclusions is accurate?
    F. Shaun White will earn nearly $10 million over the next 10 years.
    G. Ryan Sheckler has been more successful than White through his first few years of competition.
    H. Ryan Sheckler will eventually overtake Shaun White as one of the world's best X-Game competitors.
    I. Tony Hawk probably feels comfortable leaving the sport of skateboarding in the hands of these two young stars.

Reading Strategy

Summin' Up

Search the article for as many words as you can find that describe Shaun White, Ryan Sheckler, and Tony Hawk. Write those words on the small skateboards below. Then write a summary of the article in the decal. Use at least five of the descriptive words you have written in the skateboards AND the following words in your summary: laziness, image, athlete, skateboarding, snowboarding.

This activity helps you learn how to summarize, a key habit of effective readers. Summarizing also helps you search out the details that help you determine the main idea.

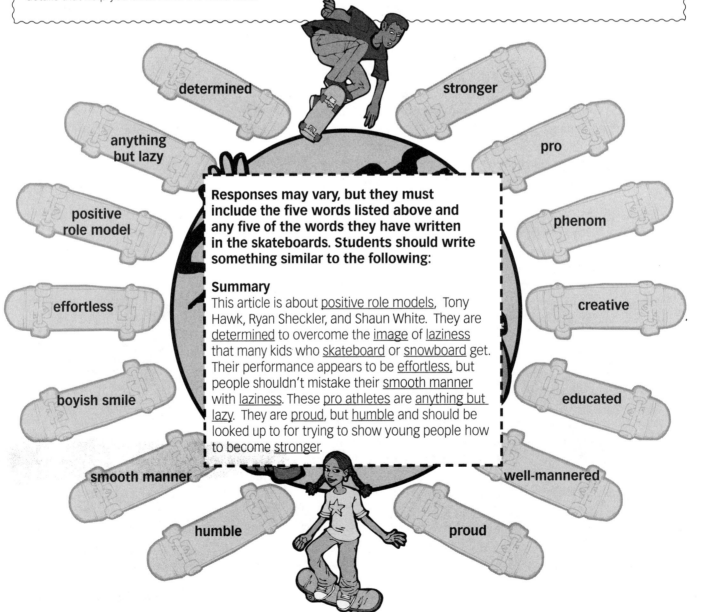

determined

stronger

anything but lazy

pro

positive role model

phenom

effortless

creative

boyish smile

educated

smooth manner

well-mannered

humble

proud

Responses may vary, but they must include the five words listed above and any five of the words they have written in the skateboards. Students should write something similar to the following:

Summary
This article is about <u>positive role models</u>, Tony Hawk, Ryan Sheckler, and Shaun White. They are <u>determined</u> to overcome the <u>image</u> of <u>laziness</u> that many kids who <u>skateboard</u> or <u>snowboard</u> get. Their performance appears to be <u>effortless</u>, but people shouldn't mistake their <u>smooth manner</u> with <u>laziness</u>. These <u>pro athletes</u> are <u>anything but lazy</u>. They are <u>proud</u>, but <u>humble</u> and should be looked up to for trying to show young people how to become <u>stronger</u>.

Interpreting the Data

PART I

Snowboarding is a sport closely associated with skateboarding. It struggled with image problems in its first years. When it was first introduced, some ski resorts reportedly wouldn't even let people snowboard on their slopes. The sport had to work hard to be recognized by the Olympics. Now it is becoming more popular and was one of the featured sports in the 2006 Winter Olympics. Shaun White led the charge for the Americans in their attempt to dominate the sport.

Look at the table below that indicates the medal winners in each of the snowboarding events.

2006 Winter Olympic Snowboarding Medal Winners		
Medal	Winner	Country
Men's Halfpipe		
Gold	Shaun White	USA
Silver	Daniel Kass	USA
Bronze	Markku Koski	Finland
Women's Halfpipe		
Gold	Hannah Teter	USA
Silver	Gretchen Bleiler	USA
Bronze	Kjersti Buaas	Norway
Men's Snowboard Cross		
Gold	Seth Wescott	USA
Silver	Radoslav Zidek	Slovakia
Bronze	Paul-Henri Delerue	France
Women's Snowboard Cross		
Gold	Tanja Frieden	Switzerland
Silver	Lindsey Jacobellis	USA
Bronze	Dominique Maltais	Canada
Men's Parallel Giant Slalom		
Gold	Phillip Schoch	Switzerland
Silver	Simon Schoch	Switzerland
Bronze	Siegfried Grabner	Austria
Women's Parallel Giant Slalom		
Gold	Daniela Meuli	Switzerland
Silver	Amelie Kober	Germany
Bronze	Rosey Fletcher	USA

15. Fill in the chart below to tally the number of medals each of the winning countries accumulated in snowboarding.

Snowboarding Medals			
Country	Gold	Silver	Bronze	Total
USA	3	3	1	7
Finland			1	1
Norway			1	1
Slovakia		1		1
France			1	1
Switzerland	3	1		4
Canada			1	1
Austria			1	1
Germany		1		1

16. Rank the top four countries according to the total number of medals they won in snowboarding. In the case of a tie, consider numbers of gold, silver, and bronze medals to rank the countries. Write the countries in their order below. Explain how you arrived at your answer. Use numbers from the table you have created to support your claim.

COMPREHEND ANALYZE EXPLAIN

Student answers may vary somewhat.

The countries should be ranked in the following order:
1) USA
2) Switzerland
3) Slovakia
3) Germany

The USA had seven total medals, and three of them were gold. Switzerland had three gold medals, but a total of only four. Slovakia and Germany each won one medal, but their medals were silver. The other countries only won bronze medals, so Slovakia and Germany would be tied for third.

Use the short-response rubric in the Appendix to reference the criteria and determine the number of points to award.

Look at the following graph which shows the total number of medals won by the top-performing countries in the 2006 Winter Olympics.

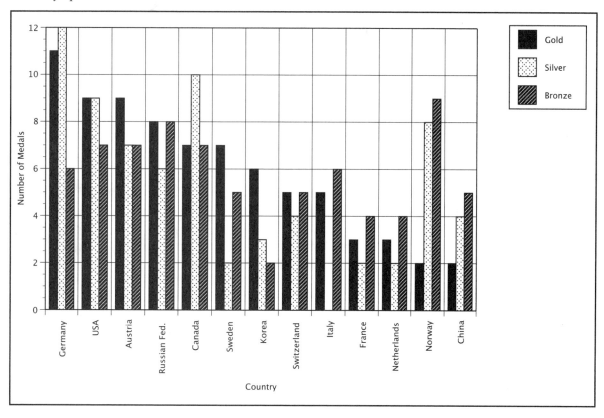

17. Compare the performances of Austria and the Russian Federation. Decide which country performed better overall. Consider the total number of medals won and the types of medals won. Use numbers from the table to support your answer.

COMPREHEND ANALYZE EXPLAIN

Austria won more gold and silver medals than the Russian Federation. Austria also won a total of 23 medals, while the Russian Federation won only 22. Therefore, Austria performed better overall.

Use the short-response rubric in the Appendix to reference the criteria and determine the number of points to award.

18. Use the preceding bar graph to tally the total number of medals each of the winning countries accumulated overall.

		Overall Medals		
Country	Gold	Silver	Bronze	Total
Germany	11	12	6	29
USA	9	9	7	25
Austria	9	7	7	23
Russian Fed.	8	6	8	22
Canada	7	10	7	24
Sweden	7	2	5	14
Korea	6	3	2	11
Switzerland	5	4	5	14
Italy	5	0	6	11
France	3	2	4	9
Netherlands	3	2	4	9
Norway	2	8	9	19
China	2	4	5	11

Now go back to the Snowboarding Medals table you filled out for the total number of medals each country won in snowboarding. Compare it to the Overall Medals table you filled out above to answer the following questions.

19. Of all the medals won by the United States, calculate the percentage of gold, silver, bronze, and total medals that were won by the snowboarding team. Show your work below.

COMPREHEND ANALYZE EXPLAIN

3 / 9 = .33 = 33% of gold

3 / 9 = .33 = 33% of silver

1 / 7 = .14 = 14% of bronze

7 / 25 = .28 = 28% of total

Use the short-response rubric in the Appendix to reference the criteria and determine the number of points to award.

20. If snowboarding were not an event in the 2006 Winter Olympics, where would the United States have ranked in the overall medal standings? Base your ranking on total number of medals won, and consider types of medals when needed to break a tie. Use the preceding tables to determine your answer. Show your work on the space beside the tables or in the box below. Explain how you came to your conclusion.

COMPREHEND APPLY EXPLAIN

Student answers may vary.

If snowboarding had not been an event in the Olympics, the United States would have won 7 less medals, for a total of 18. Germany would have lost 1 medal, for a total of 28. Canada would have lost 1, for a total of 23. Austria would have lost 1, for a total of 22. The Russian Federation would have lost 0, for a total of 22. Norway would have lost 1, for a total of 18.

So, if snowboarding were not an event, the United States would have been fifth in the overall medal ranks instead of second. (The United States would not have been tied with Norway for fifth because they won more gold medals than Norway.)

Use the extended-response rubric in the Appendix to reference the criteria and determine the number of points to award.

PART II

Use the following data table to answer the questions in Part II.

	2003 Estimated Population (in millions)	# of skate-parks per state (data from skate-board.com 2002)	# of people per skatepark	Tony Hawk Foundation Grants (2005 - 2005) (*tonyhawkfoundation.org, 2006)			
				$25,000	$15,000 - $10,000	$5,000	$1,000
California	35.5	200	21. **177,500**	2	7	11	16
Illinois	12.7	115	22. **110,435**				6
Massachusetts	6.4	105	23. **60,952**		1	2	2
Florida	17.0	85	24. **200,000**				2
New York	19.2	80	25. **240,000**		1	3	6
Colorado	4.6	73	26. **63,014**			1	2
Washington	6.1	58	27. **105,172**	1	2	4	9
Wyoming	0.5	10	28. **50,000**				1
Louisiana	4.5	8	29. **562,500**		1		
Hawaii	1.3	8	30. **162,500**				2
North Dakota	0.6	7	31. **85,714**				3
Alaska	0.6	7	32. **85,714**			2	2
Delaware	0.8	5	33. **160,000**				1
Wash, DC	0.6	1	34. **600,000**		1		
Tennessee	5.8	0	35. **0**			2	1

36. According to the table above, in which state do you believe skateboarding is most popular, based on the number of skateparks?

California

37. Determine the number of people there are per skatepark in each state. Fill in your answers in the third column. Examine the table to determine which three states actually have the most skateparks when you consider the state populations. Use the box below to show your work.

ANALYZE EVALUATE EXPLAIN

Students should divide the population in each state (in millions) by the number of skateparks.

Wyoming, Colorado, and Massachusetts have the most skateparks considering their populations. You come to this conclusion by dividing the number of people in millions by the number of skateparks. Wyoming has 50,000 people per skatepark. Colorado has 63,014 people per skatepark, and Massachusetts has 60, 952 people per skatepark.

Use the extended-response rubric in the Appendix to reference the criteria and determine the number of points to award.

*Quick*thought

Be a leader! Make everything that is positive about you shine through. Make others look at you and say, "I want to be just like that person."

PART III

Read the following information to answer questions in Part III.

The Tony Hawk Foundation gives money to communities that wish to build skateparks. This money is referred to as a "grant." The community must be in a low-income area, have strong community support for the project, and be available for "at-risk" children (those who are most likely to get in trouble due to their environment). The community must also fill out an application showing why they are most in need and send it to the Tony Hawk Foundation. As many as 450 applications are sent to the Foundation each year, which makes it very difficult for the Foundation to decide who deserves the grants. Look at the data above for the number of grants awarded to the states that applied over the last few years.

38. Examine the data in the table from Part II and decide which states need to become more involved in increasing the availability of skateparks in their communities. Explain how this might help problems they may have with street skating. Use actual numbers from the table to support your answer below.

ANALYZE EVALUATE EXPLAIN

Student answers may vary.

Florida, Washington DC, and Louisiana have few parks per total number of people. Florida has only one park for every 200,000 people but has applied for and received only two grants. DC has one park for every 600,000 people, and Louisiana has one park for every 562,500 people, but each has only applied for and received one grant. If they would put more effort into creating community skateparks, kids could skate in the skateparks rather than on the street where they can damage things.

Use the extended-response rubric in the Appendix to reference the criteria and determine the number of points to award.

39. Use the table to deduce which state seems to be the most involved in trying to make skateboarding a popular sport in its communities. Use data and details from the table to support your answer.

COMPREHEND ANALYZE EXPLAIN

California has 200 skateparks and has applied for and received 36 grants. This is far more than any other state.

Use the short-response rubric in the Appendix to reference the criteria and determine the number of points to award.

Look Inside and Grow

40. If you had to choose the top two things about yourself that you think annoy others, what would they be? On the other hand, what do you think are your two best characteristics? Do those two characteristics outweigh the two things that may bother others? Do you think you continually try to grow as a person and use your strengths to help others? Or are your weaknesses dragging you down and keeping you from positively affecting others? Explain how you try to positively affect others and continually work on your weaknesses.

Student answers may vary.

The student should address each section of the question to the best of his/her ability. The question is meant to elicit strong classroom conversation about character. Students should be able to demonstrate that they have learned a lesson about the value of others' perceptions.

Use the character-education rubric in the Appendix to reference the criteria and determine the number of points to award.

Notes

He also advises …: Cave, Steve. "Ryan Sheckler Interview." About.com. http://skateboard.about.com/od/proskaters/a/RyanShecklerMin.htm.

2006 Winter Olympics (charts)…: XX Olympic Winter Games 2006 website. www.torino2006.org.

Technical Extension

The Physics of *Snowboarding*

It's obvious when you learn about snowboarding that those who have risen to the top of their field can't be lazy. The physical aspect of competing in snowboarding requires athletic training for hours a day. But the educational aspect is perhaps even bigger. Snowboarders have to know a gigantic amount about science and physics to get the best results when they're riding. Not only do snowboarders not have lazy bodies, but they don't have lazy minds either.

Snowboarding is a sport that requires lots of skill and agility. Snowboarders strap their feet to a fiberglass board that resembles a large skateboard. Perhaps the most difficult part is maintaining balance while strapped to the board. Riders then use their whole body to manipulate physics and fly down a ski slope or custom-made course called a pipe while staying on their feet.

Because they often use the same courses, many people have a tendency to compare snowboarding to skiing. Unlike skiing, where skiers shift their weight from one leg to another, snowboarders shift their weight from heels to toes and from front to back on the board. In fact, snowboarding has more in common with skateboarding or surfing than with skiing.

Snowboarding has a lot to do with physics, a science that explores the interactions between matter and energy. Matter is anything that takes up space. In snowboarding, this can refer to the snowboarder, the board, the snow, the course, and any other physical thing that occupies space. Energy is the capacity to do work or activity. In snowboarding this includes everything from how a rider moves down a course to how he or she stops. In physics, you talk about matter and energy by singling out forces.

Gravity is the first physical force at work in snowboarding. It might be the easiest to understand. Gravity works in snowboarding the same way it does any other place on Earth.

The force of gravity not only pulls the rider down the mountain or slope, but it also keeps the board on the snow. Think of it this way: If a rider did an aerial stunt (a trick in the air) without the presence of gravity, that rider would stay suspended in the air forever.

Speed (or velocity) is the second force at work. Velocity is another way of explaining the distance traveled over a certain amount of time. Scientists find the velocity of an object by calculating the distance it has traveled divided by the time it takes to go that distance. The equation looks like this: $V = D/T$. V is velocity, D is distance, and T is time. Snowboarding would not be possible without velocity. Snowboarders measure their velocity using a combination of distance and time measurements. For example, they measure their speed in miles per hour (M/H) or kilometers per hour (Km/H).

Also involved is acceleration. Basically, it is the rate of change of velocity with respect to time. Acceleration refers to an object getting faster. This force makes a snowboarder go faster on the course and tells a snowboarder the change in speed over a given amount of time. A decrease in speed is called negative acceleration.

The final force at work in snowboarding is friction. Friction is the resistance that happens when one body of matter is moved against another body. In snowboarding, there is friction between the board and the snow. In other words, friction affects the speed of the snowboarding run and allows the rider to slow or stop the board. Snowboarders apply wax to their boards and like to ride on icy slopes in order to decrease friction and increase speed. To slow down and turn, the rider digs into the snow with the edge of the board he is riding on and leans in the direction he wants to move. This creates friction. At the bottom of a slope, he uses friction to stop by putting pressure on the board against the snow.

Snowboarders might not confess to thinking about physics while they ride down a mountain at lightning speeds. In fact, if you ask Olympic champion Shaun White what he's thinking when he takes the slopes, chances are his first answer won't include the equation for velocity. What he would tell you he's thinking about would probably include how to ride the fastest, how to get the most height on his jumps, and where his weight needs to be on his board. That's all physics—just in different words. Knowing the physics of snowboarding helps Shaun White be the best snowboarder in the world.

Reading Comprehension

After reading "The Physics of Snowboarding," choose the options that best answer questions 1-14.

1. Read this sentence.
   Energy is the capacity to do work or activity.

   What is the meaning of the word *capacity* as it is used in this sentence?
   A. ability
   B. failure
   C. position
   D. inability

2. Read this sentence.
   Not only do snowboarders not have lazy bodies, but they don't have lazy minds either.

   What does the author mean by this sentence?
   F. Snowboarders have bigger brains than most people.
   G. Snowboarders are energetic because they love their sport.
   H. Snowboarders have to study hard and be knowledgeable to do well.
   I. Snowboarders do not need to learn because their sport is only physical.

3. According to the article, which physical force is used when a rider wants to stop?
   A. gravity
   B. friction
   C. velocity
   D. acceleration

4. What is the role of gravity in snowboarding?
   F. It suspends the rider in the air when he jumps.
   G. It measures the relationship between matter and energy.
   H. It pulls the rider down the mountain and keeps the board on the snow.
   I. It affects the speed of the run and allows the rider to slow or stop at any time.

5. What does the author conclude is the reason Shaun White is the best snowboarder in the world?
   A. He knows the equation for friction.
   B. He isn't physically lazy, and he trains hard.
   C. He thinks about physics while he rides, although he might not realize that's what he is doing.
   D. He uses different, non-scientific words to explain physics to others, although they do not understand.

6. The author organizes this article by
   F. presenting a chronological list of events linking physics to sports.
   G. listing the best snowboarders and how they use physics in their sport.
   H. comparing how science is used to improve performance in different sports.
   I. describing the different physical forces in snowboarding and how they work.

7. What was the author's purpose in writing this article?
   A. to describe why snowboarders need a good education
   B. to explain to the reader the basics of how to snowboard
   C. to demonstrate the large role physics plays in snowboarding and briefly explain physical forces
   D. to introduce the reader to the sport of snowboarding and show how it is different from all other sports

8. What is the main idea of the article?
    F. Snowboarding requires both physical and mental energy.
    G. Shaun White is the best snowboarder in the world right now.
    H. Snowboarding is based on physics, and understanding physics improves riding ability.
    I. Snowboarders are constantly measuring their results using physics as a basis for their placement.

9. What is difficult about snowboarding with regard to the snowboard?
    A. The board is often too slippery to maintain control.
    B. Riders can use only their feet to control their ride on the board.
    C. The board is hard to use because it is much larger than a skateboard.
    D. Riders have to maintain balance while their feet are strapped to the board.

10. Why does a snowboarder accelerate when he goes down a hill?
    F. The snowboarder experiences an increase in gravity over a certain amount of time.
    G. The snowboarder experiences an increase in friction over a certain amount of time.
    H. The snowboarder experiences a decrease in velocity over a certain amount of time.
    I. The snowboarder experiences an increase in velocity over a certain amount of time.

11. Skiing and snowboarding are ALIKE in that they
    A. use the same or similar courses.
    B. have similarities to skateboarding.
    C. require riders to shift weight from foot to foot.
    D. require riders to shift weight from front to back.

12. Which statement about velocity is LEAST accurate?
    F. Velocity is calculated by dividing time by distance (T/D).
    G. A snowboarder might say his velocity was 40 miles per hour.
    H. Velocity helps determine acceleration and is used in its equation.
    I. Velocity explains the distance traveled over a set amount of time.

13. Which of the following is NOT an example of matter?
    A. rider
    B. stopping
    C. snowboard
    D. pipe course

14. Based on the article, which statement is most accurate?
    F. Knowing physics will automatically create a champion athlete.
    G. Physics is a difficult subject, and only professional scientists truly understand it.
    H. Understanding physics helps athletes better understand and perform in their sport.
    I. Shaun White is so busy training that he doesn't have time or a need to learn about science.

Vocational Extension

Job Description

On the Ball Advertising is looking for full-time energetic and self-motivated people to fill entry-level positions in Sports Marketing and Account Management. Positions are open to college graduates who have experience or interest in marketing. Several degree fields are helpful, including advertising, journalism, business management, marketing, and communication. Applicants must possess computer skills, including Microsoft Office Suite and desktop publishing skills. The salary will range from $30,000 to $65,000 per year with opportunities for advancement. If you fit the above criteria and are interested, please e-mail your resume to info@ontheball.com.

Walk into a football stadium. Chances are one of the first things you'll notice is the display of huge banners advertising Coca-Cola or any number of other companies who use sports to advertise. Did you notice the commercials during the 2005 Olympics? Major-name athletes endorsed companies like McDonalds and Visa with the Olympic rings. Or take a look at Shaun White, the gold medal winning snowboarder. You'll see him sporting sunglasses by Oakley, one of his sponsors, while riding a snowboard by Burton, another sponsor. In sports, advertisements are everywhere. Welcome to the world of sports marketing.

Sports marketers handle the business side of sports. There is no shortage of jobs in this arena. Some work for professional organizations such as the National Football League. Others work for individual teams like the NBA's Orlando Magic. Some work for major companies, like Gatorade, who advertise their products in conjunction with athletics. Still others work as agents for professional athletes to negotiate contracts and endorsement opportunities. There are also marketers who organize events on behalf of organizations, teams, or companies. Sports marketing firms seem to be popping up everywhere.

As new sports take the spotlight, even more marketing opportunities have surfaced. Extreme sports, such as snowboarding, have produced new athletes, new venues, new equipment, and new sponsors.

Sports management jobs may include any of the following responsibilities:

- negotiating contracts and endorsements for athletes
- planning and coordinating sports events
- conducting research and analysis for the sports market
- producing promotional materials, including print and multimedia
- monitoring sports activities and trends
- developing new merchandise and products associated with clients

There are jobs at every level of training and education in the sports management field. It takes a great deal of work, willingness to learn, and drive to succeed in this type of job. But the rewards can be great. Sports marketing can be fun and exciting, but it can also require strong work ethic and skills. The job description above lists some of the requirements for a job in this field, including college training. There are other things a person interested in sports marketing can do to set himself apart. Look at the resume on the next page and try to identify what background activity sets this candidate apart.

Sample Resume for a Sports Marketing Candidate

Jill Jones
1234 Washington Rd.
Jacksonville, FL 32223
904-222-3344
jilljones@sportscareer.com

OBJECTIVE	To obtain a challenging job in sports management.

EDUCATION

University of Florida
Gainesville, FL, May 2006
- Bachelor of Arts in Business Marketing
- GPA: 3.8

EXPERIENCE

Student Manager, UF Soccer Team
    Gainesville, FL, 2004-2006
- Worked with Sports Information Director at college to handle information needed for game days

Intern, The Daniels Company
Atlanta, GA, Summer 2005
- Assisted Marketing Manager in handling the marketing needs of the organization
- Trained with individual account managers

Student Worker, UF Fitness Center
Gainesville, FL, 2003-2004
- Fitness center supervisor
- Ensured safe workout environment, enforced procedures

HONORS

Michael P. Wilson Leadership Award, May 2003
Dean's List, 3 semesters

CAMPUS ACTIVITIES

Intramural Soccer League
Fellowship of Christian Athletes
Student Honor Society

COMMUNITY ACTIVITIES

Volunteer for LIVESTRONG Challenge, 2004-2006

REFERENCES

Dr. Mark Goldberg, Business Professor
goldbergm@ufl.edu, (352) 556-5556

Coach Bill Raymond, UF Athletic Department
raymondg@ufl.edu, (352) 113-4477

Looking Forward

15. You're a high school student who knows you want to become a Sports Manager. Identify at least three activities you could participate in during high school and college to gain experience. Next, decide what type of Sports Management you would like to pursue (i.e., business, promotion, media). Use the job description, article, and sample resume along with your experience to complete your answer.

Looking Forward

Student answers may vary.

The student should address the question to the best of his/her ability using the article and personal experience. The question is meant to encourage students to explore areas of interest for their future and begin to determine how they will prepare for a future career.

Use the extended-response rubric in the Appendix to reference the criteria and determine the number of points to award.

Ethical Dilemma

16. You're a sports marketing executive in charge of a major new promotion for kid's basketball shoes. The manufacturer has chosen a successful but troubled basketball star to promote the product. The company knows this star has been suspended multiple times for breaking the rules and has even had some legal trouble. On the other hand, they are sure he will make their product popular. Do you encourage this athlete to be a role model for young players by making him the product spokesperson? Explain you answer.

Ethical Dilemma

Student answers may vary.

The student should address the question to the best of his/her ability using background knowledge from the article as well as personal opinion and experience. The question is meant to encourage students to contemplate scenarios and make ethical decisions.

Use the character-education rubric in the Appendix to reference the criteria and determine the number of points to award.

Reading Instructional Guide

BEFORE READING

Front-Loading Background Knowledge Through Read-Aloud-Think-Aloud

Search the internet for recent articles on video games and use them to model the effective habits of readers through a Read-Aloud-Think-Aloud.

Check out articles at the following websites to determine if they would be appropriate for your RATA:

- http://www.seattlepi.nwsource.com/videogameviolence/plyr14.shtml
- http://www.seatllepi.nwsource.com/videogameviolence/jrmy14.shtml

(Please keep in mind that it is the responsibility of the teacher to determine if articles from suggested sites are appropriate. The sites may have changed content since this publication. The publisher takes no responsibility for the current content of the site.)

Looking at the Words

Determining How the Word Sounds (Phonics)

With your students, use one of the sets of steps from the Syllable Guide in the beginning of the book to determine how to break a word into manageable parts. The goal is to break the words into syllables that the students can say. Then they can put those parts together to "sound the word out." However, remember that the rules for syllabification do not always work because our language is so diverse. The rules can also become rather complex for low readers, so keep in mind that their overall objective is just to figure out how the word sounds. They may not be able to break the word into its syllables perfectly, but they should at least be able to figure out how to say the word based on their attempt at following one of these sets of steps. Lesson One is a more basic set, while Lesson Two attempts to give the students the more specific rules without becoming too complicated. Take your time when teaching either set, and understand that many of the lower readers are not going to understand right away. It will take time, practice, and repeated application before many of them are able to make use of these strategies on their own.

Determining What the Words Mean (Vocabulary)

After students have spent time breaking the words apart to figure out how they sound, use the lists of prefixes and suffixes and their meanings found in the Syllable Guide to have students try to add whatever meaning they can to the words before actually looking at their definitions. After giving the students the definitions, have them see if they can figure out which words truly apply the meaning of any of the prefixes or suffixes.

Words to Study	Breaking into Syllables	Short Definition
Inappropriate	in-ap-pro-pri-ate	(adj.) not suitable
Psychologists	psy-cho-log-ists	(n.) those who are educated and trained to study human behavior
Aggressive	ag-gres-sive	(adj.) boldly hostile
Hostile	hos-tile	(adj.) unfriendly
Criticized	cri-ti-cized	(v.) analyzed and judged
Irresponsible	ir-re-spon-si-ble	(adj.) not responsible
Deemed	deemed	(v.) judged

Activating Background Knowledge

Anticipation Guide
Mark each of the following statements True or False:

1. _____ Madden NFL is the number-one selling video game.

2. _____ There are five different ratings for video games.

3. _____ There has been a significant increase in violent crimes over the past 20 years.

4. _____ Children who play a lot of video games are more likely to get into fights.

5. _____ The Columbine tragedy may have been a reenactment of a video game.

Starter Questions
After completing the Anticipation Guide, have a group or class discussion with the students using the following questions:

1. What video games do you like to play?

2. How much time each week do you spend playing video games?

3. What is the Entertainment Software Rating Board (ESRB)?

4. Why might video games be dangerous for some children to play?

5. What is the Columbine tragedy?

Make a prediction about what you think the article will be about.

DURING READING

- Have the students skim the article. Give them about 45-60 seconds to do this.

- As they skim the article, tell them to circle any words they don't know how to say.

- When they are finished, talk about how to chunk the words they don't know how to say by sounds they now know and then sound them out.

- Have the students skim the questions. Give them only about 30-45 seconds to do this.

- Ask the students to predict what the article is about.

- Have the students read the article. They should question, summarize, clarify, and predict as they read. Instruct them to jot their questions, summarizations, clarifications, and predictions in the margins as they read.

- Remind students to constantly ask themselves if they know what the article is about right now. If they don't, they must reread to clarify. This is called monitoring for understanding.

- After they have finished reading the article, they are ready to answer the questions.

The Strategy Sheet

You may choose to have students complete the strategy sheet for each section before they answer the multiple-choice questions. Or you could have them complete the questions, work on the strategy sheet with a partner, and then go back over the questions to see if the use of the strategy sheet helped them more easily find the answers to any of the questions.

AFTER READING

Discussion Starter Questions

1. Should children be able to purchase and play adult-rated video games? Why? Why not?

2. In sports such as wrestling and football, should children be allowed to play in activities that have physical contact and may promote violence? Why? Why not? Is that fair?

3. What other types of entertainment could be blamed for aggressive behavior?

4. What are some of the positive ways video games promote learning?

5. What effect does gaming have on the community?

Teacher Reflection

When you are finished with the article, strategies, and questions, ask yourself the following:

1. Did I get the students to THINK about what they have read?

2. Did I teach them (even a little bit) about how to read more effectively?

If you answered "Yes" to both questions, you can feel good about the day.

Violent Video Games: *Who Is Raising Our Children?*

A muscular man runs around in front of you. He is swinging a baseball bat and tossing objects around. But he's not playing baseball. He is actually throwing hand grenades. He is destroying everyone in his path. If the graphics on the screen were any clearer, they would make many of us sick.

Two decades ago, a little round yellow man harmlessly gobbled up pink and purple ghosts on the screen. That little man was Pac-Man. He, along with Space Invaders, Galaga, and Super Mario Brothers, was starting a revolution. Little did he know at the time that it wasn't only the ghosts that would catch up with him, but also goblins, monsters, soldiers, and cold-blooded killers. Those violent creatures have taken over video games, and some people fear they've taken the youth of America with them.

Today, 79% of American children play video games on a regular basis. According to David Walsh, a man who studies video games and their effects, children between the ages of 7 and 17 play video games for an average of eight hours a week. Some psychologists believe, however, that they are not just playing video games. Some believe children are actually being trained

to kill. The problem is that some video games are packed with violence, strong language, and themes that are inappropriate for kids.

These psychologists know that repetition increases the chance a child will learn something. A child who studies his multiplication tables over and over is more likely to learn them than a child who reads through them once or twice. These psychologists say the same goes for video games. When a child plays a killer on a video game over and over again, he is more likely to become an aggressive or more hostile person. In studies conducted by David Walsh, he has proven that the least hostile children who play lots of violent video games are more likely to get in fights than hostile children who do not play violent video games.

The producers of these video games are not willing to take the blame that easily for youth violence. To begin with, they claim that violent crime rates have actually been going down over the last 20 years. This must mean that the video games they are creating have no effect on the young people of America. They also claim that in the studies they have conducted, they find no proof that kids who play violent video games act more aggressively after they play them.

They say that the games themselves constantly remind the kids that video games are not real. They use a joystick, attached to a cord, plugged into a television. The games are somewhat like cartoons, not real life. They say that kids know the difference between real life and the fantasy world of video games the same way an audience knows not to rush the stage during a play when a murder is about to take place.

Video game producers also point to facts like the violent crime rate in 2004 was the lowest it has been in 40 years. The top-selling video game that year? Grand Theft Auto: San Andreas, a video game criticized for its amount of violence. They argue that this game

Best-Selling Video Game Franchises (since 1995) as of 12/2005, according to Wikipedia, the online encyclopedia		
Game Franchise	Ratings on Majority of Games	Units Sold (in millions)
Mario Series	E	184
Pokémon	E	109
Final Fantasy	T	60
Tetris	E	50
The Legend of Zelda Series	E	47
Grand Theft Auto	M	44
Donkey Kong	E	44
Gran Turismo	E	40
Sonic the Hedgehog Series	E	38
Dragon Quest	T	35
Command & Conquer Series	T	35
Resident Evil	M	30
Tomb Raider	T	30
Madden NFL	E	30
Crash Bandicoot	E	30

obviously didn't have an effect on the nation's young people.

The video game industry decided several years ago to try to help people decide which games would be appropriate for younger people. They formed a group called the Entertainment Software Rating Board (ESRB) to put ratings on all video games sold. The ratings range from E to AO. E-rated games are okay for everyone to play. AO-rated games are deemed appropriate for adults only.

One group thinks that violent video games are the cause of bad behavior in young people. The other group can brandish their own facts and statistics to seemingly prove that those claims just aren't true. So the two sides just can't agree, right? Actually, they do agree on one thing, and it is probably the most important point of all: parents are the last line of defense.

Both sides repeat over and over in their arguments that parents concerned about their children and what they learn should not allow their children to play games that are inappropriate for them to begin with.

One could argue that video game makers are being irresponsible for making violent video games. But the video game industry produces violent video games for a more mature audience, not for children. They expect the parents to be responsible enough to monitor what their children are playing.

Video game producers send the same theme in all of their messages: Children should not be raised and taught by video games. Children should be raised and taught by caring and responsible adults.

Video Game Ratings of the Entertainment Software Rating Board

EC: Early Childhood

Games have content that may be suitable for persons ages 3 and older. Titles in this category contain no material that parents would find inappropriate.

E: Everyone

Games have content that may be suitable for persons ages 6 and older. Titles in this category may contain minimal violence, some comic mischief, and/or mild language.

T: Teen

Games have content that may be suitable for persons ages 13 and older. Titles in this category may contain violent content, mild or strong language, and/or suggestive themes.

M: Mature

Games have content that may be suitable for persons ages 17 and older. Titles in this category may contain mature sexual themes, more intense violence, and/or strong language.

AO: Adults Only

Games have content suitable only for adults. Titles in this category may include graphic depictions of sex and/or violence. Adults Only products are not intended for people under the age of 18.

Tragedy in Colorado
On April 20, 1999, Columbine High School in Littleton, Colorado was changed forever. Two young men went on a rampage throughout the school. Dressed in trench coats and armed with guns, they killed 13 people and wounded 23 before killing themselves. No one knows for sure what caused them to do this. However, many people pointed out later that both boys enjoyed playing a particularly bloody video game. The same game has been used at times by the military to train soldiers to kill. To make matters worse, the two boys had modified the game into an even more violent version. Some believe the boys were performing a real-life account of the game itself.

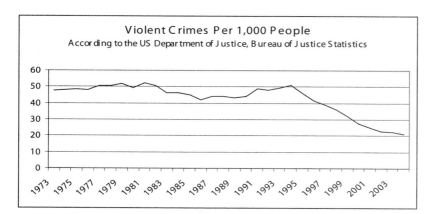

Violent Crimes Per 1,000 People
According to the US Department of Justice, Bureau of Justice Statistics

Reading Comprehension

After reading "Violent Video Games: Who Is Raising Our Children?" choose the options that best answer questions 1-14.

1. Read this sentence.
   The other group can brandish their own facts and statistics to seemingly prove that those claims just aren't true.

   What is the meaning of the word *brandish* as it is used in this sentence?
   A. argue or fight with
   B. reciting memorized facts
   C. repeating something over and over again
   D. find false information in a list of many different sources

2. Read this sentence.
   Actually, they do agree on one thing, and it is probably the most important point of all: Parents are the last line of defense.

   What does the author mean by this sentence?
   F. Parents are the only people defending kids against video games.
   G. Parents and video game manufacturers can't agree on who is responsible.
   H. Parents don't know how to defend their kids against video game companies.
   I. Parents must monitor the content of the video games their children play.

3. According to the text box on Video Game Ratings, which of the following game ratings would be suitable for a 15-year-old boy to play?
   A. E, T, and M
   B. EC, E, and T
   C. T, M, and AO
   D. EC, T, and AO

4. What is the significance of the video game industry's rating system?
   F. It gives parents a guideline for games appropriate for their children.
   G. It isn't a reliable measure of how appropriate a game is for young children.
   H. The guideline does not allow parents with young children to buy mature games.
   I. It decreases the units sold of video games rated Teen, Mature, and Adults Only.

5. With which statement would the author of the passage most likely agree?
   A. Video games are too expensive.
   B. Violent video games are harmless parts of today's society.
   C. Violent video games always cause children to be aggressive.
   D. Parents need to take an active role in determining what video games are appropriate for their children.

6. The author organizes the article by
   F. listing the pros and cons of violent video games.
   G listing the reasons people like to play video games.
   H. discussing different views on the effects of video games.
   I. presenting a chronological list of the development of video games.

7. What is the purpose of the text box about Columbine High School?
   A. to show that video games affect crime rates
   B. to explain that video games are often used to train killers
   C. to point out a possible connection between violent tragedy and violent video games
   D. to show that the boys involved in the Columbine shootings committed the crime because of the video game they played

8. Which statement BEST expresses the main idea of this article?
   - F. American children spend too much time playing video games.
   - **G. Parents should be cautious of the games their children play and the messages the games might send.**
   - H. Violent video games are a dangerous part of society and are responsible for the violent behavior of young teens.
   - I. The video game industry is concerned only with making money and not with the safety of the children who purchase their games.

9. Which person or group would be most likely to believe that the students in Littleton, Colorado shot their classmates because they frequently played violent video games?
   - **A. David Walsh**
   - B. middle school teachers
   - C. the producers of violent video games
   - D. the Entertainment Software Rating Board

10. Why do video game producers refuse to take the blame for youth violence?
    - F. They put the blame on television.
    - G. They say video games don't ever imitate reality.
    - H. They acknowledge that video games cause violence in children but don't think it is their job to monitor it.
    - **I. They say there is no research proving a correlation and crime has actually gone down in the past decade.**

11. The major difference between video games and cartoons is that
    - A. cartoons are life-like, and video games are pretend.
    - B. video games are life-like, and cartoons are pretend.
    - C. video games come to life, and cartoons stay on the screen.
    - **D. video games are controlled by the player, and cartoons are watched.**

12. Which statement about the video game industry is LEAST accurate?
    - F. It is a major industry among American children.
    - **G. It claims responsibility for the Columbine tragedy.**
    - H. It tries to regulate age-appropriateness for video games with a rating system.
    - I. It thinks that parents are the ultimate authority on what games are appropriate for their kids.

13. What can you conclude about the top 15 video game franchises after looking at the information entitled "Best-Selling Video Game Franchises (since 1995)"?
    - **A. There are nearly five E-rated games for every M-rated game.**
    - B. T-rated games have made nearly as much money as M-rated games.
    - C. For every E-rated video game franchise, there are four T-rated franchises.
    - D. Tetris, Dragon Quest, and Madden NFL might be games most suitable for a 10-year-old boy.

14. According to the information entitled "Video Game Ratings of the Entertainment Software Rating Board" and "Best-Selling Video Game Franchises (since 1995),"
    - F. violent games sell better than games rated for everyone.
    - **G. games suitable for people 6 and older outsell games suitable for those 17 and older by about eight times as much.**
    - H. Sonic the Hedgehog, Dragon Quest, and Resident Evil each contain intense violence, but they are suitable for kids 13 and over.
    - I. Resident Evil, Tomb Raider, and Madden NFL have sold the same number of units because they can be sold to people from 6 years old to 17 years old.

Reading Strategy

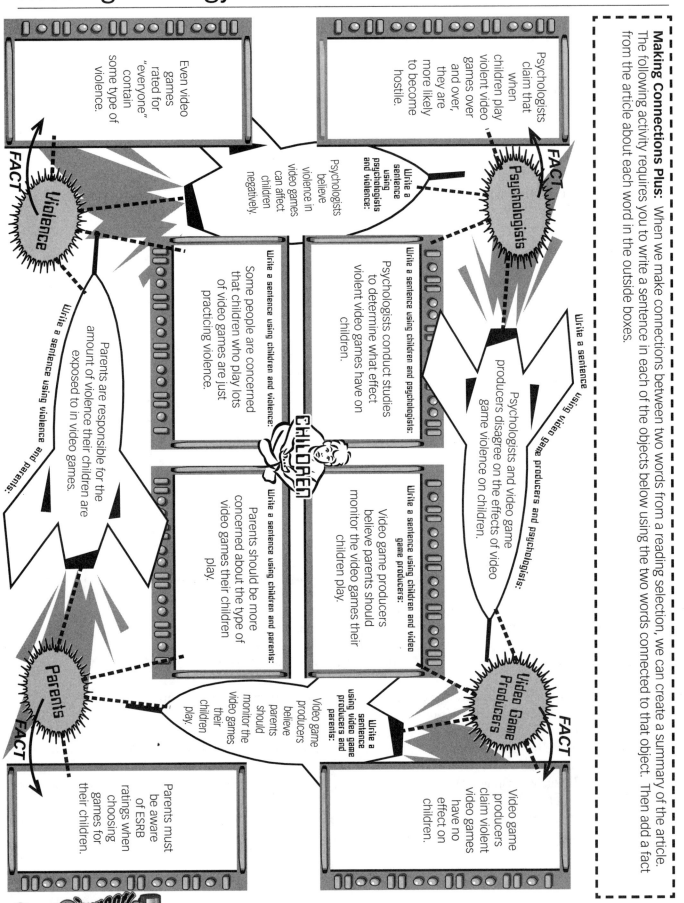

Making Connections Plus: When we make connections between two words from a reading selection, we can create a summary of the article. The following activity requires you to write a sentence in each of the objects below using the two words connected to that object. Then add a fact from the article about each word in the outside boxes.

FACT

Even video games rated for "everyone" contain some type of violence.

FACT

Psychologists claim that when children play violent video games over and over, they are more likely to become hostile.

Write a sentence using psychologists and violence:
Psychologists believe violence in video games can affect children negatively.

Violence

Psychologists

Write a sentence using children and psychologists:
Psychologists conduct studies to determine what effect violent video games have on children.

Write a sentence using children and video game producers:
Video game producers believe parents should monitor the video games their children play.

Write a sentence using children and violence:
Some people are concerned that children who play lots of video games are just practicing violence.

CHILDREN

Write a sentence using children and parents:
Parents should be more concerned about the type of video games their children play.

Write a sentence using video game producers and psychologists:
Psychologists and video game producers disagree on the effects of video game violence on children.

Write a sentence using violence and parents:
Parents are responsible for the amount of violence their children are exposed to in video games.

Write a sentence using video game producers and parents:
Video game producers believe parents should monitor the video games their children play.

Parents

FACT

Video Game Producers

FACT

Parents must be aware of ESRB ratings when choosing games for their children.

Video game producers claim violent video games have no effect on children.

110

©2006 PRINCIPLE WOODS, INC.

Interpreting the Data

PART I

Below is a chart indicating the top 20 computer and video games most searched on the Internet during the four weeks ending November 20, 2004.

	Top 20 Most-Searched Video Games	E	T	M
1	Dragonball Z: The Legacy of Goku	■		
2	The Sims 2		■	
3	Grand Theft Auto: San Andreas			■
4	NBA 2005	■		
5	Halo 2			■
6	Star Wars Knights of the Old Republic II: The Sith Lords		■	
7	Grand Theft Auto: Vice City			■
8	Doom 3			■
9	Star Wars Galaxies		■	
10	Unreal Tournaments 2004			■
11	Warcraft III		■	
12	EverQuest 2		■	
13	Final Fantasy X2		■	
14	Half Life 2			■
15	Mortal Kombat: Deadly Alliance			■
16	Dragonball Z: Budokai 3		■	
17	Madden 2005	■		
18	Gundam Wing		■	
19	Need For Speed Underground 2	■		
20	Tony Hawk's Pro Skater 4		■	
	Totals	4	9	7

15. What percentage of the 20 most-searched video games from November 2004 were rated M? Show your work in the box below.

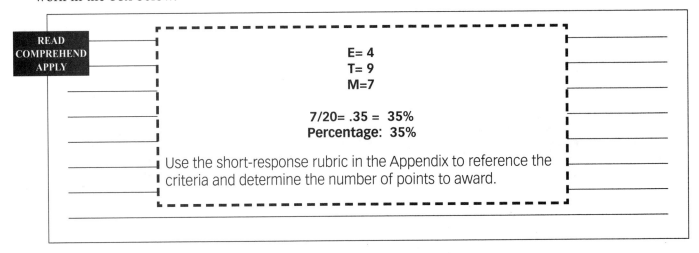

READ
COMPREHEND
APPLY

E= 4
T= 9
M=7

7/20= .35 = 35%
Percentage: 35%

Use the short-response rubric in the Appendix to reference the criteria and determine the number of points to award.

16. What percentage of the top 20 most-searched video games from November 2004 were rated for children 13 and over? Show your work in the box below.

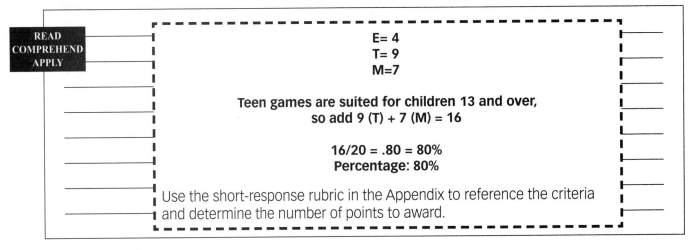

READ
COMPREHEND
APPLY

E= 4
T= 9
M=7

Teen games are suited for children 13 and over,
so add 9 (T) + 7 (M) = 16

16/20 = .80 = 80%
Percentage: 80%

Use the short-response rubric in the Appendix to reference the criteria and determine the number of points to award.

17. Make a conclusion about the type of video games people in our society are apparently most interested in playing and describe them below. Support your answer using details and information from the chart on the preceding page and the box from the article entitled "Video Game Ratings of the Entertainment Software Rating Board."

COMPREHEND
ANALYZE
EXPLAIN

Based on the data from the chart on the preceding page, people in our society are most interested in playing Teen and Mature games. Those types of games contain violent content, mild or strong language, and suggestive or mature themes.

Use the extended-response rubric in the Appendix to reference the criteria and determine the number of points to award.

PART II

The following chart depicts the top movies of the week of November 19, 2004.

		Rating Motion Picture Association of America (MPAA)	Movie content according to the MPAA rating						
			Crude humor	Brief crude language	Strong language	Drug use	Some violence or intense action	Strong violence	Mature sensual content
1	National Treasure	PG					■		
2	SpongeBob SquarePants	PG	■				■		
3	The Incredibles	PG					■		
4	The Polar Express	G							
5	Bridget Jones: The Edge of Reason	R		■					■
6	After the Sunset	PG-13		■	■			■	
7	Ray	PG-13			■	■			■
8	The Grudge	PG-13						■	
9	Seed of Chucky	R						■	■
10	Saw	R			■			■	
11	Shall We Dance	PG-13		■					■
12	Sideways	R			■				■
13	Finding Neverland	PG		■					
14	Alfie	R			■				■
15	The Motorcycle Diaries	R			■	■			■
16	Kinsey	R			■				■
17	Shark Tale	PG	■						
18	Veer-Zaara	NR							
19	Friday Night Lights	PG-13		■					■
20	Ladder 49	PG-13		■			■		
	Totals		2	6	7	2	4	4	9

Quickthought

Throughout history, societies that have lived by violence have met violent ends. When we become violent, we lose control of who we are truly meant to be.

18. What percentage of the top movies in November 2004 had strong violence, strong language, and/or mature sensual content? Show your work in the box below.

READ COMPREHEND APPLY

Eleven of the movies had strong violence, strong language, or mature sensual content.

11/20 = .55 = 55%
Percentage: 55%

Use the extended-response rubric in the Appendix to reference the criteria and determine the number of points to award.

19. Examine the data on the preceding pages. What is a recurring theme in the content of movies and video games sold to the public? Use statistics and data to show what content seems to be most popular.

ANALYZE EVALUATE EXPLAIN

Based on the data on preceding pages, the most popular games and movies seem to have recurring violence and mature themes. We know this because Teen- and Mature-rated video games have mild or strong violence, and they make up 35% of the most popular games in November 2004. Over half of the most popular movies during November 2004 also had strong violence or mature themes.

Use the extended-response rubric in the Appendix to reference the criteria and determine the number of points to award.

The following table summarizes the information about the percentages of the ratings on video games and movies in the year 2004.

Video Game Ratings			
	R A T I N G S		
Industry	E	T	M
VIDEO GAMES	54%	33%	12%
	R A T I N G S		
	G	R	
MOVIES	8%	55%	

20. Based on information from the table above, explain which industry may have more of an effect on violence in society. Use data and statistics to support your claim.

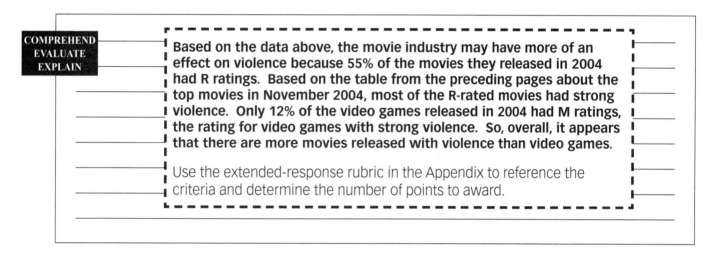

COMPREHEND EVALUATE EXPLAIN

Based on the data above, the movie industry may have more of an effect on violence because 55% of the movies they released in 2004 had R ratings. Based on the table from the preceding pages about the top movies in November 2004, most of the R-rated movies had strong violence. Only 12% of the video games released in 2004 had M ratings, the rating for video games with strong violence. So, overall, it appears that there are more movies released with violence than video games.

Use the extended-response rubric in the Appendix to reference the criteria and determine the number of points to award.

PART III

Look at the table below from the US Department of Justice, Bureau of Justice Statistics entitled "Violent Crimes per 1,000 People."

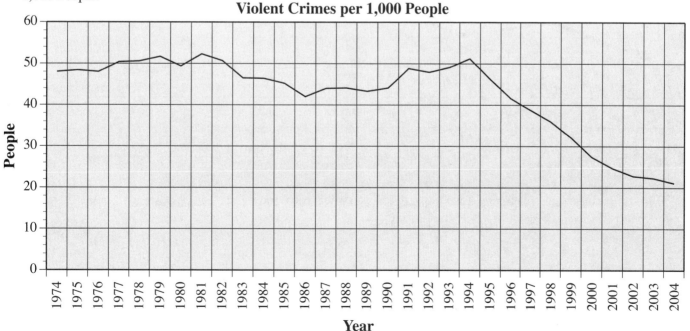

Violent Crimes per 1,000 People

21. Look at the preceding graph and tell how you would use it if you were a video game producer attempting to prove that your products don't have a negative effect on society. Use data from the graph to support your claim.

ANALYZE EVALUATE EXPLAIN

Based on the data in the graph above, the violent crime rate has gone down from about 1995 to the present. This suggests that our society is becoming less violent, which could help a video game producer prove that violent video games don't have a negative effect on society.

Use the attached rubric in the Appendix to reference the criteria and number of points to award for each element for the extended-response box.

The following graph is a summary of information on youth violence as reported by the Surgeon General.

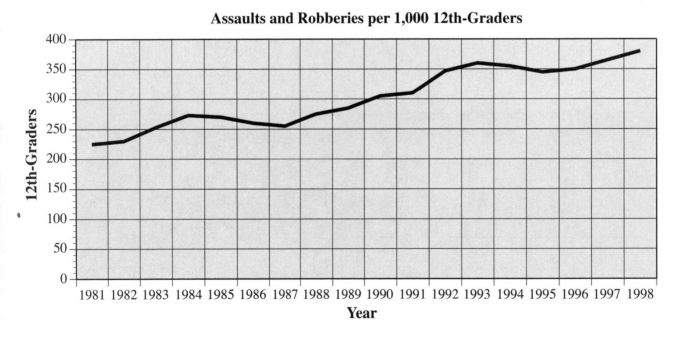

Assaults and Robberies per 1,000 12th-Graders

22. Compare the two preceding graphs. How would you use the information from the Assault and Robberies graph to argue against the point made by video game producers that video games haven't had a negative effect on society? Use facts from the graphs to support your answer.

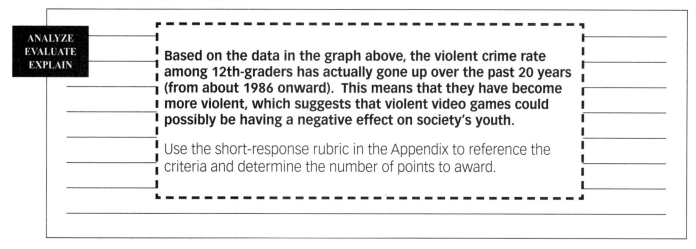

ANALYZE
EVALUATE
EXPLAIN

Based on the data in the graph above, the violent crime rate among 12th-graders has actually gone up over the past 20 years (from about 1986 onward). This means that they have become more violent, which suggests that violent video games could possibly be having a negative effect on society's youth.

Use the short-response rubric in the Appendix to reference the criteria and determine the number of points to award.

The following table summarizes the information about parental supervision of the use of television and video games.

Percentage of parents who regularly supervise their children's...	
use of television	88%
use of video games	48%

23. Look at the information above. Compare it to each of the graphs and information provided on the previous pages. What would you tell parents of children to ensure that their children aren't affected by violent video games? Use data, statistics, and information from the previous pages to support your answer.

ANALYZE
EVALUATE
EXPLAIN

Based on the table above, parents don't supervise their children's use of video games as much as they do their use of television. In fact, they supervise their use of television about twice as much as they supervise their use of video games. Because about 80% of the top 20 video games in November 2004 had some form of violence, parents should understand that they still need to pay attention to the types of games their children are playing because some of the games may be too violent. The number of assaults with injuries has gone up over the last 20 years among 12th-graders, which means that group of our youth is becoming more violent. Parents need to ensure that their children aren't being trained by video games to become more violent.

Use the short-response rubric in the Appendix to reference the criteria and determine the number of points to award.

Look Inside and Grow

24. Pretend you work for a video game producer. Your company is ready to unleash their next video game, and they expect it to make millions. The ESRB has rated it M due to strong violence and language. Write the content for a flyer you would place inside the box to warn parents against the dangers of allowing children under the age of 17 to play this game. Consider everything you have read in the article, your own background knowledge, and the data you have seen on the preceding pages.

Student answers may vary.

The student should address each section of the question to the best of his/her ability. The question is meant to elicit strong classroom conversation about character. Students should be able to demonstrate that they have learned a lesson about the effect of violent video games on society's youth.

Use the character-education rubric in the Appendix to reference the criteria and determine the number of points to award.

Notes

Today, 79% …: Walsh, David. "Video Game Violence and Public Policy." National Institute on Media and the Family, 2001. http://culturalpolicy.uchicago.edu/conf2001/papers/walsh.html.

According to David Walsh …: Walsh.

In studies conducted …: Walsh.

Best-Selling Video (text box chart)…: "List of best-selling computer and video games." Wikipedia.org. http://en.wikipedia.org/wiki/List_of_best_selling_video_games.

Video Game Ratings (text box chart)…: "Game Ratings & Descriptor Guide." Entertainment Software Rating Board. http://www.esrb.org/ratings/ratings_guide.jsp.

Violent Crimes per (graph)…: "Violent crime rates declined since 1994, reaching the lowest level ever recorded in 2004." U.S. Department of Justice, Bureau of Justice Statistics, Page last revised September 25, 2005. http://www.ojp.usdoj.gov/bjs/glance/viort.htm.

Top 20 Most (chart)…: "Top 20 Most Searched Computer and Video Games." Lycos Entertainment. http://50.lycos.com/112604.asp.

Top Movies (chart)…: "The Top Movies, Weekend of November 19, 2004." The Numbers.com. http://www.the-numbers.com/charts/weekly/2004/20041119.html.

Video Game Ratings (chart)…: "Caution: Children at Play: The Truth About Violent Youth and Video Games." Game Revolution website. http://gr.bolt.com/oldsite/articles/violence/violence.htm.

Violent Crimes per…: (see note above.)

Assaults and Robberies (graph)…: "Youth Violence: A Report of the Surgeon General." United States Department of Health and Human Services. http://www.surgeongeneral.gov/library/youthviolence/chapter2/sec1.html#epidemic.

Percentage of Parents (chart)…: "Media Violence Facts and Statistics." National Youth Violence Prevention Resource Center. http://www.safeyouth.org.

Technical Extension

Video Game Production

Have you ever thought about how your favorite video game was created? Believe it or not, it didn't just spring to life on your television screen. The exact process of its creation is unique to the particular game, but the idea is the same. Making a video game is a complex, exciting task. Let's learn how it's done!

Types of Video Games
3D Action/Adventure
Simulation
Sports
Strategy/Role-playing/Adventure
Fighting
Puzzle
Shooter
Platform
Racing
Conversion

The first part of creating a video game is coming up with an idea. Ideas can come from well-known stories, previous game characters, or even from thin air. Once an idea is selected and accepted by the person in charge of the project, a preproduction team is assembled. This team normally includes at least one of each of the following people: director, designer, software engineer, artist, and writer. Each member of the preproduction team is vital to the game's success.

The first thing a preproduction team develops is the story line for the game. The complexity and design of the story varies depending on the type of game. In order to develop the story line, the team must have the game designer identify the nature of the game. Generally, three points must be addressed:

- What will the features of the game involve?
- What type of play will result from user interaction?
- What type of technology is needed?

Once the story line has been developed, the team creates a set of storyboards. Storyboards are a series of drawings done by the team artist, and they include words

and technical instructions. Each individual storyboard describes a scene or part of a scene in the game.

Next, designers map out each different level of play, or the different worlds that signify advancing through the game. Once the storyboards and game designs are complete, the production phase begins. Many animated video games use 3D models that are also used to depict scenes before electronic programming begins. Engineers and programmers then begin writing code in C programming language. This provides the framework for the game. Finally, the game design is fed into the computer by a tool chain which creates one long piece of electronic code. A game has been created!

Now the fun really begins. After the basics are in place, the production team looks for ways to refine the game. They add special effects and hidden parts. The engineer adds life to the game by adding texture, 3D effects, and shading. He or she also cleans up the game code so that the final product on the screen looks as good as possible.

Once a game is finished, it enters the postproduction phase. The first part of this phase is to have users test the alpha (first) version of the game. Once any problems are fixed, the game is released in a beta (second) version to be tested again. After any items in the beta version are corrected, the final product is released for sale. Sometime during postproduction the game is sent to the Entertainment Software Rating Board to be rated for age-appropriateness. This way, when the game is released, it can be marketed to the suitable audience.

The last step involves you! Consumers purchase new games and try them out for themselves. Many people see this as the beginning of the game's life. Little do they know it's actually the middle of an already long journey!

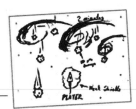
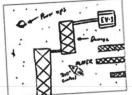
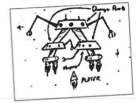

Reading Comprehension

After reading "Video Game Production," choose the options that best answer questions 1-14.

1. What is the meaning of the phrase *nature of the game* as used in the third paragraph?
    A. what message the game sends
    B. what features the game involves
    C. how the game is developed
    D. how the game works

2. Read this sentence.
    This provides the framework for the game.

    What is the meaning of the word *framework* as it is used in this sentence?
    F. information
    G. background
    H. border
    I. structure

3. According to the article, a game is created when
    A. the computer creates one piece of electronic code.
    B. the beta version is released and tested by users.
    C. the storyboards are mapped out.
    D. engineers and programmers write the code in C programming language.

4. Which task is NOT the job of the preproduction team?
    F. The team comes up with the idea for the game.
    G. The team develops the story line of the game.
    H. The team creates a sequence of storyboards for the game.
    I. The team determines the nature of the game.

5. In the author's opinion, which member of the preproduction team is most important?
    A. The director is most important.
    B. The artist is most important.
    C. The engineer is most important.
    D. All members are equally important.

6. The author organizes this article by
    F. presenting a story about how video games are created.
    G. presenting a series of questions about video games to be answered.
    H. describing the development of a video game in chronological order.
    I. comparing the process of creating a video game today to the process ten years ago.

7. What was the author's main purpose in writing this article?
    A. to explain how video games are marketed to their target audience
    B. to describe the weakness in the video game rating
    C. to explain the complex process of creating a video game
    D. to convince the reader that video games cause violence

8. Which title BEST fits the article?
    F. Are Video Games Safe?
    G. Video Games: A Complex Process
    H. How to Become a Video Game Producer
    I. Video Games and Education

9. Why do storyboards make production easier?
    A. They are 3D versions of each screen in the game.
    B. They start to incorporate the code used in the game.
    C. Storyboards only involve the artist and the designer.
    D. They map out exactly what will happen in the game.

10. Why can't storyboards be created until the preproduction team determines the nature of the game?
    F. The team has to first decide what components the game will involve.
    G. The artist has to first decide what to draw.
    H. The engineer won't know what code to enter.
    I. The designer has to have detailed sketches before the storyboards are created.

11. What is true of BOTH storyboards and 3D models?
    A. Their creation requires artists, writers, and engineers.
    B. They help depict scenes before they are programmed.
    C. They are vital parts of the preproduction process.
    D. They are optional parts of the production process.

12. Which statement about postproduction is LEAST accurate?
    F. The alpha version is the first to be tested.
    G. In the beta version, many problems have already been corrected.
    H. The final game has already been through two sets of human testing cycles.
    I. The game is rated before postproduction begins.

13. Which fact from the article provides the best evidence that the entire process of creating a video game is unique to the particular game?
    A. The preproduction team involves many different types of workers who contribute to creating the game.
    B. Designers must determine what will be involved in the game before production can begin.
    C. Animated video games often use 3D models before the code is created.
    D. Technology is an integral part of the production process.

14. Based on the article, which statement is most accurate?
    F. Creating a video game is a complex process that begins well before consumers are allowed to purchase it.
    G. Video games are created quickly and simply by a few very intelligent people.
    H. The process that occurs before a game is released isn't really important as long as the game sells many copies.
    I. Video games are constantly under scrutiny for not being rated correctly.

Vocational Extension

> ## *Job Description*
>
> Graphic Magic will be on the campus of Southwest Florida College on May 15, 2006 to interview for three entry-level Graphic Design training positions. These positions are geared toward future graduates interested in learning about design in an active working environment. Interested applicants should contact Mary White at mwhite@gmagic.com.

One of the most integral parts of a video game production team is the graphic designer. In the production of a video game, the graphic designer works closely with the artist and the software engineer to first create storyboards and then program the design. In short, the graphic designer helps create all of the effects that make the video game so fun to play on the screen.

However, graphic designers aren't limited to working with video games. Graphic designers don't necessarily work with video at all. Some designers might create only 2D products like pamphlets, signs, or graphics for books. Others create websites using computer-aided graphic design. While some designers specialize in one area, many work with multiple types of media.

A graphic designer produces image solutions bringing to life the ideas their clients communicate. Typical work activities for a graphic designer might include the following:

- meeting with clients to discuss objectives of the project and interpret their needs
- calculating quotes for clients
- developing a cost-effective design plan for each client balanced with time management
- thinking creatively to produce new ideas and concepts
- designing 2D and/or 3D designs using design software such as QuarkXpress, FreeHand, Illustrator, Photoshop, 3D Studio, Dreamweaver, and Flash
- working with a team toward a final product
- presenting finalized ideas to clients

The training to become a graphic designer can take years, beginning in high school. Because of the nature of the job, it is important for anyone interested in a design career to get a well-rounded high school education including English, math, science, computers, art, and communications. Later, both technical colleges and four-year universities have programs in graphic design. The sky is the limit! The more experience and education a designer gets, the more leadership he or she can take on projects.

Designers must possess imagination, awareness of current advertising fashions, and expert knowledge of graphic computer software. As you can probably tell from the activities listed above, an important part of graphic design is having a good relationship with clients. Communication is an important part of being able to understand what each client wants and being able to verbalize the process it will take to get the final product.

Sample Cover Letter

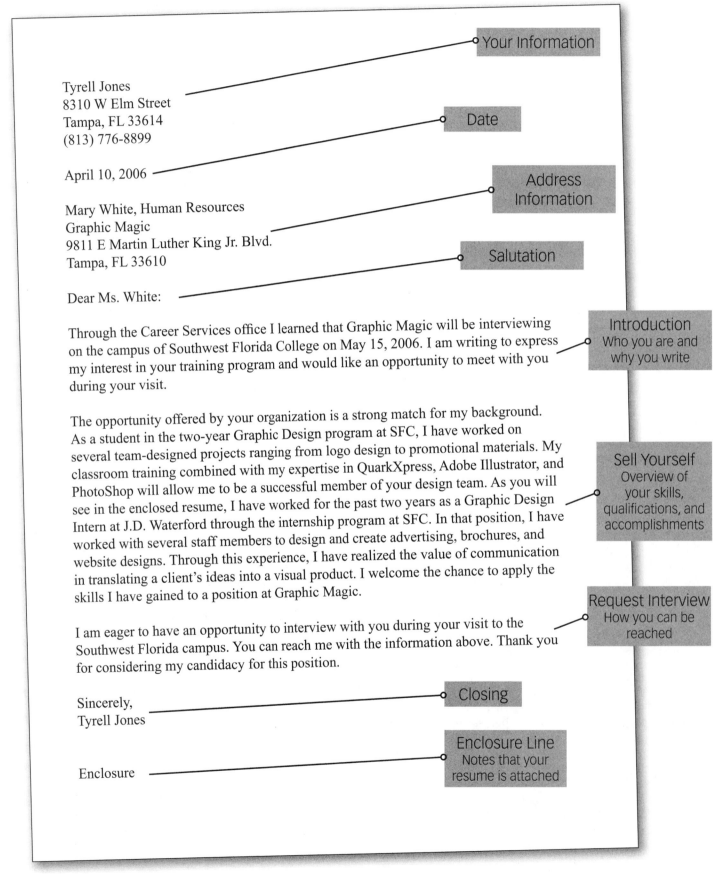

Tyrell Jones
8310 W Elm Street
Tampa, FL 33614
(813) 776-8899

April 10, 2006

Mary White, Human Resources
Graphic Magic
9811 E Martin Luther King Jr. Blvd.
Tampa, FL 33610

Dear Ms. White:

Through the Career Services office I learned that Graphic Magic will be interviewing on the campus of Southwest Florida College on May 15, 2006. I am writing to express my interest in your training program and would like an opportunity to meet with you during your visit.

The opportunity offered by your organization is a strong match for my background. As a student in the two-year Graphic Design program at SFC, I have worked on several team-designed projects ranging from logo design to promotional materials. My classroom training combined with my expertise in QuarkXpress, Adobe Illustrator, and PhotoShop will allow me to be a successful member of your design team. As you will see in the enclosed resume, I have worked for the past two years as a Graphic Design Intern at J.D. Waterford through the internship program at SFC. In that position, I have worked with several staff members to design and create advertising, brochures, and website designs. Through this experience, I have realized the value of communication in translating a client's ideas into a visual product. I welcome the chance to apply the skills I have gained to a position at Graphic Magic.

I am eager to have an opportunity to interview with you during your visit to the Southwest Florida campus. You can reach me with the information above. Thank you for considering my candidacy for this position.

Sincerely,
Tyrell Jones

Enclosure

Labels:

Your Information

Date

Address Information

Salutation

Introduction
Who you are and why you write

Sell Yourself
Overview of your skills, qualifications, and accomplishments

Request Interview
How you can be reached

Closing

Enclosure Line
Notes that your resume is attached

Looking Forward

15. A cover letter is sent with a resume to set the potential employee apart from his or her competition. Look at the different parts of the sample cover letter. It was written as a response to the job description at the beginning of the article. Using each part of the sample letter and your experience, write a cover letter for the following job description.

SignsPlus! is looking for an energetic worker to train in the field of Graphic Design. High school candidates are welcome, as hours will be flexible to allow for in-school and after-school activities. Candidates should have good computer skills and be willing to work hard. Course credit is available. If you are interested, contact:

DeShaun Jackson
1460 Oak Street
Jacksonville, FL 32223

Student answers may vary.

The student should address the question to the best of his/her ability using the article and personal experience. The question is meant to encourage students to explore areas of interest for their future and begin to determine how they will prepare for a future career.

Use the extended-response rubric in the Appendix to reference the criteria and determine the number of points to award.

Ethical Dilemma

16. You are a graphic designer who has been hired to create a website for a medical supplier. Part of the website is a video download of a revolutionary new product the company offers that promises to enhance the lives of those who use it. You discover that the video is fabricated and the product doesn't really do what it says it should. When you discuss this with the company's marketing manager, she shrugs and says it's just business. On one hand, no one will be physically hurt by this fib, but you aren't sure if you want to help the company advertise falsely. What do you do?

Ethical Dilemma

Student answers may vary.

The student should address the question to the best of his/her ability using background knowledge from the article as well as personal opinion and experience. The question is meant to encourage students to contemplate scenarios and make ethical decisions.

Use the character-education rubric in the Appendix to reference the criteria and determine the number of points to award.

Reading Instructional Guide

BEFORE READING

Front-Loading Background Knowledge Through Read-Aloud-Think-Aloud

Search the internet for recent articles on the charities and legal troubles of celebrities.
Check out articles at the following websites to determine if they would be appropriate for your RATA:

- http://www.childrens-express.org/dynamic/PUBLIC/role_model_260204.htm

- http://www.warm2kids.com/guest/teen/30/90/index.htm

(Please keep in mind that it is the responsibility of the teacher to determine if articles from suggested sites are appropriate. The sites may have changed content since this publication. The publisher takes no responsibility for the current content of the site.)

Looking at the Words

Determining How the Word Sounds (Phonics)

With your students, use one of the sets of steps from the Syllable Guide in the beginning of the book to determine how to break a word into manageable parts. The goal is to break the words into syllables that the students can say. Then they can put those parts together to "sound the word out." However, remember that the rules for syllabification do not always work because our language is so diverse. The rules can also become rather complex for low readers, so keep in mind that their overall objective is just to figure out how the word sounds. They may not be able to break the word into its syllables perfectly, but they should at least be able to figure out how to say the word based on their attempt at following one of these sets of steps. Lesson One is a more basic set, while Lesson Two attempts to give the students the more specific rules without becoming too complicated. Take your time when teaching either set, and understand that many of the lower readers are not going to understand right away. It will take time, practice, and repeated application before many of them are able to make use of these strategies on their own.

Determining What the Words Mean (Vocabulary)

After students have spent time breaking the words apart to figure out how they sound, use the lists of prefixes and suffixes and their meanings from the Syllable Guide to have students try to add whatever meaning they can to the words before actually looking at their definitions. After giving the students the definitions, have them see if they can figure out which words truly applied the meaning of any of the prefixes or suffixes.

Words to Study	Breaking into Syllables	Short Definition
Pessimist	pes-si-mist	(n.) one who expects the worst
Optimist	op-ti-mist	(n.) one who takes the most hopeful view of matters
Dabbled	dab-bled	(v.) to do something superficially
Scrappy	scrap-py	(adj.) having an aggressive spirit
Perception	per-cep-tion	(n.) the act of realizing or understanding

Activating Background Knowledge

Anticipation Guide

Mark each of the following statements True or False:

1. ____ Kurt Busch was number three on GQ Magazine's list of Top Ten Most Hated Athletes.

2. ____ Percy Miller is Master P's real name.

3. ____ Jake Plummer is considered one of the top NBA players.

4. ____ Kurt Busch quarterbacks the Denver Broncos.

5. ____ Master P has been arrested on more than one occasion for carrying an unregistered firearm.

Starter Questions

After completing the Anticipation Guide, have a group or class discussion with the students using the following questions:

1. What qualities make a celebrity?

2. Who is Jake Plummer?

3. Can you name any NASCAR drivers?

4. What do T.I. and Master P have in common?

5. Who is Kurt Busch?

Make a prediction about what you think the article will be about.

DURING READING

- Have the students skim the article. Give them about 45-60 seconds to do this.

- As they skim the article, tell them to circle any words they don't know how to say.

- When they are finished, talk about how to chunk the words they don't know how to say by sounds they now know and then sound them out.

- Have the students skim the questions. Give them only about 30-45 seconds to do this.

- Ask the students to predict what the article is about.

- Have the students read the article. They should question, summarize, clarify, and predict as they read. Instruct them to jot their questions, summarizations, clarifications, and predictions in the margins as they read.

- Remind students to constantly ask themselves if they know what the article is about right now. If they don't, they must reread to clarify. This is called monitoring for understanding.

- After they have finished reading the article, they are ready to answer the questions.

The Strategy Sheet

You may choose to have students complete the strategy sheet for each section before they answer the multiple-choice questions. Or you could have them complete the questions, work on the strategy sheet with a partner, and then go back over the questions to see if the use of the strategy sheet helped them more easily find the answers to any of the questions.

AFTER READING

Discussion Starter Questions

1. Should we judge celebrities for what they do during their personal life? Why? Why not?

2. Why do we tend to remember the negative qualities of a person rather than the positive attributes?

3. Name another celebrity that has had their endorsement revoked because of their behavior. Is that fair of endorsement companies to fire him/her when job performance is not the motivating factor behind the termination?

4. Describe qualities of a role model. Should celebrities have an obligation to their fans to be role models?

5. Everyone needs someone they can rely on. Name mentors/role models in your community. How have they influenced you in your life?

Teacher Reflection

When you are finished with the article, strategies, and questions, ask yourself the following:

1. Did I get the students to THINK about what they have read?

2. Did I teach them (even a little bit) about how to read more effectively?

If you answered "Yes" to both questions, you can feel good about the day.

What's the Message???

A recent poll conducted by *USA Weekend* revealed a lot about teenagers that many adults may not have; expected. When teens were asked if they typically give more thought to a special cause (like Hurricane Katrina relief) that is endorsed by a celebrity, 78% of them responded "no." Further, 70% of them said they don't respect that celebrity more because they support such a cause. And 52% of them said they think the celebrity is actually just trying to promote himself/herself by supporting the cause. What this tells us is that teens may not be influenced by celebrities as much as we may like to think. This is a good thing in some cases, because some celebrities leave us wondering what message they are trying to send in the first place.

Take a look at both sides of the following celebrities. If you are an optimist, you may believe that everyone is entitled to a few mistakes, and those mistakes can be washed clean by learning from them and trying to become a better person. However, if you are a pessimist, you may not be convinced that these people are decent role models. You may believe that when people make bad decisions, it just allows us to see what kind of people they really are, which may not be pretty.

Look for a little piece of yourself in each story, and then ask yourself what you can learn from the mistakes.

Jake Plummer

Jake Plummer is considered one of the top quarterbacks in the National Football League. His scrappy style of play has led his team, the Denver Broncos, to nearly two dozen exciting victories decided in the final minutes of the games.

Not only has he excelled on the field, he has done what he can to provide for people off the field as well. He established The Jake Plummer Foundation in 1999. His grandfather suffered from Alzheimer's disease, so Plummer's

organization focuses primarily on raising money and awareness for Alzheimer's patients. He has also been known to take kids shopping for Christmas presents, providing them each with $200 from his foundation to help them experience the Christmas season.

On April 20, 2006, he donated $100,000 to Family Tree, an organization in Denver that fights child abuse, homelessness, and domestic violence.

Unfortunately, a month later, Jake was given a summons to appear in court. It appears that on the night he delivered the check to Family Tree, he was driving dangerously and another driver began honking at him. When they stopped at a stop light, witnesses say Plummer backed his car into the other man's car and then got out and kicked his headlight. Plummer claims the other man bumped into him.

There have been other cases in Plummer's past where he has made poor decisions. He directed an obscene gesture at someone in the crowd at one of his games. He has also criticized Denver Broncos fans on the radio.

He has done a lot of good things for people; however, Plummer needs to determine how to deal with people's perception of his aggressive behavior.

T.I.

He proclaims that he is the "King of the South." Clifford Harris, known on stage as T.I., cracked open his hip-hop celebrity status with his album *King*. The CD debuted at number one on the *Billboard* 200 chart.

T.I. has used his fame to encourage young kids to become educated. He has gone into Georgia's Paulding Detention Center to speak with over 150 kids about the evils of drugs and violence and about the value of giving back to the community. He has even provided scholarships for single-parent families at the Boys and Girls Club. He has also participated in concerts to raise money for the victims of Hurricane Katrina and has personally donated $50,000 to the relief effort.

In 1998 he was convicted for having controlled substances and giving false information. In 2003 he was arrested for battery on a law enforcement officer, trespassing, and disorderly conduct. He later had additional time added to his sentence of community service when he was caught driving with a suspended license. Eventually, he was sentenced to prison time for violating his probation after he had been caught with drugs and firearms on different occasions.

Following these incidents, he was taken to court in 2006 for his involvement in a fight on New Year's Eve. That case was dismissed. However, officials stopped him as he left the court. They realized he still hadn't served all of his community service from 2003. He will likely serve a consequence for this most recent mistake.

Kurt Busch

Speed. Kurt Busch thrives on it. He has to in his world. He is one of the nation's top NASCAR drivers. In 2004 he won the top award for NASCAR when he was named the Nextel Cup champion. No one denies his level of dominance in his sport. But many NASCAR fans have a hard time overlooking his attitude and style. In 2006 he was named number three on GQ magazine's list of the 10 most hated athletes.

Busch has gotten into fights with other drivers after races. During one race, he even threw a water bottle that hit an official. Finally, he was arrested in 2005 for reckless driving and was suspected of being intoxicated. When he was pulled over, he was disrespectful to the arresting officers. The manner in which he handled himself cost him his job. The president of his racing team basically fired him, saying they were "officially retiring as Kurt Busch's apologists." It was later confirmed that Busch was not intoxicated, and some of the police charges were dropped. Regardless, it seemed Busch had reached his final straw with NASCAR.

Since then, he has decided it is time to do something about his image. He joined a new racing team and created the Kurt Busch Foundation. In May 2006 he donated $1 million to the Victory Junction Gang Camp. The organization helps seriously ill children enjoy camping and recreational activities. His donation will help pay for a sports facility that will be called the Kurt Busch Superdome.

Master P

Master P's real name is Percy Miller. He was born into a life of poverty but has since let nothing stand in his way. He has created a business empire called No Limit Entertainment. The company has allowed him to become a master of all trades in the entertainment world. He acts. He directs. He produces films. He produces music. He has even dabbled in becoming a professional basketball player. His sense of business has allowed him to turn his poverty into incredible wealth.

Despite his fame, he hasn't forgotten his roots. Every Thanksgiving he helps feed families in need in Louisiana. He makes a $100,000 donation to them through his Master P Foundation. He has even been known to give $250,000 to churches and schools in his home state.

He originally started the Master P Foundation to supplement the Stop the Violence peace campaign. Through his foundation, he has helped find 7,000 jobs for inner-city kids around the country.

In spite of all of the good he has done, he has allowed a negative influence to creep into his life. In 2003 he was arrested at an airport when he tried to check his handgun through security. The weapon included eight bullets known as "cop-killers" because of their hollow tips. These bullets are illegal in many states. In 2005 he was arrested on a felony charge for carrying an unregistered and loaded gun. He pleaded no contest to a lower charge and was fined $700 for the offense. His brother, Vyshonne "Silkk the Shocker" Miller was arrested with him at the time. He pleaded guilty and was sentenced to three years of probation, 40 hours of community service, and a $700 fine.

Your opinion of each of these celebrities may tell you something about yourself. If you tend to focus on the positive things, you may be one of those teens who looks at a celebrity as a role model. You may center your life on an understanding that no one is perfect, but everyone should set high goals to make a difference in the world. If you can't get past the negative side of each celebrity's story, then you may think that celebrities were never meant to be role models in the first place. You may think that famous people should never be expected to be perfect, so we shouldn't allow ourselves to be influenced by these people.

Remember, it is important not to judge others by their faults, but to learn from their mistakes.

Reading Comprehension

After reading "What's the Message?" choose the options that best answer questions 1-14.

1. Read this sentence.
   Not only has he excelled on the field, he has done what he can to provide for people off the field as well.

   What is the meaning of the word *excelled* as it is used in this sentence?
   A. exerted
   B. hindered
   C. surpassed
   D. exhausted

2. Read this sentence.
   Remember, it is important not to judge others by their faults, but to learn from their mistakes.

   What does the author mean by this sentence?
   F. You should continue being a pessimist.
   G. You should judge a person for their blunders.
   H. You should allow yourself failure before achieving success.
   I. You should not criticize, but understand and grow from others' shortcomings.

3. According to the article, why might teenagers not be influenced by celebrities?
   A. Teenagers believe celebrities are promoting their own causes.
   B. Teenagers believe celebrities buy their way out of their mistakes.
   C. Teenagers believe celebrities do not have to work as hard as everyone else.
   D. Teenagers believe celebrities are less likely to be punished for their crimes.

4. Which statement about Kurt Busch is LEAST accurate?
   F. Kurt Busch created his foundation for publicity.
   G. Kurt Busch is one of the top drivers of NASCAR.
   H. Kurt Busch is most likely remorseful for his behavior.
   I. Kurt Busch is not a crowd pleaser with NASCAR fans.

5. With which statement would the author of the passage most likely agree?
   A. Jake Plummer, T.I., Kurt Busch, and Master P are positive role models.
   B. Each celebrity has taken his own organization and promoted his own agenda.
   C. Jake Plummer and Kurt Busch are both talented athletes who like to live dangerously.
   D. Regardless of image, Master P, T.I., Kurt Busch, and Jake Plummer have helped their communities.

6. The author organizes the article by
   F. comparing four celebrities' crimes.
   G. describing four celebrities' images.
   H. listing the reasons why you should not like celebrities.
   I. listing the celebrities' accomplishments and their crimes.

7. Why does the author include both entertainers and athletes in the article?
    A. to show how role models come in all shapes and sizes
    B. to encourage the reader to keep an open mind toward celebrities
    C. to tell the reader that athletes are better role models than entertainers
    D. to expand the reader's own expectations on what defines a role model

8. What statement best expresses the main idea of the article?
    F. Celebrities support a cause to promote themselves.
    G. Role models are celebrities who have polished images.
    H. People should decide for themselves what defines a role model.
    I. Because of their mistakes, celebrities should not be considered role models.

9. Why might Master P be considered a master of all trades?
    A. He likes to take risks with his money.
    B. He can transform singers into superstars.
    C. He has taken his life of poverty and made it into a life of wealth.
    D. His many talents have given him an edge in the entertainment world.

10. Why might T.I.'s behavior be confusing to some?
    F. T.I.'s behavior does not reflect his own teachings.
    G. T.I. has devoted much of his time and money to the community.
    H. T.I.'s carefree behavior has encouraged others to duplicate his actions.
    I. T.I.'s positive influence has encouraged young kids to contribute to their communities.

11. Jake Plummer and Kurt Busch are different in that
    A. both have tempers.
    B. Kurt Busch has tried to clean up his image.
    C. Jake Plummer has been arrested for his aggressive behavior.
    D. Jake Plummer donates more money to charity than Kurt Busch does.

12. Which statement about T.I. is LEAST accurate?
    F. T.I. is a talented performer.
    G. T.I. raises drug awareness in his community.
    H. T.I. has broken the law on several occasions.
    I. T.I. donates profits from his album *King* to charities.

13. What can you conclude from the president of Kurt Busch's racing team stating that they are "officially retiring as Kurt Busch's apologists"?
    A. The president feels sorry for Kurt Busch.
    B. The president is a loyal fan of Kurt Busch.
    C. The president is tired of making amends for Kurt Busch's behavior.
    D. The president wants to hire Tony Stewart as his new NASCAR driver.

14. Based on the article, which statement is most accurate?
    F. Celebrities are remorseful for their behavior.
    G. Most people endorse celebrities if they support a cause.
    H. Celebrities should not define what makes decent role models.
    I. Most people believe looking at the positive in a situation is better than looking at the negative.

Reading Strategy

Organizing the Details of Modern-Day Dr. Jekylls and Mr. Hydes

In the boxes marked *Who*? fill in the names of each of the celebrities described in the article. Fill in the details of the good things that celebrity has done in the column under Dr. Jekyll. Fill in the details of the bad things that celebrity has done under Mr. Hyde. To answer *Why*? you may have to make inferences. Using the details and any other conclusions you come to, write the theme of the article in the middle vertical column.

Answering *Who*? *Did What*? *When*? *Where*? and *Why*? helps a reader summarize as he/she reads. It is also a good way to Monitor for Understanding. As you read, stop and ask yourself those questions. If you can't answer them, go back and clarify what you have read.

Teacher's Notes: You may need to give the students some basic background knowledge of Dr. Jekyll and Mr. Hyde. Student answers may vary for this activity, but could include the information provided below.

Who?	Dr. Jekyll	What is the overall message or theme of the article?	Mr. Hyde	Who?
Jake Plummer	**Did What?** Donated $100,000 to Family Tree. **When?** April 20, 2006. **Where?** In Denver. **Why?** To give back to the community and help fight child abuse, etc.	Some of the celebrities we have today could be good role models, but some of them run into problems. We need to make sure we aren't quick to judge them by their mistakes, but learn from them instead.	**Did What?** Was accused of backing into and kicking a car. **When?** On his way to donate the money to Family Tree. **Where?** In Denver. **Why?** He may have been angry and lost control of his emotions.	Jake Plummer
T.I.	**Did What?** Has spoken to kids about the dangers of drugs, violence, etc. Has provided relief to the victims of Katrina. **When?** Following Hurricane Katrina. **Where?** Georgia and Louisiana. **Why?** He wants to encourage kids to do the right thing.		**Did What?** Has been arrested for having drugs, battery, and disorderly conduct. **When?** Different times from 1998-2006. **Where?** Exact details aren't provided. **Why?** He apparently has had difficult controlling his actions.	T.I.
Kurt Busch	**Did What?** Donated $1 million to the Victory Junction Gang Camp. **When?** May 2006. **Where?** Exact details aren't provided. **Why?** To help pay for a sports facility for sick children.		**Did What?** Has gotten into fights during races and has been arrested for reckless driving. **When?** In 2005. **Where?** On the racetrack and on the public streets. **Why?** He lets the "attitude" he needs on the racetrack overtake him.	Kurt Busch
Master P	**Did What?** Gives donations through the Master P Foundation to needy people. **When?** Thanksgiving and other times when people are in need. **Where?** Louisiana. **Why?** He doesn't want to forget his roots.		**Did What?** Has been arrested for having illegal bullets and for illegal gun possession. **When?** In 2003 and 2005. **Where?** At an airport and somewhere else. (We aren't given the exact details.) **Why?** He has let himself be influenced by a negative force.	Master P

Impact

Interpreting the Data

PART I

Examine the following data about important events that have occurred in rapper T.I.'s life over the last decade.

Awards Certification Status of T.I.'s Albums & Singles						
Title	Format	Release Date	Certified Gold[1]	Certified Platinum[2]	Certified Multi-Platinum (2)[3]	Certified Multi-Platinum (3)[4]
Trap Muzik	Album	8/19/03	12/08/03			
Urban Legend	Album	11/30/04	12/17/04	03/03/05		
Bring 'Em Out	Single	10/19/04	05/27/05	10/25/05		
King	Album	3/28/06	04/25/06	04/25/06		

The Gold® and Platinum® Awards are certified by the Recording Industry Association of America® through an extensive process of auditing sales information for each album or single.

1 Sold 500,000 units.
2 Sold 1,000,000 units.
3 Sold 2,000,000 units.
4 Sold 3,000,000 units.

Events Occurring in the Life of Rapper T.I.	
1998	Arrested and convicted for possession of controlled substances and giving false information.
2003	Arrested for battery on a law enforcement officer.
4/2004	Stated, "I've got a lot of loose ends to tie up, legitimately, before I can further my career."
4/2004	Sentenced to three years in prison for violating the terms of his probation. He was offered the ability to apply for a work-release program after serving a minimum of one year.
4/21/2005	Spoke to youth at Georgia's Paulding Center about the dangers of drugs and living a life of crime.
9/2005	Assisted with the Heal the Hood Relief Concert to provide money and relief to victims of Hurricane Katrina.
2006	Went to court over an altercation on New Year's Eve.
2006	Charged (during his court appearance for the New Year's Eve altercation) for failing to serve all of his community service from 1993.

			Best Position of Title by Categories/ Charts						
Year	Title	Format	Billboard Hot 100	Hot R&B/Hip-Hop Songs	Pop 100	Hot Rap Tracks	Billboard 200	Top R&B/Hip-Hop Albums	Top Rap Albums
2006	Ride Wit Me	Single			78				
2006	What You Know	Single	3	1	10	1			
2006	Why You Wanna	Single	31	6	52	5			
2005	ASAP	Single	75	18		14			
2005	Bring 'Em Out	Single	9	6		4			
2005	Get Loose	Single				70			
2005	Motivation	Single		62					
2005	U Don't Know Me	Single	23	6	65	4			
2004	Let's Get Away	Single	35	17		10			
2004	Rubber Band Man	Single	30	15		11			
2003	24's	Single	78	27		15			
2003	Be Easy	Single		55					
2006	King	Album					1	1	1
2005	Urban Legend: Chopped & Screwed	Album						42	20
2004	Urban Legend	Album					7	1	1
2003	Trap Muzik	Album					4	2	
2001	I'm Serious	Album					98	27	

15. Create a timeline below using at least a dozen major events that have occurred in T.I.'s life over the past few years. Write the event above the line if it was a good thing. Write the event below the line if it was a bad thing.

Above the line:

- Urban Legend ranks #1 on two charts.
- Urban Legend goes Platinum.
- Spoke to youth at Georgia's Paulding Center.
- Gave money to a Hurricane Katrina charity.
- Single "Bring 'Em Out" goes platinum.
- Album King goes #1 on three charts.
- Album King goes platinum.
- Single "What You Know" goes #1 on two charts.

Timeline years: 1998 | 2003 | 2004 | 2005 | 2006

Below the line:

- Arrested for controlled substances and giving false information. (1998)
- Arrested for battery on a law enforcement officer. (2003)
- Sentenced to three years for violating probation. (2004)
- Goes to court over a New Year's Eve altercation. (2006)
- Charged for failing to serve all his community service. (2006)

16. Which one of T.I's albums has had the most and quickest success? Support your answer with details from the preceding tables.

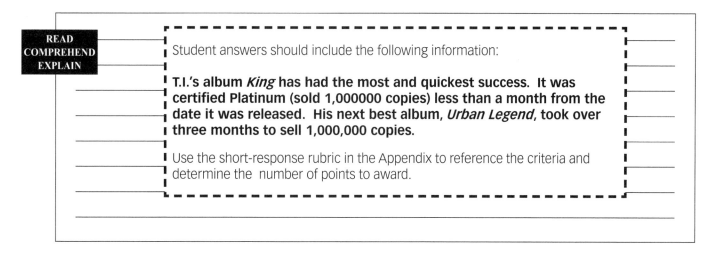

READ COMPREHEND EXPLAIN

Student answers should include the following information:

T.I.'s album *King* has had the most and quickest success. It was certified Platinum (sold 1,000000 copies) less than a month from the date it was released. His next best album, *Urban Legend*, took over three months to sell 1,000,000 copies.

Use the short-response rubric in the Appendix to reference the criteria and determine the number of points to award.

Using the tables on the preceding pages, compare the timing of the negative things in T.I.'s life with the positive things. Then answer the following question.

17. In April 2004 T.I. stated, "I've got a lot of loose ends to tie up, legitimately, before I can further my career." How does the timeline show that his efforts to "tie up loose ends" may have helped his career? Use details and facts from your timeline to support your answer.

ANALYZE EVALUATE EXPLAIN

Student answers may vary, but they should demonstrate an ability to use data and details to make inferences. They should also support their claims with data and details from the tables. Their answers could include the following information:

After being arrested in 1998, his career amounted to little until 2004 when *Urban Legend* reached number one on the charts. In 2004 he was sentenced to a year for violating his probation. That is when he said, "I've got a lot of loose ends to tie up, legitimately, before I can further my career." A year later, he visited youth in Georgia's Paulding Center and spoke to them about the dangers of crime. He also helped out the victims of Hurricane Katrina. By 2006 he had a number-one song and also a number-one album in *King*. These could have been as a result of him getting focused on his career. Unfortunately, during his ride to success, he was taken back to court for crimes from his past.

Use the short-response rubric in the Appendix to reference the criteria and determine the number of points to award.

PART II

Analyze the data in the following table and use it to answer the questions on the following pages to determine how Kurt Busch stacks up against some of NASCAR's best drivers over the past seven years.

> Student should use the total column in this chart to help them complete the math for the questions on the following pages. Data has been included to assist you in guiding students.

Results of Top NASCAR Drivers (2001-2006)								
		2001	**2002**	**2003**	**2004**	**2005**	**2006***	**Totals**
Group One	**Jimmie Johnson** Ranking	52	5	2	2	5	1	67/6
	Winnings (millions) (rounded to .1)	$0.1	$2.8	$5.5	$5.7	$6.8	$5.3	26.2
	Wins/ Starts	0/3	3/36	3/36	8/36	4/36	3/15	21/162
	Top-10 Finishes	0	21	20	23	22	12	98
	Tony Stewart Ranking	2	1	7	6	1	6	23/6
	Winnings (millions) (rounded to .1)	$3.5	$4.7	$5.2	$6.2	$7	$3.1	29.7
	Wins/ Starts	3/36	3/36	2/36	2/36	5/36	1/15	16/195
	Top-10 Finishes	22	21	18	19	25	8	113
	Kurt Busch Ranking	27	3	11	1	10	16	68/6
	Winnings (millions) (rounded to .1)	$2.2	$3.7	$5	$4.2	$6.5	$2.2	23.8
	Wins/ Starts	0/35	4/36	4/36	3/36	3/34**	1/15	15/192
	Top 10 Finishes	6	20	14	21	18	4	83
Group Two	**Matt Kenseth** Ranking	13	8	1	8	7	2	39/6
	Winnings (millions) (rounded to .1)	$2.3	$3.9	$4.0	$6.2	$5.8	$3.3	25.5
	Wins/ Starts	0/36	5/36	1/36	2/36	1/36	2/15	11/195
	Top-10 Finishes	9	19	25	16	17	10	96
	Jeff Gordon Ranking	1	4	4	3	11	11	34/6
	Winnings (millions) (rounded to .1)	$6.6	$5	$5.1	$6.4	$6.9	$2.5	32.5
	Wins/ Starts	6/36	3/36	3/36	5/36	4/36	0/15	21/195
	Top-10 Finishes	24	20	20	25	14	6	109
	Dale Earnhardt, Jr. Ranking	8	11	3	5	19	4	50/6
	Winnings (millions) (rounded to .1)	$5.4	$4.6	$4.9	$7.2	$5.8	$2.5	30.4
	Wins/ Starts	3/36	2/36	2/36	6/36	1/36	1/15	15/195
	Top-10 Finishes	15	16	21	21	13	7	93

*As of Week 15 (June 18, 2006)

**Busch missed the last two races as a result of his November arrest.

Create a line graph for the Group One drivers that shows the history of their rankings among fellow NASCAR drivers over the last six years.

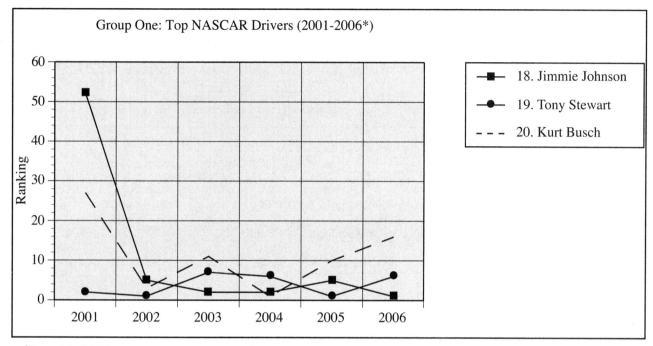

*as of June 18, 2006

Create a line graph for the Group Two drivers that shows the history of their rankings among fellow NASCAR drivers over the last six years.

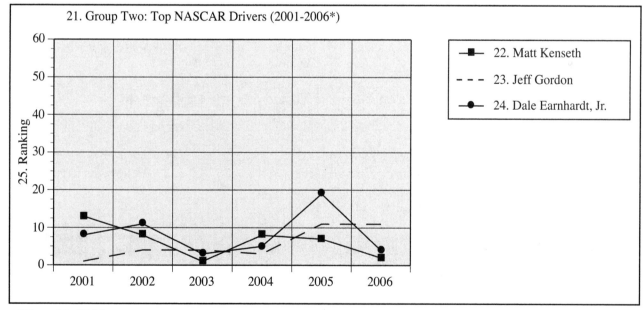

*as of June 18, 2006

Analyze the data from the preceding table and graphs to answer the following questions.

26. Which driver(s) has the most number of wins over the past six years?

Jimmie Johnson and Jeff Gordon

27. Which driver has the best winning percentage for all of the races he has started over the past six years? Round your answer to the nearest whole number. Use the box below to show how you determined your answer.

Jeff Gordon

READ
COMPREHEND
APPLY

Driver	# wins	# races	Wins/races	Percentage
Johnson, J.	21 (divided by)	162	.1296	13%
Stewart, T.	16	195	.0820	8%
Busch, K.	15	192	.0781	8%
Kenseth, M.	11	195	.0564	6%
Gordon, J.	21	195	.1077	11%
Earnhardt, Jr.	15	195	.0769	8%

Which driver has the best winning percentage per starts? **Jimmie Johnson**

Use the short-response rubric in the Appendix to reference the criteria and determine the number of points to award.

28. Which three drivers have won the most money over the past six years per race they have started? Use the box below to show how you determined your answer.

READ
COMPREHEND
APPLY

Driver	$ (millions)	# races	$ Winnings / races
Johnson, J.	26.2	162	$161, 728/ race
Stewart, T.	29.7	195	$152,308 / race
Busch, K.	23.8	192	$123,958/ race
Kenseth, M.	25.5	195	$130,769/ race
Gordon, J.	32.5	195	$166,667/ race
Earnhardt, Jr.	30.4	195	$155,897/ race

Three drivers who have won the most money per race:
1. **Jeff Gordon** 2. **Jimmie Johnson** 3. **Dale Earnhardt, Jr.**

Use the short-response rubric in the Appendix to reference the criteria and determine the number of points to award.

29. Which three drivers have averaged the best rankings over the past six years? Round your answers to two decimal points. Use the box below to show how you determined your answer.

READ
COMPREHEND
APPLY

Driver	Combined Ranks	# years	Average ranking over the past six years
Johnson, J.	67	6	11.17
Stewart, T.	23	6	3.83
Busch, K.	68	6	11.33
Kenseth, M.	39	6	6.5
Gordon, J.	34	6	5.67
Earnhardt, Jr.	50	6	8.33

Use the short-response rubric in the Appendix to reference the criteria and determine the number of points to award.

30. Which three drivers have the highest percentages of top-10 finishes for each of the races they have started? Round your answer to the nearest whole number. Use the box below to show how you determined your answer.

READ COMPREHEND APPLY

Driver	Top-10 finishes	# races	Top-10 finishes/ race	Percentage
Johnson, J.	98 (divided by)	162	.61/ race	61%
Stewart, T.	113	195	.58/ race	58%
Busch, K.	83	192	.43/ race	43%
Kenseth, M.	96	195	.49/ race	49%
Gordon, J.	109	195	.56/ race	56%
Earnhardt, Jr.	93	195	.48/ race	48%

Three drivers who have the highest percentages of top-ten finishes:
1. **Jimmie Johnson** 2. **Tony Stewart** 3. **Jeff Gordon**

Use the short-response rubric in the Appendix to reference the criteria and determine the number of points to award.

31. List the top drivers from best to worst based on the table, the graphs, and the answers to the preceding questions. Use data from the tables to explain why you ranked Kurt Busch where you did.

ANALYZE SYNTHESIZE EXPLAIN

Student answers may vary, but they must be able to support their claims using the data from the tables and graphs. Students should be able to discuss why they chose the rankings they did based on the data given. A possible list is shown below (along with reasoning for each driver's ranking. Students are required only to explain their ranking of Kurt Busch):

1. **Jimmie Johnson (Most consistent ranks over the last five years. Most consistent top-ten finishes and most consistent wins.)**
2. **Jeff Gordon (Most money per race. Second in rankings over the last six years. In top three in the top-10 finishes.)**
3. **Tony Stewart (Higher % of top-10 finishes. Higher rankings overall than Earnhardt, Jr..)**
4. **Dale Earnhardt, Jr. (Higher average of wins than Kenseth. 3rd in money per race.)**
5. **Matt Kenseth (Slightly higher average money per race than Busch. Slightly higher top-10 finishes % than Busch.)**
6. **Kurt Busch (Lowest amount of winnings per race out of the six drivers. Lowest ranking over the last five years. Lowest percentage of top-10 finishes over the last six years.)**

Use the extended-response rubric in the Appendix to reference the criteria and determine the number of points to award.

Analyze the data in the following table showing Kurt Busch's finishes in his first 15 races of 2006.

2006 Race Results of Kurt Busch (as of June 25, 2006)				
Week	Date	Race	Finish	Winnings
1	2/19/06	Daytona 500	38	$280,366
2	2/26/06	Auto Club 500	16	$144,558
3	3/12/06	UAW-DaimlerChrysler 400	16	$126,583
4	3/20/06	Golden Corral 500	37	$99,153
5	3/26/06	Food City 500	1	$175,858
6	4/02/06	DirecTV 500	11	$111,683
7	4/09/06	Samsung/RadioShack 500	34	$124,633
8	4/22/06	Subway Fresh 500	24	$103,833
9	5/01/06	Aaron's 499	7	$143,233
10	5/06/06*	Crown Royal 400	29	$105,008
11	5/13/06	Dodge Charger 500	19	$115,633
12	5/23/06	Coca-Cola 600	39	$122,858
13	6/04/06	Neighborhood Excellence 400 presented by Bank of America	16	$122,658
14	6/11/06	Pocono 500	2	$193,258
15	6/18/06	3M Performance 400 presented by Post-it Picture Paper	9	$117,583
16	6/25/06	Dodge/Save Mart 350	5	$145,433
			Total	$2,232,331
			Average Winnings/ Race	$139,520

*Busch donated $1 million to charity in May 2006.

32. Based on the table above, does it appear as though Busch has been affected in 2006 by his 11/05 arrest? Compare his results so far this year to his results over the past six years to support your answer.

ANALYZE EVALUATE APPLY

Student answers may vary, but they should demonstrate an ability to use data and details to make inferences. They should also support their claims with data and details from the tables. Their answers could include the following information:

Busch has won more money per start this year ($139,126) than he has averaged from 2001-2005 ($134,463). This could indicate that he is actually doing better than he was before his arrest. However, only 31% of his finishes are in the top-10 so far this year as opposed to 45% from 2001-2005. This is quite a fall-off, which could indicate he has been affected by his lack of focus following his arrest.

Use the extended-response rubric in the Appendix to reference the criteria and determine the number of points to award.

33. After examining the data in the table, does it appear that giving the donation has made Kurt Busch a better, more focused driver? Use data from the table to support your claim.

ANALYZE EVALUATE APPLY

Student answers may vary, but they should demonstrate an ability to use data and details to make inferences. They should also support their claims with data and details from the tables. Their answers could include the following information:

At first, he did not perform as well, finishing 29th, 19th, and 39th. But about a month later, he dropped down to 16th, 2nd, 9th, and 5th. This may indicate that he is getting more focused again, which is resulting in better performance on the track.

Use the extended-response rubric in the Appendix to reference the criteria and determine the number of points to award.

---

*Quick*thought

You may not always see a positive consequence for doing the right thing, but it will keep your life focused and allow you to enjoy more success in the long run.

Look Inside and Grow

34. Can you control your own fate? Do you believe that if you do something bad, something bad will happen to you? Do you believe that if you do something good, you will be returned in kind? Give an example of when you have done something good and something good has happened to you.

> Student answers may vary.
>
> The student should address each section of the question to the best of his/her ability. The question is meant to elicit strong classroom conversation about character. Students should be able to demonstrate that they have learned a lesson about the value of having strong morals and character all the time, regardless of whether it will pay immediate results.
>
> Use the character-education rubric in the Appendix to reference the criteria and determine the number of points to award.

Notes

A recent poll …: Majewski, Lori. "Teens & Celebrities." *USA Weekend*, May 19-21, 2006.

The president of …: Fleischman, Bill. "Busch Siblings Not Cozy With NASCAR Brotherhood." *Philadelphia Daily News*, June 1, 2006. http://www.philly.com/mld/dailynews/sports/14712965.htm.

Awards Certification Status (chart)…: Recording Industry Association of America®,
The Gold® and Platinum® Awards Searchable Database.
http://www.riaa.com/gp/database/search_results.asp.

Stated, "I've got…: "T.I. Hasn't Been Hiding Out Lately — He's Been In Jail." MTV.com News, April 19, 2004.
http://www.mtv.com/news/articles/1486451/04192004/t_i_.jhtml.

T.I.'s Top Singles (chart)…: "T.I. Top Albums." Billboard.com.
http://www.billboard.com/bbcom/retrieve_chart_history.do?model.chartFormatGroupName=Albums&model.
vnuArtistId=447490&model.vnuAlbumId=763690.

Results of Top (chart)…: Official Driver Standings, NASCAR.com.
http://www.nascar.com/races/cup/2006/data/standings_official.html,
http://www.nascar.com/races/cup/2005/data/standings_official.html,
http://www.nascar.com/races/cup/2004/data/standings_official.html,
http://www.nascar.com/races/cup/2003/data/standings_official.html,
http://www.nascar.com/races/cup/2002/data/standings_official.html,
http://www.nascar.com/races/cup/2001/data/standings_official.html,
http://www.nascar.com/races/cup/2000/data/standings_official.html.

Results of Top (chart)…: "Kurt Busch, In-Depth Statistics." Offical Driver Standings, NASCAR.com, 2006.
http://www.nascar.com/drivers/dps/kbusch00/cup/data/2006/index.html.

Technical Extension

How a Nonprofit Is Formed

A nonprofit organization is an organization or company established as a charity and not for the purpose of making money. This doesn't mean that a nonprofit doesn't make any money. If that were true, the charity

501c3
donation

would never be able to do any good! It also doesn't mean that the people who work for the charity don't get paid. Being a nonprofit organization simply means that the main purpose of the company is to fulfill its mission—whether that is to feed the homeless, provide medical supplies to the needy, or educate at-risk youth. The bulk of the money raised by the organization will go to the charity it supports.

The major difference between a nonprofit and a for-profit company revolves around the company's

mission. While the primary purpose of having a nonprofit organization is to help the charity it supports, anyone who forms a nonprofit is also running a business. In order to achieve its mission, a nonprofit must be a strong business as well.

Below we can look at just a few of the first steps needed to start a nonprofit.

First, the organization that wants to become a nonprofit needs to determine what it will be called. To make the name official, the company has to reserve the name with its state government. The company needs a mission statement. This statement describes what the company does and why it does it. The person in charge of the organization then chooses the people who will be on the board of directors.

Most companies that want to become nonprofits hire an accountant to do the financial paperwork. Nonprofits do not have to pay income tax on the money they make and have to complete lots of paperwork with the government. There is also paperwork that must be done on a yearly basis. Many times a nonprofit will have an accountant or financial expert as a part of the full-time staff.

The company also has to open a bank account and set up a system for accepting donations. Sometimes a nonprofit charity's biggest source of income is from donations, and there have to be rules in place for what happens with that money.

The organization still needs a few more things. For example, workers need to be hired and the board of directors has to decide how much each one will get paid. The company must rent or buy office space and buy supplies.

Undertaking the development of a nonprofit is a major responsibility, but one that allows people to make a significant difference for a cause they truly care about. When people think about starting a nonprofit organization, they are really starting a small business with all the needs of a successful business. However, it's the heart of the business—its mission—that really drives the success of a nonprofit organization.

The Vocabulary of a Nonprofit

501c3—The most common type of nonprofit organization.

Audit—Looking at financial records to make sure they are correct.

Board of Directors—The group of people responsible for supervising an organization.

Donation—A gift to a fund, organization, or cause.

IRS (Internal Revenue Service)—A U.S. government agency responsible for collecting income tax.

Mission Statement—A summary describing the aims, values, and plan of an organization.

Tax-Exempt—When a company is not taxed on money made.

Reading Comprehension

After reading "How a Nonprofit Is Formed," choose the options that best answer questions 1-14.

1. Read this sentence.
   Undertaking the development of a nonprofit is a major responsibility, but one that allows people to make a significant difference for a cause they truly care about.

   What is the meaning of the word *undertaking* as it is used in this sentence?
   A. to give up
   B. to manage
   C. to try harder
   D. to over achieve

2. Read this sentence.
   It's the heart of the business—its mission—that really drives the success of a nonprofit organization.

   What does the author mean by this sentence?
   F. The heart and a mission are one and the same.
   G. The heart is the main organ that keeps the body alive.
   H. The mission is the central component in a nonprofit; it keeps it alive.
   I. The heart will eventually stop working just like a mission will eventually fail.

3. According to the article, what is the first thing a nonprofit needs in its organization?
   A. a mission
   B. donations
   C. an accountant
   D. a board of directors

4. What is the purpose of a nonprofit?
   F. A nonprofit is formed to avoid paying taxes.
   G. A nonprofit is formed to help companies it supports.
   H. A nonprofit is established to fulfill its mission statement.
   I. A nonprofit is established for the purpose of making money.

5. With which statement would the author of the passage most likely agree?
   A. The nonprofit must decide its name in the early stages.
   B. Nonprofits are complicated and difficult to understand.
   C. Once a nonprofit's mission is achieved, its work is over.
   D. Working for a nonprofit is easier then working for a for-profit company.

6. The author organizes the article by
   F. listing the vocabulary of a nonprofit.
   G. describing a nonprofit and how one works.
   H. placing events in order of how to establish a nonprofit.
   I. comparing a for-profit organization with a nonprofit organization.

7. Why does the author compare a nonprofit with a for-profit organization?
   A. to show how confusing running a business can be
   B. to encourage you to apply for a company that makes money
   C. to describe the similarities and differences of the two organizations
   D. to show how much money you could make if you were working for a for-profit organization

8. What statement best expresses the main idea of the first paragraph?
   F. A nonprofit's goal is to make money.
   G. A nonprofit organization runs a business.
   H. A nonprofit is formed to support a charity.
   I. A nonprofit feeds the homeless and provides medical supplies.

9. What is significant about a nonprofit's financials?
   A. They do not have to pay taxes on money earned.
   B. They require less paperwork then a for-profit organization.
   C. They have the same paperwork as a for-profit organization.
   D. The person in charge of a nonprofit decides how the money will be spent.

10. Why is it important for a nonprofit to hire an accountant?
    F. The accountant decides who should be hired.
    G. The accountant decides how much money each of the employees will get paid.
    H. The accountant prepares and completes all necessary paperwork required by the government.
    I. The accountant's responsibility is to open a bank account for the non-profit organization.

11. What is true of both for-profit and nonprofit organizations?
    A. A nonprofit has its employees work for free.
    B. A for-profit organization requires a board of directors.
    C. For-profit and nonprofit organizations both pay income taxes to the government.
    D. For-profit and nonprofit organizations both have money in their budgets to pay employee salaries.

12. Nonprofit organizations are important today
    F. because they support groups in the community.
    G. because they hire many people that cannot find jobs.
    H. because they allow their employees to work less then a regular job.
    I. because the government makes as much money from them as they make from for-profit companies.

13. According to the article and the box entitled "The Vocabulary of a Nonprofit," who would be responsible for providing correct paperwork for an audit?
    A. an employee
    B. an accountant
    C. a board of directors
    D. the person who receives the donations

14. How does the vocabulary text box help the reader understand the article?
    F. It doesn't make it any easier to understand.
    G. It makes the reading more difficult to understand.
    H. It provides the reader with terms that are commonly associated with a nonprofit.
    I. It provides the reader with the necessary background information for establishing and maintaining a nonprofit.

Vocational Extension

Have you ever heard of an accountant? You might hear your parents talking about their accountant between January and April of any given year. This is because one of the primary jobs of an accountant is to help prepare income tax documents. But accountants do so much more.

A certified public accountant (CPA) records and examines the financial records of an individual or business. A CPA prepares income tax reports and other financial reports. He or she must be very familiar with tax laws and business economics.

Can you picture an accountant now? Are you picturing a middle-aged man staring through his bifocals at a stack of books? This might be one example of an accountant, but there are so many more. Accountants are smart and creative. They enjoy working with numbers. Accountants are men and women. They have strong written and verbal communication skills. They are organized, and they understand detailed processes.

Often, people who enjoy business and math classes in middle and high school decide to look into accounting. After college, accountants must take a certification exam. Accountants who have passed the Uniform Certified Public Accountant Examination are certified as CPAs. The CPA exam was developed to set the standard of knowledge for accountants. It is a two-day exam with four sections. The test checks for understanding of four major areas:

- Auditing
- Financial Accounting and Reporting
- Regulation (business ethics and professional responsibility)
- Business Environment & Concepts

Accountants can be employed in various types of jobs. Some work for public accounting firms. These CPAs generally contract services to many different clients. Because of their education, CPAs usually have a good understanding of business. They are often employed by companies in roles that require them to give general business recommendations. Many work as analysts or management executives in small and large companies. Other accountants work in governmental roles performing audits. Still others work for nonprofit organizations. In this role, they help the company solve tax problems, set up a budget, or prepare data for fundraising. Finally, accountants often find themselves teaching a new generation of potential accountants. They work in universities and business schools across the country.

In recent years, accountants have been able to use technology to increase their effectiveness. They no longer have to spend large amounts of time manually recording and calculating numbers. Therefore, they have been able to take on more responsibilities in their jobs.

Accounting is a career field with so many possibilities. The field is growing, and dedicated workers are needed. Helping a person or company understand and plan finances is important. It's fulfilling. It's a great career path.

Looking Forward

15. Whether or not you decide to become an accountant, it is important to understand your finances as you go through life. Starting after you graduate from high school, you will likely be responsible for earning, spending, and understanding money. Answer the following questions: What can you do now to prepare for your financial future? What do you think you need to learn in school to be ready? What do you imagine your financial life will be like when you are on your own? Use the job description and article along with your experience to complete your answer.

Looking Forward

Student answers may vary.

The student should address the question to the best of his/her ability using the article and personal experience. The question is meant to encourage students to explore areas of interest for their future and begin to determine how they will prepare for a future career.

Use the extended-response rubric in the Appendix to reference the criteria and determine the number of points to award.

Ethical Dilemma

16. You're a successful accountant working for a large company. You are in charge of the financial paperwork for the company and give financial advice to the CFO (Chief Financial Officer). When you are working on the financial books, you notice that there is a small amount of money that isn't accounted for. When you look further, you discover that one of your colleagues has been taking some of the company's profits to help pay medical bills for her sick child. It isn't much money, and you don't want to get your colleague in trouble, but you know that what she is doing isn't right. Should you take action?

Ethical Dilemma

Student answers may vary.

The student should address the question to the best of his/her ability using background knowledge from the article as well as personal opinion and experience. The question is meant to encourage students to contemplate scenarios and make ethical decisions.

Use the character-education rubric in the Appendix to reference the criteria and determine the number of points to award.

Reading Instructional Guide

BEFORE READING

Front-Loading Background Knowledge Through Read-Aloud-Think-Aloud

Search the internet for recent articles on Shakira and use them to model the effective habits of readers through a Read-Aloud-Think-Aloud.

Check out articles at the following websites to determine if they would be appropriate for your RATA:

- http://www.shakiramedia.com/?page=bio

- http://en.wikipedia.org/wiki/shakira

(Please keep in mind that it is the responsibility of the teacher to determine if articles from suggested sites are appropriate. The sites may have changed content since this publication. The publisher takes no responsibility for the current content of the site.)

Looking at the Words

Determining How the Word Sounds (Phonics)

With your students, use one of the sets of steps from the Syllable Guide at the beginning of the book to determine how to break a word into manageable parts. The goal is to break the words into syllables that the students can say. Then they can put those parts together to "sound the word out." However, remember that the rules for syllabification do not always work because our language is so diverse. The rules can also become rather complex for low readers, so keep in mind that their overall objective is just to figure out how the word sounds. They may not be able to break the word into its syllables perfectly, but they should at least be able to figure out how to say the word based on their attempt at following one of these sets of steps. Lesson One is a more basic set, while Lesson Two attempts to give the students the more specific rules without becoming too complicated. Take your time when teaching either set, and understand that many of the lower readers are not going to understand right away. It will take time, practice, and repeated application before many of them are able to make use of these strategies on their own.

Determining What the Words Mean (Vocabulary)

After students have spent time breaking the words apart to figure out how they sound, use the lists of prefixes and suffixes and their meanings found in the Syllable Guide to have students try to add whatever meaning they can to the words before actually looking at their definitions. After giving the students the definitions, have them see if they can figure out which words truly apply the meaning of any of the prefixes or suffixes.

Words to Study	Breaking into Syllables	Short Definition
Resonates	res-o-nates	(v.) to produce strong sounds; reverberate
Acquainted	ac-quain-ted	(adj.) familiar
Humanitarian	hu-man-i-tar-i-an	(adj.) devoted to promoting the welfare of humanity
Humble	hum-ble	(adj.) modest
Ambition	am-bi-tion	(n.) a strong desire to achieve something
Consequence	con-se-quence	(n.) a result or effect
Ambushed	am-bushed	(v.) to attack by surprise

Activating Background Knowledge

Anticipation Guide
Mark each of the following statements True or False:

1. _____ Shakira is second to Jennifer Lopez as the most popular Latin American singer.

2. _____ Shakira has been writing her own music since the age of 8.

3. _____ English was the primary language in Shakira's household.

4. _____ Shakira has used her fame to help children in her native Mexico.

5. _____ Shakira is the youngest singer to sign with Sony records.

Starter Questions
After completing the Anticipation Guide, have a group or class discussion with the students using the following questions:

1. Who is Shakira Isabel Mebarak Ripoll?

2. Name some of Shakira's music.

3. Can you name other Latin entertainers?

4. What does it mean to be self-driven?

5. What makes Shakira successful?

Make a prediction about what you think the article will be about.

DURING READING

- Have the students skim the article. Give them about 45-60 seconds to do this.

- As they skim the article, tell them to circle any words they don't know how to say.

- When they are finished, talk about how to chunk the words they don't know how to say by sounds they now know and then sound them out.

- Have the students skim the questions. Give them only about 30-45 seconds to do this.

- Ask the students to predict what the article is about.

- Have the students read the article. They should question, summarize, clarify, and predict as they read. Instruct them to jot their questions, summarizations, clarifications, and predictions in the margins as they read.

- Remind students to constantly ask themselves if they know what the article is about right now. If they don't, they must reread to clarify. This is called monitoring for understanding.

- After they have finished reading the article, they are ready to answer the questions.

The Strategy Sheet

You may choose to have students complete the strategy sheet for each section before they answer the multiple-choice questions. Or you could have them complete the questions, work on the strategy sheet with a partner, and then go back over the questions to see if the use of the strategy sheet helped them more easily find the answers to any of the questions.

AFTER READING

Discussion Starter Questions

1. Think of a time when you struggled to do something. What happened next? Did you succeed? Did you fail? How did you ultimately feel when it was over?

2. How do you measure success?

3. Think of a time when you were told you were not allowed to do something. Did that make you want to do it more? Why? Why not?

4. How do you envision your life in 1 year? 5 years? 10 years?

5. What plans can you make now to help pave the way for the future?

Teacher Reflection

When you are finished with the article, strategies, and questions, ask yourself the following:

1. Did I get the students to THINK about what they have read?

2. Did I teach them (even a little bit) about how to read more effectively?

If you answered "Yes" to both questions, you can feel good about the day.

Building Bridges

Golden-blond tresses of hair fall over her shoulders and down her back. Her voice resonates with emotion, touched slightly by the accent of her native Colombia. No one would believe such a powerful sound could come from the mouth of the 5-foot-2, 29-year-old Latino. It is so robust, in fact, that when Shakira Isabel Mebarak Ripoll stood in front of her school choir director at the age of 10, he dismissed her for having a voice that was too strong. Her classmates reportedly teased her the rest of her school days, saying she had the voice of a goat.

None of that matters to her anymore because Shakira Isabel Mebarak Ripoll grew up to be known simply as Shakira. Now she stands on top of the world as the most popular Latin American singer of record.

"I can think in English, true, but I feel in Spanish."

Shakira is considered to be the first singer who has released two versions of the same album in Spanish and English at the same time. Anyone who has seen Shakira perform or be interviewed knows she is full of the passion for which the Latin culture is known. She grew up in Barranquilla, Colombia surrounded by a variety of cultural influences. Throughout her life, she has attacked her career full-force and has let nothing get in her way. By releasing her CDs in English as well as Spanish, she is showing

the world how determined she is to make everyone respect the different cultures around us.

Following her negative experiences with her school choir, Shakira looked elsewhere to show off her talents. She became a celebrity in her hometown when she performed on a local television show. Then she somehow managed to cross paths with an executive for Sony, the music company. Some stories say she just happened to be sitting next to him on a flight to Bogotá, Colombia, where she was going to try modeling. Others say she and her parents "ambushed" him in the lobby of a hotel in Barranquilla and sang for him. Regardless of the truth, the executive loved her and pushed to get her signed with Sony. However, the company's music director called her a "lost cause." But the executive knew a star when he saw one and refused to give up. He finally convinced his company to sign her. By the time Shakira was 13, she had a contract to do three albums.

Shakira had been writing her own music since she was 8. Her first album included those early songs. For a variety of reasons, the album was doomed from the start. However, she did not lose her ambition. She released her second album in 1993 at the age of 15. This collection of songs did much better than her first album, but not as well as she'd hoped. Although she was still set on becoming a star, she decided she needed to take time off to graduate from high school.

When she returned to the music scene in 1995, she tasted immediate success. She released the album *Pies Descalzos* (Bare Feet). It has sold over 5 million copies worldwide. Following this album, her career took off. She became acquainted with Gloria and Emilio Estefan, Jr., two legends of the Latin music scene. Emilio helped her produce her next album, *Where are the Thieves?* This album displayed her Latin roots, but it was also influenced by the rock bands she'd listened to while growing up, like Led Zeppelin, the Beatles, and Nirvana. It sold over 7 million copies around the globe.

Her success inspired her to attempt to break into the English-speaking market. So she began studying the English language. With the help of the Estefans, she released *Laundry Service*, her first album aimed at English-speaking countries. She was criticized by some people who said her language skills were too weak to write and sing in English. Even MAD TV performed a skit poking fun at the way she spoke English. But Shakira got the last laugh. The CD sold more than 13 million copies around the world. To top it all off, she performed live on MAD TV a few years later, and the audience loved her. So, instead of striking back at them, she took sweet revenge. It was the type of revenge that success provides.

"I'm slow and I take my time, like fruit takes time to ripen. You can't throw rocks at fruit so they can ripen faster."

Shakira's career has been a display of independence. She writes almost all of her lyrics and music. This is rarely seen in today's pop-music scene. When she decided to release her albums in Spanish and English, she knew it would be a great challenge. So she took her time before releasing another CD. She began learning the English language about five years ago and now considers herself fully bilingual. This education led to her release of two albums at about the same time. The first was the Spanish version of the CD, *Fijación Oral Vol. 1*. The next was *Oral Fixation Vol. 2*, the English version.

Her patience and determination paid off. In February 2006 she won a Grammy Award for Best Latin Rock Album for *Fijación Oral Vol. 1*. Early in 2006 she released the single "Hips Don't Lie," featuring Wyclef Jean from *Oral Fixation Vol. 2*. It has spent over 40 weeks on the Top 40 USA Singles Chart and has been as high as number 16. The album itself has done just as well, peaking at number 5.

The years 2005 and 2006 have been very good to Shakira. She was awarded a Grammy and was named Outstanding Female Performer at other awards shows. Some of her songs are even being played in Spanish on American Top 40 radio stations. For Shakira, this is a big step in building bridges for immigrants in America.

"If I want to die in peace, I've got to do it [be a good person]."

Shakira has used her fame to benefit the young people of Colombia. She created the Fundacion Pies Descalzos (Barefoot Foundation) to help improve the lives of thousands of children in Colombia who are affected by poverty, violence, and turmoil. She has promoted education and is aiming to use her foundation to build better schools for the people of Colombia.

Her charity has even been recognized by the United Nations. They honored her recently for her humanitarian work in Colombia, a country they have had difficulty providing aid for themselves. In 2003 she was named a goodwill ambassador for UNICEF, a children's charity. Her job with them is to make people more aware of the issues faced by children around the world.

"I'm just a consequence of the moment. I'm not the cause."

Although Shakira is pleased with her accomplishments, she is humble about them. Possibly the greatest accomplishment of her career has been her ability to succeed when others told her to quit. Because of her passion, she has helped build part of the bridge between Latin and American cultures. It is a bridge that, in the long run, will help strengthen both areas of the world.

Reading Comprehension

After reading "Building Bridges," choose the options that best answer questions 1-14.

1. Read this sentence.
   Her voice resonates with emotion, touched slightly by the accent of her native Colombia.

   What is the meaning of the word *resonates* as it is used in this sentence?
   A. echoes
   B. rumbles
   C. resolves
   D. commends

2. Read this sentence.
   I'm just a consequence of the moment. I'm not the cause.

   What does Shakira mean by this sentence?
   F. Everything in Shakira's life has happened by accident.
   G. She is only successful because society needs someone like her right now.
   H. Shakira works for many charitable causes in hopes of getting more attention.
   I. Shakira's time spent on many worthy causes has made people like her even more.

3. According to the article, Shakira's current success has been most influenced by
   A. Gloria and Emilio Estefan, Jr..
   B. English speaking rock bands like Led Zeppelin and Nirvana.
   C. an urge to show her critics how successful someone from Colombia can be.
   D. a desire to connect Latin American countries to the rest of the world through music.

4. What has Shakira done that it is believed no other artist has?
   F. She writes and sings her own lyrics and music.
   G. She recorded music that she wrote at an early age.
   H. She sold over seven million copies of a single album.
   I. She released an English and Spanish version of the same album simultaneously.

5. With which statement would the author of the passage most likely agree?
   A. Shakira has been popular non-stop since her career started.
   B. Shakira uses the United Nations for publicity to become more popular.
   C. Shakira is building bridges between American and Latin American cultures.
   D. Shakira's mission is to become the most popular Latin American singer in American history.

6. The author organizes the article by
   F. comparing Shakira to several other Latin American singers.
   G. describing Shakira's career and her ability to confront obstacles and overcome them.
   H. listing the incidences of cultural prejudice Shakira has had to overcome to be successful.
   I. starting with Shakira's personal qualities and showing how she demonstrates them through her charities.

7. What is the author's purpose in writing this article?
   A. to show how one person can have a wildly successful career
   B. to encourage others to contribute to Shakira's Barefoot Foundation
   C. to show how Shakira overcame obstacles and went on to make a difference
   D. to show how Shakira's fame has brought her honor in her own country and around the world

8. Which statement BEST expresses the main idea of this article?
   F. Shakira didn't let the opinions of others stop her from having an effect on millions of people.
   G. Shakira wants to be recognized for building bridges for immigrants and for helping her native Colombia.
   H. Shakira has reached her biggest goals in life by winning a Grammy and releasing many albums of original material.
   I. Shakira is better than most other pop musicians today because she can sing and dance and writes almost all of her music.

9. What two qualities has Shakira used to become successful?
   A. weakness and revenge
   B. weakness and patience
   C. determination and revenge
   D. determination and patience

10. Why did Shakira aim her album *Laundry Service* at English speaking countries?
    F. She was influenced by rock bands like Led Zeppelin and Nirvana.
    G. She was inspired by the world-wide success of her previous album which was influence by English-speaking rock bands.
    H. She was determined to overcome her weak English language skills and wanted to enjoy sweet revenge for MAD TV's skit about her.
    I. Emilio Estefan, Jr, the husband of Glorida Estefan, helped her produce *Where Are the Thieves?* and he was impressed with its display of Latin roots.

11. Shakira's early and late albums are SIMILAR because they
    A. were all immediate successes.
    B. all contain tracks written mostly by her.
    C. were all released in English and Spanish.
    D. all gave a portion of their proceeds to charity.

12. Which statement provides the best evidence that Shakira has had to overcome not only personal obstacles, but cultural obstacles as well?
    F. She must write all of her lyrics in Spanish and in English.
    G. Her classmates teased her, saying she had the voice of a goat.
    H. The people of her native country have been affected by poverty, violence and turmoil.
    I. She grew up in Colombia, a country where she was surrounded by a variety of cultural influences.

13. Which statement from the article supports the idea that Shakira values education?
    A. She has become fully bilingual in about five years.
    B. She took time off from her career to graduate from high school.
    C. She has been named a goodwill ambassador for UNICEF, a children's charity.
    D. She is showing the world how determined she is to make everyone respect all the different cultures around us.

14. What information does the author use to support the idea that Shakira is full of passion for making everyone respect different cultures?
    F. She took time to learn the English language.
    G. She won a Grammy Award for Best Latin Rock Album.
    H. Her music is played in Spanish on some American Top 40 radio stations.
    I. She sold more than thirteen million copies of *Laundry Service* after she was poked fun of on MAD TV.

Reading Strategy

Five Questions for the Main Idea

(Who? Did What? When? Where? Why?)

Answering the five questions listed above can help you organize the details of an article in order to find the main idea. Answer the questions for three different events in Shakira's life and then summarize the information to write the main idea in the box at the bottom of the sheet.

Did What? Learned the English language.

When? Over the last five years.

Where? Colombia/United States.

Why? So people in the United States could be exposed to music from Latin America.

Did What? Released the same album in two different formats—one in English, the other in Spanish.

When? 2005.

Where? United States/the rest of the world.

Why? To help build relationships for America's immigrants by exposing the United States and the rest of the world to another culture.

Did What? Created the Barefeet Foundation.

When? Possibly around 2003 when she was named a UNICEF ambassador.

Where? Colombia.

Why? To help improve the lives of thousands of children in Colombia.

What is the main idea of the article? Shakira has been strong enough to overcome obstacles throughout her life and career in order to build cultural bridges between Latin America and the rest of the world and to provide a better life for those in need.

Impact

Interpreting the Data

PART I

Analyze the following table of top hits from the spring and summer of 2006. You will use it to create line graphs that will help you interpret the data to determine which artist is most successful, which one is least successful, and which one is on the rise.

		6/24	6/17	6/10	6/03	5/27	5/20	5/13	5/06	4/29	4/22	4/15	4/08	4/01
Group One	SOS Rescue Me Rihanna	11	6	5	3	1	1	1	40	35	28	25	25	31
	Bad Day Daniel Powter	5	5	2	2	2	2	2	1	1	1	1	1	2
	Ridin' Chamillionaire	4	2	1	1	3	4	4	4	Fell off the Top 40 Chart		32	33	32
	Temperature Sean Paul	16	14	9	4	4	3	3	2	2	2	2	2	1
Group Two	Hips Don't Lie Shakira and Wyclef Jean	1	1	7	38	25	22	24	16	20	27	36 New		
	Where'd You Go Fort Minor	8	7	4	5	5	5	10	38	39 New				
	It's Goin' Down Yung Joc	3	4	11	20	29	30	40 New						
Group Three	Unfaithful Rihanna	6	10	21	22	15	16 New							
	Snap Yo' Fingers Lil' Jon	10	11	10	6	6	10 New							
	Me & U Cassie	9	9	6	11	35 New								

Table title: Spring and Summer 2006 Top Hits and Their Spots on the USA Singles Top 40 List (from top40-charts.com)

Fill in the missing elements on the following line graph using the information for the songs in Group One from the preceding table.

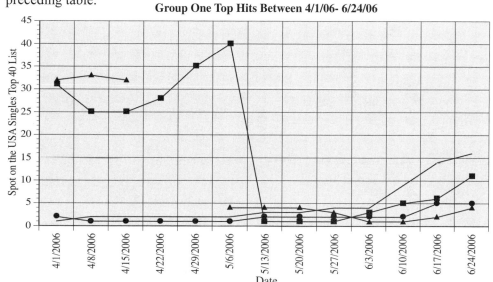

Group One Top Hits Between 4/1/06- 6/24/06

Fill in the missing elements on the following line graph using the information for the songs in Group Two from the table.

Group Two Top Hits Between 4/01/06-6/24/06

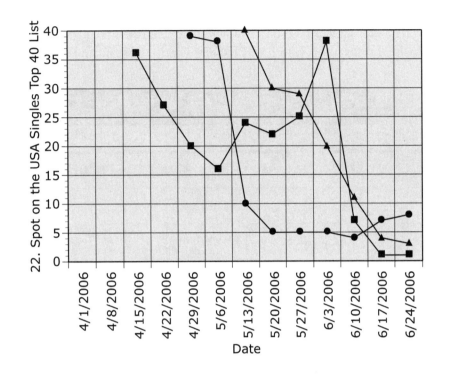

Now create the graph for the songs in Group Three from the table on the preceding pages.

23. Group Three Top Hits Between 4/01/06-6/24/06

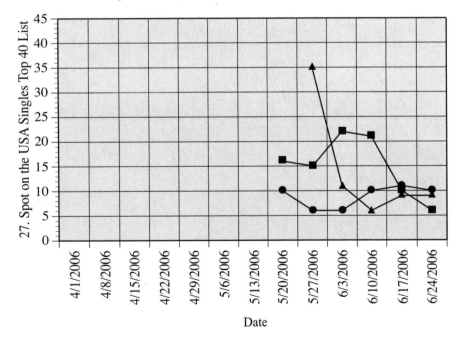

28. Compare the data for each song (include all three groups) from April through June. Decide which two songs had the strongest showing. Use data from the graphs and table to support your claim.

ANALYZE EVALUATE EXPLAIN

Student answers should include the following information:

"Bad Day" had the best showing from April through June. It was never rated above fifth, and it spent six weeks at number two and five weeks at number one. "Temperature" was the second strongest hit. It spent ten weeks in the top five singles.

Use the short-response rubric in the Appendix to reference the criteria and determine the number of points to award.

29. Compare the data for each song from April through June. Decide which two songs had the weakest showing. Use data from the graphs and table to support your claim.

ANALYZE EVALUATE EXPLAIN

Student answers should include the following information:

Shakira's "Hips Don't Lie" actually had the weakest overall showing between April and June. The song had six weeks over the top 20. For the second weakest showing, Rihanna's "SOS Rescue Me" also spent six weeks above number 20, but Rihanna had five weeks at number five or below between April and June while Shakira had only two weeks at number five or below.

Use the short-response rubric in the Appendix to reference the criteria and determine the number of points to award.

30. Which artist from the table would Shakira need to be the most concerned about if she were competing for the title of Best Artist of 2006? Use data from the graphs and table to support your claim.

ANALYZE EVALUATE EXPLAIN

Student answers should include the following information: Answers could vary, but must be supported by the information given in the table.

Shakira would need to be most concerned about Rihanna because she has already had two songs in the top 40 between April and June. If her song "Unfaithful" continues to follow its trend, it may wind up being her second number-one hit of the summer.

Use the short-response rubric in the Appendix to reference the criteria and determine the number of points to award.

31. Analyze all of the data from the table. Create a list that ranks the songs given in the table in order from weakest to strongest. Explain why you ranked Shakira's song "Hips Don't Lie" where you did. Use data from the graphs and table to support your claim.

ANALYZE SYNTHESIZE EXPLAIN

> Student answers should include the following information:
> **Answers could vary slightly, but they should demonstrate an ability to make a decision based on the data given in the table and graphs.**
>
> **A possible list might be:**
> | | |
> |---|---|
> | 1. "Bad Day" | 6. "Unfaithful" |
> | 2. "Temperature" | 7. "Snap Yo' Fingers" |
> | 3. "Ridin'" | 8. "Me & U" |
> | 4. "It's Goin' Down" | 9. "SOS Rescue Me" |
> | 5. "Where'd You Go" | 10. "Hips Don't Lie" |
>
> **Shakira's song is ranked 10 because "Hips Don't Lie" has spent the least amount of time at number one compared to the other songs that have been on the chart as long as it has. Students could argue that "Me &U," "Unfaithful," and "Snap Yo' Fingers" were the weakest, but they are relatively new songs to the chart, and each one has actually spent more time in the top 10 or so than "Hips Don't Lie."**
>
> Use the short-response rubric in the Appendix to reference the criteria and determine the number of points to award.

PART II

Gloria Estefan was the first break-out Latin American singer. Her popularity among the Spanish-speaking community spread to the English-speaking community when she released her first English-language album, *Primitive Love*, in October 1985. Estefan paved the road to the worldwide popularity of singers of Latin-American heritage.

Begin looking at the table below that compares old and new stars Estefan and Shakira, along with another new artist, Rihanna, originally from Barbados and known for her Caribbean, dance-pop sound.

Awards Certification Status of Albums & Singles of Today's and Yesterday's Stars							
Artist	Title	Format	Release Date	Certified Gold[1]	Certified Platinum[2]	Certified Multi-Platinum (2)[3]	Certified Multi-Platinum (3)[4]
Rihanna	Music of the Sun	Album	8/30/05	1/11/06			
Rihanna	Pon De Replay	Single	10/11/05	1/30/06	1/30/06	1/30/06	2/15/06
Shakira	Oral Fixation 2	Album	11/29/05	2/27/06	4/04/06		
Shakira	La Tortura	Single	8/02/05	10/27/05	10/27/05		
Shakira	Hips Don't Lie	Single	5/09/06	*			
Gloria Estefan	Primitive Love	Album	10/85	4/28/86	10/08/86	3/08/90	5/09/96
Gloria Estefan	Let It Loose	Album	6/1/87	8/11/87	5/09/88	8/05/88	12/04/91
Gloria Estefan	Turn the Beat Around	Single	10/18/94	1/19/95			
Gloria Estefan	Conga	Single	10/85	9/11/89			

Shakira

The Gold® and Platinum® Awards are certified by the Recording Industry Association of America® through an extensive process of auditing sales information for each album or single.

[1] Sold 500,000 units.

[2] Sold 1,000,000 units.

[3] Sold 2,000,000 units.

[4] Sold 3,000,000 units.

* At the time this piece was written, Shakira's "Hips Don't Lie" had not yet been certified for Gold, but she had set a record for the one-week digital download record. Her fans downloaded the song 266,500 times during the first week of June. The previous record had been held by D4L when it sold 175,500 copies of its song "Laffy Taffy" through digital download.

32. Gloria Estefan's *Primitive Love* and Shakira's *Oral Fixation Vol. 2* are their first "crossover" albums in which they sing primarily in English. The Gold and Platinum Awards are given for American sales. Which singer had quicker success in America? Use data and information from the table to support your answer.

> **ANALYZE EVALUATE EXPLAIN**
>
> Student answers should include the following information:
>
> **Shakira's album reached success more quickly. It took her album only three months to reach gold and five months to reach platinum. It took Gloria Estefan's album six months to reach gold and twelve months to reach platinum.**
>
> Use the extended-response rubric in the Appendix to reference the criteria and determine the number of points to award.

33. Shakira and Rihanna are considered two of today's hottest young music stars. Based on the data you have seen in this unit, decide which singer could be considered the most successful so far. Use information from both tables to support your answer.

> **ANALYZE EVALUATE EXPLAIN**
>
> Student answers should include the following information:
>
> **Shakira could be considered the most successful singer because she has had an album reach platinum (sell over 1,000,000 units) while Rihanna has not. Shakira's album also reached gold nearly a month and a half more quickly than Rihanna's album. Rihanna has had two hits in the top 40 in the summer of 2006, but Shakira's album has enjoyed more success overall.**
>
> Use the extended-response rubric in the Appendix to reference the criteria and determine the number of points to award.

34. Analyze the data given in this unit. Create a list that ranks the three artists on the table from most successful to least successful. Explain how you determined your ranking. Use data and information from the table to support your answer.

ANALYZE SYNTHESIZE EXPLAIN

Student answers should include the following information:

1. **Gloria Estefan**
2. **Shakira**
3. **Rihanna**

If one went strictly with the data on the table, Gloria Estefan would win the number-one spot because she has had more albums and singles go multi-platinum (sell over 3,000,000 units). Shakira would come in second because she has hit platinum with an album while Rihanna has not. Rihanna has gone multi-platinum with one of her singles, but Shakira has also set a record for the number of downloads with her single "Hips Don't Lie."

Use the extended-response rubric in the Appendix to reference the criteria and determine the number of points to award.

*Quick*thought

The world belongs to you and everyone in it. No matter who you become, you still have the duty to share your talents with others in order to make the world a better place.

Look Inside and Grow

35. According to her publicist, Shakira's name is Arabic for "woman full of grace." Other sources translate the name to mean "thankful" or "grateful." Either way, the name is appropriate for this pop star who has chosen to use her celebrity status to help the children of Colombia through her Fundacion Pies Descalzos (Barefeet Foundation). If you were given a foreign name, what English word(s) would you like it to represent? Would it be *proud*? Would it be *forgetful*? Would it be *lazy*? Choose a word that best represents you and give examples to prove it.

Student answers may vary.

The student should address each section of the question to the best of his/her ability. The question is meant to elicit strong classroom conversation about character education related issues. Students should be able to demonstrate that they have learned a lesson through the inspirational model Shakira provides by trying to cross over cultures with her music. They may have also learned something from the way Shakira uses her success to help society.

Use the character-education rubric in the Appendix to reference the criteria and determine the number of points to award.

Notes

I can think…: Fuchs, Cynthia. "Shakira." PopMatters Film& TV. http://www.popmatters.com/music/videos/s/shakira-underneath.shtml.

Some stories say…: "Shakira." Wikipedia, May 7, 2006. http://en.wikipedia.org/wiki/Shakira.

Others say she…: Wright, Evan. "Shakira." RollingStone.com, April 11, 2002. http://www.rollingstone.com/artists/shakira/articles/story/5937750/shakira.

I'm slow and…: Gurza, Agustin. "Shakira's Bilingual Approach."ShakiraMedia.com, November 26, 2005. http://www.shakiramedia.com/?page=articles&art_id=807.

If I want…: Wright.

I'm just a …: Gurza.

Spring and Summer 2006 (chart) …: Top40-charts.com. http://top40-charts.com/chart.php?cid=27.

Awards Certification Status (chart) …: Recording Industry Association of America, 2003.
http://www.riaa.com/gp/database/search_results.asp.

At the time …: Hasty, Katie. "Digital Explosion Drives Shakira's 'Hips' To No. 1." Billboard.com, June 8, 2006. http://billboard.com/bbcom/news/article_display.jsp?vnu_content_id=1002650537.

According to her …:
http://www.babynamewizard.com/sampleentries.html,
http://www.babynameworld.com/s-girl.asp,
http://www.absolutely.net/shakira/bio.htm.

Technical Extension

Immigration in the United States

Throughout its history, America has served as the destination point for a steady flow of immigrants. The first European immigrants came from England and northern European countries. Their numbers declined

number of people already living in each country. In 1965 this changed to eliminate quotas based on nationality. The government then gave preference to relatives of citizens and workers with specific skills. In 1978 the

during the Revolutionary War in the 1770s, but immigration later picked up again strongly during the 1840s and 1850s. The United States government set up a special port of entry on Ellis Island, which is today a part of the Statue of Liberty National Monument. A gift from the people of France in 1866, the Statue of Liberty became a symbol of political freedom and democracy. For reasons varying from political and religious freedom to rumors of economic opportunity, immigrants poured into the "New World." Between 1820 and 1979, the United States received more than 49 million immigrants.

In 1924 the United States government set limits on how many people each country could send, based on the

United States government set a single annual world quota of 290,000, and this ceiling was raised again in 1990 to 700,000. Certain categories of people were exempted from the limit in an attempt to draw skilled workers and professionals. The United States accepts more immigrants than any other country.

The U.S. Immigration and Naturalization Service estimates that approximately 5 million people are living in the United States illegally, a number which continues to grow. Some Americans think that illegal immigrants take jobs from citizens, especially young people and minority groups. Illegal immigrants also create a burden on taxpayers, especially in the field of social services. An

immigration debate has existed since government began to regulate the admittance of foreigners to the United States. Immigration laws change almost annually. The basic requirements for immigration can be confusing and complex. The immigration process involves multiple steps and includes the following:

• A person must determine that he or she is eligible for U.S. immigration.

• The U.S. Citizenship and Immigration Services (USCIS) must approve an immigrant visa petition.

• If the person is seeking to become a lawful permanent resident based on employment, his or her U.S. employer will submit a labor certification request with the Department of Labor's Employment and Training Administration.

• An immigrant visa number, through the State Department, must be immediately available.

• The person may apply to adjust to permanent resident status after a visa number becomes available, or applicants outside the United States must then go to their local U.S. consulate to complete processing.

Following is an overview of the terms commonly used in the immigration process. Becoming familiar with the terminology will allow you to more thoroughly understand the process.

Visa

A visa allows a non-citizen to travel in the United States. There are two types of visas: immigrant and non-immigrant. Immigrant visas are for people who intend to permanently live in the United States. There are over 60 types of non-immigrant U.S. visas for people with permanent residence outside the United States. These include visas for students, workers, family members, those needing medical treatment, and even visas for extended vacations. Visas are generally for limited time periods ranging from months to years.

Green Card

A permanent resident card, or Green Card, refers to the official card issued by the U.S. government to lawful permanent residents as evidence of their authorization to live and work in the United States.

Citizenship

Immigrants who decide to make their permanent home in the United States often choose to become citizens. This allows them to fully participate in U.S. democracy by voting and guarantees them that they will be allowed to reside in the United States forever. There are certain eligibility requirements to become a citizen:

• Residing in the United States for five continuous years after becoming a resident

• Spending at least half of the permanent residency time in the United States

• Living for at least three months in the place where the application is filed

• Having good moral character and attachment to the principles of the U.S. Constitution

• Possessing basic English skills and knowledge of U.S. history and government

Naturalization

Naturalization means that a person has obtained U.S. citizenship by a legal process of obtaining a new nationality.

Reading Comprehension

After reading "Immigration in the United States," choose the options that best answer questions 1-14.

1. Read this sentence.
   The government then gave preference to relatives of citizens and workers with specific skills.

   What is the meaning of the word *preference* as it is used in this sentence?
   A. value
   B. priority
   C. eligible
   D. overlooks

2. Read this sentence.
   Throughout its history, America has served as the destination point for a steady flow of immigrants.

   What does the author mean by this sentence?
   F. Immigrants point to America to relieve economic disparity.
   G. Immigrants have continuously moved to America through the years.
   H. History has shown that America has a complex immigration process.
   I. Most immigrants transitioned to other countries after visiting America.

3. According to the article, what is one reason immigrants come to the United States?
   A. political freedom
   B. economic disparity
   C. promote education
   D. religious persecution

4. What change took place in immigration in the late 1970s to early 1990s?
   F. the annual quota was revoked
   G. the annual quota was reduced
   H. the annual quota was increased
   I. an increase in the number of immigrant rights'

5. With which statement would the author of the passage most likely agree?
   A. Immigration will continue to decrease in America.
   B. The immigration requirements are difficult and confusing.
   C. There are not enough laws governing immigration in America.
   D. Most illegal immigrants come from northern European countries.

6. The author organizes the article by
   F. describing immigration and its process.
   G. listing the reasons immigration is successful.
   H. comparing earlier immigration to later immigration.
   I. placing events in the order in which they occur to show why immigration has failed.

7. Why does the author include terminology in the article?
   A. to explain to the reader unfamiliar terms
   B. to emphasize the importance of the immigration process
   C. to encourage the reader to further research the immigration process
   D. to prove that defining words increases your knowledge about the immigration process

8. What is the main idea of the first paragraph?
   F. United States set up Ellis Island as the official entry site.
   G. Immigration is a five-step process.
   H. United States had an influx of immigrants between 1820 and 1979.
   I. United States has housed immigrants since before the Revolutionary War.

9. What is significant about a student visa?
   A. The student visa allows the student to receive a Green Card.
   B. It allows the student to permanently reside in the United States.
   C. The student visa allows the student temporary residence in the United States.
   D. The student visa allows the student to participate in U.S. democracy by voting.

10. Why was the immigration law changed in 1965?
    F. The law was unconstitutional.
    G. The new law allowed more student visas.
    H. The law changed to eliminate quotas based on nationality.
    I. The law changed to set limits on the number of non-immigrant visas.

11. The major difference between an immigrant visa and a non-immigrant visa is
    A. nationality.
    B. length of stay.
    C. place of employment.
    D. where the application was filed.

12. Which statement about immigration in the United States is LEAST accurate?
    F. Citizenship is a lengthy process.
    G. A person becomes an immigrant upon application.
    H. The United States leads other countries in the number of immigrants.
    I. There are more illegal immigrants than legal immigrants in the United States.

13. Which statement is correct, according to the article?
    A. An illegal immigrant is a person who has a Green Card.
    B. A person who is applying for citizenship must meet eligibility requirements.
    C. A visa refers to the official card issued by the U.S. government to lawful permanent residents.
    D. Most immigrants that come to America become a citizen of the United States without getting a visa.

14. Based on the article, which statement is most accurate?
    F. Immigration is a multi-step process that is often difficult to understand.
    G. Immigration gives power to non-U.S. citizens to participate in our democracy.
    H. Understanding that immigration laws change annually will help immigrants gain citizenship.
    I. Knowing immigration is a complex process will guarantee an immigrant entry into the United States.

Vocational Extension

Job Description

Jackson County School District is looking for several teachers certified in ESL (English as a Second Language) to work as Elementary School ESL program directors. Teachers will be responsible for all ESL students in their assigned schools. Valid teaching certificate and course work in ESL are required. Spanish language skills are a plus. To request an interview, send an e-mail with resume and cover letter to Judy Bonners at bonnersj@jackson.fl.us.

One of the most important jobs in the world is that of a teacher. There's a cliché saying that "teachers shape the future." That saying is true. If it weren't for teachers, children would never learn what they need to know to become future physicists, business people, doctors, lawyers, and, yes, future teachers.

When you picture a teacher, chances are you picture your third-grade teacher drilling your class in multiplication tables, or your middle school history teacher lecturing about the Civil War. These are two good examples of the kinds of jobs teachers have, but there are many more types of teaching jobs you may not think of. In teaching, there is an infinite number of fields a teacher can choose from. Elementary school teachers get the opportunity to teach a variety of subjects, while secondary teachers usually specialize in one or two areas.

A great deal of attention has been given lately to the extremely specialized areas of teaching. These areas include exceptional education, reading remediation, and English as a Second Language (ESL). Teachers who specialize in areas such as these generally have very specialized training. Many have taken post-graduate (after college) classes to learn about their specialties.

Becoming a teacher always requires a person to attend college. In college, he or she earns a bachelor's degree. Most four-year colleges have a school of education to prepare students to become teachers. A person studying to become a teacher studies a wide variety of subjects. He or she will take many classes about teaching, as well as classes in a particular content area. A content area is the specific subject a teacher will teach, such as mathematics or communications. If the teacher wishes to have a specialty, he or she takes additional classes dealing with that area. An example is a teacher who will become an ESL Specialist. Many teachers go on to continue their education in graduate school, earning a master's degree in Education. Some even complete a PhD program to earn a doctorate degree. These teachers are now eligible to teach in a college.

Many young people never consider the possibility of becoming a teacher because it isn't one of the most glamorous jobs. Teaching involves a lot of dedication, hard work, and flexibility, without much public acknowledgement of a job well done. Teaching isn't easy. However, teaching is perhaps one of the most rewarding careers. For those who want to make a difference in the future, teaching is an option with limitless possibilities.

Looking Forward

15. What is your favorite school subject? What part of learning excites you? Imagine that you are preparing to become a teacher. Write about what you would choose as your specialty, what you think you would teach, and what you would need to learn in school to effectively teach that subject. Use the job description and article as well as your experience to complete your answer.

Student answers may vary.

The student should address the question to the best of his/her ability using the article and personal experience. The question is meant to encourage students to explore areas of interest for their future and begin to determine how they will prepare for a future career.

Use the extended-response rubric in the Appendix to reference the criteria and determine the number of points to award.

Ethical Dilemma

16. You're an English as a Second Language teacher in a middle school. You have a particularly bright 7th-grade student who has recently moved to your school from the Dominican Republic. In her old school, she was working several grade levels above 7th grade, but she has limited English skills. Because of this, she does poorly on the end-of-the-year assessments. Several teachers on her team want to hold her back a grade because of the language issue. Her parents are afraid this will not challenge her educationally and will hurt her socially. Either way, something will suffer. What do you recommend?

Ethical Dilemma

Student answers may vary.

The student should address each section of the question to the best of his or her ability. The question is meant to elicit strong classroom conversation about character education related issues.

Use the character-education rubric in the Appendix to reference the criteria and determine the number of points to award.

Reading Instructional Guide

BEFORE READING

Front-Loading Background Knowledge Through Read-Aloud-Think-Aloud

Search the internet for recent articles on football celebrations and use them to model the effective habits of readers through a Read-Aloud-Think-Aloud.

Check out articles at the following websites to determine if they would be appropriate for your RATA:

* http://www.nfl.com/news/story/7204087
* http://www.msnbc.msn.com/id/10309548/

(Please keep in mind that it is the responsibility of the teacher to determine if articles from suggested sites are appropriate. The sites may have changed content since this publication. The publisher takes no responsibility for the current content of the site.)

Looking at the Words

Determining How the Word Sounds (Phonics)

With your students, use one of the sets of steps from the Syllable Guide in the beginning of the book to determine how to break a word into manageable parts. The goal is to break the words into syllables that the students can say. Then they can put those parts together to "sound the word out." However, remember that the rules for syllabification do not always work because our language is so diverse. The rules can also become rather complex for low readers, so keep in mind that their overall objective is just to figure out how the word sounds. They may not be able to break the word into its syllables perfectly, but they should at least be able to figure out how to say the word based on their attempt at following one of these sets of steps. Lesson One is a more basic set, while Lesson Two attempts to give the students the more specific rules without becoming too complicated. Take your time when teaching either set, and understand that many of the lower readers are not going to understand right away. It will take time, practice, and repeated application before many of them are able to make use of these strategies on their own.

Determining What the Words Mean (Vocabulary)

After students have spent time breaking the words apart to figure out how they sound, use the lists of prefixes and suffixes and their meanings from the Syllable Guide to have students try to add whatever meaning they can to the words before actually looking at their definitions. After giving the students the definitions, have them see if they can figure out which words truly apply the meaning of any of the prefixes or suffixes.

Words to Study	Breaking into Syllables	Short Definition
Enthusiasm	en-thu-si-asm	(n.) great interest or excitement
Excessive	ex-ces-sive	(adj.) beyond proper limits
Feigned	feigned	(v.) to pretend
Equivalent	e-quiv-a-lent	(adj.) equal in value
Appreciation	ap-pre-ci-a-tion	(n.) grateful recognition
Humility	hu-mil-i-ty	(n.) the state of being modest
Obscene	ob-scene	(adj.) offensive

Activating Background Knowledge

Anticipation Guide
Mark each of the following statements True or False:

1. _____ The NFL fines players for excessive celebration.

2. _____ Deante Culpepper was fined $10,000 for an obscene gesture.

3. _____ Chad Johnson leads in NFL fines for excessive celebration.

4. _____ When Larry Fitzgerald was a kid, his father did not allow him to celebrate in the end zone

5. _____ NFL owners disagree with the league about enforcing celebration fines.

Starter Questions
After completing the Anticipation Guide, have a group or class discussion with the students using the following questions:

1. What sport do you enjoy playing?

2. What sports teams do you enjoy watching?

3. What gestures do you make when you score, make a great play, or win a game?

4. Who are your favorite NFL players?

5. Who is Chad Johnson?

Make a prediction about what you think the article will be about.

DURING READING

- Have the students skim the article. Give them about 45-60 seconds to do this.

- As they skim the article, tell them to circle any words they don't know how to say.

- When they are finished, talk about how to chunk the words they don't know how to say by sounds they now know and then sound them out.

- Have the students skim the questions. Give them only about 30-45 seconds to do this.

- Ask the students to predict what the article is about.

- Have the students read the article. They should question, summarize, clarify, and predict as they read. Instruct them to jot their questions, summarizations, clarifications, and predictions in the margins as they read.

- Remind students to constantly ask themselves if they know what the article is about right now. If they don't, they must reread to clarify. This is called monitoring for understanding.

- After they have finished reading the article, they are ready to answer the questions.

The Strategy Sheet

You may choose to have students complete the strategy sheet for each section before they answer the multiple-choice questions. Or you could have them complete the questions, work on the strategy sheet with a partner, and then go back over the questions to see if the use of the strategy sheet helped them more easily find the answers to any of the questions.

AFTER READING

Discussion Starter Questions

1. Should players be fined for celebrating with their teammates? Why? Why not?

2. Should there be standard, accepted celebration gestures throughout sports? What about standard fines?

3. Should coaches make players sit out of games for excessive celebrations? Why? Why not? Is that fair?

4. Should team owners punish players for their behavior by taking away part of their salaries? Why? Why not?

5. In what ways can we demonstrate humility in our lives?

Teacher Reflection

When you are finished with the article, strategies, and questions, ask yourself the following:

1. Did I get the students to THINK about what they have read?

2. Did I teach them (even a little bit) about how to read more effectively?

If you answered "Yes" to both questions, you can feel good about the day.

HARD TO BE HUMBLE

A student studies all week for a test. A day later, the teacher returns his test with a big, fat, red A at the top. He jumps up, spins around, does a somersault, and high-fives all of his fellow classmates in Algebra II. The school newspaper staff sits in the corner of the room, waiting for his next zany move. The other students sit with Cs and Ds on the tops of their papers, wondering if this stellar student will ever become a little more humble.

Over the past few years, some football players have also become quite creative in their celebrations. They'll dance, spin, and shuffle when they score a touchdown or make a tough tackle or difficult catch. Chad Johnson of the Cincinnati Bengals and Terrell Owens of the Dallas Cowboys have become two of the National Football League's top entertainers. Johnson has been known to do a "Riverdance" and pretend to ask a cheerleader to marry him after scoring. Lately it seems cameramen chase players around more to see what they are going to do after they score than to actually watch them make the touchdown.

The NFL makes no apologies about the fact that it is all about entertainment. The more flash the better. It is a business that relies on excitement. Excitement puts fans in the seats. Fans in the seats equal dollars—millions of them. If a defensive player pulls a quarterback down from behind, making him drop the ball, fans expect to see a celebration. If the players walked off the field with no enthusiasm, it would take away from the moment. Owners want electricity.

On the other hand, the league wants the public to know that it frowns on excessive individual celebrations. The NFL fines players if it thinks the

showboating goes too far. The first fine can be up to $5,000. Some players don't seem to care about the fines. Some news reports claim one wide receiver had even set aside $100,000 at the beginning of the year to pay fines during the season.

When Joe Horn of the New Orleans Saints was fined recently, he said he had expected the league to fine him $10,000 to $15,000. He claimed it was worth it. Before the game, he had placed a cell phone in the padding on the goal post. When he scored a touchdown, he pulled the cell phone out and pretended to make a call on it.

Randy Moss, of the Minnesota Vikings at the time, was fined $10,000 two seasons ago for making an obscene gesture toward the Green Bay Packers fans during his touchdown celebration. He seemed to miss the point of the fine when he later asked the media, "What's 10 grand to me?" His agent explained that Moss had committed the act in response to the way the Green Bay fans acted toward his team's bus in the parking lot. He did not think the fine was fair in that case.

Players who engage in the excessive celebrations claim they are just expressing themselves. They think they should be able to do so with personal style and flair. They think they have the right to act as creatively as they wish while playing a game that is as difficult and dangerous as football is. They say they aren't doing it to offend anyone, but just to add more fun to the game. They are concerned that others want to take away their freedom of being individuals. However, those who don't agree with them say that is just the point. Football is not meant to be a game of individuals, but a team sport. They say when players are allowed to express themselves in such a creative way, they are ruining the game.

Some players, like Larry Fitzgerald of the Arizona Cardinals, simply hand the ball to the referee after they score and go to the sideline to celebrate with their teammates. Fitzgerald said his father was opposed to the dances when he was young, so it "broke him right there."

Chad Johnson says it is all part of his culture. He grew up in the Liberty City section of Miami. In a quote from *USA Today*, he says that a baby's first words from that area are not "Mommy" or "Daddy," but some type of trash talk. He says one needs to learn to act the way he does in order to survive. He points to all of the NFL players that come from Miami as proof. It is a competitive city, and people learn to play sports with passion in order to survive. So, acting this way is not something he can just turn off. It is part of him. And he enjoys it. Most of all, he seems to love it when his fans respond to his antics. And they do. His fans argue

that if he is not directly insulting someone, his actions shouldn't be a big deal. They say even though some people find him annoying, he has always been positive in his approach. No one, they claim, wants to win more than Johnson. And that is where he is showing how much of a team player he is, no matter how much it looks like he is putting on his own personal show.

When it comes right down to it though, no one likes to be shown up. And this is the biggest complaint players and coaches have about these celebrations. The NFL owners recently voted 29-3 to penalize a team 15 yards on the ensuing kickoff for excessive celebrations. They will still allow players to spike the ball, dunk it over the goal post, jump into the waiting arms of fans, or do a simple dance or spin. However, the days of allowing a feigned proposal of marriage to a cheerleader or cradling the football like a baby and then wiping its "bottom" are over. Chad Johnson claims this won't stop him though. He says that he will just have to be more creative now. He told a Cincinnati reporter after the rule was handed down that he will have to form a committee with Terrell Owens and Keyshawn Johnson, another player known for his lack of humility, to come up with better ways to celebrate.

The league will continue to fine Johnson and others if they keep up their showiness. Of course, those large fines would hurt the average citizen. But they don't mean much to these guys. If a man is making $5 million a year, a $5,000 fine doesn't amount to much. That fine would be the equivalent of $50 to a person making $50,000 a year. The fines also go to charities. So, if Johnson is fined $10,000, it isn't like the money is just being thrown away. Someone eventually benefits from it. It just won't be Johnson.

Or maybe he does benefit. He's being given the attention he wants. It is just at a cost. Unfortunately, he can't just accept the fact that he is already one of the best players in the league. His pure talent would get him all the attention he needs without his rubbing it in the face of the opposing team.

The point of the fines and penalties is that the league has to maintain a balance between entertainment and sportsmanship. They are trying to make the statement to the next Chad Johnson, some 13-year-old boy watching from his couch at home, that football is a team sport, and displaying humility is the best way to show appreciation for your fellow teammates and the role they play in the total team victory.

Reading Comprehension

After reading "Hard to be Humble," choose the options that best answer questions 1-14.

1. Read this sentence.
    The NFL owners recently voted 29-3 to penalize a team 15 yards on the ensuing kickoff for excessive celebrations.

    What is the meaning of the word *ensuing* as it is used in this sentence?
    A. proactive
    B. following
    C. offending
    D. preceding

2. Read this sentence.
    Owners want electricity.

    What is the meaning of this sentence?
    F. Owners of football teams are afraid of power outages.
    G. Owners of football teams are worried about showboating.
    H. Owners of football teams profit when players celebrate emotionally.
    I. Owners of football teams have to pay large amounts for their electric bills.

3. According to the article, owners want to penalize end-zone celebrations because
    A. they want to teach players humility.
    B. they find players who celebrate annoying.
    C. they want to emphasize that football is a team sport.
    D. they want players to concentrate on developing their skills.

4. What is one reason that the owners of football teams may want players to have fun when they are celebrating?
    F. It adds excitement to the game.
    G. It makes the other team feel worse.
    H. It encourages the other players to perform just as well.
    I. It can make the other team feel like they have been shown up.

5. With which statement would the author of the passage most likely agree?
    A. Players that show off don't see football as a team sport.
    B. The players being charged fines feel like their money is going to waste.
    C. NFL players should keep showboating as long as the money continues to be given to a charity.
    D. NFL players should form a committee to figure out a way around the new excessive celebrations rule.

6. The author organizes the article by
    F. providing a chronological list of the evolution of celebration rules.
    G. giving examples of the ways players celebrate while discussing the purposes of rules and penalties.
    H. comparing the careers of those players who focus on the game with those who focus on entertaining.
    I. listing the accomplishments of Terrell Owens, Chad Johnson, and Randy Moss and how entertaining fans has helped their careers.

7. What is the purpose of the information about fines?
   A. to compare them to fines in other sports
   B. to prove that fines are not always enforced
   C. to show that fines aren't a large percentage of a player's salary and therefore aren't effective
   D. to emphasize how important it is to fine players in order to stop them from celebrating excessively

8. Which statement BEST expresses the main idea of this article?
   F. Football players cannot be expected to be humble when they are constantly made celebrities.
   G. Celebrating is part of the entertainment of football, but in excess it takes away from the game.
   H. Football players should not be allowed to show any type of individual celebration during a game.
   I. NFL players have always found ways to celebrate, so it is not worth trying to stop them in the future.

9. Why does Chad Johnson feel justified in celebrating the way he does?
   A. He doesn't realize he is annoying other players.
   B. He thinks the NFL expects him to act this way to entertain the fans.
   C. Other players on the field make it necessary for him to act this way.
   D. Growing up in a competitive city has made his behavior a part of him he can't change.

10. Why did the NFL need to vote to penalize players' teams if they want them to stop excessive celebrations?
    F. Players don't want to be shown up.
    G. Fines don't affect the players too much.
    H. Players need a way to express themselves.
    I. A player's talent can get him enough attention without rubbing it in a team's face.

11. The major difference between Larry Fitzgerald's and Chad Johnson's feelings about celebrating is that
    A. Fitzgerald doesn't want a fine, and Johnson doesn't care about being fined.
    B. Fitzgerald cares more about his team, and Johnson cares only about himself.
    C. Fitzgerald was raised with the idea that showboating was wrong, and Johnson was raised with the idea that it's the only way to get attention.
    D. Fitzgerald is shy and doesn't like having attention drawn to him, while Johnson is outgoing and tries to get as many people as possible to notice him.

12. Which statement provides the best evidence that Chad Johnson is not willing to change?
    F. He doesn't like to be shown up by other players.
    G. He says he needed to act this way to survive where he came from.
    H. He is not directly insulting anyone, and he is positive in his approach.
    I. He jokingly told reporters he would form a committee to come up with better ways to celebrate.

13. What point was Randy Moss trying to make when he said, "What's ten grand to me?"
    A. It was okay to do what he did.
    B. He makes so much money that a $10,000 fine isn't that much money to him.
    C. $10,000 is a lot of money to him and he wonders if what he did was worth it.
    D. A $10,000 fine was better than being penalized during the play for his actions.

14. Based on the article, which of these conclusions is LEAST accurate?
    F. The NFL is trying to discourage any type of celebration.
    G. Players will try to find new ways around the newly strict rules.
    H. The point of having rules about celebrations is to balance entertainment and good sportsmanship.
    I. NFL players who continue to celebrate excessively despite penalties are getting the attention they want.

Reading Strategy

WHAT'S THE ISSUE?

Students should write something to the effect that the commissioner of professional football along with the team owners must determine a way to deal with the touchdown dances and excessive celebrations that bring a lot of personal attention to individual players in a sport that relies on players working together as a team.

FOR

AGAINST

FACE-OFF

Students could include the following types of arguments for allowing the celebrations to continue as they have in the past:

- **Professional football is about entertainment.**

- **Football relies on excitement to draw fans. The fans put big money in the pockets of the owners and the players.**

- **Owners want electricity and excitement.**

- **Players are just being creative and expressing themselves.**

- **Players are just trying to add more fun to the game.**

- **Players aren't trying to directly insult other individual players.**

Students could include the following types of arguments against allowing the celebrations to continue as they have in the past:

- **Professional football is about entertainment.**

- **Football relies on excitement to draw fans. The fans put big money in the pockets of the owners and the players.**

- **Owners want electricity and excitement.**

Players are just being creative and expressing themselves.

- **Players are just trying to add more fun to the game.**

- **Players aren't trying to directly insult other individual players.**

WHAT'S THE ISSUE? Some articles show the reader both sides of an issue. To complete the following strategy activity you must summarize and infer to compare and contrast two sides of an issue.

Follow these steps to complete the strategy activity:

🏈 Use facts and details to determine what the issue is in this article.

🏈 Write the issue in the football between the goalposts.

🏈 Then consider the issue and decide what arguments the author makes *for* and *against* it. Write the arguments in the appropriate columns above.

🏈 After you are finished, write no more than 30 words to summarize the article on another sheet of paper. Use the information you have written on this sheet to help you.

HARD TO BE HUMBLE

Interpreting the Data

PART I

Look at the following table to help answer questions in Part I.

Eight of the Most Famous End-Zone Celebrations	
Machine-Gun Celebration 10/19/03	After scoring a touchdown while beating Atlanta 45-17, Joe Horn was fined $30,000 when he pretended to "machine-gun" his teammates who "fell down dead."
Cell-Phone Celebration 12/14/03	During a 45-7 win over the Giants, Joe Horn pulled a pre-planted cell phone out of the goal post padding and pretended to make a phone call while still on the field.
Twirl-Into-End-Zone Celebration 11/19/01	While playing the NY Giants, Randy Moss caught a pass and was running toward the end zone with no opposing players near him. He slowed down three yards before scoring the touchdown and did a twirl while falling into the end zone. He was fined $10,000. His team won the game 28-16.
Directing-His-Backside-at-the-Opposing-Fans Celebration 1/09/05	While beating the Green Bay Packers in their stadium, Randy Moss scored a touchdown, turned his backside to the crowd, and pretended to pull down his pants. After he was fined $10,000, he was quoted as asking, "What's ten grand to me?"
"Please Don't Fine Me" Celebration 12/14/03	In a 41-38 victory over San Francisco, Chad Johnson scored a touchdown and then held up a sign that read, "NFL, please don't fine me again." He was subsequently fined for the sign.
Riverdance Celebration 9/25/05	In a game in which Chad Johnson's Bengals beat the Chicago Bears 24-7, Johnson scored an 18-yard touchdown and proceeded to do a "Riverdance" celebration in the end zone. He was fined for the dance.
Sharpie-Marker Celebration 10/14/02	Terrell Owens pulled a Sharpie marker from his sock and signed a ball after scoring a touchdown against Seattle. He was not fined for the move, but it caused NFL officials to begin looking at making a stricter policy for end-zone celebrations.
Mocking-Ray Lewis Celebration 10/31/04	In a game with the Baltimore Ravens, Terrell Owens scored a touchdown and then openly mocked a linebacker on the opposing team, Ray Lewis, by performing Lewis's trademark celebration dance.

15. Some fans and NFL officials are concerned that players have gotten carried away with end-zone celebrations over the past few years. Based on the information in the article and the table in this section, are those fans and officials right? Use details to support your answer.

READ COMPREHEND EXPLAIN

Student answers may vary but should include information such as the following:

The end-zone celebrations seem to be getting more extravagant. In 2001 Randy Moss was fined for twirling into the end zone. In 2005 his celebrating progressed to directing an obscene gesture at the Packers fans. Also, two of the three most recent celebrations seem to be more personal, directed at players or fans rather than just being "celebrations."

Use the short-response rubric in the Appendix to reference the criteria and determine the number of points to award.

Use the following table to help answer the remaining questions in this section.

Famous End-Zone Celebrations and the Players' Statistics the Game After		Catches	Total Yards Gained	Touch-downs Scored	Win/ Loss
Joe Horn	10/19/03: Machine-Gun Celebration	8	133	1	W
	Game after: 10/26/03	6	74	2	L
	12/14/03: Cell-Phone Celebration	9	133	4	W
	Game after: 12/21/03	2	39	0	L
Randy Moss	11/19/01: Twirl-Into-End-Zone Celebration	10	171	3	W
	Game after: 11/25/01	4	25	0	L
	1/09/05: Directing-His-Backside-at-the-Opposing-Fans Celebration	4	70	2	W
	Game after: 1/16/05	3	51	0	L
Chad Johnson	12/14/03: "Please-Don't-Fine-Me Celebration	6	91	1	W
	Game after: 12/21/03	7	115	0	L
	9/25/05: Riverdance Celebration	3	77	2	W
	Game after: 10/02/05	7	67	0	W *
Terrell Owens	10/14/02: Sharpie-Marker Celebration	6	84	2	W
	Game after: 10/20/02	4	61	1	L
	10/31/04: Mocking-Ray Lewis Celebration	8	101	1	W
	Game after: 11/07/04	7	53	0	L

*Against Houston (a team that won two games and lost fourteen during that season)

HARD TO BE HUMBLE

16. Use the table on the preceding page to determine which player performed the worst in the game after his end-zone celebration. Use statistics to support your claim that he had the worst game.

**COMPREHEND
EVALUATE
EXPLAIN**

Student answers may vary, but they should demonstrate an ability to use data and details to make inferences. They should also support their claims with data and details from the tables. Their answers could include the following information:

Joe Horn played the worst game after his end-zone performance. Randy Moss came in a close second. During the game of Horn's cell-phone celebration, he had nine catches, but he dropped to only two catches in the following game. In his celebration game, he scored four touchdowns with 133 yards, but he dropped to zero touchdowns and 39 yards in the next game.

Use the short-response rubric in the Appendix to reference the criteria and determine the number of points to award.

Determine how well the players did on average during the games in which they performed their end-zone celebrations. Fill in the data from the preceding table and do the math to compute the totals and averages.

Performed Their End-Zone Celebrations		Catches	Total Yards Gained	Touch-downs Scored	Win/ Loss
Joe Horn	10/19/03: Machine-Gun Celebration	8	133	1	W
	12/14/03: Cell-Phone Celebration	9	133	4	W
Randy Moss	11/19/01: Twirl-Into-End-Zone Celebration	10	171	3	W
	1/09/05: Directing-His-Backside-at-the-Opposing-Fans Celebration	4	70	2	W
Chad Johnson	12/14/03: Please-Don't-Fine-Me Celebration	6	91	1	W
	9/25/05: Riverdance Celebration	3	77	2	W
Terrell Owens	10/14/02: Sharpie-Marker Celebration	6	84	2	W
	10/31/04: Mocking-Ray Lewis Celebration	8	101	1	W
	Totals	**17.** **54**	**19.** **860**	**21.** **16**	# Wins **23. 8**
	Averages	**18.** **6.75/game**	**20.** **107.5/game**	**22.** **2/game**	**24.** **8/8**

Now determine how well the players performed on average during the game after their end-zone celebration games. Fill in the data from the table on the preceding pages and do the math to compute the totals and averages.

		Catches	Total Yards Gained	Touch-downs Scored	Win/ Loss
Statistics of Players For the Games After the Game in Which They Performed Their End-Zone Celebrations					
Joe Horn	Game after: 10/26/03	6	74	2	L
Joe Horn	Game after: 12/21/03	2	39	0	L
Randy Moss	Game after: 11/25/01	4	25	0	L
Randy Moss	Game after: 1/16/05	3	51	0	L
Chad Johnson	Game after: 12/21/03	7	115	0	L
Chad Johnson	Game after: 10/02/05	7	67	0	L
Terrell Owens	Game after: 10/20/02	4	61	1	W
Terrell Owens	Game after: 11/07/04	7	53	0	L
Totals		25. **40**	27. **485**	29. **3**	**# Wins** 31. **1**
Averages		26. **5/game**	28. **60.6/game**	30. **.38/game**	32. **1/8**

33. Use the information in the two tables you have created to determine how many yards the players gained as a group per catch. Determine their combined yards per catch (a) for the games in which they performed their end-zone dances and (b) for the games after they performed their end-zone dances. Round your answer to the nearest whole number. Use the box below to show how you determined your answers.

KNOW COMPREHEND APPLY

860 total yards gained / 54 catches = 15.9 yards gained per catch

(a) Combined yards/catch during the game they performed their end-zone dances: <u>16</u>

485 total yards gained/ 40 catches = 12.1 yards gained per catch

(b) Combined yards/catch after the game they performed their end-zone dances: <u>12</u>

Use the short-response rubric in the Appendix to reference the criteria and determine the number of points to award.

34. Use the data in the preceding tables you have created to tell whether showing off pays off for the player and his team. Use data and statistics from the table to support your answer.

COMPREHEND ANALYZE EVALUATE

Student answers may vary, but they should demonstrate an ability to use data and details to make inferences. They should also support their claims with data and details from the tables. Their answers could include the following information:

Players have played worse overall in the games after they performed their famous end-zone celebrations. Overall, they averaged two touchdowns per game during their end-zone performance games, while scoring an average of .4 touchdowns per game the week after. Their yardage per catch also went down by four yards. Most importantly, the teams the players played on all lost their games the following week with the exception of the Bengals, who beat Houston (although, that is a game they should have won anyway due to Houston's 2-14 record). So, overall, the showing off did not pay off.

Use the extended-response rubric in the Appendix to reference the criteria and determine the number of points to award.

PART II

Fill in the missing data in the table below to determine the combined averages of the four players from this section. Round your answers to the nearest two decimal points (.00).

Players' Career Statistics				
	Games	Catches	Yards Gained	Touchdowns
Joe Horn	142	539	7822	53
Randy Moss	125	634	10147	98
Chad Johnson	76	379	5556	34
Terrell Owens	142	716	10535	101
Totals	35. 485	36. 2,268	37. 34,060	38. 286
Averages		39. 4.68 Catches/ Game	40. 70.22 Yards Gained/ Game	41. .59 Touchdowns/ Game

Source Two

42. Compare the players' data for the games after they performed their end-zone performance with their combined career statistics. Tell whether the group performed better as a whole or worse compared to their combined career statistics? Use the data in the tables to support your answer.

COMPREHEND ANALYZE EVALUATE

Student answers may vary, but they should demonstrate an ability to use data and details to make inferences. They should also support their claims with data and details from the tables. Their answers could include the following information:

As a group, the players performed slightly better in the category of catches/ game during the game after the end-zone performance than they did over their whole careers. However, they performed worse in the game after their end-zone performances than they did in their whole careers in yards gained per game and touchdowns per fame, gaining 70.22 yards per game in their careers versus only 60.6 yards per game in the game after. During their careers, they scored .59 touchdowns per game versus only .38 touchdowns in the game after. These statistics show that the players were not as effective overall for their teams the week after showing off with their end-zone performances.

Use the extended-response rubric in the Appendix to reference the criteria and determine the number of points to award.

---

*Quick*thought

The greatest achievements are enjoyed most by everyone involved when accomplished with humility and dignity. Pride can be dangerous.

Look Inside and Grow

43. Using the data in tables and the information given in the article, what can you infer about showing off? How does showing off seem to affect these professional athletes? What can you learn from their example? Support your claim with details and facts from this unit.

Student answers may vary.

The student should address each section of the question to the best of his/her ability. The question is meant to elicit strong classroom conversation about character education related issues. Students should be able to demonstrate that they have learned a lesson about the value of humility and the consequences of displaying too much pride.

Use the character-education rubric in the Appendix to reference the criteria and number of points to award.

Notes

He seemed to miss …: "'What's 10 Grand, to Me?' Moss Asks After Fine." MSNBC SportsTicker, January 14, 2005. http://www.msnbc.msn.com/id/6807933/.

Fitzgerald said …: Calvisi, Paul. "Wide Right with Paul Calvisi, Week 14." Official Site of the Arizona Cardinals, December 9, 2005. http://www.azcardinals.com/news/news_details.html?iid=3306.

In a quote …: Corbett, Jim. "Bengals' Johnson Talks the Talk But Walks the Walk." *USA Today*, October 19, 2005. http://www.usatoday.com/sports/football/nfl/bengals/2005-10-19-johnson-feature_x.htm.

He told a …: Clayton, John. "NFL Votes to Rein in NFL Celebrations." ESPN.com, March 30, 2006. http://sports.espn.go.com/nfl/news/story?id=2389062.

Famous End-Zone (chart)…: NFL Players Page. Game Logs (2001-2005). NFL.com. http://www.nfl.com/players/playerpage.

Players' Career Statistics (chart) …: Players. Pro-Football-Reference.com. http://www.pro-football-reference.com/players/.

Technical Extension

Football Science

When a quarterback throws a football across the field to a teammate, science is the essence of what's happening. He makes adjustments for all of the scientific factors: distance, wind, and weight of the ball. The farther away the receiver is, the harder the quarterback has to throw the ball. The quick calculations are done in the quarterback's head, and he may not even realize what he is doing. Watching or playing football can teach you a lot about science.

In physics, there is a division of science called mechanics. Mechanics is the study of motion and the causes of motion. There are two ways a ball moves during a game of football:

- the throwing of the ball through the air
- the motion of players running on the field (carrying the ball)

We'll take a look at these two categories of motion as they relate to the science of football.

A Football in the Air

When a football travels through the air, it moves in a curved path. Sometimes this path is also called a parabolic path, as shown in the diagram. As the ball travels through the air, gravity causes it to slow down and then come down after it reaches its peak. If it weren't for gravity, the ball would simply fly in a straight line and never come down. The motion of a football or any other object thrown or launched into the air is called projectile motion.

Think about a football punt. The ball is kicked by the punter at a certain angle, force, and speed. These variables determine how high and how far the ball will go. When the ball reaches its peak in the air, gravity causes it to complete the curve and return to the ground. The same is true when a ball is thrown.

Players Running

The first important part of the science of motion on the field is where the players line up to start a play. The line of scrimmage (where the ball is) is between the two teams. To begin a play, players on both sides usually line up away from the line of scrimmage. This lets them speed up, or accelerate, from their starting positions of non-motion. The farther back a player is, the higher the speed he can reach.

Players also use direction change when on the ground. This allows them to avoid being blocked or tackled. To change direction, a player pushes down on the ground with one foot. Because of Newton's Third Law of motion, "For every action there is an equal and opposite reaction," the ground "pushes" back, forcing the player in the opposite direction.

Players running on an open field do not have to stop or change direction to avoid other players. These players are able to reach their maximum momentum. Momentum is a combination of a player's weight and speed. Momentum is important for tackling or blocking runners on the field.

How many college or NFL players do you think study their science books as a part of training camp? Probably not many, but these scientific lessons are likely a large part of conversation in locker rooms. When a coach helps a player by suggesting an angle of kickoff or practicing direction changes when running, he's teaching mechanical science.

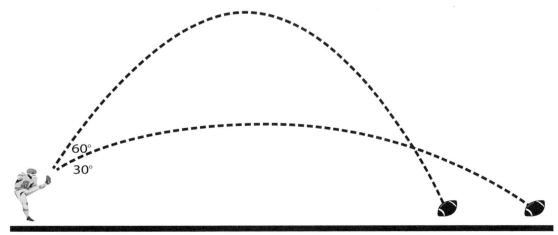

Reading Comprehension

After reading "Football Science," choose the options that best answer questions 1-14.

1. Read this sentence.
   These variables determine how high and how far the ball will go.

   What is the meaning of the word *variables* as it is used in this sentence?
   A. rules
   B. teams
   C. players
   D. changes

2. Read this sentence.
   The quick calculations are done in the quarterback's head, and he may not even realize what he is doing.

   What does the author mean by this sentence?
   F. The quarterback uses science subconsciously.
   G. The quarterback is not sure if the answer is correct when doing calculations.
   H. The quarterback is using a calculator prior to the game to ensure the correct answers.
   I. The quarterback has completed complicated math problems without the help from others on the team.

3. According to the article, what is one scientific lesson football players use but don't realize they are using it?
   A. Energy is the property that enables it to do work.
   B. Velocity is a physical quantity of an object's motion.
   C. For every action there is an equal and opposite reaction.
   D. The application of force on an object which rotates around an axis perpendicular to the force is called torque.

4. What is the purpose of teaching mechanical science in football?
   F. to help football players throw and kick farther
   G. to increase the ability to solve complex mathematical problems
   H. to decrease the number of mistakes players make during a game
   I. to change the number of positions that one person can play on a team

5. With which statement would the author of the passage most likely agree?
   A. Football coaches study science books before games.
   B. A punter uses science more than any other player on the field.
   C. Most football players do not realize how much science is involved in football.
   D. Quarterbacks calculate the use of a parabolic path to ensure they complete a pass to their receivers.

6. The author organizes the article by
   F. listing events that occurs during a football game.
   G. describing different scientific lessons that relate to football.
   H. listing Newton's Third Law of Motion as it applies to football.
   I. comparing the motion of throwing a football with punting a football.

HARD TO BE HUMBLE

7. What is the purpose of the illustration in the article?
   A. to entertain the reader with a colorful picture
   B. to show how the football curves when traveling in the air
   C. to encourage the reader to go outside and practice kicking
   D. to explain to the reader why the punter must kick the ball at a certain angle

8. What statement best expresses the main idea of the first paragraph?
   F. Science is a part of football.
   G. Football is a very complex sport.
   H. A football can be thrown farther by adjusting to the wind.
   I. The quarterback constantly makes adjustments in a football game.

9. What is significant about momentum?
   A. It causes the football to slow down or stop.
   B. It forces the player to go in the opposite direction.
   C. It is important for tackling or blocking runners on the field.
   D. It is the most important factor in punting a football in a straight line.

10. Why is the law of gravity important in football?
    F. The law of gravity launches the ball through the air.
    G. The law of gravity causes the football to return to the ground.
    H. The law of gravity changes the ability of a player to make blocks or tackles.
    I. The law of gravity adjusts to the player's weight to ensure he can push off the ground.

11. What advantage do players have by using science in football?
    A. They are less likely to get hurt on the field.
    B. They are more likely to miss a winning field goal.
    C. They are likely to be the first to score on their team.
    D. They are likely to make the most out of each game play.

12. Which statement about science in football is LEAST accurate?
    F. Mechanical science can be applied to other sports besides football.
    G. Players can improve their game performance by studying mechanical science.
    H. Coaches spend most of their time teaching mechanical science to their players.
    I. A spiral football thrown through the air to a receiver is known as projectile motion.

13. According to the article and the diagram, what would a punter need to do to make the ball go on the other side of the field?
    A. start closer to his team's end zone
    B. punt the ball higher to avoid a blocked kick
    C. kick the ball at a smaller angle to make it travel farther in the air
    D. kick the ball at a higher angle so it is able to travel farther in the air

14. Based on the article and the diagram, which conclusion is most accurate?
    F. Football players should devote their time to learning mechanical science.
    G. Football players use and apply mechanics on the field to enhance their game.
    H. Football players should go back to school and take a class in mechanical science.
    I. Football players who study mechanical science will be the best players on the field.

Vocational Extension

Job Description

Highland College is seeking a Certified Athletic Trainer to perform the following tasks for college athletes:
- Prepare athletes for practice and competition
- Develop conditioning programs
- Evaluate injuries to determine treatment
- Implement rehabilitation programs and provide referrals when necessary

Applicants must have a degree in the field, NATA Board Certification, and eligibility for a FL state license. (Highland College will help out-of-state applicants complete licensing paperwork.)

Sports Medicine is a wide field encompassing many different jobs and levels of employment. Those interested in sports medicine often enjoy competitive sports and have an interest in medicine or therapy. They must have good skills in observation, attention to detail, and problem solving. Formal education is almost always a requirement, but the amount of education needed varies from job to job. Those in sports medicine might work in college athletic departments, for professional sports teams, or in middle and high schools. They might have their own private practices or contract out their services to a variety of schools or teams.

Here are just a few of the avenues someone interested in sports medicine can look into:

Sports Dietician/ Nutritionist

A sports dietician plans diets for athletes to help them eat the correct balance of foods needed for their particular regimen of physical activity. They also take into account the athlete's body type and general physical health when creating the nutritional plan. Dieticians work closely with athletes and coaches to create programs that are maximally effective. Dieticians and nutritionists generally have a college degree or higher.

Sports Physiotherapist (Physical Therapist)

A sports physiotherapist treats and rehabilitates muscle, ligament, and joint injuries sustained by athletes in their sport. They use both manual therapy, such as stretching, and electrical equipment to stimulate damaged tissue and restore full mobility to an injured athlete. Physiotherapists also work with athletes to teach proper techniques athletes can use to avoid injury. Physiotherapists generally have a college degree and may have done graduate work.

Athletic Trainer

An athletic trainer is a certified medical expert in preventing, recognizing, and treating injuries resulting from physical activity. Athletic trainers usually work as part of a team under a licensed physician with coaches, athletes, and administrators. Athletic trainers generally have a college degree and have tested for certification.

Sports Medicine Practitioner

Sports medicine practitioners treat and prevent sports injuries caused by overuse or accidents. They both monitor athletic performance and provide on-site medical attention to prevent or treat injury. Medical practitioners can also diagnose injuries and create treatment programs. Medical practitioners have a college degree and have been to some medical school.

Sports Psychologist

Sports psychologists help athletes achieve optimum mental health through psychological treatments designed to enhance sporting performance. They conduct research to understand how participation in sports and injury affect an individual's psychological health. Psychologists have a college degree and a graduate degree.

Sports Medicine Physician

Sports medicine physicians treat mainly sports injuries. They generally specialize in a specific area of medicine and offer specialized treatment for athletes. These areas may include family practice, pediatrics (children), physical therapy, and orthopedic (bone, muscle, and joint) surgery, among others. Sports medicine physicians have a college degree, a four-year medical degree, and have completed a residency and fellowship in a hospital.

No matter what avenue you take, sports medicine is a rewarding and challenging career.

Looking Forward

15. Pretend you're a college graduate about to pursue a career in sports medicine. Write about which specialty you have chosen and what your education has been up to this point. Describe your dream job: what you will do, who you will meet, what further education you will need. Be specific and use the job description, article, and your experience to complete your answer.

Looking Forward

Student answers may vary.

The student should address the question to the best of his/her ability using the article and personal experience. The question is meant to encourage students to explore areas of interest for their future and begin to determine how they will prepare for a future career.

Use the extended-response rubric in the Appendix to reference the criteria and determine the number of points to award.

Ethical Dilemma

16. You are a sports medicine practitioner for a professional football team. A rookie on the team has come to you with a knee injury. You believe that his only chance of recovery is to stay off his knee for three months. Otherwise, he faces the risk of career-ending surgery. The player is afraid of losing his spot on the team. Because the team needs him, the coach wants him to play and may cut him from the team if he can't. What would you recommend to the player? When talking with the coach, how would you back up your recommendation?

Ethical Dilemma

Student answers may vary.

The student should address the question to the best of his/her ability using background knowledge from the article as well as personal opinion and experience. The question is meant to encourage students to contemplate scenarios and make ethical decisions.

Use the character-education rubric in the Appendix to reference the criteria and determine the number of points to award.

Reading Instructional Guide

BEFORE READING

Front-Loading Background Knowledge Through Read-Aloud-Think-Aloud

Search the internet for recent articles on Bono's work and use them to model the effective habits of readers through a Read-Aloud-Think-Aloud.

Check out articles at the following websites to determine if they would be appropriate for your RATA:

* http://www.time.com/time/covers/1101020304/story.html
* http://www.time.com/time/covers/1101020304/global.html

(Please keep in mind that it is the responsibility of the teacher to determine if articles from suggested sites are appropriate. The sites may have changed content since this publication. The publisher takes no responsibility for the current content of the site.)

Looking at the Words

Determining How the Word Sounds (Phonics)

With your students, use one of the sets of steps from the Syllable Guide at the beginning of the book to determine how to break a word into manageable parts. The goal is to break the words into syllables that the students can say. Then they can put those parts together to "sound the word out." However, remember that the rules for syllabification do not always work because our language is so diverse. The rules can also become rather complex for low readers, so keep in mind that their overall objective is just to figure out how the word sounds. They may not be able to break the word into its syllables perfectly, but they should at least be able to figure out how to say the word based on their attempt at following one of these sets of steps. Lesson One is a more basic set, while Lesson Two attempts to give the students the more specific rules without becoming too complicated. Take your time when teaching either set, and understand that many of the lower readers are not going to understand right away. It will take time, practice, and repeated application before many of them are able to make use of these strategies on their own.

Determining What the Words Mean (Vocabulary)

After students have spent time breaking the words apart to figure out how they sound, use the lists of prefixes and suffixes and their meanings found in the Syllable Guide to have students try to add whatever meaning they can to the words before actually looking at their definitions. After giving the students the definitions, have them see if they can figure out which words truly apply the meaning of any of the prefixes or suffixes.

Words to Study	Breaking into Syllables	Short Definition
Conquering	con-quer-ing	(v.) winning
Poverty	pov-er-ty	(n.) condition or quality of being poor
Obviously	ob-vi-ous-ly	(adv.) clearly; evidently
Jeer	jeer	(v.) to make fun of
Predicament	pre-dic-a-ment	(n.) unpleasant situation
Criticism	cri-ti-cism	(n.) act of making judgements
Publicity	pub-lic-i-ty	(n.) any information that brings a person or cause to public notice

Activating Background Knowledge

Anticipation Guide
Mark each of the following statements True or False:

1. _____ Chris Martin is the lead singer of U2.

2. _____ Bono does not believe in the cause of fighting poverty.

3. _____ Bono has met with the President of the United States.

4. _____ G-8 is the name of the President's airplane.

5. _____ Every day 1,400 newborn babies are infected with HIV/AIDS.

Starter Questions
After completing the Anticipation Guide, have a group or class discussion with the students using the following questions:

1. Who is Bono?

2. What do you think is killing the people of Africa?

3. What is poverty?

4. Can you name any people or group of people who live in poverty?

5. What are some of the methods people use to raise money for a cause?

Make a prediction about what you think the article will be about.

DURING READING

- Have the students skim the article. Give them about 45-60 seconds to do this.

- As they skim the article, tell them to circle any words they don't know how to say.

- When they are finished, talk about how to chunk the words they don't know how to say by sounds they now know and then sound them out.

- Have the students skim the questions. Give them only about 30-45 seconds to do this.

- Ask the students to predict what the article is about.

- Have the students read the article. They should question, summarize, clarify, and predict as they read. Instruct them to jot their questions, summarizations, clarifications, and predictions in the margins as they read.

- Remind students to constantly ask themselves if they know what the article is about right now. If they don't, they must reread to clarify. This is called monitoring for understanding.

- After they have finished reading the article, they are ready to answer the questions.

The Strategy Sheet

You may choose to have students complete the strategy sheet for each section before they answer the multiple-choice questions. Or you could have them complete the questions, work on the strategy sheet with a partner, and then go back over the questions to see if the use of the strategy sheet helped them more easily find the answers to any of the questions.

AFTER READING

Discussion Starter Questions

1. What can you do to help end poverty?

2. Name other entertainers who use their fame to help promote their causes. Do you agree with what they are doing? Why?

3. Should anyone who is well-known use his or her status to publicly influence others? Why? Why not?

4. Should leading nations forgive debt and offer more financial help to third world countries? Why? Why not?

5. Should we give medicine and cutting-edge technology to third world countries for free? Why? Why not?

Teacher Reflection

When you are finished with the article, strategies, and questions, ask yourself the following:

1. Did I get the students to THINK about what they have read?

2. Did I teach them (even a little bit) about how to read more effectively?

If you answered "Yes" to both questions, you can feel good about the day.

Attention:

The following article includes content of a sensitive nature. In order to prepare for any questions or class discussion that could arise teachers should thoroughly review the article and multiple-choice reading comprehension questions before choosing to teach the lesson.

Conquering the Music World,
Saving the Third World

Poverty and AIDS are destroying the people of Africa. Imagine a typical football stadium on a Sunday afternoon. Most stadiums seat about 65,000 screaming fans. In Africa, that is the amount of people who die from the HIV/AIDS virus in a week and a half. Shocking?

Consider also that every day in Africa 1,400 newborn babies are infected with HIV/AIDS during childbirth or by their mother's milk.

Now picture that same football stadium packed for a rock concert. The band is U2. Standing in the center of the stage is one of the world's most popular rock singers. He is known simply as Bono. When most people think of rock stars, they picture some wild, scraggly-haired person. They picture someone who lives a crazy lifestyle with fast cars, late nights, and parties. Bono and his rock band have been around for over 20 years, and they've had their share of late night parties, but now he stays up late for a different cause. Any extra energy he has left over after concerts and recording new albums goes to the people of Africa. He is doing what he can to reduce their poverty level. He is also helping the people of that country pay for drugs to help them fight the disease that is killing their continent—a disease that many of them never asked for. They were just unlucky enough to contract it because they live in a country where 25 million people are infected.

The awards Bono and his band have been honored with are impressive. One might argue that he and U2 have earned the title of World's Greatest Rock Band. They have been honored with Grammys in categories such as Album of the Year, Best Music Video, Record of the Year, and Best Rock Group Performance, to name a few. They were also voted to the Rock and Roll Hall of Fame in 2004. Although he has earned these awards, he is not one to rest on his success. Money and awards obviously don't mean as much to this pop star as making a difference in the world.

Over the past few years, Bono has met with many world leaders including the Pope, the Canadian Prime Minister, and the President of the United States. He looks a little strange dressed in wraparound sunglasses, jeans, and casual t-shirts next to these older, esteemed

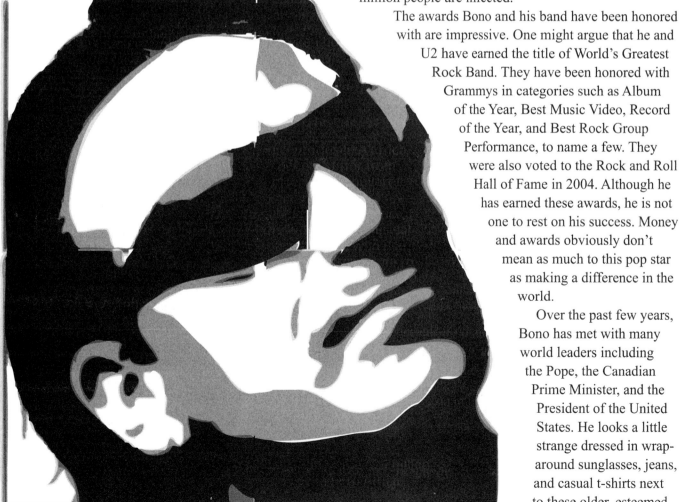

individuals dressed in their suits and formal attire. But he knows how to work a crowd. He is just as comfortable talking to wealthy and powerful people as he is talking to his fans on the streets. This comfort is mostly because he believes in his cause. He wants to help deliver Africa from the predicament it is in, and he won't allow himself to feel threatened by anyone.

Since Bono began his work, Britain has decided to spend $180 million per year until 2015 helping poor countries. The leaders of the world's richest countries have also decided to forgive the $40 billion in debt owed to them by the world's poorest countries. And the G-8, a group of the world's strongest industrialized nations, has also approved a $50 billion aid package including $25 billion to Africa. They have further promised to help 10 million people in poor countries get AIDS treatment. Now these countries can start spending money on the future of their people and not on their past.

Bono has also inspired other pop stars to get in on the act. Chris Martin, a member of the band Coldplay, has spent time doing charity work to help workers in poor countries. Alicia Keys has recently teamed up with Bono to record the single "Don't Give Up (Africa)." All of the money they have made from the song will go to an organization called Keep a Child Alive that helps provide medicine to families suffering from AIDS and HIV. Due to his efforts, Bono was named *Time* magazine's Person of the Year at the end of 2005.

However, he still receives criticism. People have openly jeered him at his concerts from time to time. Bono has said that he needs the band's drummer, Larry Mullen, to keep a watch on him during their concerts to ensure he doesn't go overboard when talking to the crowd about making poverty history.

One American writer has condemned Bono's efforts, saying the answer to settling Africa's problems is through education. He opposes the idea that Bono seems to just want to throw money at the situation. The writer is concerned that Bono is doing more harm than good by "badgering people for money." He says no one is making sure that money is going to exactly the right place, so it could be just wasted funds.

Actor Russell Crowe has been quoted as saying, "I do my bit to improve the world but I think it's very important to get things done on the quiet. I'm sick to death of famous people standing up and using their celebrity to promote a cause. If I see a particular need, I do try to help."

Even though it may sound bad, Crowe is making a good point. He seems to say that when you do something good for someone, you shouldn't try to get publicity for it. If you are trying to make people praise you for doing something for others, then you really aren't doing it for the right reasons. You are only thinking about your own popularity, not the needs of others.

However, it is difficult for famous people. Sometimes it is good for them to use their fame to make people aware of the problems of others. That is what Bono appears to be doing.

Bono is not the type to let the opinions of others get in his way, especially when his goal is to literally save the lives of millions of people. The man began his career in Ireland and has practically conquered the world music scene. Now that he has focused on a different life-long legacy, one wouldn't think that someone with so much heart would let anyone or anything stop him until he's met his objective.

Proving that he is doing it for others and not for himself is not a battle he needs to spend time fighting.

The people of Africa are happy the only fighting he is doing is for them.

Reading Comprehension

After reading "Conquering the Music World, Saving the Third World," choose the options that best answer questions 1-14.

1. Read this sentence.
   One American writer has condemned Bono's efforts, saying the answer to settling Africa's problems is through education.

   What is the meaning of the word *condemned* as it is used in this sentence?
   - A. praised
   - **B. criticized**
   - C. overstated
   - D. commended

2. Read this sentence.
   Although he has earned these awards, he is not one to rest on his success.

   What does the author mean by this sentence?
   - F. Bono is constantly looking for more ways to get awards.
   - **G. Bono focuses on what else he can do to help, rather than on his awards.**
   - H. Bono is one of the most successful entertainers because of the awards he has won.
   - I. Bono's tour schedule is so busy that he has to look for time to rest between performance dates.

3. From the article, what can the reader tell about Bono's popularity?
   - **A. He is not bothered by other people's opinions of him.**
   - B. He cares deeply about maintaining his musical popularity.
   - C. His popularity is decreasing because of his charitable work.
   - D. He works for worthy causes to increase his global popularity.

4. On which of the following has Bono seemingly had the largest influence due to its large contribution to Africa?
   - **F. Britain**
   - G. the G-8
   - H. Canada
   - I. the United States

5. With which statement would the author of the passage most likely agree?
   - A. Bono is responsible for saving Africa.
   - **B. Bono has had a huge impact on acquiring resources for Africa.**
   - C. Bono's mission is to make U2 the world's most popular rock band.
   - D. Bono immerses himself in charity work in order to gain popularity.

6. The author organizes the article by
   - F. listing the ways Bono has helped Africa.
   - **G. describing the problems Africa faces and then showing what Bono has done to help raise awareness.**
   - H. listing Bono's accomplishments so the reader can see the credibility of his charitable efforts for Africa.
   - I. comparing Bono's musical accomplishments and then showing how different entertainers have tried to duplicate his work.

7. What is the author's purpose in writing this article?
   - A. to show the reader how to help in Africa
   - B. to explain the needs of the people of Africa
   - C. to encourage others to get involved in charitable work
   - **D. to show how Bono's efforts have made an impact on Africa**

8. Which statement BEST expresses the main idea of this article?
   - F. Bono raises millions of dollars each year for Africa.
   - G. Bono has devoted much of his life to being a great musician.
   - **H. Successful singer Bono is using his fame to selflessly help reduce Africa's poverty and disease.**
   - I. Successful singer Bono does charity work for the people of Africa to gain popularity and fame.

9. What is the tone of Russell Crowe's comments about Bono?
   - **A. critical**
   - B. neutral
   - C. envious
   - D. astonished

10. Why will countries in Africa now be able to start focusing on the future?
    - **F. Much of their past debt has been forgiven.**
    - G. Popular celebrities are working to help them.
    - H. They have improved schools and begun to focus on education.
    - I. The Pope, the Canadian Prime Minister, and the President of the United States are now on their side.

11. The major difference between Russell Crowe and Bono, based on the theme of the article, is that
    - A they are from two different countries.
    - B. Russell Crowe is an actor, and Bono is a musician.
    - **C. Russell Crowe is more quiet than Bono about charitable work.**
    - D. Bono is more quiet than Russell Crowe about charitable work.

12. Which fact from the article provides the best evidence that Bono has dedicated himself to fighting for the people of Africa?
    - F. Bono has inspired others to help him.
    - G. Bono rallies fans to make poverty history.
    - **H. A majority of Bono's time is now spent helping Africa.**
    - I. Bono has raised millions of dollars for Africa and been named Person of the Year.

13. What does the author use to support the idea that Bono has conquered the Music World?
    - **A. a description of his awards**
    - B. stories about how he has inspired other musicians
    - C. a description about how he handles himself at concerts
    - D. statistics about the number of people he draws to concerts

14. Which statement BEST supports the idea that Bono's efforts go beyond just donating his own money to Africa?
    - F. People refuse to help with the situation in Africa.
    - G. He receives criticism and little help from other celebrities.
    - H. His charitable ways are conflicting with his musical career.
    - **I. He travels the world convincing its leaders to provide relief to Africa.**

Reading Strategy

Reading on Target

This article is about suffering in Africa, money, and music. Read the article again and find as many details as you can about each of these concepts. Write those details in the appropriate rings below. Then answer the question in the center ring using the information you've written in the outer rings.

Use of this strategy sheet helps you find facts and details which lead to the main idea. It also helps you summarize facts and details through answering the target question in the center.

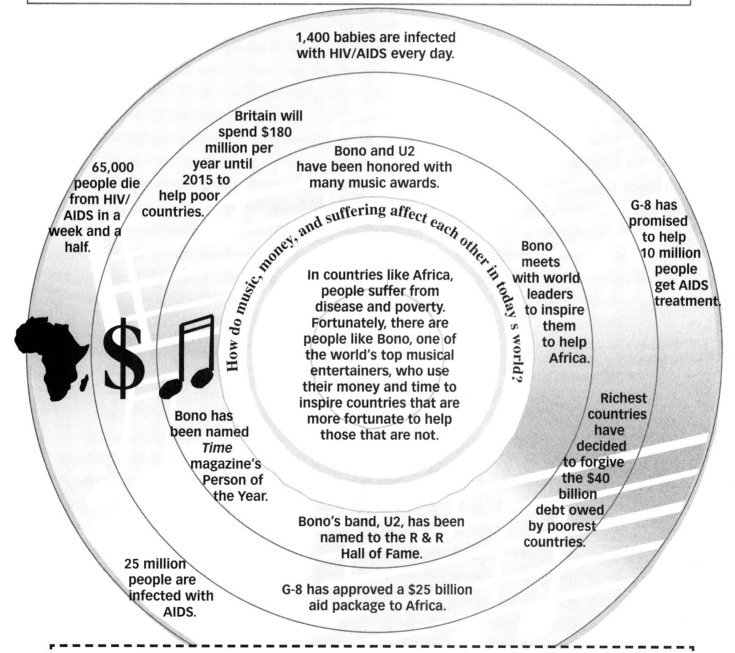

1,400 babies are infected with HIV/AIDS every day.

Britain will spend $180 million per year until 2015 to help poor countries.

65,000 people die from HIV/AIDS in a week and a half.

Bono and U2 have been honored with many music awards.

G-8 has promised to help 10 million people get AIDS treatment.

How do music, money, and suffering affect each other in today's world?

In countries like Africa, people suffer from disease and poverty. Fortunately, there are people like Bono, one of the world's top musical entertainers, who use their money and time to inspire countries that are more fortunate to help those that are not.

Bono meets with world leaders to inspire them to help Africa.

Bono has been named *Time* magazine's Person of the Year.

Richest countries have decided to forgive the $40 billion debt owed by poorest countries.

Bono's band, U2, has been named to the R & R Hall of Fame.

25 million people are infected with AIDS.

G-8 has approved a $25 billion aid package to Africa.

Teacher's Notes: Students may need some guidance in determining the number of facts and details to write in the circles. Also, remind them that by answering the question in the center, they are basically writing the main idea of the article. Possible responses are included here.

Interpreting the Data

PART I

According to DATA, the organization Bono works with to help find relief for the people of Africa, African countries still owe $293 billion in debts to foreign countries.

Forbes magazine publishes a list of the richest people in the world each year. The following people from Africa appeared on the list in 2006.

Africans Making Forbes Magazine's List of Richest People in 2006			
Name	Rank	Residence	Net Worth in $Billions
Onsi Sawiris	129	Egypt	4.8
Nicky Oppenheimer & family	134	South Africa	4.6
Johann Rupert & family	207	South Africa	3.3
Naguib Sawiris	278	Egypt	2.6
		Total	15. **15.3**

16. If the richest people in Africa had put their money together last year, would they have been able to pay the debt owed by the African countries to other countries?

Circle one: Yes   (No)

17. If those four people were worth that same amount of money every year, how many years would it take them to pay off Africa's debt if there were no interest charges?

Show your work in the box below. Round your answer to the nearest whole number.

READ COMPREHEND APPLY

Divide 293,000,000,000 by 15,300,000,000 to get 19 when rounded.

To simplify, students could reduce to 293,000 / 15,300 to get 19.

Number of Years: **19**

Use the short-response rubric in the Appendix to reference the criteria and determine the number of points to award.

Billboard magazine released a list of the top 20 musical Money Makers of 2005. They included musical groups and soloists.

The following chart includes the top 10 acts/entertainers and the amount of money those acts/entertainers earned as income in 2005. Income included the album and digital sales as well as accumulated box office receipts.

Top 10 Money-Making Acts/Entertainers in 2005 According to Billboard Magazine		
Rank	**Act/Entertainer**	**2005 Income**
1	U2	$255,022,633.35
2	The Rolling Stones	$152,356,754.40
3	Kenny Chesney	$87,731,463.50
4	Paul McCartney	$84,263,375.10
5	Elton John	$77,150,061.65
6	Celine Dion	$76,137,905.65
7	50 Cent	$75,351,514.85
8	Green Day	$71,753,415.60
9	Neil Diamond	$70,203,895.50
10	The Eagles	$67,524,283.25
		18. **$1,017,495,302.85**

19. If the top 10 entertainers in the world were to add their money together, would they be able to pay off Africa's debt right now?

Circle one: Yes   (No)

20. If each of the entertainers had this good of a year every year, approximately how long would it take them to pay off Africa's debt if they put their money together and there was no interest? Show your work in the box below. Round your answer to the nearest whole number.

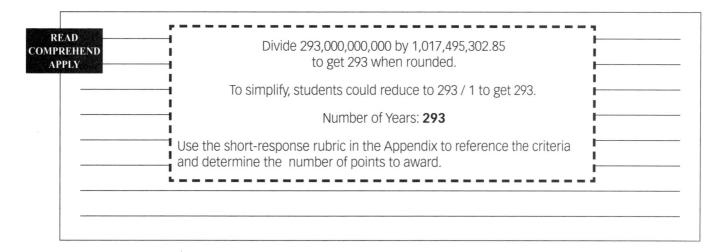

READ COMPREHEND APPLY

Divide 293,000,000,000 by 1,017,495,302.85 to get 293 when rounded.

To simplify, students could reduce to 293 / 1 to get 293.

Number of Years: **293**

Use the short-response rubric in the Appendix to reference the criteria and determine the number of points to award.

21. Consider what you have read in the article and analyze the data you have seen so far. Why is it important that Bono tries to get other countries to send money to Africa rather than just trying to talk his friends in the music industry into trying to help? Use data to support your answer.

COMPREHEND ANALYZE EXPLAIN

Student answers will vary, but should include a statement with support. Students may write something like the following:

Bono could not possibly collect enough money from just his friends in the entertainment industry. Even the top 10 richest entertainers would take 293 years to pay off the debts of Africa (assuming they lived that long and earned the same amount each year). Other countries may be able to afford more money, which is why he should enlist their support.

Use the extended-response rubric in the Appendix to reference the criteria and determine the number of points to award.

PART II

22. U2 earned $138.9 million for 78 North American shows in 2005. They sold a total of approximately 1.4 million tickets for those shows. Determine what the average ticket price was for those shows. Show your work below.

READ COMPREHEND APPLY

Divide $138.9 million by 1.4 million to get $99.21

Average Ticket Price: **$99.21**

Use the short-response rubric in the Appendix to reference the criteria and determine the number of points to award.

23. 4.7 million people in Africa need anti-retroviral (ARV) drugs to treat the effects of AIDS/HIV and other diseases. The cheapest drugs cost about $1 per day per person. If U2 sent the amount grossed on each ticket to Africa, determine how many tickets they would have to sell to supply the ARV drugs to those 4.7 million people for one day. Then determine the number of tickets they would have to sell for a year's supply. Round your answers to the nearest whole number.

READ COMPREHEND APPLY

Multiply 4.7 million people by $1 per day= $4,700,000 per day.

Each ticket costs on average $99, so divide $4,700,000 by $99 to get 47,475.

Number of tickets per day: **47,475**

Multiply 47,475 tickets per day X 365 days per year to get 17,328,375.

Number of tickets for a year's supply: **17,328,375**

Use the short-response rubric in the Appendix to reference the criteria and determine the number of points to award.

24. If 60,000 people attend each of U2's concerts and tickets cost on average the same as you determined above, figure out how many concerts U2 would have to perform to pay for a year's supply of the drugs. Round your answer to the nearest whole number.

READ COMPREHEND APPLY

Divide 17,328,375 tickets by 60,000 tickets per concert to get 289 concerts.

Number of concerts: **289**

Use the short-response rubric in the Appendix to reference the criteria and determine the number of points to award.

25. Some people like to criticize celebrities who use their fame to ask for money for different causes. Those people like to say the celebrities should just send all of their money to the cause and stop bugging them. Based on the data in this unit, determine if it would be possible for Bono to provide Africa all the money it needs to help repay its debts and help fight diseases. Use statistics and data to support your answer.

ANALYZE EVALUATE EXPLAIN

Student answers may vary, but should include statistics and data to support answers. Answers may include information such as the following:

It wouldn't be possible for Bono alone to provide Africa all of the assistance it needs. If he sent all of the money he earned through U2's concerts, he'd have to do 288 shows per year, every year. That would only pay for the medicine. It wouldn't even account for the debt Africa has. For instance, U2 earned $138.9 million in 2005, which seems like a lot, but the debt in Africa is $293 billion. Even with his $138.9 million, Bono couldn't begin to repay Africa's debt and fight diseases on his own.

Use the extended-response rubric in the Appendix to reference the criteria and determine the number of points to award.

---

*Quick*thought

Don't forget that you are not alone in the world. When you see someone fall, help him up. When you go through rough times, let others help you overcome them. No one can do it alone.

PART III

Use the map and table below to answer the questions on the following pages.

Data for African Countries							
Fill in regions below: North, North/Central, Central, South	Country	Literacy Rate (females 15-24)	# of Infant Deaths/ 1,000 Births	% of People With HIV (ages 15-49)	Average $ Earned per Person (in U.S. Dollars)	Life Expectancy at Birth (Total Years)	Population Total in Millions
26. South	Lesotho	N/A	80	28.9	730	35.6	1.8
	South Africa	94.3	54	21.5	3630	44.6	45.5
	Swaziland	89.8	107.6	38.8	1660	42.2	1.1
	Zambia	66.2	102	16.5	400	38.1	11.5
	Zimbabwe	N/A	79.4	24.6	620	37.2	12.9
	Botswana	95.6	84	37.3	4360	35.5	1.8
	Namibia	93.5	46.8	21.3	2380	47.5	2
27. Central	Congo Dem. Rep.	63.1	129	4.2	110	43.7	55.9
	Burundi	70.4	114	6	90	44.2	7.3
	Uganda	71.2	80.2	4.1	250	48.9	27.8
	Tanzania	76.2	78.4	7	320	46.2	37.6
	Kenya	80.7	78.5	6.7	480	48.3	33.5
	Cameroon	N/A	87.2	5.5	810	46	16
28. N/C	Nigeria	N/A	101.4	5.4	430	43.7	128.7
	Central Afr. Rep.	46.9	115	13.5	310	39.4	4
29. North	Sudan	71.4	62.6	2.3	530	56.5	35.5
	Chad	23.2	117	4.8	250	43.9	9.4
	Ethiopia	N/A	110.4	4.4	110	42.5	70
	Eritrea	N/A	52.2	2.7	190	54.4	4.2
	Mauritania	55.5	78	0.6	530	53.3	3
	The Gambia	N/A	89	1.2	280	56.3	1.5
	Niger	23.2	151.8	1.2	210	44.7	13.5
	United States	99	7	1	41,440	77	293.7

Analyze the table and the map on the preceding page to answer each of the following questions. Read, Comprehend, Analyze, and Evaluate to answer the questions in the table.

30. How do the southern countries compare with the central and northern countries in amount of money made per person?	**The southern countries make more money per person than the other regions.**
31. How do the southern countries compare with the other countries in literacy rate?	**The southern countries have a higher literacy rate than the countries of the other regions.**
32. What is the relationship between the amount of money people in a country make and their education?	**The more money the country makes per person, the higher their literacy rate appears to be.**
33. How do the southern countries in Africa compare to the other countries in terms of life expectancy?	**The people of the southern countries don't seem to have as long of a life expectancy as the people from the other regions.**
34. Use data from the table to determine why southern countries compare to other countries in terms of life expectancy.	**The percentage of people from the southern countries living with HIV is higher, which must cause them to have a shorter life expectancy.**
35. What seems to be the relationship between the literacy rate and the percentage of people ages 15-49 that have the HIV virus?	**It appears that the higher the literacy rate, the larger the percentage of people living with HIV in different countries.**
36. Using this data and the answers to your questions, which countries in Africa do you think Bono should target?	**Though they are richer countries, the southern ones seem to need the most help in fighting diseases like HIV.**

37. Imagine you are Bono, and you are trying to convince world leaders that Africa needs assistance. Write to convince the leaders to help certain countries in Africa. Use data from the table and information from the article to support your answer.

ANALYZE EVALUATE EXPLAIN

Student answers may vary; however, they must contain support from the data and the article.

Students should point out that money doesn't seem to have much of an effect on the AIDS epidemic, as the richer countries seem to have a higher percentage of people living with AIDS. They may also point out that the countries that seem most literate also have a higher percentage of people living with AIDS. This means that money and education alone aren't enough. Other countries must be creative in the type of support they give to help Africa overcome its problems with debt and disease. When one compares the literacy rate of many of the countries in Africa to the United States (99%), they will see that African countries are falling far behind the world. They must have help in order to help them help their own people.

Use the extended-response rubric in the Appendix to reference the criteria and determine the number of points to award.

Look Inside and Grow

38. Many of us tend to live in our own little worlds. We get so caught up in our own personal lives that we forget there is a whole world out there that suffers like we suffer and rejoices like we rejoice. Why is it important for us to look outside of our own environment to seek those who need our help? Use examples to discuss specifically how you provide for others or what your plans are to be able to make a difference in the world some day.

Student answers may vary.

The student should address each section of the question to the best of his/her ability. The question is meant to elicit strong classroom conversation about character. Students should be able to demonstrate that they have learned a lesson about the value of helping others.

Use the character-education rubric in the Appendix to reference the criteria and determine the number of points to award.

Notes

Consider also that …: DATA website, 2005. http://www.data.org/whyafrica/.

He says no one…: "Theroux Slams Bono's African Ideas." Contactmusic.com, December 19, 2005. http://www.contactmusic.com/new/xmlfeed.nsf/mndwebpages/theroux%20slams%20bonos%20african%20ideas.

If I see…: "Crowe Slams Celebrity Campaigners." Contactmusic.com, August 28, 2005. http://www.contactmusic.com/new/xmlfeed.nsf/mndwebpages/crowe%20slams%20celebrity%20campaigners.

Africans Making Forbes (chart)…: "The World's Richest People." Forbes.com, 2006. http://www.forbes.com/lists/2006/10/Rank_4.html.

Top 10 Money (chart)…: "U2 Tops Billboard's Money Makers Chart." Billboard.com, January 20, 2006. http://www.billboard.com/bbcom/news/article_display.jsp?vnu_content_id=1001882362.

Data for African (chart)…: Africa, Data and Statistics (2004). The World Bank. http://web.worldbank.org/WBSITE/EXTERNAL/COUNTRIES/AFRICAEXT/0,,menuPK:258665~pagePK:146732~piPK:146813~theSitePK:258644,00.html.

Technical Extension

HIV and the Body

HIV and AIDS are diseases that affect millions worldwide. Nowhere is the problem greater than in Africa. AIDS is the leading cause of death in sub-Saharan Africa, with approximately 2.4 million deaths in 2005 attributed to AIDS.

The fact is, HIV and AIDS are diseases that can affect anyone. There are a few common ways that HIV is spread:

- unprotected sex with someone who is infected
- sharing a needle (to take drugs) with someone who is infected
- accidental contact with body fluids from an infected person (such as a nurse being stuck with an infected needle)
- being born to a mother with HIV, or nursing from breast milk

HIV cannot be spread by casual contact such as touching or hugging someone with HIV or AIDS. It's not transmitted in bathrooms or swimming pools, nor by sharing cups, utensils, or telephones. Scientists have also recently proven that mosquitoes and other insects do not spread HIV.

HIV stands for human immunodeficiency virus. It is the virus that causes AIDS, which stands for acquired immune deficiency syndrome. The HIV virus works in the body in five basic steps as follows:

1. HIV identifies healthy CD4 cells.
2. HIV unlocks and invades CD4 cells.
3. HIV changes to enter CD4 nucleus.
4. HIV takes over CD4 cells.
5. CD4 cells reproduce HIV.

When the HIV virus first enters the body, it invades healthy CD4 cells. CD4 cells are special white blood cells that help the body's immune system protect against germs and viruses. When a person's CD4 cells don't work properly, that person is more susceptible to illnesses. Viruses can't make copies of themselves on their own, so they need healthy cells already in the body to help them. HIV has a special chemical that allows it to enter the CD4 cell. Picture the chemical as a key that unlocks the cells.

Next, HIV uses an enzyme called reverse transcriptase to hide the fact that it is a bad virus. It then uses another enzyme called integrase to enter the cell's command center, or nucleus. The nucleus is the part of the cell that tells it what to do. A healthy CD4 command center does the job of telling the immune system to protect the body against germs and viruses. When HIV controls the cell's nucleus, it tells the cell to do other things.

The worst part about the HIV virus is that it tells the cell to reproduce more and more of the HIV virus in the body. Another enzyme called protease manipulates the virus and creates new copies of it. The new copies of the virus then go into the body and seek out more CD4 cells to invade.

AIDS is the final stage of HIV. It can take many years for people with the virus to develop AIDS. When CD4 cells drop to a very low level, meaning that HIV has invaded many of those cells, a person's ability to fight infection is very low. A healthy adult generally has 1,000 or more CD4 cells. Doctors say that someone has developed AIDS when his or her CD4 cell count is less than 200. In addition, the definition of AIDS includes 26 "AIDS-defining conditions." Most AIDS-defining conditions are infections that rarely make healthy people sick. In people with AIDS, however, these infections can be severe and sometimes fatal.

This is because the immune system is so weak from HIV that the body cannot fight off certain bacteria and viruses.

Although HIV and AIDS can't be cured, science has come a long way in treating the diseases. We've learned that the HIV virus uses three enzymes in the reproduction process: reverse transcriptase, integrase, and protease. Anti-HIV medication works by attacking the virus inside the CD4 cell. The medication is called an enzyme inhibitor, meaning that it stops the enzymes used by the virus from working. Then HIV is either unable to reproduce, or it is slowed down. There are also drugs that delay the onset of AIDS-defining conditions. Usually, those infected with HIV are placed on a strict combination of these drugs and closely monitored by a doctor.

HIV and AIDS are life-threatening illnesses that have caused a lot of tragedy around the world. But the spread of HIV can be prevented by avoiding the short list of common ways people get the virus. Humanitarians and activists have spent hundreds of millions of dollars to educate people and treat the HIV virus. Hopefully, one day, we'll find a cure.

Reading Comprehension

After reading "HIV and the Body," choose the options that best answer questions 1-14.

1. Read this sentence.

   When a person's CD4 cells don't work properly, that person is more susceptible to illness.

   What is the meaning of the word *susceptible* as it is used in this sentence?
   A. unlikely
   B. vulnerable
   C. forgiving
   D. questionable

2. Read this sentence.

   Picture the chemical as a key that unlocks the cells.

   What does the author mean by this sentence?
   F. The anti-HIV medication stops the cells from reproducing.
   G. The reverse transcriptase enzyme tells which cells are infected.
   H. HIV has a special chemical that allows it to enter the CD4 cells.
   I. The command center distinguishes the healthy cells from the invaded cells.

3. According to the article, what stops the enzymes used by the virus from working?
   A. protease
   B. integrase
   C. enzyme inhibitor
   D. reverse transcriptase

4. What is the role of the CD4 cell?
   F. It copies infectious cells.
   G. It hides the fact that HIV is a bad virus.
   H. It creates another enzyme called transcriptase.
   I. It helps the body's immune system protect against germs and viruses.

5. With which statement would the author of the passage most likely agree?
   A. There is nothing you can do to prevent HIV.
   B. Low levels of CD4 cells help fight infection.
   C. Educating yourself can protect you from HIV.
   D. There are not enough HIV and AIDS cases to worry about.

6. The author organizes this article by
   F. describing the role that CD4 cells take in HIV.
   G. listing the ways the virus is spread and the stages of HIV.
   H. presenting a chronological list of events linking HIV to AIDS.
   I. comparing and contrasting how HIV and AIDS affect the body.

7. What was the author's purpose in writing this article?
   A. to emphasize the need to find a cure
   B. to show how many people have died from AIDS
   C. to explain why you should avoid someone with HIV
   D. to describe how HIV spreads and invades the body

8. What title best fits the article?
    F. AIDS and the Cure
    G. HIV, the Silent Killer
    H. AIDS, the Poor Man's Disease
    I. HIV, the Preventable Disease

9. Which phrase best describes accidental contact?
    A. hugging a person with AIDS
    B. a nurse being stuck with an infected needle
    C. sharing a needle with someone who is infected
    D. having unprotected sex with a person with HIV

10. Why is infection severe and sometimes fatal in people with AIDS?
    F. The CD4 cells rise to an unsafe level.
    G. The body cannot fight off certain viruses.
    H. The protease enzyme doesn't copy enough healthy cells.
    I. The anti-HIV medication is too strong for the body to handle.

11. What is true of BOTH unprotected sex and sharing a needle with someone who is infected?
    A. They are causes of HIV.
    B. They are illegal activities.
    C. They affect only young people.
    D. They are contracted accidentally.

12. Which statement about HIV is LEAST accurate?
    F. HIV takes over the CD4 cells.
    G. HIV identifies healthy CD4 cells.
    H. HIV changes to enter the CD4 nucleus.
    I. HIV can be cured with anti-HIV medication.

13. Which of the following is NOT a common way HIV is spread?
    A. casual contact such as touching
    B. being born to a mother with HIV
    C   unprotected sex with someone who is infected
    D. sharing a needle with someone who in infected

14. Based on the article, which statement is most accurate?
    F. People who have researched HIV cannot be infected.
    G. HIV is spreading so rapidly that it cannot be stopped.
    H. Knowing the causes of HIV will guarantee not being infected.
    I. HIV can be prevented by avoiding the ways that people can be infected.

Vocational Extension

Job Description

The United States Peace Corps is looking for volunteers with bachelor's degrees to work in HIV/AIDS education. Volunteers will work for two years in the field of prevention and treatment of HIV/AIDS in developing countries around the world. Volunteers will have the opportunity to learn a new language, live in another culture, and develop career and leadership skills. This job also includes the benefit of deferment of student loans, graduate school scholarship opportunities, and noncompetitive eligibility for employment in the federal government. Interested parties can begin the application process at www.peacecorps.org.

Have you ever wanted to travel to a far-off place? Do you feel a calling to educate or help others? Are you an educator, a business guru, a construction worker, or a nurse? Are you unsure of what you want to do with your life? Maybe the Peace Corps is for you.

In a nutshell, joining the Peace Corps means you will train to go to a foreign country and spend two years doing any number of types of service work there. While those who join the Peace Corps are called volunteers, the Peace Corps is a job. Volunteers work, teach, and learn while immersed in a foreign culture. They serve in areas such as education, social outreach, health work, community development, environmental concerns, and technology. Currently the largest numbers of volunteers work in the fields of education and health, with environment and business falling close behind.

Any American citizen over 18 years of age can apply to become a Peace Corps volunteer. The Peace Corps also encourages applicants to obtain a four-year degree or solid work experience in areas like business, agriculture, or a skilled trade. According to eligibility requirements, having a college degree by the time you're ready to leave helps your chances of acceptance. The degree can be in just about anything. The Peace Corps will match each applicant with service that uses his or her skills.

During the two-year service term, volunteers are given a living allowance to meet basic needs and live a lifestyle similar to that of the locals in the community they are serving. Medical care is provided as well as the cost of transportation to and from the service site. Most student loans from college can be deferred (or postponed) until the worker returns to the United States.

Volunteers are eligible for a stipend for readjustment to life in the United States. The Peace Corps also provides job placement support and educational support. The Peace Corps provides volunteers with three months of training before country placement and offers ongoing training throughout service. The skills learned give volunteers cross-cultural experiences and increased marketability for future employment. In addition, many graduate schools offer scholarships and grants to Peace Corps volunteers.

More than anything, the Peace Corps allows volunteers to become selfless humanitarians making a difference in the lives of others. In exchange, volunteers gain a new perspective of the world and of themselves.

Looking Forward

15. What is your dream for the future? Identify a future goal and tell how service in the Peace Corps could help you achieve it. Use personal experience and information from the article to explain your answer.

Looking Forward

Student answers may vary.

The student should address the question to the best of his/her ability using the article and personal experience. The question is meant to encourage students to explore areas of interest for their future and begin to determine how they will prepare for a future career.

Use the extended-response rubric in the Appendix to reference the criteria and determine the number of points to award.

Ethical Dilemma

16. You're a Peace Corps volunteer assigned to a remote village in a developing country. After becoming familiar with the language and traditions of your village, you come to realize that some of the sacred rituals your people participate in lead to risk factors for contracting the HIV virus. You don't know if you can educate your village without insulting their sacred traditions, but lives are at risk. What do you do?

Ethical Dilemma

Student answers may vary.

The student should address the question to the best of his/her ability using background knowledge from the article as well as personal opinion and experience. The question is meant to encourage students to contemplate scenarios and make ethical decisions.

Use the character-education rubric in the Appendix to reference the criteria and determine the number of points to award.

Reading Instructional Guide

BEFORE READING

Front-Loading Background Knowledge Through Read-Aloud-Think-Aloud

Search the Internet for recent articles on Internet safety.
Check out articles at the following websites to determine if they would be appropriate for your RATA:

- http://www.kidshealth.org/kid/watch/house/Internet_safety.html

- http://www .cybercrime.gov/rules/kidInternet.htm

(Please keep in mind that it is the responsibility of the teacher to determine if articles from suggested sites are appropriate. The sites may have changed content since this publication. The publisher takes no responsibility for the current content of the site.)

Looking at the Words

Determining How the Word Sounds (Phonics)
With your students, use one of the sets of steps from the Syllable Guide at the beginning of the book to determine how to break a word into manageable parts. The goal is to break the words into syllables that the students can say. Then they can put those parts together to "sound the word out." However, remember that the rules for syllabification do not always work because our language is so diverse. The rules can also become rather complex for low readers, so keep in mind that their overall objective is just to figure out how the word sounds. They may not be able to break the word into its syllables perfectly, but they should at least be able to figure out how to say the word based on their attempt at following one of these sets of steps. Lesson One is a more basic set, while Lesson Two attempts to give the students the more specific rules without becoming too complicated. Take your time when teaching either set, and understand that many of the lower readers are not going to understand right away. It will take time, practice, and repeated application before many of them are able to make use of these strategies on their own.

Determining What the Words Mean (Vocabulary)
After students have spent time breaking the words apart to figure out how they sound, use the lists of prefixes and suffixes and their meanings found in the Syllable Guide to have students try to add whatever meaning they can to the words before actually looking at their definitions. After giving the students the definitions, have them see if they can figure out which words truly apply the meaning of any of the prefixes or suffixes.

Words to Study	Breaking into Syllables	Short Definition
Profile	pro-file	(n.) a short vivid biography
Disclosed	dis-closed	(v.) to reveal
Inappropriate	in-ap-pro-pri-ate	(adj.) improper
Solicitations	so-li-ci-ta-tions	(n.) the act of enticement or luring

Activating Background Knowledge

Anticipation Guide
Mark each of the following statements True or False:

1. _____ The NETwork.com is a site where you can buy and sell items.

2. _____ While online you should lie about your age.

3. _____ CyberTipline.com is for reporting any kind of harassment to the police.

4. _____ The NETwork.com is a site for ages 14 and over.

5. _____ A Cyberspace safety tip is don't give out your full name.

Starter Questions
After completing the Anticipation Guide, have a group or class discussion with the students using the following questions:

1. What is a blog?

2. How much time do you spend on the computer?

3. What are some of your favorite sites?

4. What is TheNETwork.com?

5. What is MySpace.com?

Make a prediction about what you think the article will be about.

DURING READING

- Have the students skim the article. Give them about 45-60 seconds to do this.

- As they skim the article, tell them to circle any words they don't know how to say.

- When they are finished, talk about how to chunk the words they don't know how to say by sounds they now know and then sound them out.

- Have the students skim the questions. Give them only about 30-45 seconds to do this.

- Ask the students to predict what the article is about.

- Have the students read the article. They should question, summarize, clarify, and predict as they read. Instruct them to jot their questions, summarizations, clarifications, and predictions in the margins as they read.

- Remind students to constantly ask themselves if they know what the article is about right now. If they don't, they must reread to clarify. This is called monitoring for understanding.

- After they have finished reading the article, they are ready to answer the questions.

The Strategy Sheet

You may choose to have students complete the strategy sheet for each section before they answer the multiple-choice questions. Or you could have them complete the questions, work on the strategy sheet with a partner, and then go back over the questions to see if the use of the strategy sheet helped them more easily find the answers to any of the questions.

AFTER READING

Discussion Starter Questions

1. Think about a time when you were on a website and knew you should not be on it. Did you ever think you were in danger?

2. Do you know any friends that have lied or have been in trouble for being in Cyberspace? What happened to them?

3. How might you protect yourself while on social network sites?

4. Should police have the right to impersonate themselves as young girls/boys to catch sexual predators? Why? Why not?

5. Should teachers and parents be allowed to monitor Myspace accounts? Does this invade privacy?

Teacher Reflection

When you are finished with the article, strategies, and questions, ask yourself the following:

1. Did I get the students to THINK about what they have read?

2. Did I teach them (even a little bit) about how to read more effectively?

If you answered "Yes" to both questions, you can feel good about the day.

Attention:

The following article includes content of a sensitive nature. In order to prepare for any questions or class discussion that could arise teachers should thoroughly review the article and multiple-choice reading comprehension questions before choosing to teach the lesson.

Cyberspace Safety
As Careful As She Always Is

Her fingers dash around the keyboard at the speed of light. Thanks to growing up with a computer as a second best friend, her typing skills are nearly perfect. Marcia's dad once told her he thought he was eventually going to need to have the computer's mouse surgically removed from her hand.

Her father's sarcastic prediction looks less like a joke now that he has allowed her to open an account with TheNETwork.com. This social networking website allows people to set up accounts to create their own blogs. The system is set up so that only the people Marcia lists as "Friends" can access her page. She's never considered the fact that she may be in any kind of danger when she logs on. Neither have her parents, for that matter.

Marcia is really only 13 years old. TheNETwork.com makes it clear that its site is only for people 14 and over. Those from the ages of 14 to 16 have special guidelines for whom they can allow into the Friends network. There is even a list of rules and restrictions the people at TheNETwork.com have created for them. But Marcia has never read them. She didn't have to. She just lied about her age when she created her profile to make her account. In real life, she is 13-year-old honors student Marcia Lasiter, who lives at home with a younger brother, two parents, and her cat. But online she is Raven, 16-year-old party girl. One glance at her page, and someone would guess that she

lives an out-of-control lifestyle.

Her parents have never actually seen her page. With work and raising the new baby brother, they just don't have time. Besides, they trust Marcia. She brings home good grades and never really gets in trouble. She's a good girl, and they feel they really know her.

Marcia's lack of trouble may be exactly why she has created a page full of profanity and pictures that would give her mother a heart attack if she ever saw them. "My life is boring," she once told her friend Leena. "I've got to spice it up. It's no big deal. It's just my friends looking at it, and they know the real me. It's just for fun. No worries."

Bob Grimm joined Marcia's Friends network about three weeks ago. Bob Grimm has also taken advantage of the age loophole on TheNETwork.com. Online, he is 16-year-old ShyGuy, a kid who claims to play basketball for the high school in the county next to Marcia's. He gets decent grades and is athletic, but he has trouble talking to girls face-to-face. That is why he likes the time he gets to spend with Marcia online, he says. They can just chat. He doesn't have to try to impress her. He can just be himself and not worry about what she thinks about him. But Bob isn't really being himself. He is actually a 26-year-old overweight man who is going prematurely bald.

Bob does have trouble talking with girls. That much is true. He always has. But he hit a gold mine when the Internet made it possible for guys like him to meet people that he could convince to like him. He has accounts on several different websites. Along with those different accounts, he has several different identities. Each identity portrays him with a different personality. One day he is ShyGuy, and the next day he is Punkster. He is everything from the boy you'd take home to meet Mom, to the guy you'd brag about to your older sister's college friends, with his self-proclaimed washboard abs and surfer, wild-boy attitude. With each of these personas, he has managed to sneak into the Friends networks of four different girls. All of them are young teenagers.

Marcia would never use her real name on her blog. She's too smart for that. But her friend Leigh Ann sometimes forgets that others might be reading what she writes to Marcia in chats. So, from time to time, she's called her by her first name. And on her own site she's written Marcia's full name along with the names of some of her other friends in captions with pictures she's taken of them with her cell phone.

ShyGuy got into the Marcia's Friends network because he was in Leena's network. Marcia trusts Leena. She figures a friend of Leena's should be a friend of hers. Leena added him because her sister had him in her network. She liked the music he listed on his profile page. Leena's sister didn't really know him at all. But—BINGO—he got in. And now he has full access to chats with Marcia whenever he wants. She has grown to trust him. But, most importantly, she feels safe because it is all done online and she can just cut him off if he ever says something she doesn't like. But she gets the feeling he'd never do something like that.

With homework finished, Marcia's getting really bored. She's chatting with Leena and Leigh Ann online. "i'm hungry lets meet at macs," she finishes her chat. Mom has let her walk to Mac's Burgers in the past. It is only a few blocks up the road.

Marcia has disclosed the name of her high school on her profile page before. Bob Grimm knows the area she lives in. He knows her first and last name. He knows what she looks like. And he just caught the last line of the conversation in her chat room. He knows where she's headed, and now he only hopes she is walking. If she is walking, she'll probably be walking home alone.

"This is almost too easy," Bob thinks to himself as he grabs his car keys and heads for the door.

"Be back around 7:00," Marcia calls to her mom.

"Be careful," her mom replies.

The wind-muffled response barely reaches Marcia's mom, "I always am."

A cold chill runs down her mom's spine as she finishes cleaning the baby's high chair. "Must be the draft," she thinks.

Keeping out of CyberTrouble

The following are things to think about to keep yourself out of trouble online:

1. Be prepared to face the consequences if you choose to break the rules of online etiquette, the website you are visiting, or the law.
2. It is really easy to make inappropriate comments, bully people, and pretend to be someone you are not when you are sitting behind your "private" computer at home. Don't forget that computers are no longer private. Today they are very public machines.
3. Don't even pretend to make a bomb threat, physical threat, etc. online. You could easily go to jail for something that seems like a joke at the time.
4. Keep vulgar remarks to yourself, especially those directed toward other people. Kids have been kicked out of schools for making ugly comments online about their teachers. Remember, freedom of speech is not as free as you might think.
5. Don't forget, a future employer or college admissions official could be checking out your blog someday. Would you want them to base their decision to hire you or admit you into their college based on what they saw?
6. Don't post the private information of your friends online. This is often accidentally done by young people on their friends' or their own blogs or profiles.
7. Don't argue with your friends online and then begin posting their personal information. That is a battle that cannot be won. Think about what they may post about you.

The Real Deal

Believe it or not, there are few stories about young people actually being abducted, hurt, or killed by someone they met online. But the risk is out there, and it is continually increasing. The National Center for Missing & Exploited Children is an organization that seeks to protect children from all kinds of crimes. They reported that between July 2000 and July 2001 there were 2,577 arrests for Internet sex crimes against minors. When compared to the amount of people who use the Internet, that number may not seem very high. But one must keep in mind that those numbers include only the arrests. When the agency researched the number of times a child was inappropriately approached or harassed online, they found it reached over 4 million.

Police agencies are working hard to find and arrest the people guilty of taking advantage of young people on the Internet. Many times they lure those people into an encounter with an officer, who then arrests them and causes them plenty of public embarrassment. Recently, the press secretary for the Department of Homeland Security, a very important person involved in our nation's security, was arrested for engaging in inappropriate conversations and actions online with a person he thought was a 14-year-old girl. It was actually a police detective, and he was openly humiliated.

The National Center for Missing & Exploited Children also found that one in five children receive online solicitations of a sexual nature. Because of this danger, it is important for you to keep in mind that you must always remain in control. Bad things can happen to you. As long as you are smart about what you do, use common sense, and keep an open line of communication between you and your parents about what you are doing in Cyberspace, you will most likely be safe.

Following are a number of Cyberspace Safety Tips. Anytime you break one of these rules, you are causing a crack in your wall of security in Cyberspace.

1. While online, don't do any of the following:
    - Give out your full name
    - Tell the name of your school
    - Tell the names of the sports teams or activities you are involved in
    - Post your daily schedule and routine
    - Tell where you work
    - Post your phone number
    - Lie about your age
    - Break the rules of the websites you visit
    - Choose a screen name that is vulgar or makes you seem like a wild partier
    - Trust anyone online that you don't know well

2. Do not meet people in person that you met through the Internet. If you have to meet someone you've met online, do it in public with an adult you know and trust.

3. Don't give out your password. Pick a password that you won't forget, but make sure it isn't one that someone could easily guess. Think about what your friends know about you right now. Could they guess any of your computer passwords if they tried?

4. Don't go online if your virus software is not up-to-date. Also, don't open attachments from people you don't know if your virus software is not up-to-date.

5. Don't respond to unwanted e-mail. Just delete it. Responding to it lets the scammer know you have a working e-mail account.

6. Remember that when you are online, you are in charge of you. No one else can tell you what to do or how to do it.

7. Report any kind of harassment or bullying to the police. If anyone sends you material that is sexual in nature, report it to www.CyberTipline.com.

8. Be very careful when shopping online. It is better not to buy that olive-green, fuzzy lampshade with hanging crescent moons than to go through the hassle of having to cancel all of your parents' credit cards. Assume that all sites are scams. Do a little extra checking before purchasing anything from anyone online.

9. Be smart online. If something seems too good to be true, it probably is. If you get the feeling that something is "just not right," you are probably correct.

10. Don't respond to offensive comments or engage in verbal wars with anyone through your site. Just delete the comments and find out how you can block that person from making comments in the future.

11. Don't allow yourself to be stressed-out over outrageous comments or solicitations online. Just print them, report them, delete them, and forget about them. If you respond, you are doing exactly what the harasser wants you to do. Remember, you must stay in control.

12. Don't let the Internet consume your real life. It isn't healthy to spend more time talking to friends and playing games in cyberspace than in the real world.

Reading Comprehension

After reading "Cyberspace Safety: As Careful As She Always Is," choose the options that best answer questions 1-14.

1. Read this sentence.
   Her father's sarcastic prediction looks less like a joke now that he has allowed her to open an account with TheNETwork.com.

   What is the meaning of the word *sarcastic* as it is used in this sentence?
   A. jovial
   B. fawning
   C. mocking
   D. flattering

2. Read this sentence.
   But he hit a gold mine when the Internet made it possible for guys like him to meet people that he could convince to like him.

   What does the author mean by this sentence?
   F. He traded gold in his coin club online.
   G. The Internet company paid him in gold for using their service.
   H. The Internet makes it possible for otherwise shy people to have conversations.
   I. The Internet companies have become extremely wealthy by allowing customers to trade foreign currency online.

3. According to the article, Leigh Ann
   A. has befriended Bob Grimm.
   B. has considered the dangers of using the Internet.
   C. should be more cautious while using the Internet.
   D. has taken all of the necessary precautions while using the Internet.

4. What is the purpose of Cyberspace safety?
   F. to protect users online
   G. to report people who exploit children
   H. to ensure people get caught for breaking the law
   I. to provide an atmosphere for users to do whatever they want

5. With which statement would the author of the passage most likely agree?
   A. People always lie when creating a profile.
   B. Social networking sites have blockers that ensure users' safety.
   C. There are risks in social networking sites, and they are continually increasing.
   D. Online harassment rarely occurs, and only the worst cases should be reported.

6. The author organizes the article by
   F. listing safety tips for cyberspace.
   G. comparing Marcia's and Bob Grimm's lifestyle.
   H. placing events in the order in which they occur to show Marcia's daily schedule.
   I. describing an unsafe situation and stating ways to avoid potential dangers in cyberspace.

Cyberspace Safety

7. Why does the author include the website CyberTipline.com in the article?
   - A. to show how to scan for viruses
   - **B. to encourage readers to report harassment**
   - C. to explain technical difficulties to the reader
   - D. to give Bob Grimm Marcia's personal information

8. What statement best expresses the main idea of the article?
   - F. Marcia needs to be more cautious when using the Internet.
   - G. People who exploit young girls should be punished for their crime.
   - **H. Potential dangers can be avoided by taking necessary online precautions.**
   - I. Marcia's parents have taken a hands-off approach in monitoring her online.

9. What should you do to keep yourself out of cyberspace trouble?
   - **A. You should avoid offensive comments.**
   - B. You should post personal information online.
   - C. You should pretend you are someone different so others cannot track you.
   - D. You should post your friends' personal information online instead of your own.

10. What made Bob Grimm leave his home?
    - F. He was going to find Leena.
    - **G. He was going to find Marcia.**
    - H. He was going to grab a bite to eat at Mac's.
    - I. He was going to meet some of his friends at Mac's.

11. Marcia and Bob Grimm are ALIKE in that they
    - A. both eat at Macs.
    - **B. both lie about their age.**
    - C. both have younger siblings.
    - D. both listens to the same music.

12. Which statement about exercising cyberspace safety is LEAST accurate?
    - F. While online, discuss your favorite NFL team with your friend.
    - **G. While online, open and respond to attachments in your bulk e-mail account.**
    - H. While online, give your partial name to a person you have met in a chat room.
    - I. While online, tell your friend about how much fun you had at the party you attended the night before.

13. According to the article, how can Marcia increase her safety online?
    - A. Marcia should be selective in choosing the people in her circle of friends.
    - B. Marcia should give out her password only to her closest friends within her access page.
    - **C. Marcia should talk with her friends about using personal information on their blogs.**
    - D. Marcia should decide to allow only people with the same interests in her social networking site.

14. Based on the article, which statement is most accurate?
    - F. Marcia uses her Internet blog responsibly.
    - G. Leena carefully chooses whom she allows in her circle of friends.
    - **H. Bob Grimm uses information from the Internet to prey on young girls.**
    - I. Marcia's parents are at fault for not monitoring her activity on the Internet.

Reading Strategy

Safety in Cyberspace

Making Inferences and Drawing Conclusions: When we make inferences, we put two or more bits of information together to come to some conclusion. Use the questions below as guidelines to help you organize the information from the article. Use one box to describe Marcia and one to describe Bob. Then use the information you've filled in about Marcia and Bob to help you answer the question at the bottom of the page.

What does the character believe? **It is okay to mislead people to make friends.**

Describe the character's personality: **He seems like a loner. He needs to make up different identities to get friends online. He has a hard time meeting people.**

An important quotation or thought made by the character: **"This is almost too easy…"**

Character acts like: **Lies online to make friends. Has different identities online.**

Character looks like: **26-year-old, overweight man. Going prematurely bald.**

Teacher Notes: Students should be able to answer the questions and use the information to make inferences. Sample answers are given, but students may include more information.

What is the relationship between the two characters?

They become online friends. They are both comfortable with who they are in real life.

Character looks like: **13-year-old honors student.**

Character acts like: **Honors student. Lies about her age. Puts profanity and wild pictures on site.**

An important quote or thought made by the character: **"My life is boring. I've got to spice it up. It's just my friends looking at it… No worries."**

Describe the character's personality:
She thinks she is boring. She is a pretty good girl and enjoys acting "bad" online.

What does the character believe?
She is too smart to get hurt by lying on the Internet. She thinks nothing bad can happen.

What can you infer about how the story will end based on what you know about the topic and what happens in the story so far?
Bob will be able to confront Marcia and manipulate her because he already has a lot of information on her and has established trust with her online. He'll be able to hurt her if he wants.

Interpreting the Data

PART I

15. After reading the article, explain the different ways that Marcia's family members failed her. Use details from the selection to support your answer.

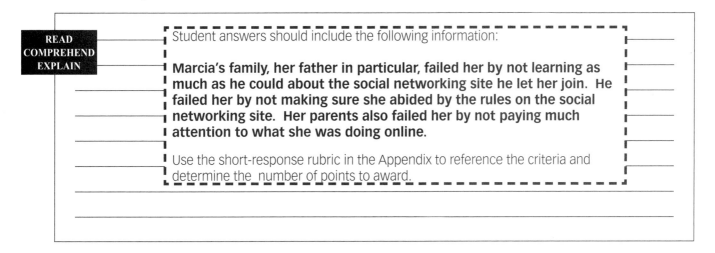

READ COMPREHEND EXPLAIN

Student answers should include the following information:

Marcia's family, her father in particular, failed her by not learning as much as he could about the social networking site he let her join. He failed her by not making sure she abided by the rules on the social networking site. Her parents also failed her by not paying much attention to what she was doing online.

Use the short-response rubric in the Appendix to reference the criteria and determine the number of points to award.

Analyze the following table created by the U.S. Census Bureau.

Percentage of Children Using Computers and the Internet			
Characteristics	Number of Children (in thousands)	Percent Using Computers	Percent Using the Internet
All persons age 5-17	53,013	89.5	58.5
Age 5-7	11,990	80.5	31.4
Age 8-10	12,455	90.5	53.5
Age 11-14	16,493	92.6	68.3
Age 15-17	12,075	93.4	77.1
Female	25,835	90.0	58.6
Male	27,178	89.1	58.3

Using the preceding table, create a line graph that compares the percentage of children using computers to the percentage using the Internet, broken down by age groups.

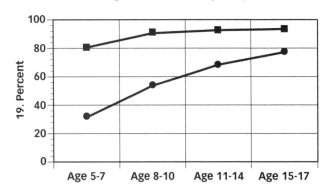

16. Percentage of Children Using Computers and the Internet

- ■ **17. Using Computers**
- ● **18. Using Internet**

19. Percent (y-axis: 0, 20, 40, 60, 80, 100)

Age 5-7   Age 8-10   Age 11-14   Age 15-17

20. One of the concerns of authorities is that the victims of child predators are no longer only the little 6-year-old children they can lure into their cars with candy. Using the table and concepts from the article, explain how the Internet has changed the face of possible victims of child predators. Use data from the table to support your answer.

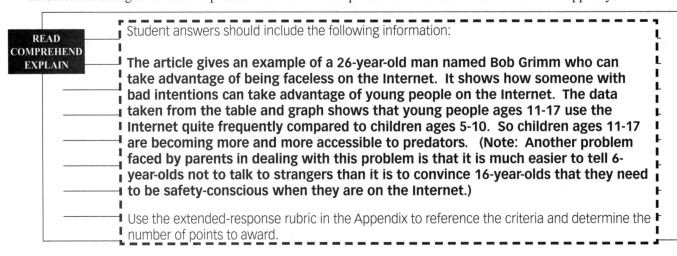

**READ
COMPREHEND
EXPLAIN**

Student answers should include the following information:

The article gives an example of a 26-year-old man named Bob Grimm who can take advantage of being faceless on the Internet. It shows how someone with bad intentions can take advantage of young people on the Internet. The data taken from the table and graph shows that young people ages 11-17 use the Internet quite frequently compared to children ages 5-10. So children ages 11-17 are becoming more and more accessible to predators. (Note: Another problem faced by parents in dealing with this problem is that it is much easier to tell 6-year-olds not to talk to strangers than it is to convince 16-year-olds that they need to be safety-conscious when they are on the Internet.)

Use the extended-response rubric in the Appendix to reference the criteria and determine the number of points to award.

Read the following statistics.

Statistics from "Parents' Internet Monitoring Survey"
30% of teens list their bedroom as the top area where they have access to the Internet.
51% of parents don't have (or don't know if they have) security software to track where their teens go online and with whom they converse online.
87% of families who have monitoring software review where their teens have gone online.
23% of parents with monitoring software daily review where their children have gone online.
33% of parents with monitoring software review where their children have gone online only once a month or less.
49% of parents don't have or don't know if they have software on their computers that blocks specific websites or key words.
61% of parents say their teen(s) participate in chat rooms and/or use instant messaging.
57% or more of parents were unable to correctly interpret the meanings of several common instant messaging abbreviations (like LOL, BRP, etc.).

21. Determine how many 11- to 17-year-olds have access to the Internet without any parental monitoring to track where they have gone online. Use the data and statistics from the two preceding tables to find your answer. (Assume that the data from both tables was taken from the same survey groups during the same time period. Also assume one child per parent.) Show your work below.

ANALYZE COMPREHEND APPLY

11- to 14-yr-olds: 68.3% (use Internet) X 16,493 (use computers [000s]) = 11,264.7

15- to 17-yr-olds: 77.1% (use Internet) X 12,075 (use computers [000s]) = 9,309.8

Add the 11- to 14-yr-olds and the 15- to 17-yr-olds together= 20,574.5 (000s)

51% of parents don't use security software, so multiply 20,574.5 (000s) by

51% and get: 10,492.99 (000s)

You also need to add the number of children whose parents have the security software but don't use it. One statistic above tells us that 87% of families who have monitoring software review where their children go online. So 13% of those who have it don't use it.

Also, assume from above that 49% of parents use some form of security software (100%- 51% who don't have or don't know if they have it= 49%).

So, multiply the total number of children using the Internet, 20,574.5 (000s), by 49% to get 10,081.5 (000s) children. Then multiply that number by 13% (the percent that have the security software but don't use it) to get 1,310.6 (000s).

Add 10,492.99 (000s) whose parents don't have the software + 1,310.6 (000s) whose parents have it but don't use it, to get 11,803.59 (000s). This is the number of children from the Census Bureau Survey who would have no real supervision on the Internet and thus are at risk.

Number of 11- to 17-year-olds without parental monitoring: 11,803,590

Use the extended-response rubric in the Appendix to reference the criteria and determine the

22. Based on the statistics given in the "Parents' Internet Monitoring Survey," what can be inferred about children's Internet safety in regard to their parents? Make a claim and support it using statistics and data from the table.

READ COMPREHEND EXPLAIN

Students should include information such as the following:

According to the table, parents aren't taking enough of an active role in ensuring their children's safety on the Internet. The table states that 51% of parents don't have monitoring software (or know if they have it). That means that many of the children using the Internet have no real supervision online and thus are at risk of being exposed to some form of inappropriate material. The table even goes on to say that a majority (57%) of parents don't know common instant messaging abbreviations (like LOL, BRP, etc.). This means that even if they do monitor what their children are doing online, many of them don't understand it.

Use the extended-response rubric in the Appendix to reference the criteria and determine the number of points to award.

PART II

Use the following data table to answer Part II questions.

Analyze the following data.

Statistics from "Online Victimization: A Report on the Nation's Youth"
One out of five children (ages 10-17) reported being inappropriately "approached" online.
One out of four children (ages 10-17) reported unwanted exposure to obscene pictures while online in the past year.
One out of seventeen children (ages 10-17) reported being harassed.
One out of four of those that were harassed reported being distressed by the harassment.
Only 17% of youth and approximately 10% of parents knew the name of a specific authority (such as the CyberTipline) to whom they could report online harassment or inappropriate conduct.

23. How might Marcia use the statistics from the table above to prove to her parents that she has no reason to be concerned about the dangers involved with using the Internet? What might she say to them? Use the tables and information given so far to support your answer.

COMPREHEND EVALUATE EXPLAIN

Students should include information such as the following:

Marcia may try to point out to her parents that only 1 of every 17 children is "harassed" online. Those numbers may not seem too bad. She may point out that 1 of every 5 children has been approached inappropriately, and 1 of every 4 has been exposed to inappropriate material. Those numbers equate to 20% and 25% of children using the Internet, which may not seem too bad to a teenager. She may also point out that the statistics don't include any numbers about children who have actually been harmed by someone as a result of their actions on the Internet. Then she could point out that if she were exposed to inappropriate material, she would know how to handle it by logging off or exiting the website.

Use the short-response rubric in the Appendix to reference the criteria and determine the number of points to award.

So far, the government has not made any laws relating to the availability of obscene pictures on the Internet. Let's put in perspective the data given in the preceding table. Assume that in a typical NFL game with 60,000 people in attendance, 20,000 of them are between the ages of 10-17. Use those numbers to answer the following question.

24. Of the children attending that NFL game, if the same percentage were subjected to obscene material at the game as are subjected on the Internet, how many young people attending the game would have been exposed to it? Show your work below.

> **READ COMPREHEND APPLY**
>
> **Using the number of 20,000 children, if one in four were exposed to obscene material, then 5,000 would have been shown the material (20,000 X 25%= 5,000).**
>
> **Number of young people exposed to obscene material: 5,000**
>
> Use the short-response rubric in the Appendix to reference the criteria and determine the number of points to award.

25. Consider how the children's parents and the newspapers would react if the situation in the preceding question had occurred. Explain why you think there might be a greater outcry against exposure to obscene material at a professional football game than there would be against the same material on the Internet.

> **READ COMPREHEND EXPLAIN**
>
> Student answers may vary, but they should support their claims with sound reasoning and data from the unit. Their answers may include the following ideas:
>
> **Parents and the newspaper would probably be more aggravated by children's exposure to obscene material in a public place.**
>
> **Parents and the newspaper have someone more visible to blame for the children's exposure (the team, the NFL, or the stadium owners). On the Internet, it is difficult to confront the responsible party.**
>
> **Children can be taught to turn the computer off more immediately than they can escape exposure to obscene material in a public place, so it may not be considered to be as much of a threat.**
>
> Use the extended-response rubric in the Appendix to reference the criteria and determine the number of points to award.

Percentage of Children Using Computers at Home and at School			
Characteristics	Number of Children (in thousands)	Percent Using Computers at Home	Percent Using Computers at School
All persons age 5-17	53,013	65.2	80.7
Age 5-7	11,990	56.4	68.2
Age 8-10	12,455	62.7	83.1
Age 11-14	16,493	68.6	85.2
Age 15-17	12,075	72.0	84.5
Female	25,835	65.7	81.6
Male	27,178	64.8	79.9

26. After analyzing the table entitled "Percentage of Children Using Computers at Home and at School," create a short memo as a principal of a middle or high school explaining why you would require your teachers to include online safety rules as part of their curriculum. Use statistics and data from any of the tables or graphs in this unit to support your memo.

ANALYZE SYNTHESIZE EXPLAIN

Student answers may vary, but they should support their claims with sound reasoning and data from the unit. They could use any of the statistics given in this unit to support their answers. Their answers may include ideas such as the following:

More children use the Internet at school than at home, making the schools responsible for their online security (at least while at school).

Only 10% of parents know where to report inappropriate activity on the Internet. This shows that adults are not as well educated as they may think they are when it comes to dealing with online security. Therefore, teachers may need to learn more about cyberspace safety and then pass it along to their students.

One in 17 children reported being harassed online. So the Internet is becoming another form of "bullying ground." Students need to be taught what is and is not appropriate to say online and how to handle it when they are bullied.

If a teacher has 30 students in his class, unless there is a 100% effective site-blocking device or security software device, he should expect that at least seven of his students will be exposed to obscene material. He needs to educate his students about what to do if they do stumble on material they shouldn't be looking at.

Use the extended-response rubric in the Appendix to reference the criteria and determine the number of points to award.

---

*Quick*thought

Staying educated about technology and how to handle potentially dangerous situations makes you stronger than those who abuse the privileges of technology.

Look Inside and Grow

27. Explain why your teachers might be concerned about your safety when you are on the Internet. Then tell why you feel safe when you are on the Internet. What precautions can you take to ensure your safety online? How would you handle someone who is using the Internet or instant messaging to harass others?

Student answers may vary.

The student should address each section of the question to the best of his/her ability. The question is meant to elicit strong classroom conversation about character. Students should be able to demonstrate that they have learned a valuable lesson about the dangers of sharing personal information on the Internet.

Use the character-education rubric in the Appendix to reference the criteria and determine the number of points to award.

Notes

They reported that…: Wolak, Janis, Kimberly J. Mitchell, and David Finkelhor.
"Internet Sex Crimes Against Minors: The Response of Law Enforcement."
Research Center, University of New Hampshire, November 2003.
Copyright 2003, National Center for Missing & Exploited Children.

When the agency…: Finkelhor, Mitchell, and Wolak. "Online Victimization: A Report on the Nation's Youth by the Crimes Against Children Research Center." June 2000.
Funded by the U.S. Congress through a grant to the National Center for Missing & Exploited Children.
Copyright 2000, National Center for Missing & Exploited Children.

The National Center…: Finkelhor, Mitchell, and Wolak. "Online Victimization."

*Cyberspace safety tips are derived in part from the Teenangels (a division of WiredSafety.org) website, http://www.teenangels.org/.

Percentage of Children (chart)…: U.S. Census Bureau, Current Population Survey, September 2001. Source: DeBell, Matthew, and Chris Chapman. "Computer and Internet Use by Children and Adolescents in 2001, Statistical Analysis Report." National Center for Education Statistics, October 2003.

Parents' Internet Monitoring (chart)…: "Parents' Internet Monitoring Study," prepared for Cox Communications and The National Center for Missing and Exploited Children and NetSmartz. Ketchum Global Research Network, 2005.

Various Statistics From (chart)…: Finkelhor, David, Kimberly J. Mitchell, and Janis Wolak. "Online Victimization: A Report on the Nation's Youth By the Crimes Against Children Research Center." Funded by the U.S. Congress through a grant to the National Center for Missing & Exploited Children, June 2000.

Percentage of Children (at Home and at School) (chart)…: U.S. Census Bureau, Current Population Survey, September 2001. Source: DeBell and Chapman.

Technical Extension

Inside the Internet

The Internet is an amazing system of networks. The networks, big and small, connect together in different ways to form what we think of as the Internet. The word *internet* is really made of two parts that describe its very essence. The prefix *inter* means between or among. The suffix *net* is just a shortening of the word *network*. Think of a fishing net and how all the pieces are connected together, and you have pictured a network. So the Internet is literally a connection between networks.

The Internet came to be in 1969 on four computer systems and has since expanded to be a part of the daily life of millions upon millions of people. In fact, there are few people in the world whose lives aren't touched in some way by the Internet. But how does it work? Although the Internet may seem like a mysterious part of technology, it is relatively simple to understand the basic functions that make it work.

Imagine the Internet as a massive highway system. Each computer is just one car on the road. Think about your neighborhood. It is probably connected by a series of small roads. You can go to lots of different houses within your neighborhood by using these same roads. This is like a network. A network allows your computer to connect to other places in the network. The neighborhood is the provider of that network or, in computer terms, the Internet Service Provider.

If all you could ever do was drive your car around in your own neighborhood, you wouldn't learn much about the rest of the world. When you are driving, small neighborhoods are connected together by larger roads called highways. Highways are often more crowded than neighborhood streets. The same is true for the computers.

Smaller networks are connected together by the Internet, allowing you to visit many different sites.

Like a highway, the Internet is a busy place. In order to keep order on the highway, we use a combination of signs and signals, like *Stop*, *Yield*, and *One Way*. These signals tell cars when and where they can go on the streets. The Internet has a way of doing the same thing, called routers. Routers make sure information gets where it is supposed to go and keep information from going where it isn't supposed to go. This keeps extra information from backing up networks. Routers are a necessity when connecting networks.

On the road, cars all look different from one another. They are different colors and shapes, and each has a unique license plate with numbers and letters. Buildings are identified by a street number and name. This helps cars find the exact building they are looking for. Computers are similarly identified by a series of numbers called an Internet Protocol (IP) Address. Like computers, websites also have an IP Address. They also have a Domain Name, such as www.pwimpact.com, that allows people to better remember how to get to them.

The processes that make the Internet work aren't hard to understand. But, like the United States interstate highways, the way they work together is mind-boggling. Each individual process is complicated and has many steps. The exact combination it takes to bring up a web page three seconds after you type it into your computer is truly amazing. If only traveling on the road were so fast!

Without the network system, there would be no Internet, and modern life would change dramatically.

Reading Comprehension

After reading "Inside the Internet," choose the options that best answer questions 1-14.

1. Read this sentence.
   The word *internet* is really made of two parts that describe its very essence.

   What is the meaning of the word *essence* as it is used in this sentence?
   A. core
   B. beauty
   C. signature
   D. complexity

2. Read this sentence.
   Without the system, there would be no Internet, and modern life would change dramatically.

   What does the author mean by this sentence?
   F. The Internet alone runs modern life.
   G. The system is required constantly to run the Internet.
   H. Modern life would collapse without computer networks.
   I. Our lives would be altered without the use of Internet technology.

3. From this article, the reader can tell that computer networks require
   A. many basic functions.
   B. one main network site.
   C. a single overseeing system.
   D. humans to type in long numbers.

4. What is the purpose of networks?
   F. to provide Internet connections
   G. to protect the computer against electrical surges
   H. to ensure safety precautions while using the Internet
   I. to serve as a communication barrier between computers

5. In the author's opinion,
   A. we rely heavily on the Internet.
   B. dial up connections are too slow.
   C. computer technology is truly amazing.
   D. URL's should be replaced with a binary code.

6. The author organizes the article by
   F. listing the contents of a network.
   G. comparing the Internet to a system of highways.
   H. listing the reasons why networking is complicated.
   I. describing the basic functions of a network and how they work.

7. What was the author's main purpose in writing this article?
   A. to describe in detail the networking process
   B. to expand the reader's computer knowledge
   C. to encourage users to stay connected on the Internet
   D. to prove to the reader Internet processes are not difficult to understand

8. What title best fits the article?
   F. Routers Rule
   G. Network Highways
   H. Life without the Internet
   I. Technology's Hidden Mystery

9. What is significant about the invention of the Internet?
   A. It started with just four computers.
   B. It has impacted millions of people.
   C. It shares the same technology as the iPod.
   D. It has now replaced the telephone as the best invention.

10. Why is it easier for us to picture routers as traffic signs?
    F. Routers are electrical just like traffic signs.
    G. We are able to locate routers and signs quickly.
    H. We spend more time in the car then on computers.
    I. Routers navigate computers just like signs navigate cars.

11. The Internet is compared to a highway because
    A. the reader is able to drive and see the network.
    B. you can travel on the highway and reach the network.
    C. the reader can imagine all of the roads that lead to the network.
    D. the reader can imagine how busy and intertwining the network can be.

12. Which statement about the Internet is LEAST accurate?
    F. Routers ensure information gets to where it needs to go.
    G. The Internet is a technology that we can not live without.
    H. The Internet is a fairly new concept, only a few decades old.
    I. The Internet has many smaller networks that are connected together.

13. Which of the following provides the best evidence the Internet is like an information highway?
    A. cars being identified by their license plates
    B. the picture showing a car driving through neighborhoods
    C. computers being identified by their Internet Protocol Addresses
    D. computer information being thought as vehicles traveling all over the world

14. Which statement is correct, according to the article?
    F. All websites have an IP address.
    G. Domain names are complex and hard to remember.
    H. Routers and modems can be expensive additions to your computer.
    I. Cable modems send data much quicker than standard dial up connections.

Vocational Extension

Job Description

Web Task Group (WTG) is seeking a Junior Level Web Developer with 1-3 years work OR classroom experience designing, developing, and maintaining web applications. Candidates must have 1+ years using one or more of the following development languages: Visual Basic, VB/C# .NET, ASP, JSP, JavaScript. This experience may have occurred in a work environment OR in an internship. Excellent oral and written communication skills are needed.

Have you ever wondered about the billions of websites that can be found when you surf on the World Wide Web? How did they get there? Who created them?

In the 21st century, website development is a growing job market. With more and more research, business, and communication being done over the Internet, the need for people to develop web application is growing by leaps and bounds.

Web developers can be employed in very different types of positions. The job description above is from a company who provides technology services to individuals or companies who need them. In this type of job, a web developer would be assigned different clients who have contacted the company, and provide services such as website development, design, and maintenance.

Another form of employment for a web developer might be in the information technology department of a specific company. For example, a large financial company might hire its own web developer to provide services to only their company. In this case, a web developer might also be required to take charge of any or all technology needs of the company.

There are many paths to becoming a web developer. Perhaps the most common path is to attend a four-year college or university and earn a degree in information technology or communications with an emphasis in web development. Classes in computer-aided graphic design are also helpful. However, this is not the only way to get a foot into the world of web development.

Many future web developers choose to attend a two-year technical school to earn their associate's degree in web development or a similar field. They then try to find entry-level positions or internships to learn the ropes of the field and progress to more advanced positions as they gain experience.

Still others who have learned programming language and graphic design basics in high school or in internships during that time choose to look for employment directly after high school graduation. They gain all of their experience while working.

Regardless of the path a web developer chooses to take, learning the requirements of the field takes hard work. But the benefits are rewarding and long-lasting, and web developers are some of the most highly sought-after employees today.

Job Information

Company:
WTG (Web Task Group, Inc.)

Location:
Tampa Bay, FL

Salary/Wage:
$40,000- $50,000/year

Status:
Full-time Employee

Job Category:
Information Technology

Contact Information

Contact:
Tammy Greenswater
rgreens@wtg.com
(813) 442-3672, ext. 56

Reference Code:
137042

Looking Forward

15. You've discovered the necessary steps and knowledge needed to become a web developer. Assume you're a high school sophomore who has decided to pursue web development as a career option. Make a plan about how you will work toward this goal and which path you will take. Be specific and use the job description, article, and job information along with your experience to complete your answer.

Looking Forward

Student answers may vary.

The student should address the question to the best of his/her ability using the article and personal experience. The question is meant to encourage students to explore areas of interest for their future and begin to determine how they will prepare for a future career.

Use the extended-response rubric in the Appendix to reference the criteria and determine the number of points to award.

Ethical Dilemma

16. You're a web developer who has been assigned to work with the account of a popular teenage website, Connections.com. Your job is not only to design the site by the specifications of the Connections.com owner, but also to maintain the site. You notice that teens are exchanging potentially dangerous personal information over the site. When you talk with the owner, he recognizes the problem but is afraid he will lose business if he takes away such a popular feature. Discuss your options based on your opinion of the subject.

Ethical Dilemma

Student answers may vary.

The student should address the question to the best of his/her ability using background knowledge from the article as well as personal opinion and experience. The question is meant to encourage students to contemplate scenarios and make ethical decisions.

Use the character-education rubric in the Appendix to reference the criteria and determine the number of points to award.

Appendix

	Reading Short-Response Rubric Created for *Impact!*
2 points	The student fully understands what is being asked for. The student's answer is correct, complete, and addresses all aspects of the assigned task. The student provides detail and support from the text in order to support his/her answer. Any additional information provided by the student is related to the assigned task and acts as support for his/her response.
1 point	The student partially understands what is being asked for. The student's answer is correct; however, it is generalized and not specific enough. The student is missing any specific details and support from the text that would prove his/her full understanding of the text and the assigned task.
0 points	The answer is completely incorrect, has nothing to do with the assigned task, or no answer is provided.

	Reading Extended-Response Rubric Created for *Impact!*
4 points	The student fully understands what is being asked for. The student's answer is correct, complete, and addresses all aspects of the assigned task. The student provides detail and support from the text in order to support his/her answer. Any additional information provided by the student is related to the assigned task and acts as support for his/her response.
3 points	The student understands what is being asked for. The student's answer is correct and addresses all aspects of the assigned task. The student provides detail and support, but it is not fully complete or directly from the text.
2 points	The student partially understands what is being asked for. The student's answer is correct; however, it is generalized and not specific enough. The student is missing any specific details and support from the text that would prove his/her full understanding of the text and the assigned task.
1 point	The student has very little understanding of what is being asked for in the task. The answer is not complete, has many things wrong with it, or addresses very little of what has been asked for.
0 points	The answer is completely incorrect, has nothing to do with the assigned task, or no answer is provided.

Interpreting the Data Short-Response Rubric
Created for *Impact!*

2 points	The student fully understands what is being asked for. The work is completed correctly and efficiently. There is a full demonstration of the know-how necessary to accurately answer the problem provided. If applicable, the explanations and interpretations are clear, complete, and concise. Any small mistakes do not take away from the overall display of understanding.
1 point	The student seems to understand what is being asked for, but the answer is only partially correct. The answer may be correct, but it is apparent that there is a lack of full awareness in the know-how necessary to complete the problem. Or there is a full awareness of the know-how necessary to complete the problem, but the answer is incorrect.
0 points	No answer is provided, the answer is completely incorrect, or there is absolutely no demonstration of the know-how necessary to complete the problem (even if the answer provided is correct).

Interpreting the Data Extended-Response Rubric
Created for *Impact!*

4 points	The student fully understands what is being asked for. The work is completed correctly and efficiently. There is a full demonstration of the know-how necessary to accurately answer the problem provided or others like it. If applicable, the explanations and interpretations are clear, complete, and concise. Any small mistakes do not take away from the overall display of understanding.
3 points	The student understands what is being asked for. The answer is essentially correct, but the demonstration of the know-how necessary to explain how the student came to the answer is slightly flawed. The answer contains some minor errors that could be due to lack of attention to detail in the demonstration of the know-how necessary to answer the problem or others like it.
2 points	The student seems to understand what is being asked for, but the answer is only partially correct. The answer may be correct, but it is apparent that there is a lack of full awareness in the know-how necessary to complete the problem or others like it. Or there is a full awareness of the know-how necessary to complete the problem, but the answer provided is incorrect.
1 point	There is a very limited understanding of what is being asked for. The answer is incomplete and has errors. There is some demonstration of the know-how necessary to answer the problem or others like it, but the answer is incomplete, totally incorrect, or inadequate.
0 points	No answer is provided, the answer is completely incorrect, or there is absolutely no demonstration of the know-how necessary to complete the problem (even if the answer provided is correct).

Character-Education Rubric
Created for *Impact*!

4 points	The student uses information from the reading selection and his/her life and formulates a strong answer that demonstrates what conclusions about character he/she has drawn from the article.
3 points	The student gives examples from either only his/her life or only the reading selection and formulates a strong answer that demonstrates what conclusions about character he/she has drawn from the article.
2 points	The student gives few examples from his/her life or the reading selection, but formulates an answer that demonstrates what conclusions about character he/she has drawn from the article.
1 point	The student does not use examples from his/her life or from the reading selection. It is difficult to determine whether the student has drawn any conclusions about character from the article.
0 points	The student has provided no response or a completely incorrect response. The student does not demonstrate that he/she has drawn any conclusions about character from the article.

Article and Extension Lexile Measures

High Interest Article	Lexile	Technical Extension	Lexile	Vocational Extension	Lexile
Failure and the Sweet Smell of Success: Queen Latifah and Mariah Carey	900	Tracking Billboard	1050	Police Officer	910
Pirates on the Sea of Technology	960	What's In a CD	1010	Sound Engineer	1090
The Founding Fathers Never Met the Paparazzi	990	Rights and Responsibilities	890	Photojournalist	980
Image: Don't Judge a Skater	920	The Physics of Snowboarding	1010	Sports Manager	1100
Violent Video Games: Who Is Raising Our Children	1000	Video Game Production	920	Graphic Designer	1180
What's the Message?	1030	How a Nonprofit Is Formed	1070	Accountant	880
Building Bridges	1020	Immigration	1140	Teacher	1020
Hard to Be Humble	1030	Football Science	910	Sports Medicine	1210
Conquering the Music World, Saving the Third World	1150	HIV and the Body	980	Peace Corps Volunteer	1100
Cyberspace Safety: As Careful As She Always Is	1060	Inside the Internet	880	Web Developer	1140